BLACK
WOLF

BLACK WOLF

JUAN GÓMEZ-JURADO

Translated from the Spanish by

NICK CAISTOR
LORENZA GARCIA

MINOTAUR BOOKS
NEW YORK

First published in the United States by Minotaur Books, an imprint of St. Martin's Publishing Group

www.minotaurbooks.com

Design by Meryl Sussman Levavi

Library of Congress Cataloging-in-Publication Data

Names: Gómez-Jurado, Juan, author. | Caistor, Nick, translator. | Garcia, Lorenza, translator.
Title: Black wolf / Juan Gómez-Jurado ; translated from the Spanish by Nick Caistor, Lorenza Garcia.
Other titles: Loba negra. English
Description: First U.S. edition. | New York : Minotaur Books, 2024. | Series: The Antonia Scott trilogy ; 2 | "Originally published in Spain as Loba negra by Ediciones B"—Title page verso.
Identifiers: LCCN 2023045838 | ISBN 9781250853691 (hardcover) | ISBN 9781250359001 (international edition) | ISBN 9781250853707 (ebook)
Subjects: LCGFT: Thrillers (Fiction) | Novels.
Classification: LCC PQ6707.O54 L6313 2024 | DDC 863/.7—dc23/eng/20231016
LC record available at https://lccn.loc.gov/2023045838

Our books may be purchased in bulk for promotional, educational, or business use. Please contact your local bookseller or the Macmillan Corporate and Premium Sales Department at 1-800-221-7945, extension 5442, or by email at MacmillanSpecialMarkets@macmillan.com.

Originally published in Spain as LOBA NEGRA by Ediciones B

First U.S. Edition: 2024

1   3   5   7   9   10   8   6   4   2

For Babs,
because I love her

For Arturo, Javi, and Rodrigo,
no matter what

BLACK
WOLF

AN ABYSS

Antonia Scott has never been faced with such a tough decision.

To others, her dilemma could seem negligible.

Not to Antonia. While she may be capable of functioning several levels into the future, her mind is no crystal ball. She may have the ability to visualize dozens of disparate pieces of information simultaneously, but her brain doesn't work like in those movies where you see a whole string of letters superimposed on the face of the protagonist as they're thinking.

Antonia Scott's mind is more like a jungle, a jungle full of monkeys leaping at top speed from vine to vine, carrying things. Many monkeys and many things, swinging past one another in midair, baring their fangs.

Today, the monkeys are carrying dreadful things, and Antonia is afraid.

This isn't a feeling she is accustomed to. After all, she has seen herself in such situations as:

- A high-speed nighttime boat chase in the Strait of Gibraltar.
- A tunnel packed with explosives, where a kidnapper was pointing a gun at the head of a particularly valuable hostage.
- What happened in Valencia.

Her astuteness saved her on the day of the speedboats (she let those in front of her crash), and her knowledge (of words for animals) in the tunnel. As for Valencia, no one knows how she came out alive (the only person who did) from that massacre. She has always refused to talk about it. But she survived. And didn't feel afraid.

No, Antonia is afraid of almost nothing, apart from herself. Afraid of life, maybe. After all, she relaxes by imagining for three minutes every day how she could kill herself.

Those are her three minutes.

They're sacred.

They're what keep her sane.

In fact, it's that time now. But instead of being immersed in the calm of her ritual, Antonia is sitting in front of a chessboard. The pieces are red and white. One of Antonia's bishops could make an easy checkmate.

Red to play and win.

A simple decision.

Not for Antonia.

Because on the far side of the board is her son, Jorge, staring at her, eyes narrowed. Behind those green half-moons, she senses all the ill humor and defiance contained within his four-foot frame.

"Make your move, Mom," says Jorge, giving a slight kick under the marble table. "I'm bored."

He's lying. Antonia may not know what to do, but she knows when someone is lying.

Jorge is waiting expectantly to see whether she moves her bishop and beats him, so that he can fly into a tantrum at losing. Or conversely, if Antonia moves a different piece, to blow his top because she's let him win.

Antonia is rescued from her paralysis by a buzz on her cell phone. A florid face appears. Redheaded and very Basque-looking. The vibrating phone makes the chess pieces dance on their squares.

Jon knows she is with Jorge. This is her third visit since the judge decided, against the wishes of the boy's grandfather, to give her a second chance. She is on probation. Jon wouldn't phone if it weren't truly urgent.

Antonia shrugs an apology and stands up to take the call. Turning her back on her son's frustration, and on the impassive social worker endlessly taking notes in a corner of the room.

However relieved she is to dodge the situation with this pretext, Antonia has already decided this was a game she couldn't win.

Which she likes even less.

Part I

ANTONIA

A man might befriend a wolf, even break a wolf,
but no man could truly tame *a wolf.*

GEORGE R. R. MARTIN

1

A BODY

Jon Gutiérrez doesn't like bodies in Madrid's river Manzanares.

It's not a question of aesthetics. This particular body is very unpleasant (apparently having spent a long time in the water), its bluish skin covered in violet blotches, its hands almost severed at the wrist. But this is no time to be finicky.

The night is unusually dark, and the streetlights illuminating the world of the living seven meters above him only make the shadows denser. The wind is producing strange rustling noises in the reeds, and the river water is decidedly on the chilly side. After all, this is the Manzanares, it's eleven o'clock at night, and February is already sliding its gray paw under the door.

None of this is what upsets Jon about bodies in the river, because he's used to freezing water (he's from Bilbao), to whispers in the dark (he's gay), and to lifeless bodies (he's a police inspector).

What Jon Gutiérrez can't stand about bodies in the river Manzanares is having to pull them out with his bare hands.

I must be an idiot, thinks Jon. *This is rookie work. But obviously, these three Madrid losers can't even find their own dicks.*

It's not that Jon is fat. But like it or not, half a lifetime of being the biggest guy in the room creates habits. A penchant for helping. Which becomes overwhelming when you see three clowns fresh out of the police academy splashing about in the reeds, trying to extricate a body from the water. And only managing to nearly drown themselves instead.

So Jon struggles into the white plastic suit, pulls on the rubber boots, and wades into the two feet of water with a *fuckyou,motherfuckers* that leaves the greenhorns' cheeks as red as if they'd been slapped.

Inspector Gutiérrez sloshes toward the corpse, displacing both water and rookies before reaching the clump of vegetation on which the body has snagged. It is caught in some roots, and is mostly submerged. Only the pallid face and one arm are floating on the surface. Stirred by the current, it's as if the victim were trying to swim away to escape the inevitable.

Jon crosses himself mentally and plunges his arms beneath the cadaver. It's soft to the touch, the subcutaneous fat jiggling under the skin like toothpaste in a balloon. He steadies his legs and prepares to yank with all his might like an *harrijasotzaile*, a Basque rock lifter who on a good day can hoist three hundred kilos.

This'll show those rookies.

His bulging arms tense, and two things occur simultaneously.

The second of them: the body doesn't move an inch.

The first: the sandy riverbed sucks in the inspector's right foot, landing him flat on his ass in the river.

Jon isn't a guy prone to tears or bellyaching. But neither the noise of the current, the rustle of the wind in the reeds, nor his own curses can drown out the rookies' laughter. So, with water up to his shoulders and his pride dented, Jon allows himself an all-too-human moment of self-pity and blames someone else for his predicament.

Where the hell are you, Antonia?

2

A CABLE

"You won't get it out like that, Inspector," a woman's voice says next to his ear.

Jon grabs hold of Dr. Aguado's forearm, and she helps him back to his feet. Normally, any pathologist's hand gives Jon the heebie-jeebies, but when your ass is stuck on a sandy riverbed, you cling on to whatever is offered.

"I thought dead bodies floated. But this one seems determined to sink."

Aguado smiles. She must be around forty years old. Long eyelashes, faded makeup, a piercing in her nose, and a sly languor in her eyes. Nowadays with an added happy spark. According to gossip, she's found a girlfriend.

"The human body is more than sixty percent water. Water doesn't float, so first of all, the body sinks. At the right temperature, bacteria start to decompose the body in a matter of hours. Right now, it's four degrees Celsius outside, and the water is around six degrees, so it'll be more like days. The stomach and intestines fill with gas, and then—*pop!*—up she comes again."

Aguado bends her knees, steadying the body with one hand while she pokes around under it with the other.

"Can I help, Doctor?"

"Don't worry. I just need to find what's keeping her down."

Jon glances at the shapeless, swollen mass floating facedown, naked. Short hair of indistinct color. Jon is wondering how the hell the pathologist knew it was a woman.

"How the hell did you know it was a woman?"

"Several reasons, Inspector," replies Aguado. "The angle of the clavicle, the lack of any occipital protuberance, and, although you can't see it, right now I'm touching what in all probability is the victim's left breast."

The forensic pathologist straightens up and hands him a small powerful flashlight. Jon shines it on her as Aguado takes a pair of blunt-tipped scissors out of the waterproof bag hanging around her neck. Leaning down again, she struggles with something under the body. Suddenly, the corpse comes free and floats to the surface.

"The murderer tied a cable to her thigh," says Aguado, pointing to an indentation at the back of the leg. "Probably with a weight attached. Help me turn her over."

The body is weightless now, and flipping it over requires no more effort than flipping a page, the final one. The eyes are gone, eaten by the fish. The face looks like a mask looking for Carnival but finding only misfortune.

Before he came to Madrid, when he was still patrolling the mean streets of Bilbao, Jon considered himself tougher. In the Otxarkoaga neighborhood, it was all broken glass and bad apples contaminating all the rest. Back then when he saw a dead body, Jon didn't feel a pang of discouragement or wonder, *What happened to you, who did this to you?*

He just felt he was doing his job.

Here he feels responsible.

That damn Antonia.

Tugging the body along under the shoulders, Jon pushes his way through the reeds and drags it to the dry part of the small island.

"No cause of death for the moment," says Aguado, talking to herself. She pauses, as if listening to something. "Elevated levels of adipocere. In the water for at least a week."

"Adipocere?"

The pathologist points to the bumps and bulges under the cadaver's bluish skin.

"Adipocere is produced when a dead body is submerged in water. The microorganisms change the subcutaneous fat into a kind of soap. I'll tell you more tomorrow: I have to get to work now before contact with the air spoils the evidence," she says, pointing to the riverbank.

Jon knows when he's being thrown out. He waves, and the three rookies come over carrying a stretcher and big transparent plastic bags. The cadaver is too far gone to put into an ordinary body bag. The inspector leaves the dirty work to them—*Go on, you can do it*. He wades back through the water to the retaining wall. There are no steps, but the police have installed a rope ladder, and Jon hauls his 110 kilos back up to street level.

The street is deserted, apart from a man leaning against a patrol car. Dark, receding hair, pencil mustache, and doll's eyes that look more painted on than real. An expensive short camel overcoat.

"It seems to be growing colder," says Mentor, blowing out a mouthful of smoke.

Jon's dented pride mends a little. No better cure for one's own humiliation than seeing someone else make a fool of himself. Mentor is *vaping*.

"What's this?" asks Jon, pointing to the gadget.

Mentor pushes the mouthpiece between his thin, almost invisible lips, inhales and then exhales again. The wind blows a mandarin-flavored cloud in Jon's direction.

"I was smoking three packs a day. Last week I even lit one in the shower. So I thought: Why not give it a try?"

"Does it work?"

"What can I say? I take in twice the amount of nicotine as before, and have three times the urge to smoke. Has Aguado come up with anything yet?"

"Only that the victim is a woman. Murdered. In the water for a week or more. And she wants to be left in peace."

"That's pretty communicative for Aguado. Have you noticed she's a lot happier recently?"

"I hear she's found a girlfriend," says Jon.

He starts to remove his plastic suit but waves away the blanket Mentor is offering.

"I hope you didn't get wet, Inspector. This part of the river isn't exactly recommended for your health."

"Meaning?"

Mentor waits for him to recover his coat and shoes, then leads him over to the riverbank.

"In 1970, a pipe from a secret experimental center ruptured near here. Apparently, Franco was determined to possess the atomic bomb, whatever it took, and had a number of scientists running experiments with plutonium. It wasn't made public until 1994, but more than a hundred liters of radioactive material ended up spilling into the Manzanares through that drain." Mentor points somewhere in the darkness. "A few hundred cancer cases here and there, nothing serious. But it's not a place where I'd choose to go swimming."

Jon doesn't react. Of course, he feels his skin itching all over and his reddish beard starting to fall out. But there's no way he's going to open his mouth. If he did, his teeth might drop out.

Mentor looks at his watch, a serious expression on his face.

"Where's Scott?"

"I called her more than three hours ago," replies Jon after realizing that the radiation poison hasn't yet affected him.

"Not that it's essential she comes. We've only dismissed the police authorities and mobilized the Red Queen unit in the middle of the night just for her."

"That's not fair," Jon protests. "She could be . . ."

This vehemence is mostly pure show. Deep down, Jon feels doubt peeping out from behind the curtains.

It's been seven months since Antonia and Jon rescued Carla Ortiz. The case made headlines around the world, first when the heiress mysteriously disappeared, and later because of what ensued between her and her father. But there wasn't a word about Antonia Scott or the Red Queen project. Nor about Jon. Emerging from the sewers with Carla, he had shielded his face from the photographers' flashes. A blurred photo, like a flower with no scent.

There are no prizes in the Red Queen project, only anonymity. A life without a name, but loads of excitement. And that was prize enough.

The loathsome Bruno Lejarreta, who had been hoping to use the scandal to launch a career in television, soon discovered he had a problem. He couldn't talk about Inspector Gutiérrez anymore. When you don't even make the regional news, it's time to go home, tail between your legs. *Oh, what a shame*, thought Jon when he heard. Then opened another beer.

The purveyors of daily garbage dug around in the Ortiz case for a few days. The body of one of the kidnappers had appeared, but the other one was still presumably under the rubble of the Goya 2 metro tunnel. The journalists speculated who it might be. This one, that one, another one. Know-it-alls and tweeters opined without knowing a thing, then went on to tweet about something else they knew nothing about. And life went on, the way things that are pretty meaningless do.

The world turned the page.

But not Antonia.

Antonia Scott *never* turns the page.

It could be her," concludes Jon, pointing to the dead body laid out on the plastic sheet on the island. The rookies have stuck six powerful halogen lamps on their orange stands in among the vegetation. The dark intimacy of death has been transformed into a distorted anatomy lesson.

Mentor shakes his head dismissively.

"Just one more unidentified cadaver. The sixth, if I remember correctly. Yet another that'll simply end up being the result of a bad trip or an abuser. Nothing of interest to us. We're wasting our time."

Antonia hasn't stopped looking for the missing kidnapper. Following every possible lead. Analyzing every scrap of information. Insisting they investigate every unidentified dead body found in or near Madrid. But despite all the time and effort she has put into the search, the woman once known as Sandra Fajardo has never turned up.

Antonia has refused to take on any more cases until she does. And that is a serious problem. However much leeway and unofficial credit they won from the Ortiz case, it's been seven months now.

The problem with unofficial credit is that it is as fickle as a politician's memory. And it's politicians who back Mentor.

"It's not as if there have been other cases," insists Jon.

"How the hell would you know, Inspector?" says Mentor, who, what with the lack of support, the cold, and the urge to smoke, is *umore txarrez*. Extremely pissed. No sign of one of those deceptive, empty smiles of his. "What would you know about the orders from above I've had to refuse? Or the dark threats she could have helped with."

Jon scratches his head and takes a deep breath. To fill that huge chest of his takes several seconds and plenty of liters of oxygen. The time he needs to calm down and not give his boss a slap that would send him cartwheeling to the bottom of the river.

"I'll talk to her. But . . ."

Jon doesn't finish his sentence. Puzzled, Mentor turns to him and follows the direction of his gaze. In the middle of the river, a phantasmagoric light is floating down with the current. If phantoms glow in bright pink. The light drifts past the island, up against the far bank. Another one follows it, closer to the center. And they glimpse a third, higher upstream.

Fifty yards from them, a fourth light seems to leap from the retaining wall a little farther up, then land in the water with a distant *plop*.

"Scott," growls Mentor, more annoyed than ever. He turns to Jon, his look telling him: *Go find her and talk some sense into her.*

The hand Jon bunches into a fist wants to reply: *What I'll do is punch you in the face.* But as it is hidden in his coat pocket, the message is not transmitted. And all Inspector Gutiérrez can do is obey and go look for Antonia Scott.

3

A BRIDGE

As a result, Jon Gutiérrez heads for the Arganzuela Bridge in a foul mood. Due to the humiliation of his soaking, the time of night, hunger, and because who the hell understands Antonia.

He's been following her upriver, catching glimpses of her ahead. A tiny figure who every few steps throws one of those lights into the water, pauses for a few moments, and then continues walking.

Jon has caught up with her slowly, going over and over in his big red head how to deal with the situation. Antonia Scott isn't exactly a reasonable person. Arguments roll off her like water off a duck's back. Especially when it's a question of finding the man who left her husband in a coma. The man who, Antonia suspects, is pulling the strings on Sandra Fajardo.

The mysterious, elusive, mythological Mr. White.

Mentor hadn't wanted to know anything about Antonia's search for White. At first, Jon thought Mentor didn't believe he existed, that he thought he was no more than a myth. Or, worse still, an obsession of Antonia's she had ended up giving a name to. But all the space Mentor had allowed her these past seven months suggested something different.

Then there were the whispers. The scared looks. And the enigmatic warning Aguado had given Jon a few days before in a hasty aside.

"Better let this one go."

Aguado disappeared before Jon could ask what she meant, leaving him as twitchy as a turkey on Christmas Eve. And none of his subsequent attempts to wheedle it out of her had gotten anywhere.

Despite all of this, Jon kept his doubts to himself and allowed Antonia to continue.

Now her time was up.

Jon reaches the Arganzuela Bridge, where night doesn't exist. The gigantic ultrametallic, ultramodern, and ultraexpensive structure is shaped like a plastic comb binder machine. It is full of powerful spotlights that glint off the metal, creating an almost perfect reflection on the surface of the water below. Jon has never been one to appreciate contemporary architecture. He's simply content that bridges bear his weight—not that he's fat. Although he does appreciate the sheer amount of light. That and the sound of his footsteps on the wooden slats of the walkway, they'll announce his arrival.

Let's see if you stop trying to escape, neska.

Antonia Scott is squatting in the center of the bridge. Thirtysomething years old. Dressed in a coat and black pants. White sneakers. On the ground beside her is a green plastic bag, one of those they give you in convenience stores.

Jon approaches her, slapping his feet on the boards a little louder than necessary.

Antonia raises a finger that warns: *Don't interrupt, it's rude.* He comes to an abrupt halt a few yards from her.

"You could have told me you were here already," says Jon. "Or at least sent a—"

At that moment, the cell phone in his pocket vibrates. He has just received a WhatsApp from Antonia. Ever since she discovered stickers, she's used them for more than half her messages. And half of those are little dogs with cute faces. Jon wonders what information she is trying to send with a sticker of a pug in a hat.

"Is this supposed to tell me you've arrived?"

"I think so."

"Great. Because I don't get it at all."

Antonia doesn't reply. She rummages in the bag, then pulls out a packet of translucent plastic glow sticks and a small bottle of water. She pours half the bottle onto the slats, and the liquid drips down into the river below. Taking one of the transparent sticks, she bends it in two. There's a quiet crack when the glass capsule inside snaps, releasing hydrogen peroxide. As it mixes with the diphenyl oxalate, the stick gives off an intense orange glow.

Has this woman come here for a murder investigation or a rave? Jon wonders.

"Approximate age of the victim?"

"Aguado hasn't told me. I was starting to—"

Antonia raises her finger again. Infuriating.

Jon is one of those who when they're infuriated go on the counter-attack. To protect himself. For sport. For his purple balls. But Antonia is behaving strangely tonight. And with her, the bar of strangeness is set very high.

Antonia puts the luminous stick inside the half-empty bottle. Screws on the top, then straightens up. She hesitates, sniffing the wind. When it dies down for a moment, she throws the bottle into the water, observing the orange glow as it floats downriver. Her eyes blink several times in succession, like a camera shutter.

Jon has seen this before. He knows Antonia is making a mental map. And now he understands why she has been throwing bottles into the water from different positions.

"Wasn't there a more ecological method?"

Staring down at the water, Antonia ignores him.

Halfway along, the current seems to lurch toward the north bank, as if that's where it wants to take the bottle. Eventually, though, the small piece of plastic runs aground among the reeds.

"Confirmed, Doctor. She was thrown from the bridge. The current changes course halfway down. The weight tied to her leg wasn't heavy enough to keep her underwater. As the body swelled up because of the gases and became more buoyant, it dragged the weight along the bottom until it reached the island."

Antonia falls silent for a few moments. Then she adds:

"I suggest you come up here with the luminol. And ask Mentor to order them to switch the bridge lights off, would you?"

She pulls her hair (black and straight, medium length) back from her ear, revealing a pair of wireless AirPods. She taps on one of them a couple of times to end the conversation, then turns toward Jon.

"So that's why neither of you paid me any attention," grumbles Jon. "You might at least have told me you were talking on the phone. I got my balls fried trying to pull that dead body of yours out of the water."

Antonia raises a quizzical eyebrow.

"Mentor told me there was a radioactive spill from that drain over there," explains Jon, pointing to it.

"That's completely untrue."

"Thank God for that," Jon says with a sigh.

"The radioactive spill was from that other one," says Antonia, pointing to the next drain, which is even closer to where Jon fell in the water.

Jon sighs again. A different sort of sigh.

"*Adiós*, fertility."

"Don't exaggerate. The amount you absorbed won't be more than the equivalent of seven or eight X-rays. Your sperm count is fine. Besides, I thought you didn't want children."

"I like to keep my options open."

"Children bring you nothing but heartache."

At that precise moment, the lights on the bridge go out, leaving their two figures in darkness. The huge silhouette stirs restlessly. The tiny one reaches for the cell phone in her bag and turns on the flashlight.

"I see the visit with your son went well," Jon says, taking a flashlight of his own out of his pocket. A real one this time. "What are we looking for?"

"Bloodstains. Especially on the metal rails."

Paradoxically, it's sometimes easier to spot bloodstains in the dark. Luminol helps a lot—a miraculous product that when sprayed on the crime scene can make blood and other organic material glow with an ultraviolet light. In the absence of luminol, when the blood is old, it can take on different hues, from brown to black, depending on the surface it has fallen onto, how long it's been there, and the effects of oxidation. In these cases, Antonia and Jon prefer to work in the dark, focusing on the small circle of light in front of them, combing the area little by little. Seeing less to see more.

"Why didn't you come down to us? We were waiting for you," Jon reproaches her as he points his flashlight at nearby surfaces.

"I can't swim."

"There's only two feet of water. Even you could stand up in it."

"That's enough to drown. Even you fell over."

Jon grits his teeth. He would have liked the Red Queen not to have seen her shield bearer fall flat on his ass. He was supposed to protect her. He'd also like to be back at home with a plate of tripe *a la vizcaina*.

And for the twenty-year-old he's been flirting with on Grindr to finally decide to meet him. And for world peace.

As Mama says, face the fucking music and dance.

That's how it is with Antonia. He has to get her dancing, even if she's the only one who can hear the music.

"It's unlike you to stay so far from the crime scene."

"Sometimes I can see better from a distance."

Out of the corner of his eye, Inspector Gutiérrez recognizes his companion's symptoms. The ones that mean her very special brain is functioning far faster than recommended. By now he has had many months to learn to read that particular stiffness in her shoulders and neck. Her ragged breathing. Her voice an octave higher than normal. Her fingers opening and closing without her realizing it.

Jon's hand moves to his jacket pocket, where he keeps the familiar square-shaped pillbox. But he doesn't take it out. Instead, he bends down and continues examining the rail meticulously. Inch by inch.

No.

Not until she asks for them.

He doesn't have any more time to think about it, because he's found something on the edge of the rail. A dry brown stain.

"Take a look at this."

Antonia turns and comes over to him. Now both of them are crouching under the rail, peering up.

"Is this what you were after?"

Antonia blinks rapidly several times. Another sign Jon has learned to interpret. Like when you hear the hard drive of a laptop humming while the disc head searches for the information.

"It might be. The bloodstain fits with the killer throwing the victim over from here."

Aguado appears at the end of the bridge, with the equipment needed to continue the job. They stand up to give her room, switching off their flashlights.

"You didn't want to commit yourself, is that it?"

Antonia nods in the darkness.

"I don't want to see the body. Not unless it's her."

Jon knows from experience that sometimes the accusing look of the dead can drag promises out of you that you have no chance of keeping. Seven months ago, an adolescent drained of his blood in a deserted mansion did that to Antonia. A promise that collided with the one she had made to Marcos, her husband, that she would never again do anything to put them at risk. She has broken both of them.

"I know what it's like to look into those dead eyes, angel. But in this case, there was no cause for worry. They were eaten by the fish."

"I don't see how that would make me worry any less," says Antonia. She is to irony what Superman is to bullets. "The absence of eyeballs greatly reduces any possibility of identification."

Jon doesn't respond at once. Because what he has to say to Antonia, what Mentor has told him to say, is something she's not going to like at all.

LOLA

Lola Moreno saves her own life thanks to a series of coincidences. The first is that the stroller she is looking at through the Prenatal store window is navy blue. If it had been light colored, the glass wouldn't have reflected the pistol raised by the man behind her. Second, if she didn't have the husband she has—and therefore know that murder is a distinct possibility in her life—it's unlikely her reaction would have been so well judged.

Instead of standing rooted to the spot or turning around to confront her attacker, Lola flings herself to the ground just as the first three shots from the Makarov smash the glass window to smithereens, destroying the stroller's hood.

She saves her life . . . for the moment. *Happiness is short-lived in a poor man's house*, her mother is always telling her. Though Lola Moreno, dressed in Balmain jeans, a soft cashmere jersey, and carrying a Prada bag, isn't exactly what you'd call poor.

She's not short of money.

She's short of time, which is a different story.

Thirty kilos of plate glass land on Lola. She immediately protects her head with her hands, confident Tole will deal with the matter. That's what he's paid for. And paid a lot.

(Lola is shouting something about it, but can't be heard).

Anatoly Oleg Pastushenko is indeed well paid. So well that he's been able to allow himself to become addicted to Starbucks coffee. In order to stay alert. The problem is that the eighteen spoonfuls of sugar in every Venti Frappuccino have made him sluggish and careless. *Fat on reflexes*, says Yuri, who sometimes mixes up words in Spanish to great effect.

Carrying a huge cup in the hand you are supposed to draw your gun with is a hindrance for a bodyguard, especially if your other hand is scrolling your cell phone to find out how Spartak, your soccer team, did last night. However quickly you toss both these things to the ground, the armed assassin will take even less time to spin around toward you before you can pull out your gun.

Tole is hit by four of the five bullets.

One in the leg, when the killer shoots first, almost without aiming. The bullet that hurt the most.

The second and third open a couple of holes in his black jacket and lodge in the left lung and spleen, ripping them apart. This means Tole is going to find it much harder to breathe and fight infection in the six seconds he has left to live. Yet these two bullets don't hurt. The adrenaline and pain from the first one leave no room for that.

Tole manages to get out his gun between his adversary's third and fourth shots. He fires only once, managing to graze the killer's arm and disturbing his aim. The fourth bullet ricochets off a sign on the wall and ends up flying harmlessly through the gap under the glass balustrade to the floor below. From where the sounds of people yelling and running come after they hear the gunfire. And where the next morning, a bored cleaner will sweep it up, along with the rest of the garbage.

The fifth bullet—the one that kills Tole—opens a perfectly round hole above his left eyebrow, plowing through his skull, then slowing down as it pushes through the brain mass before coming to a halt without reaching the parietal bone.

He drops.

Lola stops screaming in time to see Tole's face crash to the ground a few inches from her into a pool of Frappuccino. A scarlet bubble appears between his bloody lips. The friendly, loyal face of her driver and bodyguard, whom she has seen in the rearview mirror every morning for the past six years, now registers only shock and bewilderment. Tole, dead aged forty-seven without having done much in his life or having fulfilled any of his dreams.

Naturally, a thought like that doesn't cross Lola's mind then. Nor will it do so later, when she is running barefoot across the shopping mall's parking lot, feet bleeding, as she fights to survive. It will that night, when she is curled up in a bathroom wanting to weep (covered in a stolen jacket and shaking with fear) and finds she cannot.

The bubble on Tole's lips now bursts, spattering Lola's cheeks with tiny droplets of blood and saliva. And this, more than the shots or the need to protect her unborn child, is what triggers her panic reaction mode. That bubble that bursts with Tole's dying breath.

When jealous women bump into Lola on the way out of expensive restaurants and fashionable boutiques, they nudge one another. Nudges that mean "flower-vase woman" if they are Spanish. "Trophy wife" if they're English or Russian.

The fact is, Lola has more time than other thirtysomethings (according to Lola, only twentysomething) to go to the gym. And this, too, helps save her life when she:

- Shakes off the glass fragments, her hands now flat on the ground, and springs into a burpee pull-up, leaping to her feet with an explosive movement of her gluteus and rectus femoris (Zumba, Wednesdays from 11:00 to 11:45).
- Jumps over Tole's body with a vertical leap without losing her balance (Body Balance, Tuesdays from 12:15 to 1:00).
- Lands a double thrust with her elbow on the assassin's cheekbone (Cardio Boxing, Mondays and Fridays at 10:00, her favorite).

By pure chance—and because Lola stumbles a little—her double elbow jab catches him twice, although not very powerfully. Lola is tall, about five foot nine, but has never hit anybody for real in her life, and the cardio boxing is fine for a housewife for toning her butt, but not for smashing cheekbones. Even so, the confused killer staggers back a little.

And the handkerchief covering his mouth is displaced.

It takes Lola half a second to recognize him.

An entire second to realize she's in deep trouble.

Deep shit, she thinks.

When faced with a threat, the brain's adrenal medulla releases an immediate charge of catecholamine into the bloodstream, giving us instant energy for fight or flight. Lola has already fought: those two weak elbow jabs to the face were her best effort. Now terror demands she flee.

When she leaped up, she lost one of her Miu Miu sandals. As she turns in a panic, she slips on the shattered glass and falls headlong. "Belly flop," as they say in Marbella. She loses the other sandal as she tries to stand up again, and shards of glass lacerate her naked feet. She ignores the pain because she's too frightened to give in to it. As she runs to the emergency exit at the end of the corridor, she offers a perfect target to her killer.

By now he has recovered from the two blows to his face. He levels his pistol and squeezes the trigger. The pink jersey is so close it makes an easy target: but for a pistol to fire, there have to be bullets in the magazine. A Makarov contains only eight. Three bullets into the store window, four into Tole's body, one ricocheting down to the floor below. So the expected *bang! bang! bang!* turns into nothing more than a harmless *click, click.* The killer curses—he's used to other guns with more bullets—and reaches inside his jacket to pull out a second magazine he never thought he would need. Struggling with the slide, he slots the fresh magazine in, but doesn't have time to shoot at the already disappearing jersey because behind his back he hears:

"Put your hands up!"

The killer raises his eyebrows. He's probably thinking: *Seriously? Hands up? Seriously?* and spins round. The security guard from Chocrón Jewelers, revolver in hand, mustache, and beer belly, has run out of the shop and is aiming at him.

The killer gives him no chance to fire. Two shots to the chest, one to the head. That leaves five. Before the guard's knees touch the ground, the assassin has turned back to Lola. He shoots, but his first bullet simply buries itself in the doorframe of the emergency exit, which has already closed behind Lola. He cries out in frustration.

But Lola still isn't safe.

Not by a long shot.

4

A VIDEO CALL

Grandma Scott can tell Antonia is in a very bad mood.

"You're in a very bad mood. I can tell," she says.

She is in her kitchen, spreading butter and jam on a piece of toast, facing the video camera on her iPad. The soft fruit jam is homemade and packed with sugar. Antonia chooses not to remind her grandma that she's not supposed to have sugar or fats. Grandma Scott would only remind her how old she is. Ninety-three going on ninety-four next month. And fresh as a daisy.

No, Antonia doesn't mention the toast. She's given up trying to control her grandmother's sugar and cholesterol levels. What really annoys her is that her grandmother can stuff her face, whereas she has to count every single calorie. Even though very sweet tastes are the only ones that can penetrate the wall of her anosmia, they're a thing of the past for her.

Kummerspeck.

In German, that means "the bacon of sadness." The weight you gain when you're unhappy.

Since Antonia returned to work seven months ago, she's been trying not to let herself go. To make up for three years of eating processed garbage. A slice of toast like that would go straight to her skinny butt.

So she is in the kitchen of her loft in Lavapiés, with a cup of capsule coffee for breakfast, dying of envy.

"It hasn't been a good night" is all she says.

Her grandma squints and comes closer to the screen. She's just noticed something.

"You're calling me from home?"

Antonia props her iPad on the table so she can bury her face in her hands.

"I came back here to sleep. There was no point in going to the hospital so late."

She doesn't tell her grandma this is the fourth night she's slept in the loft. That increasingly she is spending less time with Marcos.

She doesn't tell her she has bought an inflatable mattress she plugs in every night and puts away every morning. That she stuffs it in the closet so the sunlight won't be a witness to her shame.

She doesn't tell her she finds it harder and harder to see her husband, take his hand, and fall asleep next to him. That his increasingly sad and wrinkled body, with its increasingly rough, cold skin, is like an unbearable accusation. That the compassion she previously felt for Marcos, the sense of guilt, the sadness, have slowly transformed into a feeling of resentment.

Empathy for other people's misfortune has its limits. You start to feel their catastrophe is an act of cruelty, with you as its victim.

She doesn't say any of this either. Antonia Scott may be the most intelligent person on the planet. But that doesn't give her the wisdom to know what to do or the strength to do it.

So Antonia says nothing, but her grandma doesn't need to hear it from her.

She knows.

"Yesterday the gas man came for the annual check. Handsome fellow."

Only Grandma Scott is capable of making *handsome fellow* sound lascivious, even with a mouthful of dentures.

"For God's sake, Grandma, you must be forty years older than him."

"Thirty-eight, my girl. And you should see his lunch box," she says, taking another bite of toast. "Plus, he's a widower, poor thing. Perhaps I'll ask him over for lamb roast with mint sauce one of these evenings."

Grandma Scott reckons her leg of lamb with mint sauce has irresistible aphrodisiac qualities. Antonia isn't shocked: she knows her grandmother would flirt with the gravedigger shoveling dirt onto her coffin.

"What I was trying to get at—" her grandma continues.

"I know perfectly well what you wanted to get at," Antonia cuts in. "I don't need a man in my life."

"Nonsense. Look what I'm reading. It has a very interesting test."

She lifts a magazine up to the screen. Antonia reads nine of the twelve letters in the headline. In their Franklin Gothic font and discreet fuchsia color. The rest of the letters are hidden by the forehead of a blond woman. Antonia can't understand how she can be smiling so much while she's biting her thumb.

"Time to grab a hunk? Find out in fifty questions."

"You're trying to dissect me with such a blunt instrument?"

"Don't play the innocent, my girl. Just look at question three . . ."

Antonia lets her go on for a while, until her grandma realizes she isn't listening.

"All right. What's the matter?"

Her granddaughter starts to talk.

About her failure to communicate with her son, Jorge. About how unbearable she finds the way he looks at her as if he can't quite trust her. She says it's something she doesn't really understand, something neither of them is accustomed to.

Her grandmother nods, but makes no comment.

Antonia describes how she feels toward her husband in a coma. She's very evasive about this. She has a black belt in lying to herself, and only a yellow one in expressing her reality.

Her grandma nods, and says nothing.

"I've been talking to myself for ten minutes."

"You've been wallowing in self-pity for ten minutes. I didn't bring you up to be a sniveling wreck. You're not going to get any compassion from me, my girl. If you want to cry, go and lean on Jon. He's being paid to lend you that big muscly shoulder of his."

"Aha," says Antonia once she's recovered from the violence of her grandma's attack. She's always frank, but this time she's wrapped her frankness in sandpaper and bludgeoned her with it. "Things aren't too good with Jon either. He's not backing me up much with Mentor. Last night—"

"Oh, you're so pigheaded!" her grandma interrupts. "Listen, and listen carefully, Antonia Scott. There's only one solution to your problems. To all of them. Let it go."

Antonia blinks in astonishment. The old woman goes on:

"You made a mistake years ago. It was your fault Marcos died."

"He's not dead, Grandma."

"We both know what it says in the medical reports. We both know you cling to him only because you can't admit you made a mistake. But your husband isn't there anymore. You made yourself ill not wanting to admit it. Your pride made you ill. It drove Jorge from you and forced your father to take him from you."

Her grandma pauses to take a sip from a glass on the table. It looks like red-currant juice, but knowing her grandma as she does, Antonia is sure it's another kind of juice. The sort that matures in oak.

"Because you haven't been with him since he was born, you've learned nothing about being a mother. Above all, the most important lesson: we never get it right. Whatever you do, it will be wrong. And when he grows up, he'll blame you for all his problems and defects. That's how it is. How we are."

Antonia understands this last part very well. After all, she blames her own father for lots of things.

"You don't pull any punches, do you?"

"As long as you don't allow yourself to make mistakes, you'll go on believing you're a bad mother. That you're letting your husband down. That you're a poor investigator because you can't find someone who nobody has ever gotten close to. You'll carry on being stuck and scared to death. Your only kingdom will be isolation and loneliness. Let it go."

It takes Antonia a few seconds to remember where she's heard that line before. Then she recalls it was the first movie Jorge asked to see when Social Services allowed her to be with him again. An incomprehensible movie with snowmen that talk and a princess who won't come out of the closet. Two hours of her life she'll never get back.

"Did you just quote Elsa, Grandma?"

"And I'm proud of it," says her grandma, raising the glass, which definitely doesn't contain currant juice.

Antonia snorts in exasperation, disturbing the bangs on her forehead. Her short hair has become a mane down below her shoulders, crying out for a cut. She hasn't even found time for that.

"I don't think you need to worry about my obsession. I only have a few hours before Aguado hands in her official report and confirms to Mentor what we all know already. That the body in the Manzanares isn't Sandra Fajardo."

"You don't even know her real name yet, do you?"

Antonia can still hear Sandra's voice ringing out in the dark tunnel. Those words whose meaning she still can't properly grasp:

With your amazing memory, you can't even recall the people you've hurt? The victims of your fight against evil?

"I don't have anything, Grandma. Everything about the Ezequiel case was a fabrication. The religious paraphernalia, the intricate modus operandi: it was all lies, smoke and mirrors. And I still don't understand why. Except that it involves White."

Her grandma takes another sip and puts on her beatific smile, the smile promising candy. She is not even remotely upset that Antonia has to give up her pursuit.

"That man is a lunatic, Antonia."

No, Grandma, he isn't. He's much more than that. Why can't anyone see it? thinks Antonia.

But she doesn't respond.

She wants to hang up.

She wants to go back to her living room and sit down, cross-legged, for her sacred three minutes. She has never needed them so much.

"Do you have any idea what Mentor has up his sleeve for you now?"

"No, I don't," says Antonia, shaking her head. "Some nonsense or other."

"Brighten up that face, my girl. It'll make you feel better."

LOLA

Lola runs down the stairs, repeating to herself some invaluable advice.

They work in pairs. When they go after someone, they always work in pairs.

A snatch of conversation she overhears in her living room as she serves eel blini and jugs of kissel, then sponges down the work surface. Conversation that becomes more animated as the night wears on and the loud voices drown out the perennial background noise of Pervý Kanal, which they get thanks to the satellite dish on the chalet roof. Dangerous loudmouths, showing off in front of her, as if she didn't exist. Yuri's pussy. Who can hardly speak Russian, it seems. Who cares what she hears?

It's true she doesn't speak Russian very well, although she's spent six years studying it, but she understands almost everything. At least enough to have heard one of the buddies—or associates, which to Yuri is the same thing—describing the way hired killers work. Never imagining she might one day be the target.

A motorbike or car waits outside. In a public space. Bang, bang, *then the gunman runs toward the waiting vehicle while the guy on the bike keeps watch and covers their exit.* Vroom, vroom *and* da svidaniya. Si te he visto no me acuerdo. (*If I saw you, I don't remember.*)

This last sentence said in Spanish, because Russians love Spanish expressions.

Lola knows the shopping mall like the palm of her hand, and so knows what she would have done. Left the car with its engine running in the parking lot near the emergency exit.

Which means she's running in the wrong direction.

A noise two floors above confirms her suspicion. The killer is on her trail. In order to make sure, Lola pokes her head out into the stairwell. The shot misses her by inches. The explosion fills her ears, echoing off the concrete walls.

Lola curses herself, then continues sprinting down. She is running out of stairs, options, space. She has reached the emergency door that leads to the parking lot.

Behind her comes the sound of the killer's footsteps as he rushes down the stairs. There's no time to lose. Lola pushes open the door, and there it is, ten yards from her, parked across the sidewalk.

A car with the engine running.

Lola doesn't stop to see who the driver is—she already knows that—but dodges among the cars parked in the lot. It's too early for there to be many of them: rush hour is at midday, when the foreigners come to have lunch first, then to burn plastic at Gucci or Valentino. So Lola has to bend down and scurry between them, trying to find somewhere to hide. Vaguely aware that her feet are leaving bloody prints on the asphalt.

She hears the emergency door opening again. She crouches behind a brand-new Prius, only too aware there are no more cars left to shield her: the nearest one is three spaces away.

It starts raining. Buckets.

Lola is paralyzed, trembling with fear, unsure what to do, when the Prius's rear window is shattered. Yelping with terror, she throws herself to the ground. She can't see the killer, it's too far for her to run to the next car. All she can do is crawl under the Prius. She pulls herself along, noting the sticky feel of motor oil on her hands and elbows (soaking through the €1,200 jersey).

The car is dripping oil.

Lola is dripping as well: dripping blood. The cuts on her feet have made her lose a lot, and she has not had any breakfast. Her idea had been to grab a coffee after buying the stroller. They say it's bad luck to buy one so soon: she is only in the third month of her pregnancy. If she wears loose clothing, it's barely visible. But she wants so much to have a baby. And she's so impatient.

It brings bad luck.

Lola is starting to feel light-headed; she can't see properly. Her arms are growing weak; the ground is pulling her down to it. Promising peace.

No, dammit, I mustn't pass out.

Something within her is tempted by the idea of losing consciousness and letting them shoot her without her being aware of it. Fade to black, *That's all, folks*. Easy, painless.

No.

She struggles up again. Mixed with the rain, the oil has left a slippery iridescent rainbow stain on her cheek, which runs into her open mouth. The taste is sweet.

Not a nice sweet.

She spits.

She crawls out and toward the next car in the row, reaching it just in time. She sees a pair of boots on the far side. Thick black boots, one of them bloodstained.

The tip of the right foot is less than a yard from her.

If he moves a bit, he'll see me.

If he crouches, he'll see me.

Someone cries for Lola, sadly and softly. It's her, of course. She doesn't make any noise and hardly moves, but she weeps disconsolately because of the huge injustice of dying like this, trapped under a car, filthy and all alone.

That's when the siren sounds. Not far away like in the movies, but very close and very loud. A block away, at most.

The boots disappear.

A door slams shut, a car engine accelerates and disappears in the distance.

Still weeping, Lola drops to the ground again, only for a short rest, as she can't stay there, the threat isn't over.

She doesn't stop crying, even when the cell phone starts vibrating in her jeans pocket.

She didn't even remember she had it with her.

It's a message from Yuri.

They're coming for me. You know what to do.

You idiot. You stupid jerk, thinks Lola. If she had her husband in front of her at that moment, she'd tear out the hair implants he'd just had done in Turkey.

Now *you're warning me?* Now?

5

IN A HURRY

What's good and what's bad about Bilbao?

The bad thing about Bilbao is that there is nowhere like Attack. Somewhere to relieve tension and aching balls in a couple of hours of cruising if you incline to starboard.

The good thing about Bilbao is there are no places like Attack, places Jon emerges from with a bruised soul and feeling far lonelier than when he went in.

But feeling lighter, I have to admit.

What he really wants is for the guy on Grindr to respond. But following a few chats, it seems as if the earth has swallowed him up. And he was very hot. Inspector Gutiérrez doesn't want to get his rocks off twice a week and feel like crying. What he wants is civilized love, but he can't find it.

Jon does up his jacket as he leaves, his hair still dripping from the sauna. He doesn't bother with his overcoat, because he's only six minutes from home. The universe putting temptation in your way, and what have you.

The eternal optimist, Jon switches on his cell phone. Inside Attack, you have to leave phones in the coatroom along with everything else, for obvious reasons. Let's see if he is lucky and a message from the young man pops up.

What pops up are five calls from Mentor.

Six, with the last one just coming in.

"It's almost two in the morning," says Jon, picking up.

"I hope you've prepared Scott as I asked."

"She already has Aguado's report," sighs Jon.

"It's as we feared. The dead woman isn't Sandra Fajardo, so I'll take you off the case."

"Couldn't this wait until tomorrow?"

"No, because something very important has come up. I need the two of you to go to Marbella."

"Okay, tomorrow first thi—"

"Right now, Inspector. Believe me, this is very urgent. And very, very big. Fetch Scott and get going. I'll send you the details on the way."

Jon's jaw drops as wide as a shark's. Either that or he's yawning—there's no way of telling the difference. This makes two nights in a row he's been to bed late. The previous one fishing out dead bodies, this one with his gay pursuits. He's not that young anymore, so he needs this order like a hole in the head.

"It's a six-hour drive."

"With that car of yours, you can make it in four if you step on it. But drive carefully."

"You're asking me to step on it and drive carefully in the same sentence?"

"They're not incompatible."

"I'm dead tired."

"If you need a chemical stimulus, you should be able to find what you want in your glove compartment."

That's all we need. Two drug addicts on the team for the price of one.

"Look here, my body is a temple."

"You can't say that with your cholesterol levels, Inspector."

"I thought medical records were confidential."

"They're confidential enough. Don't crash," Mentor orders. And ends the call.

As a result, half an hour later Antonia is sitting in the passenger seat of the Audi A8. Metallic black, tinted windows, alloy wheels, €100,000 or more. Jon has christened it "the Queenmobile," a nickname only he finds amusing.

"If you're tired, I can drive," Antonia offers, all sweetness and light.

This is the third car Mentor has provided them with. Antonia wrecked the first after a 250-kilometer-an-hour chase. Jon crashed the second one against the Rolls-Royce belonging to Sir Peter Scott, Antonia's father, in a fit of anger. But as Jon sees it, that was her fault as well.

All of which means Jon doesn't intend to let her drive until the twenty-second century at least.

"Have a rest, angel. Take a nap."

Disgruntled, Antonia leans back against the headrest, closes her eyes, and pretends to sleep.

Jon looks at the time and thinks of Amatxo, and how she must be feeling. At the age of seventy-one, and with her Arizona bingo hall closed down. What will she do to amuse herself, all alone, poor thing?

All alone, of course, because it suits her. Against all expectation, she didn't want to leave her apartment in Bilbao and follow her son to Madrid. She has no intention of going anywhere at her age. "You go if you want, I know you don't care if I die here alone." Of course I do, Ama, but duty calls and what have you. But she wouldn't budge, leaving him to iron his own shirts for the first time in forty-three years. Not really, because a laundry does that for him. Besides, Mentor pays him a fortune every month. Close to five figures. But still, he misses her.

I must call her.

The person who does call, just as they're traveling down the A-4 past Valdemoro, is Mentor. On Antonia's iPad. Using FaceTime.

She props the tablet up on the dash and accepts the call.

"You must be wondering why I've sent you to Marbella in the middle of the night."

The webcam accentuates Mentor's receding hairline and the bags under his eyes. He seems to have aged ten years all of a sudden. And he's still *vaping*.

"No, actually, we weren't. Nothing like six hundred kilometers to stretch your legs."

"Keep your eyes on the road, Inspector."

"And don't you blow smoke at the camera, we can't see a thing."

"Since we abandoned our search for Fajardo, there have been several cases where they called for Red Queen," says Mentor, ignoring him. "I've had to turn down or delay your involvement in them. But now something has come up, an opportunity we haven't had for a long time."

Mentor holds a printed photo up to the camera. From a passport, by the looks of it. A dark-haired young man, around thirty-five. Broad nose, short hair. Full lips.

I'd give him one, thinks Jon.

"This was more or less what Yuri Voronin looked like until a couple of days ago."

Mentor holds up another photo.

"This is what he looks like now."

It's a high-res photograph, taken with a flash. A bit too high-res. It shows Yuri's shoulders, and Yuri's chin. And, if you try hard to distinguish it among all the blood and bone, you can even see Yuri's hair. What you can't see are the nose, eyes, or the rest of Yuri's face, because they've been blown off by a shotgun.

Now I wouldn't give him one, thinks Jon, looking away.

"A twelve-caliber? With ceramic bullets, I think," suggests Antonia, peering closely at the screen.

"We did well investing in your education," says Mentor, confirming her opinion and showing them more photos. The body slumped over a glass table. From a distance, it looks as if half his head is missing, because half his head is missing. "For all intents and purposes, Yuri Voronin was a legitimate businessman," Mentor continues. "He had an import firm. Agrochemical products, fertilizers and acaricides, imported from Saint Petersburg to Algeciras or Málaga. And iron, aluminum, and other raw materials. In recent months, he's been concentrating on Funduk."

"What's that?"

"It means 'hazelnut' in Russian," says Antonia.

She knows Russian as well, thinks Jon. *Of course.*

"It's the Russian Nutella," Mentor explains. "Apparently, it's all the rage on the Costa del Sol. They're even exporting it to France."

"Nutella makes you fat," says Antonia, whose stomach has started to rumble at the mere mention of the name.

"Funduk is even worse. The Russians haven't pandered to the environmentalists' stupidity of taking out the palm oil, so it tastes like it should. They think that's why it's so successful."

"Let me guess," says Jon. "He wasn't murdered because he sold milk, cacao, hazelnuts, and sugar."

"No, I'm afraid not. We believe Yuri Voronin was the Orlov clan's treasurer. The main Russian Mafia in Spain."

"Why kill the treasurer? Because he skipped a column on Excel?"

"That's an important question, Inspector. Let me ask you another one. What do you know about organized crime on the Costa del Sol?"

"That it's no laughing matter," says Jon.

Even though it's not within Jon's area of expertise when he's working as a normal cop, he's been reading internal memos about it for years. He knows raids are an almost weekly event; that there are millions of euros and kilos of drugs impounded. Dozens of deaths, which are on the rise and never hit the headlines. Because above all, we don't want to bite the hand that feeds us. And in Spain, what feeds us is sun and sand.

"No, it's no laughing matter at all. It's chaos, Inspector. Colombians, Swedes, Algerians, Kosovars, all fighting for their slice of the cake. And above them all, the Russians, cutting the cake. It's a war, and we're losing it."

"For all the usual reasons?"

"No funds for the local police forces. Different factions. Rivalries. UDYCO on one side, GRECO on the other. The Civil Guard doing their own thing."

"All the usual reasons."

Mentor shows them more photographs. An auburn-haired, blue-eyed woman. An oval face. Even from her ID card, you can tell she's quite stunning. *Even if we don't fancy women.*

"Lola Moreno Fernández. Born Fuengirola in 1989. Finished one module of a secretarial course. Flirted with becoming a model, served drinks, go-go dancer. Nothing lucrative. Six years ago she married Yuri, and now she lives in a chalet worth five million euros."

"Too pretty to wear mourning clothes," says Jon. "What has she said?"

"Not much. Yesterday morning they tried to kill her in a shopping mall, at the same time that her husband was blasted. They murdered her driver and a security guard, and she has vanished."

"The police will be looking for her."

"And so will Orlov's hired killers, so now we're in a race against the clock. Your job is to win the race. That's why I'm sending you to Marbella in such a hurry, before the trail grows cold. Lola Moreno is our only link to Yuri Voronin. If you can discover why they killed her husband and tried to kill her, maybe we can open a chink in the Orlov clan's armor. Any questions?"

Jon grunts.

Antonia says nothing.

The two men know she is sulking. That what she wants is to stay in Madrid, searching for Sandra Fajardo. Or whatever her name might be.

"You don't seem very enthusiastic," Mentor reprimands her. He won't give in.

"Mafia people are boring," she says with a shrug.

"Oh, come on, this will be like Valencia."

"You and I have very different versions of Valencia."

Mentor clears his throat.

"A chaotic situation like this is the essence of why the Red Queen project was created. If anyone can clear up this mess, it's you, Antonia. I've left all the latest information on the server. Keep me up to speed," says Mentor, and hangs up.

Silence inside the car. The insulated interior of an Audi A8 is a work of art. You can't even hear the murmur of the tires as the powerful vehicle devours the kilometers.

"I always wear black," Antonia says after a while.

Puzzled, Jon looks across at her.

"You said that woman was too pretty to wear mourning clothes. What about me?"

You need to get out of mourning, Jon thinks. But he says:

"How can I explain," he says, adopting a very serious expression. "You're not the model type. But when you decide to smile, not all the Lola Morenos in the world come up to the soles of your shoes."

There, he's said it.

Antonia smiles.

Her patented ten-thousand-kilowatt smile.

Jon realizes this is the first time in months he's seen her do so, and his heart melts. Right now he has a chocolate coulis in the center of his chest.

Oh, sweetheart, how difficult you are, and how lovable.

6

A SIGN

First things first. And the first thing is breakfast.

Jon brushes Antonia's elbow to wake her. Gently. Antonia stirs uneasily.

She can't bear to be touched, but this time she says nothing.

Jon isn't sure if this is progress. He'd like to think it is.

"We're close by now. We're going to stop here."

Antonia stretches in her seat, rubs her eyes. They're parked outside a café. And it's still dark.

"This isn't the right address."

"I'm saying it is. I've got the mother of all empty stomachs. Either you allow me a coffee and a roll, or you can go to the crime scene by yourself."

Antonia reaches for the glove compartment. Beneath the car instruction manual is a red envelope. She opens it, and takes out a small strip of white pills. She shows them to her colleague.

"I don't know if Mentor told you, but—"

"Look, sweetie, don't bust balls. We've got enough going on already. Keep those for yourself."

"Diphenylmethyl-sulfinylacetamide? If you gave me one of these, my head would explode."

"Me give you drugs? Are you crazy?" says Jon, getting out of the car. Slamming the door.

Antonia catches up with him inside, perched on a stool. From behind, he looks like a gray olive on a toothpick.

"In the end, it seems you're right. This place is really expensive," says Jon, his mouth full. "Ten euros for a ham-and-cheese roll and a café con leche."

"A *pitufo mixto* and a *mitad*," Antonia orders from the waiter when he comes over.

Voices in the kitchen. Steam from the espresso machine. The sound of plates landing in front of them.

"Five euros," says the waiter.

Antonia elbows Jon for him to pay.

"Hey," says Jon, holding out the banknote. "I ordered the same, and you charged me twice as much."

The waiter points to a small sign behind him. Small. Damn small.

WELCOME TO MARBELLA

WARNING: IF YOU DON'T ORDER PROPERLY

WE CHARGE DOUBLE:

Ham and cheese roll: pitufo mixto

Café con leche: mitad

Under his breath, Jon curses all that's holy and unholy, but says nothing. To avoid trouble. Turn the page. Yet another in his long history with waiters.

"I can't believe you read the sign."

Antonia bites into the roll. She shouldn't, but . . .

"They trained me to see everything."

"Everything? Everywhere you go, every situation?"

"It's who I am."

"It's not who you are, it's what you do, pretty one. If you think any different, you'll end up crazy." He takes a sip of his coffee. "Crazier, I mean."

"It's the same thing."

"No, it isn't. If it were, you wouldn't be allowed to fail."

"I'm not."

Jon drains his coffee.

"*Tabernari*, a glass of water, if you please. And you can charge me triple."

The waiter looks daggers at him, but then considers how Jon is built, and in the end brings him the glass of water. As hot as possible.

"Antonia . . . I know you're angry with me, with Mentor, and the whole world. But failing isn't everything. We haven't found Sandra, there is no sign of Mr. White. So what? Life goes on."

Seconds pass, lulled by the sound of the TV and the chinking of the one-armed bandit. It takes Antonia about a week and a half to answer. When she does, she won't look Jon in the eye. She stares at her empty cup and the accusatory crumbs on her plate.

"You don't know how hard it is being me."

Jon guffaws. More like an indignant snort.

"Of course not, dammit. No one knows what it's like to be another person. But you possess something special. Something valuable that you shouldn't waste. The only superpower I have is being able to recognize a Manolo Blahnik at fifty yards."

Puzzled, Antonia looks across at him.

"In certain circumstances, being able to identify a suspect's exact footwear is—"

"You're impossible."

As they get up to leave, the headlines come on the Canal Sur morning news:

The police still have no leads on the failed attempt to rob a jeweler in Paradise Shopping Mall. The attackers killed a security guard and a customer who . . .

Jon and Antonia exchange looks. Neither of them says a word.

7

A TRIANGLE

Outside, the air is milder. Not swimsuit weather, but no need for overcoats either. And day is finally dawning, the sun glinting off the hoods of parked cars.

Jon drives them to the shopping mall. An hour and a half to opening time. The parking lot is deserted except for a patrol car, pulled up sideways across six parking spaces. There's nothing cops enjoy more than making it very obvious that traffic regulations don't apply to them. A plainclothes cop, lanyard around his neck and file under his arm, is waiting by the emergency exit. Access to the crime scene investigation is marked by several meters of black-and-white-striped tape.

Jon goes over and flashes his badge.

"I'm Inspector Gutiérrez."

"Oh, the people from Madrid. Come through, come through," says the cop, lifting the tape.

He is young, not yet thirty. Tall, dark complexion, muscular. Kind eyes in a sharp face. Hungry looking but handsome. Broad shoulders. He extends his hand to shake Jon's when they're both inside the tape.

"Deputy Inspector Belgrano. And you are . . . ?" he asks, turning to Antonia and stretching out his hand once more.

There is an awkward pause for five beats, namely:

Antonia stares at Deputy Inspector Belgrano's hand without showing the slightest intention of taking it.

Antonia looks at Jon.

Jon tries to make a stammering introduction, until he realizes they haven't agreed on a story for her.

The deputy inspector puts his hand in his jeans pocket.

Antonia moves her hand to her shoulder bag and takes out a dark blue ID card.

"Scott. From OCO."

Belgrano's face adopts an expression as if to say: *This should ring a bell, but it doesn't.*

Antonia explains.

"Organized Crime Office. Europol."

Europol. Like Interpol, but Euro. Europol. Good choice, angel, thinks Jon, rolling his eyes on the inside. Yes, that sounds like Mentor.

"Wow, you're the first I've met from there," says a surprised Belgrano.

"There aren't many of us." Antonia shrugs.

Not many, meaning very few, thinks Jon. *Less than a thousand in all Europe. And fewer intermediaries still with the ID Mentor provided. If anybody asks after you, it's going to seem very odd no one knows you. But at least the atmosphere here seems less hostile than with Parra.*

"Well, we're lucky you've come. We need all the help we can get. Go on up, but be careful at the foot of the stairs. There's a bloody footprint, so don't tread on it," says Belgrano, passing in front of them and holding the door open.

Definitely less hostile.

The staircase is lit only by the emergency lights. Despite this, they can spot a yellow evidence triangle on the ground by a red mark that clearly shows the print of a heel and a couple of toes. There's another triangle a few steps higher. Between them are more bloody footmarks, although few of them are complete.

"There are several prints that haven't been marked," says Antonia.

"Yes, those are all Señora Moreno's."

"How do you know? Have you compared them with the missing woman?"

Belgrano looks sheepish.

"No, but we concluded that . . ."

Antonia and Jon say nothing, but exchange a rapid look.

"To be honest, we ran out of triangles," Belgrano finally admits. "And there were lots of prints. We preferred to use the triangles we have at the main crime scene upstairs."

"Is it intact?"

"We were instructed from Madrid not to touch anything until you arrived. The examining magistrate has been by already and ordered the bodies removed, because they couldn't be left there. The rest is untouched. That part of the mall is sealed off until tomorrow."

"What about Forensics?"

"At the husband's chalet, with the other body. They started here because it's a public space. And there aren't many of us, so we couldn't cover both places at once."

The three of them start to mount the stairs, with Belgrano in the lead. Antonia in the middle. Jon last of all (he doesn't like stairs).

"I hear you're short of money."

"You're not kidding. Here in Málaga, they assign more officers to the Interior Ministry than to us. All the new recruits go to Madrid or Seville. And the ones from Interior aren't worth a cent."

From his accent, Jon guesses he isn't from Málaga, but farther inland. From Granada, maybe.

"We need at least twice the number we have. To give it a decent shot. Literally: they give us ten bullets a month for target practice. If I want more, I have to pay for them myself."

Jon, who has fought a thousand and one battles over police budgets, forgets he now earns four times as much as Deputy Inspector Belgrano and starts sounding off about the lily-livered unions and the dumbasses in the Interior Ministry, who only consider the bottom line and not people. Belgrano agrees emphatically, failing to notice that a very special person has slipped past them and is opening the staircase door with a view to doing more than complain.

"Hey! Where are you going? You can't go in there without an officer—"

Jon grabs him gently by the elbow.

"Hey, Belgrano . . . if you want to see something really interesting, stay right here and let her get to work." Then he adds, just to be sure: "And even if you don't."

8

NINE SHOTS

Antonia leaves them to their blah-blah and enters the upper floor of the shopping mall. For once, she doesn't go straight to the crime scene. Today she wants to try something different. Maybe that way . . .

She closes her eyes.

Sleep, that frontier of the life we don't have, has turned its back on her for months now. Last night was no exception. A long, disturbed doze in the car, filled with disturbing images that offered no rest or comfort. In recent weeks, rest has been a luxury she hasn't wanted to allow herself. Even when her body capitulated, when her eyes were stinging in the early hours, overwhelmed with data, exhausted from taking in hour after hour of CCTV images. Searching for Sandra, for the face peopling her nightmares, her muscles screaming at her after so many hours without moving, and Antonia was about to give in . . .

Her mind was bent on sabotaging her.

It tells her she's burned out. That she has nothing left, that she's a failure.

That's why she has fought tooth and nail against taking on new cases, on starting the old game over again before the last one was properly finished. Even going near dead bodies like the one in the Manzanares two nights earlier. Maybe out of concern—not fear, because Antonia is afraid of almost nothing—that if she rolls the dice again, she will uncover a truth she suspects about herself. That all the nonsense about duty and responsibility is nothing but empty words. That what matters, what truly matters to her, is power. Responsibility is no more than the tax included at the foot of the bill.

Then there's the other thing. The main problem.

She opens her eyes.

The early morning light is streaming through the huge glass window on the mall's eastern wall, turning it into a giant camera in which her eyelashes are the shutter and her brain the film.

She closes her eyes.

The image remains printed on her mind, as sharp as if she still had her eyes open. Less saturated. More manageable.

Her breathing becomes heavier, her pulse speeds up, the blood is pounding in her ears.

She can control it. All on her own.

She tries to classify all the elements in the scene in front of her.

The store window, smashed to smithereens.

The shards of glass like an unmade bed on the floor.

The outline drawn next to them where there had been a body, now removed.

The outline of another body, some way off.

Thebag,therearelotsofbulletcasingswhysomanyshotsthisisntanormalkillingIneedthepills.

"I don't need them," she lies to herself.

It doesn't work.

She doesn't hold out her hand or look for Jon, even though she knows he's only a few meters away, keeping a close eye on her, ready to approach when she calls for her dose, the dose of pills only he is authorized to give her.

She doesn't ask for anything.

She feels in her pants pocket, trying to hide the movement of her hand from him. She takes out two pills with her fingertips.

Please let them be enough. Please, let two be enough.

She bites through the coating and releases the longed-for bitter powder, sliding it under her tongue so that her mucous membrane will absorb the cocktail of chemical substances and take it into her bloodstream as quickly as possible. One isn't enough: she bites into the second one.

She counts to ten, breathing out after each number, descending a step at a time, down to where she needs to be.

Suddenly, the world becomes slower, smaller. The electricity tingling in her hands, chest, and face subsides.

She is back. Back to clarity. And mixed with it, a strange joy combined with a feeling of wretchedness.

Antonia combs her mental dictionary of impossible words to express what she is feeling.

Kegemteraan.

In Malay, "the joy of stumbling." The simultaneous feeling of pleasure and dismay when you realize you have done something you shouldn't have.

She'll struggle with the dismay later. For now, Antonia plunges into clarity, where the monkeys in her mind are silently crouching, awaiting her orders. They are still baring their fangs at one another and writhing around, but silently.

Antonia speaks.

"The killer fires first at the store window."

"How do you know?" says Deputy Inspector Belgrano in a low voice.

"Shhh. Keep quiet and learn," says Jon.

Antonia takes three steps toward the Prenatal store. Extending her arm, she makes a pistol of her first finger and thumb. She's so small she looks like a little girl playing cops and robbers.

She adjusts her arm, trying to get the angle right. Opposite her is the stroller with the ripped hood. There's another one to its left, a pink stroller.

"What time was the attack?"

Jon nudges Belgrano for him to respond.

"Eleven twenty-one. We know from the CCTV recording on the floor below. It's when everyone started running and calling the police."

Antonia looks down at the ground, at the shadow cast by her body and arm. Then she stares in front of her again.

"She saw him. Possibly reflected in the window. That's why she ducked down. Was the store shut?"

"The assistant was in the restroom when it happened. She'd put up a sign saying BACK IN FIVE MINUTES. Just as well, because we found one of the bullets buried in the counter."

"What about CCTV on this floor?"

"None. Someone spiked the recording," Belgrano says.

"How convenient," grumbles Jon.

Antonia steps to the side. Prenatal is the last store before the emergency exit. On the left before that, there is a corridor leading to the restrooms. On the other side, the metal and glass balustrade opens to the lower floor. The store next to Prenatal is Chocrón Jewelers. It's also cordoned off, beside the escalators. There are more stores on this floor, but they are around the corner.

The perfect place for a killing. A mousetrap, with few witnesses and an easy escape route.

Antonia raises her arm again, pointing with her finger.

"He fired. And missed."

She turns to her right. She steps over the evidence triangles.

"The first body, the one on the left, is Señora Moreno's driver, isn't it?"

Belgrano consults his notes.

"Anatoly Oleg Pastushenko. Born in Georgia in 1971. Former police officer in Riflis. Living in Spain for a number of years. We don't know exactly how many. Officially obtained residency seven years ago. He was the first employee of Señor Voronin, Lola's husband."

"Do we know how many bullets hit him?"

"Four, according to the forensic report. Two in the torso, one in the head, and one just below the left knee."

From where the killer had stood, Antonia takes three, four, five steps forward, turns around, bends down a little. Taking a pen out of her shoulder bag, she inserts it into the empty end of one of the cartridges and lifts it to eye level. She recognizes the Cyrillic characters, the three unmistakable letters: M.A.K.

"The killer's weapon was a nine-millimeter Makarov."

"Yes, that's what we've confirmed," says Belgrano. "Unfortunately, there are lots of them around here."

Not just in Marbella. Since the famous engineer Makarov designed this small pistol in the fifties, the Soviet Union and many of its satellite countries made it into the regulation weapon for their armies and police forces. And its use spread. Nowadays, from China to Cuba and from Ukraine to Zimbabwe, there are millions of them in service, all of them almost identical and using compatible ammunition. Cheap, throwaway, ideal for staying under the radar and leaving no trace.

Antonia straightens up and surveys the scene. Blinks several times.

"The driver fired as well," she announces.

Belgrano starts.

"We have no indication that the driver was arm—"

Jon silences him once more.

"And I think somebody tried to hide the fact," says Antonia.

9

A DISAPPOINTMENT

Antonia retraces her steps, then kneels down, placing her hands on the floor, and presses her nose to the tiles.

"Jon, come over here, will you?"

Inspector Gutiérrez approaches her.

"Tell me if you can smell bleach."

Jon doesn't need to bend down and sniff the floor. The smell of bleach is overpowering. He nods to Antonia.

"Even I can smell it," she says. "Did they use luminol?"

"The Forensics team was here, but there's nothing in their report about a return shot or blood that didn't belong to the two victims or the woman," says a confused Belgrano.

"The killer lost blood here. Not much, just a few drops."

Despite having worked alongside Antonia for a while now, even Jon is astonished at her assertion.

"How . . . ?"

Antonia points to the floor, then the store window.

"Count the bullet cases. Three in the first sequence."

"When the killer aimed at Lola Moreno. And missed."

"What else? Look at the pattern of the shots. The first destroys the window, but all three hit the hood of the stroller six meters away. That's a small target. What does it tell you?"

"The shots were all grouped together. With a nine-millimeter. Precision. Lots of it," concludes Jon.

"Our suspect's hand is not shaky, even though he misses. He misses his main target, and suddenly has to deal with the driver."

"The driver who, from his CV, is more of a bodyguard."

"He turns toward him. The driver was clumsy, careless. He had a cell phone in one hand and a cup of coffee in the other," says Antonia, pointing to the stain on the floor. "But the killer doesn't want to run any risks, so his first shot is instinctive. That's why he hits him in the leg."

"How do you know it was the first shot?"

"Look at the position of the body and the bloodstains on the floor. There's no backward spatter, no footprints of the driver in his own blood, no signs of dragging himself along. That means he didn't advance an inch after he was shot the first time."

"The two other bullets hit him in the chest, which again shows precision. And the third one to the head even more so."

"Exactly. So the first shot in the leg when the killer wheels around instinctively. The driver falls to his knees, then is shot once or twice in the chest. After those two shots, or in between them, he himself fires. Then collapses."

"What, you mean there's something you're not sure about?"

"I can't deduce everything," says Antonia.

"I'm disappointed."

Antonia pulls a face, but at least she recognizes Jon's attempt at humor. The pills help.

She rewards Jon with a slight stretch of her lips. Almost a half smile.

"But you still haven't explained how you know the driver fired a shot."

"Simple. Look at the casings on the floor. When the killer turns, he creates a second shot area. Now count the cases in that second area."

"Five."

"The driver was hit four times. We know the first was in the leg. The last to the head. Two hit the chest. But the killer, who is incredibly accurate, fires a shot, but we don't know what happened to the bullet. If he had fired in that direction . . ."

". . . the bullet would have ended up in the driver's body, the wall, or on the floor," both men conclude in unison.

Jon scratches his head.

"So the driver fires, hits the killer, which makes him miss once. The bullet ends up who knows where, and he is hit in the head."

"That's right."

"I'd never have guessed."

"Now I'm disappointed," says Antonia. "But someone has spilled bleach on the floor. Someone who didn't want us to find any valid DNA."

On a nonporous surface, sodium hypochlorite destroys all traces of blood. If bleach is present, luminol simply reacts to the whole area, lighting up like a Christmas tree. The blood wouldn't show up in more sophisticated tests such as phenophthalein or immuno-hemoglobin either.

"Has anybody else had access to the crime scene?" Jon asks Belgrano.

"No, of course not," the deputy inspector protests. "When we got the call, a patrol car came at once, but it was too late: the killer had disappeared. And since then, there have been police guarding the scene."

"So the killer himself spilled bleach on his own blood? Or did he have an accomplice who managed to slip through your net?"

"It wasn't the security guard," says Antonia, pointing to the second body outline.

Belgrano reads his notes.

"Mateo Lorente. Native of La Rioja. He came to live in Marbella with his wife and daughter a couple of years ago, when he got the security job. Now look at him."

"Collateral damage," Antonia says coldly. "Let's get on with it."

"Hey, security guards are human beings too," Belgrano bridles.

Inspector Gutiérrez takes a deep breath and tries to sound mellow, like when you have to reassure a nervous Chihuahua.

"If Pope Francis had been pissing behind a flower pot and died in the crossfire, Señora Scott would consider that collateral damage."

Antonia leans over to Jon and whispers.

"Maybe if it were an international dignit—"

"You're not helping."

"Sorry." Then, raising her voice again, "We know the victim, Señora Moreno, fled down the stairs."

"She left her sandals," says Belgrano, pointing to them to show he, too, has powers of observation. "She ran off barefoot and with cut feet. And her car was at the door. The dead driver still has the keys on him."

"I don't get it," says Jon. "They try to kill you and you run off with no money, bag, car, or shoes."

Antonia approaches the shattered glass again. In the center is Lola Moreno's bag, half its contents strewn across the floor. She rummages among them with the tip of her ballpoint until she comes across a half-hidden blue plastic bag. Inside are two red tubes. On one of them she reads: TIMESULIN.

"And you don't go to the police," Jon insists. "She must be very scared. Or hiding something very bad."

"No sign of her since last night?" asks Antonia.

"No, señora. We've broadcast her description to all units and sent patrol cars to comb the surrounding area, but no one has seen her."

Antonia takes out her iPad and finds the Paradise Shopping Mall on Google Maps. She turns on the 3D view. South of the mall is the AP-7 highway. To the west, a housing development. The two other directions show hilly terrain. Kilometer upon kilometer of hills leading to the slopes of the Sierra Blanca. The only signs of habitation are the San Pedro funeral parlor and the Virgen del Rocío cemetery.

"Well, if you don't want her to end up in either of these," says Antonia, pointing to the two macabre dots on the map, "we'd better find her within forty-eight hours. Señora Moreno is diabetic and pregnant."

"Not a good combination," says Jon, clicking his tongue.

LOLA

There was once a little girl who grew up in a sad, loveless home where the food tasted of ashes and the future was black. A little girl whose parents soon abandoned her. A little girl who, when she grew up, met her Prince Charming, who had come from far-off lands and took her away to live in a white marble palace with too much furniture . . .

Lola's father was a bookkeeper; her mother is a hairdresser. When she was little, they gave her all the affection their work hours permitted. There was always a plate of white rice with anchovies to eat, and a sweaty embrace. That was every day. At Christmas, warm gazpacho, poached eggs, baby goat, and apple cake for dessert, all prepared by Mom. And embraces perfumed with Farala and Brummel. Under the tree, a Furby toy, Playmobil farm, or a Tamagotchi, depending on the year. If times were hard, nothing more than a thousand-peseta banknote. Her aunt Julia died, blind and half deaf, and one of her grandmothers, half blind and stone-deaf. Then her father, the previous year. A heart attack. In his sleep.

That's all the drama she had known in her family.

Hardly worthy of Dickens.

There was once a little girl who grew up in a sad, loveless home where the food tasted of ashes and the future was black, Lola repeats to herself. It's just one version of the stories she tells herself at night when she finds it impossible to sleep, when she is pursued by doubts or remorse. She starts telling herself this story, and sleep finally comes.

Although on this particular night, she is being pursued by people who want to kill her.

I just knew it, Lola moans.

Let's rewind.

When the police sirens are almost on top of her (and the noise of the killers' car is dwindling), Lola crawls out from under the car, crosses the parking lot, and begins to walk across the fields. She doesn't look back; she doesn't worry about her bloody feet until half an hour later, when pain wins out over fear and adrenaline.

By then she is in the middle of nowhere. She has traveled across a muddy stretch of land and along a dirt track without meeting a single person. The ground is soft after the recent rain, and there is no one to be seen for kilometers around.

A few minutes pass, then she hears a car engine. Without giving it a second thought, she rushes to hide. On one side of the track is a small wood of holm oaks and fir trees; on the other, an embankment where the ground slopes away steeply for ten or twelve meters. Lola slides down the embankment and hides behind some bushes. Just in time. The car engine stops, and a door opens. Somebody walks to the edge of the track; Lola doesn't dare look to see who it is. She simply listens to him breathing heavily. Should she stand up and call for help? But Lola senses the dark figure is searching for her, *sniffing her out*, and is sure she doesn't want him to find her.

So she stays stock-still.

The only movement she makes is to twist her wedding ring with the tip of her thumb to try to calm her anxiety.

After the dark figure returns to his car and drives off, Lola remains crouching behind the bushes for a long while before straightening up. She is afraid the man wasn't alone, but left behind an accomplice who could leap on her as she comes out of hiding.

When she finally steels herself to stand up, nothing happens.

There is only silence, disturbed by the chirping of a few early cicadas. They shouldn't be out until spring, but climate change has disrupted their internal clocks, the ones that make them sleep underground for precisely seventeen years. If they emerge too soon, they're easy prey for predators.

Lola knows all of this because she saw it in a TV documentary. She is far more intelligent than you would guess from her appearance, her curriculum, or her meek demeanor.

There's a small stream at the bottom of the embankment. Normally it's dry, but in February it gurgles along lazily. Lola has little choice but to hobble down to it and walk along the bank until she can find somewhere to recover. Upstream, a slightly larger boulder offers a smooth surface wide enough to accommodate one and a half buttocks. Lola plunges her feet into the water. It's so cold it cuts like razor blades between her toes. But Lola grits her teeth. She has no intention of dodging bullets only to die of sepsis.

She takes off her grease-stained sweater, then her blouse. Nine hundred euros from Michael Kors. Now she's going to put it to a different use. She rips it into long uneven strips with her teeth. The silk fibers are hard to tear apart.

Why the hell didn't I wear a pair of sneakers today? she moans to herself. Not for the last time.

Pulling her feet from the water, she examines her wounds. There are still some shards of glass in one of them. Two square pieces that have lodged in the heel. Lola tugs at them with slippery fingers. As they come loose, she allows herself a dull howl that rebounds off the sides of the embankment and the water's surface. The only answer is a brief interruption of the cicadas' loud singing. Very slowly, she wraps the strips of material around her feet. She tries to fashion them into a spiral, but the improvised bandages, soaked in blood and water, roll up at the sides. It takes her nearly an hour to bind them on tightly. She can just about move her toes, which is the only thing she can remember you have to do, from the time when her mother sprained her ankle after slipping on hair clippings on the floor of her salon.

It would have been easier if Lola had dared use her cell phone to look things up on the internet, but she has it switched off. She can't let them trace her.

Once she has finished, she slips the sweater back on and dozes off. Passing out rather than napping. By the time she wakes up, it's late afternoon. Her stomach is rumbling, and the blood is pounding in her temples. She bends down to drink directly from the stream: the water tastes acidic and polluted. She belches, her stomach full of water for lack of anything else, and strokes her belly, where her boy child—it has to be a boy, of course, a little Yuri—is demanding to take nourishment from her.

Even in this sorry state, she can last for several hours without food. But if she can't get her insulin shot, things will get complicated. Lola is well aware of the symptoms of hyperglycemia: her mother made her repeat them over and over when she was little, as soon as she had been diagnosed. She has never suffered from them, because she has always been careful. But she knows what they are.

It starts with a headache, then thirst, a desire to urinate a lot, she thinks, massaging her temples.

She resolves the last of these behind a tree, then gets going again.

She has no idea where she's headed, but she can't stay by the stream. The temperature at the moment is mild, but at night it will drop to eight degrees Celsius. Lola feels the cold; without shelter she could die.

So she walks back up to the track, and from there to the highest point she can see. The ground rises and falls sharply—a geological aperitif before the main course of the Sierra Nevada in the background. In between, a low red-roofed building.

That is where Lola is now.

She has a hard time deciding to go in: she's very aware that she looks a mess. Even with the sweater on inside out, she can't hide the grease stains. So she paces outside the front door at the corner of the parking lot, until a few women with red eyes come out for a smoke. Lola puts her trust in fate and strides into the funeral parlor. She doesn't glance in the direction of the receptionist, who is busy trying to swindle a widow by selling her flowers for the price of a printer ink cartridge, or at anyone else. Praying no one looks at her muddy, dusty bandaged feet.

Although to be honest, when was the last time you looked at somebody's shoes?

The funeral home has several parlors, each with a dead body inside and living mourners outside, sitting on sofas that look significantly less comfortable than the caskets. There is nobody outside the room at the far end, but there are a couple of raincoats and jackets left on the sofas. No bags. Lola quickly approaches the first jacket (navy blue, it won't match her jeans, but what can you do?), grabs it, wraps it round her shoulders. She hunches over like someone overcome by a loved one's death, retraces her steps, and hides in the women's restroom. The third cubicle. She locks the door. Lifts her feet whenever she hears somebody come in.

There was once a little girl who grew up in a sad, loveless home where the food tasted of ashes and the future was black, she tells herself as she waits.

The hours go by. Funeral homes never close while there are families keeping vigil. The mourners in rooms one and two shuffle in with their dear departed, leaving the coast clear for Lola. By now it's nearly one o'clock in the morning. She stumbles, hardly able to stand. Her head is exploding.

The receptionist has her back turned and is watching something on television. The volume is low, but Lola thinks she recognizes one of those music programs looking for talent where there isn't any.

She walks on to the third room, which is empty and there is no casket behind the glass. A few chairs. A table. A landline.

Lola dials Yuri's cell phone, holding her breath. She is expecting confirmation of what she already knows.

It's switched off, or there is no coverage.

"He's dead," she says in a low voice. "He's dead, the jerk."

There was once a little girl who was left all alone.

10

A DIFFERENT SCENE

Around the time Lola is sitting semiconscious on the banks of the stream, Antonia Scott and Jon Gutiérrez reach the gates of her husband's property. Jon has had to drag Antonia there.

"We ought to be searching for that woman," protests Antonia.

"How likely is it that the people who killed her husband are those who tried to shoot her, angel?"

"Quite likely. Very likely."

"Well then?" says Jon, wrinkling his nose. It's unlike her to behave so illogically.

"I just want to get back to Madrid as fast as possible," says Antonia, folding her arms.

The place is decked out like a cruise ship. With about as much taste.

A quarter of an hour by car from the center of Marbella, the Urbanización Solfiesta is not an exclusive development like La Zagaleta, for top executives and Arab billionaires. Solfiesta is merely expensive. The residences seem to have been plonked down in the middle of nowhere, their urban planning done by a child upending his toy box. They are scattered higgledy-piggledy on a hillside, their brick and whitewashed walls protecting access to homes that compete with one another to see who has the ugliest, most ostentatious display of marble.

These are folkloric houses for mid-table soccer players, or Eurovision winners.

"The paradise of tackiness," says Jon as he pulls up at the gate. The humid, overcast afternoon is threatening a storm, which merely adds to the depressing atmosphere.

Antonia barely looks up from the documents Deputy Inspector Belgrano has passed her.

"Houses are houses."

"Go on, admit you're at least a bit shocked by it," says Jon, leaning out of the window to speak into the intercom. "You always wear white T-shirts and black jackets. Style is style."

Antonia waits until she has read the last word on the last page of the dossier—fifty pages in nine minutes—and closes the file wearily.

"Before I met Marcos, I used to choose my own clothes. He was the one who convinced me to stop."

"Is that why you always dress the same?" says Jon, overwhelmed by a wave of tenderness as he imagines Antonia going into Primark and picking up the first thing she comes across. Combining God only knows what. All of a sudden, he understands her a little better. That's the way it is with Antonia: to get to know her, you have to fit together pieces of the puzzle with the small details you pick up on.

And don't blink or you'll miss it.

"Apparently, people used to stare at me in the street. According to Marcos, you can't go wrong with black."

What there is a lot wrong with, however, is the Voronin Moreno chalet, as Antonia and Jon can immediately tell when the gate opens with a hum. In the garden there's a statue of *Manneken Pis*; a doormat with the Spartak shield in the entrance, and a doorbell that plays "Kalinka" when pressed.

"Come in," says Belgrano, opening the door for them.

Inside, more delights. Roman columns in the living room, a beer barrel next to the billiard table at the back. A pole for pole dancing. The sofa coverings are fake cowhide.

My God, I'm in hell, thinks Jon.

He leans down to Antonia when she gently tugs on his sleeve.

"I think I understand what you meant," she says, pointing at the pink LED lights under the center table. Or the Asian good-luck cat figurine with one paw bobbing up and down.

"There's hope for you yet, angel."

One small detail: the mansion has been turned upside down.

The cushions have been slashed, the stuffing scattered everywhere. The beer barrel ripped from the wall and emptied. If there had been any books, they would have been tipped from the shelves. The only concession to culture is the hundred or more movies and video games carpeting the floor, their covers opened and trampled on. Pirated copies, of course.

"Did your people do this?"

"It was like that when we arrived," says Belgrano. "Somebody was desperate to find something. Follow me, I'll take you to the body."

Antonia and Jon walk round the sofa, trying hard not to tread on the Blu-rays. Above all, trying not to slip on the checkerboard floor.

"No fingerprints?" asks Antonia, noticing the remains of print powder on the blue-tinged disc covers.

"Only the house owners. The others wore gloves."

They walk past the ninety-eight-inch TV set. Still tuned to a Russian news channel.

Jon feels a stab of envy: he's a couch potato when it comes to binge-ing TV series. *You must sleep like a baby in front of one of those*, he thinks.

A sliding glass door leads to the back garden. Still more horrors: a lot of artificial grass, cheap plastic seats with green cushions. A fountain where a pair of leaping dolphins spit water into one of the two swim-ming pools. The big one.

Yes, there are two. One is kidney shaped. The smaller one is circular, and fenced off.

"Ask me what that small pool is for. Go on, ask me," says Belgrano.

"For the dog," says Antonia.

"How . . . ?"

Antonia points to a painting on the living room wall. A family por-trait of Yuri, Lola, and a dog the size of a bus. With thick brown fur and a black mask over face and snout.

"It's a Caucasian shepherd dog. They're born in the mountains and can't stand heat."

"I thought you didn't like dogs," says Jon.

"I don't. But for some reason, they like me. So I try to find out all I can about them."

Jon opens the gate to the small pool and pokes a finger into the water.

"It's cold."

"The housekeeper told me they keep the pool at twenty-two degrees all year round to refresh the dog," says Belgrano, somewhat put out that his revelation didn't have the desired effect.

"Where is the dog now?"

"It was shut in the pool area when we arrived. In a rage. It slammed into the fence several times when we approached. The dog unit had to sedate it to take it to the dog pound."

"What about the body?"

"It's over here."

They turn a corner on the far side of the garden and come to a barbecue and a glass table smashed to pieces, with a dead body lying on what remains of it. Someone has considerately covered the body in a thermal blanket. All that can be seen are the bare feet. With dirty soles.

Jon turns to Antonia, awaiting instructions. Her body is stiffer than normal, but even so, she isn't asking for her red pills. The inspector is puzzled. He can feel the tension, the energy of her superpowered brain filling the air around her with static electricity. Or maybe it's simply about to rain, and he's imagining all the rest. *That's probably it.*

What he isn't imagining is that she hasn't asked him for anything.

Something's wrong, he deduces.

Antonia nods her head gently, almost beseechingly, and Jon pulls off the blanket covering the body.

Yuri is a man well into his thirties, with the muscular body of an adolescent. Six-pack abs. Bare chest. Obliterated face. Flies buzzing round what's left of it.

All he has on is a pair of Superdry trunks. Black, contrasting with his pallid torso. His back is purple. He's been dead for thirty hours, and since the blood is no longer being pumped by his heart, it has drained from the upper parts of the body and accumulated in the lower regions.

The blood that isn't spattered on the wall, the ground, the shattered table, and the bag of charcoal, that is.

Jon flinches, in a mixture of revulsion and horror. Close to gagging.

"Your first corpse?" asks a female voice behind him with a hint of mockery.

"My first shotgun death, smart-ass," says Jon, wheeling around.

Behind them stands a middle-aged woman in uniform. Stocky rather than tall, black hair done up in such a tight bun it's painful to look at. Dark eyes with uneven pupils, like spilled ink. A stern face. She has an air of rigor about her. When she extends her hand to greet Jon, it's with a brief, rapid gesture, as though not to waste any effort. As if she were saving herself for something.

"You don't know how lucky you are. Captain Romero. From UDYCO Costa del Sol."

"I'm Inspector Gutiérrez. And this is . . ."

Jon points to Antonia, but she hasn't made any attempt to turn around to greet the new arrival and is still taking in the crime scene.

"I already know who you are. Madrid has assured me you'll be a great help. You better be, I've had to argue with the examining magistrate to leave the body here until you arrived. It's highly irregular."

"And we thank you for it, Captain."

"Señor Voronin should be in the morgue by now, being examined by the pathologist."

"There isn't any doubt about the cause of death, is there?"

Romero gives a meaningful smile.

"No, not really. Can your colleague speak?"

"Yes, she's just shy. You see, Señora Scott has her own methods. They're somewhat unusual, but they get results."

"I've been told that too. I hope it's true. We need results."

"Yes, we heard you're a bit stretched here."

The captain lets out a laugh. Harsh, without any trace of amusement.

"Inspector Gutiérrez, sit down for a moment, and I'll tell you a horror story."

11

AN ACCELERATION

Antonia has barely registered the conversation going on behind her. She's too busy trying to make the world slow down.

That morning, the monkeys in her head were sufficiently calm for her to be able to process the scene in the shopping mall. But when she enters the chalet, the monkeys make it plain that it was just a snack break. As soon as she sees the ransacked living room, her brain is bent on trying to absorb, classify, order. To find a meaning.

It doesn't work.

In her head

> (the monkeys clamor. The monkeys fight
> to get her full attention, screeching,
> holding things aloft),

the jungle has become a wretched insane asylum.

Left on her own with Yuri Voronin's corpse, Antonia Scott clasps her elbows, trying to hug herself to stay calm, to pacify the monkeys. Her body's only response is an overwhelming desire to take more pills.

She has already taken two that morning.

A third won't be enough. Or a fourth.

She knows she must talk to Jon about what's happening to her. But she can't.

There's a word that defines what she is feeling.

Bakiginin.

In Karelian, a language spoken from the Gulf of Finland to the White Sea, it means "the sadness of a wall builder." The contrast between the need to keep the world away from your life, and the impossibility of doing so.

Invoking this word helps Antonia momentarily. She takes her hand out of her pocket, where her fingertips had already been feeling for another red pill.

She tries to focus on the corpse.

There's something odd about its position.

On his back on top of the table, which must have shattered when he fell on it. The shot fired at point-blank range, spattered blood

    (the monkeys raise the objects, howl,

        trying to make themselves heard.

      One of them should not be there)

and brains on the wall, the swimming trunks, the skin's pallor.

Something doesn't fit. There's something wrong, very wrong.

All the information she is assimilating overwhelms her. Trapped inside her own head, she closes her eyes. Surrounded by

                  (monkeys)

the data, which now signify only noise and confusion.

She flees the scene.

12

A WARNING

Captain Romero gets comfortable (in a manner of speaking) on one of the garden chairs on the far side of the swimming pool. Jon does likewise.

"You have an odd accent, Inspector."

"I could say the same."

The captain gives him a lingering stare.

"I was just wondering what someone from so far north is doing down here."

"Lending a hand. Are we going to keep playing Eight Basque Family Names, or will you tell me the horror story?"

Romero pulls her cell phone from her pocket, switches it off, and puts it away again.

"As I understand it, you've been asked to help find Señora Dolores Moreno, the victim's wife. Do you know why?"

Jon shakes his head.

"We were only told it's important for the investigation."

"Look, Inspector. Our job in UDYCO is a bit different from the rest of our colleagues. We're more . . . relaxed about regulations. We aren't so concerned with the day-to-day issues: we concentrate on the long term. If you don't mind my asking, how many cases have you worked on?"

Jon shrugs.

"You only have to look at my file to see."

"That's not my style," says Romero. "I prefer to hear it from you."

"A few."

"Important ones?"

"Some."

"I'm asking because we hear things down here. Rumors in forums, chat rooms, and WhatsApp groups. Like about the anonymous inspector who rescued Carla Ortiz from a sewer. Red-haired, big and strong, they say."

"I wonder who could fit that description," says Jon, all innocence.

The captain is starting to make him nervous. Apart from when she switched off her cell phone, she hasn't moved in her chair. Straight-backed, hands resting on her thighs. As stipulated in police regulations, she has the uniform cap tucked under her left arm. In the fading light it's as if she doesn't move anything except her lips and jaw.

She's like a ventriloquist's dummy with batteries.

"Don't think I'm trying to interrogate you, Inspector. We're very grateful they're listening to us in Madrid for a change. But I wanted to explain to you that things aren't the same here. Let's imagine, for example, that a rich heiress has disappeared. You two are given the task of finding her. You follow the trail, find her alive. Along the way, six colleagues die. But I guess to you that's just part of the job."

Aha, thinks Jon, who's beginning to see where she's coming from.

"I can assure you that—"

"Don't assure me of anything," the captain interrupts him. "Things are different here. We don't need to go looking for the bad guys. We know who they are. We meet them every day in the street, in the bars. In the supermarket. Their children and grandchildren go to the same schools as ours."

"What happened with—"

"Be quiet, Inspector, I haven't finished yet. You're called on to arrest a serial killer, and that's what you do. I can't hope to put a stop to the Russian Mafia. Our job here is to collect evidence against them, little by little, slowly. To find witnesses, step by step. To get them to testify. Keep them alive until they do. And afterward, if it makes sense and doesn't cost too much."

"It's a job that takes years."

"It's a war," Romero corrects him. "When they first came here twenty years ago, they were like a group of happy pensioners who came to pig out on seafood and dance 'Los Pajaritos.' It turned out they were up to much more than that. They began setting up businesses. Buying football teams. Building kitschy mansions like this. And everyone was over the moon. Russian money is inexhaustible. The problem, of course, is where they get it."

Jon knows that. The mafioso's holy trinity.

"Drugs, extortion, and prostitution."

"The crimes their colleagues commit in Russia produce a lot of cash. The dirty money travels to Belize, the Cayman Islands, Delaware. It rebounds from the tax havens and comes back to Europe laundered through an impenetrable web of companies. Not as profitable as those of Google and Apple, but almost."

"Then it's turned into marble," says Jon, pointing to the chalet's façade.

"This is nothing. The icing on the cake. The Mafias have got a money-laundering franchise here. Marbella and Málaga are the last, but one stop before the money goes back to where it came from. Saint Petersburg, Moscow. Putin's dacha."

"Everybody knows Russia is a Mafia state." Jon nods with the authority of someone who has seen an HBO documentary.

"Did you know Litvinenko was in Marbella before the Kremlin took him out?"

Jon remembers the case. Litvinenko was a KGB spy who spilled the beans about the connection between the Mafia and the Russian government. Somebody sweetened his tea with radioactive polonium and turned his kidneys into an offshoot of Chernobyl.

"I thought he died in London."

"He came through here a few months earlier. I interviewed him myself. Back then I was an inspector, like you. He taught us many things, and we've learned many more over the past fifteen years. We know the Russian Mafia doesn't exist as such. That it's a hundred or more organizations in thirteen countries. With a thousand complicated alliances. The Georgians hate the Uzbeks, but support them against the Tambóvskaya. The Tambóvskaya is at war with the Malyshevskaya, but only inside Russia. Over here, they tolerate one another."

"Quite a maze."

"I could continue all night, and by breakfast time, half the info would be out of date. Do you understand what I'm trying to say, Inspector?"

Jon scratches his head, weighing up what he has just heard.

"I think so. You don't want us to set the cat among the pigeons."

Romero nods slowly. Given her usual lack of movement, this is the equivalent of a dramatic display.

"Last year we had forty-six deaths, Inspector. Four more than in Madrid, in a province with a million and a half inhabitants."

"How many of those involved the Mafias?"

"We had two settlings of scores with bombs. Shootings from bicycles, motorcycles, attacks on places like this one. Abductions, facial mutilations à la Joker, holdups with Kalashnikovs in restaurants . . . and when people were leaving a baptism ceremony."

"Like in *The Godfather*?"

"Yes, like in *The Godfather*. Things are getting very complicated around here. Buried hatreds. Feuds about to break out."

"If they haven't already," says Jon, gesturing with his chin toward the corpse.

"Do you know how many officers I've lost since I was promoted captain?"

Jon hasn't a clue. He knows how many have died in the Basque Country since he took the oath. But they weren't killed by Russians. He and the other officers were given a similar speech. It began with courage, tenacity, and strict observation of the regulations and ended with don't ruffle any feathers.

"I guess none," says Jon. He elongates his words like stretching elastic.

"And that's how I want to keep it, Inspector. This is a village. There's nowhere to hide. Whenever we get a piece of relevant information, we have to conceal it from the Civil Guard, the GRECO, even from other police forces in case they rat on us to the bad guys. Whenever we try to prosecute, we're told we don't have sufficient proof. Whenever we carry out a raid and impound a ton of coke, it doesn't appear on TV. Whenever we manage to get someone on the witness stand, we nearly always lose. And we never get any assistance, except when someone in Madrid has a bright idea. Or wants to make a name for themselves. So tell me, Inspector, why did they send you here, you and that woman we both know isn't from Europol?"

The change of topic is so sudden you can practically hear the needle scratching the vinyl.

"I've already told you." Jon meets her gaze unsteadily. "We've been told Lola Moreno is important, and she has to be found."

Romero delays her response for the time it takes to put it under a lamp and poke half a dozen holes in it.

"It's true Lola Moreno is important. What you can't imagine is how important, and why."

"And you aren't going to tell me."

"No, not unless I decide I can trust you. Until then . . ."

She doesn't finish her words, because at that moment Antonia rushes past them. Jon doesn't ask permission from his superior or make an excuse. He simply nods briefly and goes after his colleague.

11 (B)

A SCREECHING HALT

Antonia runs out of the house. Leaning against the car, she feels in her pocket and does something she hasn't done for years of her own free will. Since the days of her training. Since the days when control of her capabilities was a battle she never won.

She takes out a blue capsule.

Chomps down on it.

Six seconds go by.

Seven.

Ten.

The monkeys scamper away.

The world becomes a flat, gray, uniform place.

Suddenly, Antonia is empty. No more deafening noise, no more speed.

For as long as its effect lasts—the complex blue capsule is designed to cancel her out—Antonia is no more than a normal person. Freshly awoken.

Her power has disappeared, but not her anguish. Her mind is restricted to one idea at a time. And right now she can focus on just one thing.

I'm losing it, thinks Antonia as she struggles to get her breath back. She feels herself retch, greedily gasps for air. Tears stream down her cheeks and trickle into her mouth.

It's not just that I can't control it. It's that I'm losing it completely.

13

A SILENCE

Jon Gutiérrez doesn't like Antonia Scott.

This has nothing to do with love. It goes without saying that Jon loves her. Beyond her eccentricities, Antonia has many virtues. She can never do harm, and is adorable in her awkwardness. She is irritatingly stubborn. She is generous and courageous beyond reason. And she belongs to a species at risk of extinction: one that believes justice should be defended, not expected.

It's complicated: she also has some unpleasant habits. She is silent when she shouldn't be, and speaks out of turn, usually putting her foot in it. On the rare occasions she shows something akin to affection, within thirty seconds she has offended you. *She gives, only instantly to take away.*

None of this upsets Jon about Antonia. He would die for her.

What Jon hates about Antonia Scott is that he has no way to comfort her.

You see your partner, your friend, collapsed in a heap, weeping all alone in a car, hugging her knees. That affects you: your chest feels tight, your forearms tingle. Your feet are restless, as if all of a sudden, they resent contact with the ground.

If this were anybody else, you would go and embrace them. *Come here.* You bury her in your enormous arms, with which you can lift huge rocks or crack walnuts in the crook of your elbow.

What can you do with a person who hates to be touched, who shies away from all contact or displays of affection?

What do you do with Antonia Scott?

You do nothing. And inside, the *larritasun* intensifies. Anguish, dammit, anguish.

You try to understand her, but you can't. Because you know there's an insurmountable gulf between you. Defended by walls she has built herself. And you wonder what it is this time. What is happening in that impossible, marvelous head of hers? What is she seeing, what battles is she fighting?

So you tap gently on the car window. To see if you're in luck and she unlocks the door.

Ping! the buttons fly up.

You're in luck.

Jon climbs in behind the steering wheel. Senses the sadness in the air. Viscous, almost palpable. Antonia's eyes are bloodshot, her skin pale as parchment.

The temptation to stretch out your hand and touch her is overwhelming, but Jon knows that isn't the way.

So is the temptation to talk. To explain to her she has to keep going, that whatever is preying on her mind might not go away, and all she can do is resist. But Jon knows that isn't the way either.

So he doesn't say:

Our demons never leave us, Antonia. All we can do is be even stronger.

And she doesn't reply:

I'm tired, Jon. Tired of people who are cruel to others. Tired of all the pain I see. It's like pieces of glass in my head I can't pull out.

And he doesn't reply:

I may be a stupid gay guy. I may even be fat. But, thank God, I'm here. I'm here.

They say none of these things to each other, because life isn't a movie, where a million complex emotions are neatly packaged in impeccable dialogue while Michael Giacchino, Thomas Newman, or Quincy Jones underlines everything with a dramatic soundtrack.

They don't say anything, but simply sit together in the car. In silence.

14

A CODE

The tears dry up.

Jon lowers the window. While they were sitting in the car, there's been a rain shower. A fragrant smell wafts in through the open window, relieving the sadness. Or sending it elsewhere. With one small consolation: when nothing remains of a past that is now our present, smells will last, and fill our memory.

"Petrichor," says Antonia.

"What's that?"

"The smell after rain. It's called petrichor."

Jon doesn't know why exactly, but he senses that what has just happened—this word that Antonia has shared with him—is important. He doesn't want to spoil something he doesn't understand, so he goes on waiting for her to talk some more.

To give her time, he drives the car away from the development. It's already dark. He travels several kilometers in no particular direction, then stops at an empty service station. The Marbella coastline in the distance resembles a glittering, idyllic string of beads. It helps that you can't see any of the buildings. Closer by, a Repsol sign acts as a light shield, allowing them to see their faces.

"There's something very wrong here," Antonia says at last.

"Okay, honey, let's see what we've got: we have a man with his head blown off. And two more in the morgue, riddled with bullets. All three in one morning."

"It's not just that. The Mafias are violent, but they're never this public about it. There's something else going on."

"I met a very intriguing woman. Captain Romero."

"Is she hostile?"

It's always the same whenever the two of them arrive somewhere. There's always somebody, among those on their side, who is uneasy about having them there.

"She's watching and waiting. She won't cause trouble so long as we don't. From what I understood, a war could break out here at any moment."

"Why do you say she's intriguing?"

"She asked me a very strange question. Not the usual crap. She wanted to know why we're here."

"They never ask that."

"No. They ask who you are. They ask where we're from, how we're going to help. Above all, they ask us when we're leaving."

But never *why*. That's usually goddamned obvious.

Antonia blinks. She usually does this very fast, five or six times, at the speed of a hummingbird's wings. This time, it's in slow motion. That and her languid tone of voice set off Jon's consummate-policeman alarm bells.

"Call Mentor."

If I hadn't spent several nights in the parking lot at Fever, seizing bags of pot from gangs, I'd swear this girl was high as a kite, thinks Inspector Gutiérrez.

"Are you feeling okay, angel?"

"Of course I am," she replies after a long delay.

Jon says nothing, simply puts the cell phone on hands-free and does as she told him.

Mentor picks up on the sixth ring. His voice booms out from the eight speakers as though he were inside the Audi with them.

"This isn't a good moment."

"Listen, we're surrounded by corpses here."

"And I'm in Brussels, Inspector. At a meeting of team leaders. Some . . . problems have cropped up."

Jon and Antonia exchange puzzled glances.

"What sort of problems?"

"Problems with colleagues from other countries. Nothing I can discuss on the phone. I'll explain when you get back. And now, if you'll excuse me—"

"Why are we here?" asks Antonia.

A pause. From the other end of the line, they hear the distant murmur of alarmed voices.

"What's wrong with your voice, Scott?"

He's noticed it too, thinks Jon with a pang of envy. It took Mentor just four words on a telephone, two thousand kilometers away, to spot it. Some relationship they have. With its sorry string of cases that veil more than they disclose.

"Scott," Mentor insists.

Antonia waves her hand for Jon to answer.

"We don't want to keep you from your meeting. But you told us to keep you informed. And Antonia is—"

"It was her I asked, Inspector," snaps Mentor.

Another pause. In the car there's the sound of Jon's heavy breathing. Which he might be exaggerating because he can't stand silence.

"I'm tired, that's all," says Antonia.

A longer pause this time. The voices at the other end diminish, as if Mentor were walking away down a carpeted corridor.

"All right. What can I do for you?"

He doesn't mean it. And I don't believe him.

"We'd like to know why you're so interested in Lola Moreno," says Jon.

"Still no sign of her?"

"None at all. But we've seen how keen they were to get rid of her and her husband. In short: exceedingly keen."

Mentor gives the sigh of an addict worthy of several Marlboro ads, the kind they no longer show because killing people isn't nice.

"It seemed like a simple case, Scott," says Mentor, more to himself than to them. "Find a housewife and get the hell out of there. Something easy, to help you forget your obsession with that phantom of yours."

Antonia doesn't respond.

"We only want to know what we're getting into," says Jon. "Why choose this particular case?"

"He won't tell you."

"You know I can't, Scott. Least of all by phone."

Antonia glances at Jon, then at the cell phone screen.

"I assume responsibility."

"That's not a decision for you to make, Scott."

"So just tell me the alphanumeric code. I'll explain the rest to him."

A pause. An endless one. At the other end of the line, it seems as if Mentor is retracing his steps. The voices sound ever closer.

"If I ask you to come back, you won't listen to me, will you?"

Jon has a flashback of images of a boxer dog, in a kitchen, with a ham bone. A boxer that has to be put down before it will relinquish its prey.

"You already know the answer."

The worried voices have become worried shouts. Maybe that is what makes Mentor give in.

"To hell with it. On one condition: find her quickly, and return to Madrid as soon as possible. I'm going to need you. Okay?"

"We want to come back."

Mentor pauses one last time, as though evaluating whether this is sufficient guarantee. His reply is equally brief.

"One. Five. Foxtrot." With that, he hangs up.

15

A FINE-TUNED EAR

Jon turns to look at his partner. Eyebrows raised, hands clutching the wheel. His face is a study of astonishment, a picture of befuddlement. The world is coming at him one way, his understanding going in the opposite direction. On a one-way street. With Antonia Scott in the driver's seat, of course.

"Would you mind explaining, angel?"

Antonia sniffs, and strokes her thighs.

"It's possible we haven't quite told you everything."

"It's possible I've realized that," says Jon gently.

An exquisite gentleness. One of those concealing thunder.

"I don't feel very well," says Antonia, pinching the bridge of her nose.

"It's possible I've realized that as well."

"But I don't want to talk about it."

"Could we skip that whole bit?"

"What bit?"

"The bit where you pause to choose what you're going to tell me. You go off somewhere deep inside those little green eyes of yours and return half a minute later with half-truths. Omissions. Euphemisms."

"I don't do that."

"Yes, you do."

Antonia takes thirty seconds to think how she can refute what he's said about her always taking half a minute to respond.

"There's a software program," she says eventually.

"What are you saying?"

"A computer software program. When the Red Queen project began, they started a parallel project in Brussels. A much more secret one."

"More secret?"

Antonia waves a hand for him not to interrupt her. She's become a Fiat 600 without brakes trundling down a hill. Slow, but unstoppable.

"The people in charge of the project realized that the mere existence of the teams wasn't enough. It was having a gun without a target. So they created a special software program. It's called Heimdal."

"Like the big Black guy in the Marvel movies?"

Antonia, who hasn't been to the movies this century, ignores him.

"The story goes that Odin fell for nine giant women while he was strolling by the shore. He slept with all of them, and they combined to present him with a single son."

"They combined. Like a Power Ranger?"

"I don't understand the ins and outs of it, either, so let's forget it," Antonia continues. "The nine women gave birth to Heimdal, and fed him the choicest food they had. When he grew up, Heimdal discovered he could see to the ends of the earth, and had such fine-tuned hearing that he could hear the grass grow. So Odin made him the guardian of Bifröst, the rainbow bridge that leads to Asgard, the home of the gods. Heimdal had to warn them if the giants were approaching."

Jon is listening closely now, because he's starting to understand what a program named after a Nordic god with such fine-tuned hearing can do.

"The program also had nine mothers. Nine states in the European Union, including Spain. They invested two hundred million euros in its development, and a further five hundred in setting up the biggest supercomputer in Europe. They installed it in Barcelona, buried fifty meters beneath MareNostrum V."

Jon has heard of MareNostrum, the scientific supercomputer. And to bury a supercomputer underneath another one made a lot of sense.

"That way, they could justify the energy consumption, personnel coming and going, and so on. Not bad."

"I suppose you can guess what it does."

Jon can guess.

And it's a nightmare.

But he wants Antonia to spell it out.

Which she does. Every time anybody goes on the internet, Heimdal is watching. It knows what we are doing, what we are looking for, what we buy. Every email we send, every photo we share in our WhatsApp group. Every text message, every post on Facebook. All of it is analyzed, stored, measured, and weighed up. Every loving gesture, every hateful phrase, every pose in front of the camera. Every cat video, every order we give Siri, every song, every retweet, every like.

Everything.

"I knew the U.S. did that with their citizens. But I never thought we'd do the same here," says Jon, his voice as weary as his soul.

"Europe wasn't about to be left behind, Jon."

"I can't believe you're saying that."

"It's true. The system isn't perfect yet. They brought an expert in image identification from the States, and lots of mathematicians to help with the codes, but we're still way behind the Americans. We can't analyze everything. But at least we can access key information when we have to."

Jon shakes his head. He still can't believe what he's hearing. He feels as if he's watching an episode of *Black Mirror*.

All of a sudden, a little piece of the jigsaw falls into place. *Eureka!*

"Tell me something. When you hacked into Carla Ortiz's email to find her phone number, you told me she had the password stuck on a Post-it on the back of a drawer in her desk. Like everybody, you said. But there was no Post-it, was there? You used Heimdal."

Antonia doesn't reply. Not after her regulation thirty seconds, or after fifty, or after a minute and a half.

Jon gets out of the car. He leaves the door open and strides round the Audi.

He needs to get some air.

"Fuck, fuck, fuck! Jesus F. Christ and all his shitty saints!" he shouts to no one in particular. To the night. To the Repsol sign. To the graffiti on the gas station wall.

His necktie is suffocating him. His jacket also. He yanks them both off, throws them on the ground. Stretches his arms. The seams of his white Egyptian-cotton shirt strain when he folds them again, flexing biceps the size of footballs. Then he sits on the hood of the Audi. The suspension groans.

Antonia gets out of the car and joins him. The suspension is unfazed.

"I would have preferred you not to tell me," says Jon, and it's true. In some way, the awkward but somehow comforting silence just now, the silence of someone simply waiting for things to sort themselves out on their own, was preferable to having to bear the burden Antonia has just placed on his shoulders. "I need to process all of this."

"Think of all the good we can do."

That's not exactly what Jon is thinking of.

"Have you any idea what Heimdal can do to people like me?"

"Basques?"

"Queers, angel."

"This is the twenty-first century. Things aren't the way they used to be."

Jon lets out a sarcastic laugh.

"If there's one thing I know for sure, it's that there's always somebody who wants things to go back to the way they used to be. Always."

He stoops to pick up his jacket and tie. He pats them clean in the xenon headlights. A thousand dust motes dance wildly in the beams of light.

"There's something else," says Antonia.

Of course there is.

"Tell me."

"Heimdal doesn't only monitor communications. Its primary function for the Red Queen project is to coordinate us. To combine all the databases of the hundred and eleven police forces into one."

"One to which only a very few of you have access. That's why you carry your iPad with you everywhere you go."

"For that and *Angry Birds*."

Jon dedicates five seconds to her clumsy attempt at humor.

"All right. So there's a database. Is that it?"

"Heimdal analyzes cases where we might be useful. Police files, reports of crimes, emergency calls. Not just for the information they provide, but for what could happen next."

"Hold on a minute. You're telling me an artificial intelligence decides where you should go?"

"It doesn't decide. It advises. It's for Mentor to decide. No computer can replace actual people."

"And what is it advising this time?"

"Mentor never told me why we're here. He tells me as little as possible to begin with, so as not to influence me."

"That's why you asked him for the code: 15F. What does that mean?"

"Possible top-level undercover informer."

"Holy shit," says Jon with a whistle.

Suddenly everything takes on a different meaning. One with sharp edges.

"Heimdal was keeping watch on Yuri Voronin. His death triggered an alarm in the software program. Voronin was the Orlov clan's treasurer. Orlov is the branch of the Tambóvskaya in Spain. We've never had such a valuable informer."

"If Voronin was an informer, that would explain the brutality of his execution. And why they wanted to kill his wife," Jon reasons.

"And also why Captain Romero is so keen to know why we're here."

"I doubt she'll tell us anything. If her informer was killed, she'll be desperate to find out who blabbed."

"So it's imperative we find Lola Moreno. She's the only one who can shed light on this mess."

Jon gets into the car and starts the engine.

"This mess? No, angel, that's not the word. This isn't a mess. It's a minefield."

LOLA

In an empty funeral parlor, Lola wants to weep over the absence of the man with whom she's madly in love. She wants to weep over herself, for not knowing what to do. Over the soon-to-be-born boy. Over her fear and exhaustion.

She wants to weep, but she can't.

There was once a little girl who lost what she loved most, an enchanting, brave, and generous prince.

Lola likes to brag about her husband. Not for what he buys her— that would be vulgar. She says there's no problem she has that he can't solve. How funny he is. His performance in bed.

"My husband eats me as if I had a plate of grilled prawns down there."

"Small guys are specialists in muff-diving. I suppose they try harder to compensate," declared the hairdresser.

A different hairdresser, not her mother. Lola won't let her mother anywhere near her hair. Not that she gets along badly with her, yet familiarity breeds contempt. But, hey, they love each other. Lola calls her every day. Nearly always to praise Yuri.

"He's very tender and affectionate."

Or:

"The other day he brought me flowers."

Or:

"He left me a note on the fridge saying he loves me, before he went off to work." On the telephone, with a cup of coffee in her hand.

And her mother:

"Are you sure? You know Russians have sticky fingers."
And her mother:
"You know Russians all have short fuses."
And her mother:
"You know Russians are . . ."

Lola thinks no one can be more racist than a person from Andalusia. Or than her mother, at any rate, who is always saying how wonderful it is there. What she wanted for her daughter was a nice boy from Málaga, a doctor or dentist, who would buy her an apartment in Torremolinos for summer vacations.

Lola did, too, mind you. But then she met Yuri.

There was a little girl who danced in a discotheque, and some guys tried to rape her on the way out, thinks Lola. They had her pinned against a wall, her pants around her knees, no matter hard she fought. And Yuri happened to be passing by. There were seven of them. From Málaga, for sure. Possibly dentists—they weren't wearing white coats.

Yuri arrived like a whirlwind, no questions asked. He got away with a stab wound and a punch. Lola was punched too. The other seven received worse beatings, and scattered as best they could.

While they are waiting to be attended to in the ER, Yuri asks her name. Tells her she has skin to die for and the body of a doll. Tries to steal a kiss.

A moment later, his cheek stinging from a slap and his hip smarting from a knee he dodged just in time, he understands Lola has marked the limits of her gratitude.

A month later, they are married.

Lola is the happiest woman in the world.

There was once a little girl who helped a prince build his castle, Lola tells herself, trying in vain to find a less uncomfortable position. Her backside is stiff as a board, her hip numb.

The terrazzo floor is not much better than the first bed she shared with her husband. Yuri didn't have a penny to his name. He lived in an apartment near the beach, with three low-life Georgians who didn't speak a word of Spanish.

Madly in love, for the first month Lola doesn't care where they live. The second time she gets her period and has to put up with the men banging on the bathroom door while she's changing her sanitary pad, she's had enough and calls Yuri to order.

"We need an apartment just for the two of us."

"My boss doesn't pay me much."

"Get him to pay you more."

"It's not that simple."

"What exactly do you do for him?"

Yuri tells her. In his Slav accent, full of drawled, musical *r*'s. But in a Spanish many would be proud of. Clear as anything.

"I give beatings."

"What do you mean, *beatings*?"

"Beatings. Somebody not pay my boss, my boss send me. Pow! I give him a good thump, *da*?"

Lola looks Yuri up and down. He measures less than five foot six, and a size S is baggy on him. But Lola believes what he says. Sure, he doesn't look it, but inside his head, he's nuts, totally nuts. When he's angry, he sees red and would take on seven or twenty-seven. Sometimes he arrives home and the first thing he does is fill the salad bowl with ice and plunge his hand in it.

"Well, you're moving up. Tell your boss to find you something else."

"But, Lola—"

"You're moving up. We're not earning chicken feed."

That was six years ago. Six years and four months. Lola remembers the date well. It was just before her birthday, and Yuri swore on it as his gift to her.

There was once a little girl who six years ago had nothing.

Lola thinks finally she is going to be able to cry. She can feel the tears welling in her eyes. The sob coiled in her throat like a greedy, choking tapeworm.

Her thoughts are interrupted by a noise.

Lola hears voices coming in to the funeral home, asking questions. Arrogant, unmistakable voices.

They're coming for me.

How is that possible?

Lola wastes a few precious seconds trying to work out how they have found her. She's been so careful: she didn't switch her cell phone on. She even called Yuri on the . . .

The landline.

The landline in the funeral home.

I'm such an idiot.

The voices come closer, mingling with those in the next room. No time to lose. She has to get out of there. The problem is how?

There are no windows in the room, and nowhere to hide.

The only door opens into the vestibule. To go out that way would be to throw herself into the arms of her pursuers.

Heart pounding, Lola can hear that the voices muffled by the adjoining wall are now moving toward the door. They are louder, not only because they're closer. There seems to be a row going on.

Then Lola discovers there's another door. The one leading to the glass-partitioned room where the caskets are displayed. She crosses the room and turns the knob, praying it isn't locked. It isn't.

Lola slips inside and closes the door just as the outer one opens. A rectangle of light is thrown on to the floor, across the gurney. It briefly illuminates Lola's face. She glimpses a pair of strong hands, a pistol, a dark figure, possibly the one that got out of the car on the dirt track. She knows when they find her, she's done for.

She doesn't stay around to give them the opportunity.

She crouches down and hides behind the faded maroon drapes eaten away by time and dust that conceal the passage to a service tunnel. There's no door here, just an opening where the funeral parlor employees slide the caskets. The same one Lola wriggles through toward the back of the building. Hungry, exhausted, dehydrated. Adrift, but not lost. Not hopeful, but not hopeless.

There was once a little girl who would not let herself be caught.

16

A PROMISE

The hotel was good, their night's sleep wasn't.

Jon didn't get much shut-eye. Twisted sheets between showers. A lot of sweating, a lot of tossing and turning.

What Mentor told him the day he was recruited now bounces around his head like a *pilotak* in a pelota court. Except that now it has acquired a much darker meaning.

The Red Queen project was created with very special objectives. Serial killers. Particularly elusive violent criminals. Pedophiles. Terrorists. No ties, no hierarchies.

No responsibilities to the public, thinks Jon.

That's why he wanted someone like me. Or at least like the me who planted the drugs in that pimp's car. Someone who cares more about justice than the law.

The problem is, who decides what is just?

The problem is, I'm not sure I am that person anymore.

What Antonia has told him is terrifying. And yet it's real. In a world where the boundaries of good and evil are increasingly blurred, where we have surrendered our privacy and our intellect to a social network and a search engine, the existence of Heimdal was inevitable.

Companies are already doing it. If you mention cheese to your partner in front of your voice-activated speaker, in no time at all you're bombarded by an ad for Idiazabal Basque cheese while you're driving.

But Heimdal isn't there to sell cheese. It's there to identify dangerous citizens.

And of course, history teaches us that this could never ever end badly, thinks Jon.

He takes these concerns with him to breakfast and then to the car, where he waits for Antonia for a couple of hours. They agreed to meet at ten, but he's already downstairs before eight. Playing CD after CD of Joaquín Sabina, learning that some betrayals are drugs against heartache.

Jon doesn't know what to do. At times he's tempted to start the engine and drive off.

To get the hell out of there.

In only ten hours, he'd be at home with his mother. Having to put up with her shouting at him for a while, of course. Then a dinner of *kokotxas*, and sousing everything with *ardo beltza*.

But Jon isn't like that.

And that bastard Mentor figured as much when he picked me. That my mother didn't raise a coward, a lily-livered yellowbelly. He knew it.

Of course, Jon regards what he is caught up in as monstrous. But— and he is painfully aware of the incongruity and cynicism of the idea as soon as it enters his mind—if Heimdal really has to exist, it's better *we* have it.

Oh, it's all so difficult, goddammit . . .

Jon is accustomed to dealing with incongruities. To be a cop and homosexual is tough, although it shouldn't be. You are judged twice. And, counting the earlier incident with the planted drugs, three times. You could be shot or spat on. The contours of your life are sharper than those of others. And you accept this, because you have to. Because you chose it, and because you know that if you fall, you'll fall fighting, with a *kagoendios* on your tongue.

And if you can't hold back the river with your hands, you'll still try to catch fish. And above all, you won't let your companions drown.

Here comes Antonia. Ten minutes early. For somebody who always arrives late, this is something to be thankful for.

They don't say good morning to each other. In fact, they never do, but today they're aware they don't.

"Are you sure you want to go to Voronin's funeral? Wouldn't you prefer us to go looking for Lola Moreno?"

"The police are already watching all the usual places. Her mother's home, her friends. No, let them do the spade work. I prefer to meet the man she's running from. When was the ceremony due to start?"

"At eleven. We have time: this way we can get a look at who turns up."

He says, "Let's go," yet they don't move. There's still an elephant on the back seat, propping its feet on their headrests.

Jon doesn't know how to broach the subject. In the end, it's Antonia who does so, in the most ridiculously adorable way possible.

"Are you annoyed with me?"

Jon smiles. There are many ways to be annoyed. You can harbor rage. Bear a grudge. Feel bitter. Or you can be certain someone you love has been playing you for a fool for months. What he needs now is to make Antonia Scott understand this. What to him is self-evident, to her is a brainteaser.

"I'm still processing what you told me last night. To me it's a big deal. I need to think it over and make decisions. But I want you to promise me something. Think about it carefully, because whether we stay here or head straight back to Madrid depends on your answer."

Antonia nods slowly. She's not sure she knows what he means.

Jon isn't either. But he's willing to give her this opportunity.

"I'm a big boy now," he says. "They let me carry a gun. I'm the one who covers that elusive ass of yours."

"I know."

"I do it because I want to, nobody says I have to."

"I know that too."

"Well, if you want me to keep doing it, don't lie to me anymore. From now on, no more secrets. Help me, and I'll help you. Agreed?"

And of course, what can she possibly say?

ASLAN

First and foremost, Aslan is an affable man.

You only have to look at him now. Sitting on the terrace at the Kristin, as he does every morning. Staring at the sea while he eats whole-grain toast, bratwurst, and fried eggs. There's no sun today, so his bodyguards have folded away the parasol. The occasional tourist strolling along the promenade sees him hunched over his plate, intent on his breakfast. If he raises his head and his gray eyes meet someone else's, he gives a polite smile and a nod of the head.

It's a slow, refined nod. Aristocratic. Aslan has a deep tan, the tan of a spry pensioner. It contrasts sharply with his white mane, brushed back off his forehead. Carefully groomed to collar length. He's never lost a hair in his life. That mane and his name—Aslan, the lion—inevitably led to his nickname *vor v zarkone*, "thief in law."

Aslan Orlov, the Beast.

His food arrives on a platter, and he transfers a portion to his plate, his long creamy-white fingers working with great precision. After each mouthful, he rearranges his plate, leaving not a crumb near the edges, knife and fork carefully realigned, then dabs his mouth with a corner of the white napkin before returning it to his lap.

He always thanks people for every courtesy, every service, always leaves a gratuity. He's polite, almost affectionate.

"Would you like anything else, Señor Orlov?"

"No, thank you, Karina."

As the waitress removes the dish, she accidentally knocks the nearly full glass of water. It tips over, spilling onto the tablecloth and on Aslan's pants.

The waitress withdraws her hand and shrinks back, as though afraid she might lose it. Almost as if she knows who this man she serves every morning really is. She does.

Aslan gives her a yellow-toothed smile.

"Don't worry, it's only water. It'll dry, see?"

He is very insistent about manners. He always has been, from when he was a youngster. In the eighties, he ran a brothel in Saint Petersburg. Whenever a new slave arrived, abducted from the farms of Pskov or Chuduvo, he always treated her kindly. Before raping her for the first time—an indispensable requirement to prevent her rebelling—he always rinsed his mouth with mint mouthwash. Failing that, he gargled vodka.

"It has to be done, but there's no reason they should suffer unnecessarily."

A subordinate once mistook his affability for weakness, making an inappropriate remark at dinner. Aslan smiled faintly, then stuck his fork in the man's throat. Three times. The last jab twisted the tines of the fork, opening a gaping hole through which the disrespectful upstart was able to breathe once or twice more, gasping hideously, before collapsing. Aslan simply wiped the fork and went on eating.

After that, nobody ever misinterpreted Aslan's affability.

Another time, another country. No better. Just different.

More serious, poorer, freer.

Aslan used to be as strong as an oak, but nothing lasts forever. Now he has to ask his knees' permission whenever he hoists his long thin body to his feet. The suit he is wearing today is new. Black and tailored, to match the occasion. A little tight around the waist. He would have preferred something more casual, one of the tracksuits he usually buys in the local Carrefour for fifteen euros. Comfortable clothes that are kind to his seventy-year-old joints. But he has to keep up appearances.

It's important.

He doesn't choose the Lexus or the Ferrari to travel in. The elegant gray Maserati Quattroporte is better. Two hundred thousand euros on wheels, but classy. Kiril will drive him, of course. And he'll take another six *bojevík* in cars in front and behind. Six soldiers. He's asked them to dress soberly. To show their presence, but not to cause trouble.

With every passing year, Aslan is increasingly concerned with his image. He doesn't like being reduced to a stereotype. When he exits the Maserati in front of the Orthodox church, he can sense the looks of the people on the far side of the street, those attending the funeral, the police. He knows most of them, but some are new. There's a big man and a small woman sitting in an Audi. He hasn't seen them before. From the CNI perhaps. He imagines them searching through their notes in the police files, checking the photographs.

The woman points to him. She's only eight meters away, but he can't tell if her lips are moving. While his sight isn't what it once was, he thinks they are moving. She must be reading his biography to her companion. It will say something like:

> Aslan Orlov, born Leningrad 1951. Studied at the Lenin Maritime Academy. Between 1967 and 1980, numerous jobs, as a cadet in the Naval School, and in the navy reserve. Sentenced to six years in prison in 1985. This gives him the status of *vor*, an officer in the Russian Mafia. Between 1991 and 1998, unstoppable rise through the Tambóvskaya, eliminating many of his rivals in the dark days when Saint Petersburg becomes a lawless city. Thought to have committed 23 murders, none of them proved. In 2000 is sent to Spain on a Greek visa to head up the money-laundering branch of the Tambóvskaya.
>
> We have nothing on him.

The only part of all of that Aslan would like is that last sentence. The rest is *vakuum*, empty. A meaningless collection of dates and places, verbs and nouns. They don't convey anything of the man, or the essence of what took place.

That annoys him.

How can a handful of words explain what it was like to grow up in Leningrad, hungry and surrounded by rats? How can a few syllables convey the brutality of the Soviet Union and of Communism? How can you expect someone who is wrapped up warm to understand somebody who is suffering from the bitter cold? To understand what they have to do to survive?

People point a finger at him. Claim to judge him, when the fact is that they don't even know him, let alone comprehend him.

Aslan Orlov feels contempt as well as anger toward his pursuers, who have been hounding him for so many years. The faces change, the failures continue. He waves at the car with the little woman and the bulky man. He has to keep up appearances.

It's important.

By now the street is a mass of luxury cars, cheap suits, and bad taste. Middle-aged men with bulging waistlines. Behind them, younger women, heavily made-up and silent, totter on the grooved Marbella paving, which is not kind to high heels.

They are all there. A convention of mafiosi, the worst from each clan. The sidewalk is packed, some of them are smoking, others are telling jokes or conspiring in hushed tones. It's like an atlas of the Russian underworld.

Aslan walks through the crowd, greeting them in order of importance or size of business.

First the *vor* of other *bratvá*, other clans. Rivals. Arrogant.

Then the Colombians. They hire hit men, organize kidnappings, import cocaine. Clients. Obsequious.

The Algerians, to whom he lends money for importing hashish. Subordinates. Liars.

The Swedes, who pay triple to import a kilo of cocaine to the North. Always begging for a reduction. Disposable. Tight-fisted.

The Kosovars and Romanians. Thieves, counterfeiters, arms importers. Cannon fodder. Unpredictable.

Once he's made sure he has greeted everyone important, Aslan pauses outside the church, smooths his jacket, and places one foot on the entryway step. This is an unwritten, tacit signal recognized and respected by everyone there. Aslan becomes the crest of the criminal wave flooding into the church.

Inside are the sheep, the plebs. The few of Yuri's friends who have dared to show their faces. The Orlov clan's employees, who didn't dare stay away. These are the messengers, the managers of the clan's restaurants, the men who drive their trucks, fix their cars, the women who dance in their discos, who clean their mansions.

Those who eat the crumbs that fall from the Beast's mouth.

The instructions that spread instantly on Telegram groups in Russian and Spanish were crystal clear: compulsory attendance.

The church is full to overflowing.

Aslan had it built and paid for it out of his own pocket. He brought over an Orthodox pope from the motherland. The icons, some of them from the sixteenth and seventeenth centuries, were bought or stolen from parishes and museums in the Ukraine and Belarus. In a side chapel stands the Rock of Pochaiv, a priceless holy relic. According to legend, the hollow in its center was left by the foot of the Virgin Mary in 1675, when she descended from heaven to aid the faithful in their war against the Turks. Three centuries of the faithful's kisses have deepened the hollow and made its guardian monks all the richer.

I'm not surprised they didn't want to part with it. It took fifteen men armed with submachine guns to convince them, Aslan remembers as he stoops to kiss the relic reverently.

He walks to a seat in the front row.

It's a strange funeral. The only reminder of the dead man is a photograph propped on a stand.

No coffin, no flowers, no widow.

The ceremony isn't for them. It's for Aslan, so he can convey the right message.

When the pope asks for a volunteer to say a few words in honor of the deceased, nobody stirs. The atmosphere inside the church is heavy, dense. Not because of the profusion of candles, the dim light, the low ceilings, the incense, the canticles still echoing among the stone columns, refusing to fade away completely.

Who is going to stand up?

What are they going to say?

"Yuri Voronin helped me ship six hundred kilos of cocaine in customized trucks."

"Yuri Voronin set up the corporate structure I use to launder my earnings from prostitution."

"Yuri Voronin helped me lie, bribe, cheat."

"Yuri Voronin hired me as a killer."

Nobody is going to deliver a eulogy for Yuri Voronin.

Nor is Aslan, who gets up and heads for the pulpit, a bronze eagle on a Baltic red marble pedestal. On it lies a Peshitta Bible, a direct translation from the Syriac. Purer, closer to the word of God.

Aslan Orlov rests his long creamy-white fingers on the open book. He starts to speak in Russian.

"Yuri was my friend. A very beloved friend, a son to me. When Yuri left our motherland, he had nothing. He wasn't fleeing the enemies who sought to kill him over a few rubles. He was fleeing poverty. He worked hard; he gave me all he had."

Aslan pauses to take a breath. He studies the faces closest to him—his sight isn't what it was—and not everything he sees pleases him. When he greeted each of the special guests, he could sense respect and fear, but it's impossible—as well as inadvisable—not to feel those things when Aslan Orlov shakes your hand.

But now, protected by the crowd, the looks reveal what's hidden in people's hearts.

What Aslan sees is doubt. Crisis. Opportunity.

Orlov is old, they are thinking.

The Beast has lost its teeth, they are thinking.

Orlov's deputy was a traitor, an informer, a rat.

Aslan clears his throat.

Lessons have to be given clearly.

"Yuri won my trust, and that of all of us. He was good at his work. He prospered. On one occasion, a deal went especially well. When I went to his home to congratulate him personally, I saw he had bought a new car. A beautiful gray Maserati Quattroporte."

Whispers in the audience. They have all seen the *vor* arrive in that car. Those who didn't, find out now.

"I said to him: 'Yuri, that's a very pretty car.' He told me all about the speed it could do, the horsepower. The leather upholstery. I let him talk. When he finished, I told him: 'Your car is more expensive than mine, Yuri.'"

Aslan pauses again, letting the sense of danger float in the air.

"Do you know what Yuri did then?"

The whispering has stopped. The only sound to be heard in the church is fabric rubbing against seats as people shift uncomfortably.

"He stood up. Tottered slightly, he'd been drinking a little, not a lot. He picked up the car key and gave it me. 'Here, *vor*. It's yours.'"

Now for the lesson. In Spanish, so that everyone will understand.

"Yuri was a good kid. He knew what honor meant. Until he forgot. We are here today to make sure no one else forgets."

Aslan steps down from the pulpit.

Gently strokes Yuri's portrait as he passes it.

He walks along the central nave that divides the sepulchral silence in two, the breath everyone's holding as Aslan's footsteps ring out implacably. Nobody moves, unsure whether to follow him or stay where they are.

Aslan walks past the police standing by the front door. The captain and her subordinates. The two new faces: the small woman and the big man.

They know what has just happened, but they are powerless to do anything.

They step aside to let him through.

As Aslan emerges alone into the street, the pope begins to chant once more. The chants are stifled when the door closes behind the *vor*.

Kiril is waiting for him by the car.

The elderly *vor* does not climb into the back but into the front passenger seat. The performance is over.

"Where is she?"

"We can't find her," says Kiril.

"If she doesn't appear, we're in trouble. That damned Yuri. That damned slippery vixen."

"I've got all my men searching for her."

Aslan thinks. He thinks about the police, about the attention Yuri's death has created. About people's looks, reflecting their doubts. Doubts he can't tolerate.

The punishment for those who betray the Bratvá is without appeal. Death for that person and their family.

How can Orlov continue to rule his empire if he's unable to enforce the rule of the brotherhood?

How can Orlov continue at the head of his empire if he's unable to catch a lousy housewife?

Maybe the time has come to replace him, those looks tell him.

"Call off your men, Kiril. We need somebody else. Someone who won't fail."

"Who?"

Aslan says two words.

Chernaya Volchista.

Kiril turns toward him.

They have been together more than thirty years. Aslan has seen him slit throats, disembowel, shoot, or chop up some fifty human beings. Inflict pain, smiling all the while, without even a flicker behind those blue eyes of his. Seen him laugh his head off as he takes on armed men with his bare hands.

But he has never seen this look before.

His deputy is a born psychopath, but now in his eyes he sees fear. And this is what Aslan wants.

"Are you sure, *vor*?"

I'll have to ask Pakhan's permission. And it'll be very expensive. And dangerous.

Let them fear me. Let them know what happens if they defy me.

"I'm sure. Call her. Call the Black Wolf."

Part 2

THE WOLF

If you speak in favor of the wolf,
also speak against it.

ALEKSANDR SOLZHENITSYN

She doesn't know who she is, or where she is.

There is only pain.

No awareness. No memories of what she has dreamed. No warm sheets, no soft caress from the pillow. No gentle breathing of a partner, a lover. No hangover from the night before, or the infuriating buzz of the cell phone alarm.

There is only pain.

An overwhelming, unbearable pain. An electric current that leaves no space for self. It seizes on every bone, every muscle, every centimeter of skin. Every nerve ending of her body. There is no shred of her left. Only the injustice of not knowing what sins she has committed to deserve this.

This extreme suffering lasts no more than a few seconds. Then it eases sufficiently for her to remember who she is. What she has done. The lives she has cut short. From her parched throat comes a rasping howl, half laugh, half lament. If this pain she feels on waking every morning is punishment, she's thankful it's nothing compared to the harm she has inflicted on others.

Her body's sensations slowly begin to tell her where she is. On a hard floor. A parquet floor. Naked except for a thong. On her back. Sweat is trickling down her breasts, along her ripped abdominal muscles, forming a salty pool in her navel. She senses the draft coming in under the door, the vibrations of footsteps on the floor. A maid knocks at the door of the adjoining room. She recognizes the language, Spanish.

Madrid. I'm in Madrid.

There is no time for her to remember. She must try to move. Her body doesn't respond: it's paralyzed.

Like every morning.

It takes her an eternity to move her right arm. She starts with the fingers, one by one. Then bends her wrist, her elbow. Getting her shoulder to obey her is a triumph. Now she can lower her hand to her thighs. Beneath the skin, the muscles are as taut as steel cables. She massages her right quadriceps as hard as she can.

The limb doesn't respond. She persists. The effort is exhausting. Tedious. All she can see in the dark room is the digital clock display on the television set. Eleven minutes past seven. She concentrates on watching the minutes tick by. Nineteen pass before she can loosen her leg.

She places one hand on the small wooden bed. The mattress is soft. Unslept in. She can only fall asleep on the floor. She levers her body around. Crawling on her elbows and right knee, she succeeds in reaching the bathroom.

The shower is next to the bathtub. She only ever stays in modern five-star hotels. An independent shower is indispensable.

Leaning on one elbow, she raises herself up. After several attempts, she manages to turn on the controls with her fingertips. The water gushes out, nearly scalding. She edges under it as best she can, trying to make the stream of water hit the exact point on her back where the pain radiates throughout her body.

Time goes by. After the exhausting effort, she even falls asleep for a while. She stirs, manages to sit up. The hot water has made her skin red and tender. After she has obtained all the comfort she can from the shower, she crawls back to the bed. Lifting herself onto it involves further suffering. A negotiation between her body, pain, and gravity. All three demand their due.

She feels immense relief as she flops onto the mattress. The pressure eases. But the torture isn't over, it has only abated for a while.

By the time the door opens, it is almost nine o'clock. He is punctual: that's rare for a Spaniard. Of course, he is half Slav, the son of a Ukrainian woman. So it doesn't count.

She surveys him from the bed. She is lying on her side, but makes sure it's him. She watches the man take off his coat.

"Turn around."

The man does as she tells him, hands in the air. He's young, not yet thirty, but his hair is already receding at the temples and on top. A thin mustache sits astride his upper lip.

"You know what to do."

The man removes his coat and jacket. Raises his shirt, exposing a roll of flesh hanging over his belt. Incipient, but unstoppable.

Once she has checked he is unarmed, she motions to him to approach. She already knows who he is: this is the third time they've met. But in her helpless state, it's better to be safe than sorry.

"Come over here."

The man picks up his bag and walks toward the bed. His eyes register desire as he surveys the woman's body, but he doesn't make the slightest gesture. Nor does he say anything, although a discernible bulge has appeared in his pants.

She takes her right hand out from under the pillow. Grips the pistol as tight as she can. Too tight. But she isn't going to fire it. She simply wants to remind the man what he is there for.

He begins to take things out of his bag and lay them on the bedside table. He switches on the lamp, draws back the drapes. He needs as much light as possible for what he is about to do.

"When did it get worse?"

"The day before yesterday," she replies. "I was almost well until then. At least during the day."

Two of her vertebrae are to blame. They never mended properly after a botched leap from a third-floor window onto a moving truck. To repair them would take one or more operations and several years' rehabilitation. But she isn't willing to go through that.

Her time is invaluable, as are her skills. She knows her body is screaming to her that it wants to stop what it's doing, but she's not open to discussion.

This requires exceptional measures.

"When was the last injection?"

She turns over, offering him her back. Stifling a cry of pain.

"Amsterdam. Four months ago."

That's a lie. It was in Belgrade, three weeks earlier. But the injection didn't work as it was supposed to. She's not going to tell him that, either, because she's afraid he won't give her what she needs.

It doesn't really matter anyway, as the mark of the needle is still visible on her white skin.

"It's very dangerous," says the man. "It's too soon. You could destroy your spine marrow completely. And then . . ."

She already knows it's dangerous. That she could end up paralyzed. She doesn't need to be told by a rookie doctor with a sideline.

"Do it."

"But—"

"The money's on the table."

The man turns and looks at the table. Sees the four €500 banknotes peeping out of the open envelope.

"It's your body," he says.

The alcohol-soaked cotton gauze is cold on her back. The man carefully wipes her lumbar region. As he removes the gauze, he notices the scars. A scrapbook of her way of life.

"This one's new," he says, tracing along a red line just below her shoulder bone.

A knife. She can still feel the blade. The face of the man who did it continues to torment her at night. It hasn't yet merged into the crowd of other faces lying in wait for her in the darkness.

"Warn me when you're going to stick the needle in. I wouldn't want to shoot you by accident."

The man laughs nervously, then feels with his fingertips for the exact spot. Warns her before he pricks her with the needle. She clenches her teeth, takes her finger off the trigger. Feels the metal plunge into her back.

The man holds his breath. The needle must enter the dural sac without touching the spinal cord. One millimeter shy, and the injection won't work. One millimeter proud, and she will never walk again.

He pushes very slowly until he finds the exact spot. Intensifying the pain.

She doesn't allow herself to cry.

When he begins to press the hypodermic, the cocktail of cortisone, analgesics, and other steroids enters her body with a promise of relief. Of strength, of time regained.

When he takes the money and leaves, she doesn't say goodbye. After a few minutes, she gets up and walks over to the window. The sun's rays shine on her naked skin as she surveys the rooftops facing her suite. A phoenix stares back at her from the building opposite, its spread wings silhouetted against the impossibly blue Madrid winter sky. She envies the bronze bird its indestructible strength.

Just then her cell phone buzzes on the bedside table. An email in her inbox.

She opens it. There's an encrypted attachment. The program is installed on the phone itself, so it can only be read there.

Her green eyes scan the Cyrillic text. Instructions. Photographs.

She smiles.

They're summoning the Black Wolf.

1

A MOTHER

The funeral didn't give them much to go on, apart from filling an album of mafioso mug shots. They wasted the afternoon driving round the city. Antonia in the passenger seat, trying to control an imperceptible shake of the hand.

Without saying a word.

The next morning, they meet in the hotel lobby.

Antonia pulls out her iPad and shows Jon the photo of Yuri's dead body. Her hand is almost completely steady.

"I've been thinking about this the whole night."

"I'm glad you slept well."

"It doesn't add up. Why kill him and then ransack the house?"

Jon studiously scratches his head.

"It might have been easier to convince him to talk first."

"Orlov is looking for something. Desperately."

"Possibly this isn't simply the execution of a rat," says Jon.

Antonia nods.

"We could try asking Captain Romero."

"She won't tell you anything about her informer. She made it abundantly clear that as far as she's concerned, we're here to see if Lola Moreno just happens to step into our car."

"Then we'll have to go and see the mother."

"The police have already spoken to her, angel."

"I don't have any other ideas."

"Can't you use that fascist magic on your iPad?"

"To do what?"

"I don't know, realign satellites to see if they can spot Lola Moreno. Magic fascist satellites."

Antonia spends several minutes explaining to Jon exactly how Heimdal works, how it can help Red Queen's investigations, what it can and cannot do. Hack into databases, hack into emails, use facial algorithms in security recordings, and a few other things. All of them still in beta phase. In other words, fallible.

"So you're saying there is no magic fascist function."

Jon listens closely, in earnest. A skeptical Basque. Then he presses a button on his cell phone and speaks into the microphone.

"Hey, Siri. Do magic fascists exist?"

I've found Fast and Furious Seven. *Would you like me to play it?* is Siri's suggestion.

"You see? It's as useless as yours," says Jon.

Antonia smiles. One of her good smiles, bringing a dimple to each cheek to form a perfect triangle with the one in the middle of her chin. A smile Jon hasn't seen for some time.

She is feeling much better this morning. She has shed the heavy cocoon of anxiety that enveloped her the day before.

Jon knows there's something wrong. But the morning has done what all mornings do when they arrive: promise us a few special hours, free of the usual chores and sorrows. As every freckled orphan knows, the sun will come out tomorrow. Then the day takes it upon itself to remind you that you still have no parents—but, hey, the sun will come out tomorrow.

So Jon sweeps his concern under the carpet.

And they go off to visit the mother.

All the housefronts on Calle de Salvador Rueda are painted white. Except for Tere's hairdressing salon, which is painted a lurid mauve. The inside, too, in case you hadn't had enough of it.

Tere the hairdresser isn't painted mauve. Except her fingernails. And a lock of hair. *When you're fiftysomething, mauve doesn't really cut it*, thinks Jon. He doesn't say this out loud, because you don't insult people who are helping with an investigation. However, he does pick up a business card so he can send an anonymous email protesting in the name of good taste.

"When did you last see your daughter?" asks Antonia.

"Again! I already told the police. Six days ago. I just want to be left in peace. I don't know anything," Tere responds, standing stiffly and fluffing up her hair. "You're scaring away my clients."

Antonia and Jon look around the empty salon and the deserted February Marbella street. You can almost see tumbleweed blowing along it.

"You're having a quiet morning," says Antonia.

"Things will liven up once you two have gone. Would you like a coffee? I've got a Nespresso."

"Could I have a *mitad*, please?" asks Jon.

"Since you ask so nicely."

Tere is a beautiful woman. Not just for her age: she's a beautiful woman, period. Her beauty shimmers beneath the tacky hairdo. She isn't dazzling like her daughter, but it's easy to see where Lola gets it from.

And she's one of those beauties that like to be the center of attention, thinks Jon. He has conducted far too many interviews to be taken in. *Now that she's gone through the motions of telling us she wants to be left in peace, she's delighted we're here.*

The hairdresser croons softly while the coffee machine hums at nineteen bars of pressure.

"Your colleagues have been here several times. They told me to contact them if she gets in touch with me."

If her daughter turns up here, they won't need contacting. Two plainclothes policemen are sitting in a car a few meters down the street. In the building opposite, two Slavic-looking gentlemen have rented an apartment across from the obscenely mauve façade of Tere's salon. They're sitting on plastic chairs out on the terrace, in their SOBAFRESH T-shirts and with their tattooed arms. They're smoking and drinking without taking their eyes off the hairdresser's.

If Lola shows up here, you'll be the fifth person to know, thinks Jon, staring out the window.

"Tell me about your relationship with your daughter," says Antonia.

"It's good. We have a good relationship. Well, you know how kids are. If you have kids, you'll know what I'm talking about."

"I have one. And no, I don't know."

"You will. You give them all the love you can, then when they're grown up, they go off and do their own thing. But we get along fine."

"I take it you're not close, then?"

"No, she calls me every day. But she does what she wants. Didn't I keep telling her over and over that fellow was no good for her?"

"So you didn't approve of Yuri?"

"He's Russian, isn't he?"

Antonia tilts her head.

"I don't follow."

"Well, it's obvious. What good could come of that?"

"There are twenty thousand Russians in Marbella. I'm guessing you know all of them."

Tere waves her hand, dismissing unwelcome possibilities.

"And with all the nice boys there are here. Full-blooded Spaniards. My daughter is a catch. She could be with whoever she likes, all the men are after her. But the girl had to get involved with an outsider . . . And look where it's got her. Pregnant and widowed. Now nobody will touch her with a barge pole."

"Were things going badly with her husband? Didn't they love each other?"

"No, on the contrary! She was crazy about him. Yuri this, Yuri that. That's all she spoke of all day long. Bored the pants off me. He was hers to change. We women all want a man to change. That's how we amuse ourselves. Then life gets in the way. And zilch."

"I'd like to ask you about the day when—"

An alarm bell goes off in Jon's head. He raises his hand to interrupt Antonia.

"Sorry. What do you mean he was hers to change?"

"That boy was a good-for-nothing until my daughter made a man of him."

"In what way?"

"What way do you think? He didn't have a dime. Now look how they're living, with their fancy house in a development, like rich people. As I always say: in marriage, the man is the head, the woman is the neck. Where does the head look? Where the neck decides."

"So she knew about her husband's business affairs."

At this, Tere clams up. Slamming on the brakes like someone who has passed a red light and has to reverse on the pedestrian crossing.

"Oh, I know nothing about that."

"What did Yuri do? Do you know that?"

"He imported things from Russia. That funny Nutella of his is actually delicious. Look, I have some here," she says, taking out a jar from next to the Nespresso machine. She hands Antonia a clean spoon. "Go on, go on. Dip in, if you want."

Jon observes the struggle between two invisible forces. The gravitational pull of the jar versus Antonia's willpower. Her chin swivels from shoulder to shoulder, her eyes fixed on the brown paste.

"I'll try it, if you don't mind," he says.

Mortal hatred. Bitter envy. The sourest resentment. Antonia gives her colleague a look that contains all these things. Making the Funduk taste even richer.

"Oh my God, it's amazing!" says Jon, licking his lips.

"What did I tell you? I said to Yuri, 'Concentrate on that, it'll make you a fortune.' It's much better than ours, which doesn't taste of anything anymore."

Antonia raises her hand to take the spoon, but Tere goes ahead and tosses it onto a dish next to the cup Jon drank his coffee from. The clank of metal on crockery is the sound of Antonia's heart breaking.

"Aren't you concerned about your daughter?"

"Oh, yes, of course. Extremely concerned," says Tere. "But I know she'll be fine. She's always been able to look after herself."

2

A MESSAGE

"**Did you see those men on the terrace across the way?**" Jon says as they are leaving.

"Yes, if they keep staring at that storefront, they're going to overdose on mauve."

"They're Russian. They were probably immunized against it back home."

Jon wants to stretch his legs, so they leave the car on the promenade and take a walk. There's a damp salty tang in the air that's not unpleasant. It even makes Antonia slightly receptive to her colleague's sarcasm.

"I could see they made you nervous."

"Spain at its best."

"I'm more concerned about Tere's state of mind."

"She was sick with worry, right?"

"When you've no idea where your child is, you don't react like that."

Antonia gives the impression of staring into a very dark hole.

Jon doesn't have any children. And he's never lost anything bigger than a lovebird he had as a child. One morning its cage was empty. Disaster. *It must have flown off to have fun, don't worry.* Years later, his *amatxo* confessed the cat had eaten it, but she hadn't said anything so as not to traumatize him. *But then I turned out queer, Ama,* he moaned.

A few months earlier, during the most stressful time of Antonia's life, she thought she'd lost her son, Jorge. What took place in the Goya 2 tunnel changed her. Jon knows this. What remains to be seen is exactly how.

"Have you talked to your boy?"

She shakes her head.

"The next visit is in eleven days. While I'm still on probation, they told me our daily contact has to be limited."

"Everything will be all right, you'll see."

"I'm not sure. The last visit was . . . complicated. He was very odd. Trying to provoke me all the time. Wanting me to make a mistake."

"Maybe he just wanted you to react."

"Maybe I'm not cut out to be a mother."

"Angel, none of you are cut out to be mothers. You get this thing inside you, then *pop*, out comes a creature who turns your life upside down, and you think your hormones will arrive like the cavalry to turn you into supermoms. Spoiler: no."

"It's just that I don't understand him. And I'm terrified of doing something wrong."

"You don't need to understand him. Or to be in control all the time, Antonia. You only need to love him. That's already more than a lot of people have."

From where they are now, they can see the sea. It's gray and menacing. A danger barely restrained by weary gods about to throw in the towel. A storm on the horizon is sweeping toward them. They speed up to reach the car before it breaks.

"Do you think she's in touch with her daughter?" asks Antonia, getting back to the hairdresser.

"Back in the Basque Country, in the days when quite a few people were hiding from the police, families were worried too," says Jon, breathing heavily from their brisk walk. "But they didn't call or send letters or emails when they appeared. They did what they've always done in the villages. They used the jungle telegraph. Tell the *aitas* I'm fine, *mux-utxus, agur*. And that person would pass the message on to someone else. The greengrocer, a neighbor's daughter. Anyone you might bump into who could whisper the message in your ear while they're kissing cheeks."

"That would explain the mother's attitude," says Antonia after a moment's thought. "So, Lola Moreno is still in hiding. With no bag and no credit cards."

"And without any known relatives, apart from her mother, who, as far as we can tell, isn't helping her."

"She's pregnant, and diabetic. She has to inject insulin every day."

"And if she doesn't?"

"Convulsions, loss of consciousness, death. Obviously in that order," says Antonia.

"Well, unless we start staking out pharmacies—"

"I already thought of that. There are thirty pharmacies in Marbella, so it's impossible."

"And we can't assume she would get it herself."

"Maybe we should watch the pawnshops. She has to get money from somewhere."

"In any case, it's the mother's money we need to keep an eye on."

"What makes you say that?"

"Angel, I've never seen a hairdresser with such a clean floor."

A lightning flash illuminates Antonia's face, the car windshield, and the glass front of the empty souvenir shop, outside of which the car is parked. The thunder that follows releases a bucketful of water, fat raindrops that rebound off the Audi's hood. Jon hurriedly opens the car door, but Antonia doesn't move.

The monkeys are screaming for her attention.

Jon jumps into the car, takes off his jacket, and throws it on the back seat. He fastens his seat belt and turns on the windshield wipers. He stares at them chasing each other across the glass: *tick tock*. He presses a button, and the passenger window descends slowly, to reveal Antonia still standing motionless in the rain.

"Aren't you getting in? Or do you really want to catch pneumonia?"

Antonia appears to wake up and realize she is getting soaked.

"You're a genius," she says, sliding in.

"I know that. But tell me why."

"The sign on the salon door. The one with the opening hours."

Antonia gathers her hair and wrings it out. A stream of water falls onto the upholstery and rug.

"Thank heavens for that photographic memory of yours. What did it say?"

"Mondays, Tuesdays, and Thursdays. From eleven to one."

"A workaholic."

"There's no hairdresser in the world that doesn't open on Fridays, Jon. That place is a front for money laundering."

It makes sense, thinks Jon. *Voronin sets the place up. Tere goes in a couple of hours a day, three times a week. No problem if there are no clients. She declares earnings of thousands of euros, because nobody ever asks for a receipt for a haircut. Her son-in-law pays her a small wage, and the "profits" go straight to one of the Orlov clan's companies.*

"We need to find out who actually owns the hairdresser."

"Let's ask Siri," says Antonia, pulling out her iPad and typing Heimdal.

Jon looks across at her.

Good for you, Scott. She's learning, slowly, the sly minx, he thinks, chuckling to himself.

LOLA

There was once a little girl in a sad, loveless home, where the food tasted of ashes and the future was black, Lola repeats to herself. She has come to believe it. It's not one of those spongy lies you keep squeezing to see if it is believable. No, this lie is as hard as rock, stiff with Viagra and smothered in coke. She's told it to herself so often, with so many layers of complicated detail, she can no longer determine the truth. Did they really go hungry at night in her home? Was her mother about to be evicted when Yuri set her up in the salon? Did the woodcutter save Little Red Riding Hood? Did Goku find the Dragon Balls? All these questions are identical.

If there is one thing Lola has learned in this modern world of ours, it's that the truth doesn't matter. The only important thing is the version of reality that coincides with your desires and aspirations.

Except when you find yourself with no money, sleeping on the sofa of a friend you haven't seen for seven years because you decided you were too good for her.

It's seven in the morning when Yaiza comes in. She's in a bad mood, exhausted and weary. She throws down the sports bag with the clothes she wears in the discos. She still has traces of glitter on her face.

"I've been sacked," she says as she enters.

"That's impossible. You're the best," says Lola when Yaiza collapses onto the spot where her head was until a few minutes earlier.

"I'm thirty-three. An old woman. And I'm fat."

Yaiza has put on weight. This is normal when you sleep in the daytime, eat out of containers, and drink to forget the day you decided to quit school because who but an idiot would study when they can earn lots of dough shaking their ass to the rhythm of "Dragostea Din Tei."

"Who sacked you? Samir?"

She remembers the manager of Copacabana being a moron from the time when they both danced there.

"That son of a bitch just wants fresh meat. Little girls he can fuck in the dressing rooms," says Yaiza. Her eyes are bloodshot, the pupils dilated. She needs more and more stuff every night to keep going, dancing to one song after another for hours, with only two fifteen-minute breaks.

"What will you do?"

"Go back to my parents' place in Estepona."

"But you don't even talk to them."

"I can't stay here. I owe two months' rent. I paid a three-month deposit, so the landlord will still have to give me back one if I hand him the keys tomorrow."

Lola feels her chest begin to heave.

"For fuck's sake, Yaiza. Couldn't you have hung in a bit longer?"

Yaiza stares at her, open-mouthed.

"Look, I'm sorry if my personal problems inconvenience you."

"You leave me in the lurch, and for what? A five-hundred-fucking-euro deposit?"

Lola is being unfair, and she knows it. The only dealings between them since she stopped being a go-go dancer are a few Likes on Facebook. She was lucky Yaiza took her in two nights ago when she turned up, freezing cold and barefoot. Her feet cut to ribbons. The hours she spent sitting on the front doorstep waiting for Yaiza to appear seemed eternal. She had never felt so happy her friend had such a shitty life. A life that meant she was still stuck in that apartment in Albarizas. One bedroom, kitchenette, and a two-seater couch so close to the TV you could change channels with your eyelashes.

"Five hundred bucks might be nothing to you, sweetheart, but it's all I've got."

"I have nowhere else to go!"

"Well, neither do I. I have no job, no qualifications, and both my parents are out of work. I'll have to clean houses or shake my ass on the Guadalobón traffic circle. So don't give me that shit."

"I'm in a fix and I can't seem to find a way out."

"Look, you've been living the life of a princess for years. All those Instagram photos of you with a new car, or at a spa. Or pregnant. I've helped you enough. Fix your own crap and leave me in peace."

There's no way I can fix what I've broken, thinks Lola.

"I'm sorry," she says, but it's too late. Yaiza gets up and moves away, heading for the bedroom.

"You have until tomorrow morning."

"Listen, I—"

Yaiza sends her a Don't Like in the form of a slamming door that rattles the mirror above the sofa.

Lola gets dressed. All the clothes are lent by Yaiza: a hoodie, cargo pants with multiple pockets. Cheap sneakers from Decathlon that are a little tight. A week earlier, Lola would have been horrified by things like these. She still is, but puts them on anyway. The top is loose enough to fit over her belly, which is growing by the day.

She has one dose of insulin left. She hesitates over whether to inject herself or to wait. In the end she decides she will, because she feels dizzy and dehydrated. She doesn't have her hemoglobin monitor, but she doesn't need it to realize her glucose level is too high.

Lowering her pants a little, she sticks the needle into her buttock. It hurts more than in the arm, but she read on the internet once that the effect lasts longer.

Hopefully it's true.

She can't buy more. Without a prescription, insulin is very expensive. She was able to get some because Yaiza gave her forty euros, but that option has gone. Nor can she steal any, because insulin is always kept in a freezer at the back of any pharmacy.

Besides, she wouldn't know where to start. It's been fifteen years since Lola stole anything from a store. The days when she went with her girlfriends to El Corte Inglés to slip lipsticks into her bag are long gone. Back then she already knew what mattered most was being hot. And that she was incredibly hot. She was smart, but that didn't matter as much. She only had to seize her chance.

There was once a girl who was waiting for her Prince Charming . . .

Lola shakes her head. This isn't the time for daydreaming.

It's the time to think about what to do.

She has no money. No time.
Few options.
Only one, in fact.
But it's very dangerous.

3

A LITTLE CANDLE

"And now the version for dummies, angel."

Antonia sighs and begins to explain for the fourth time. Doing her best to simplify as much as possible. They are sitting in La Bodega del Mar having something to eat, now that the storm has passed. Jon ordered swordfish with ratatouille, which tastes divine. Antonia has a chicken salad she has hardly touched because she's too preoccupied with Yuri's affairs.

"Voronin creates a company in the Cayman Islands called Balalaika Limited. And he doesn't need to take a plane to the Caribbean: it's all done on the internet. To set it up costs him less than two hundred euros."

"Balalaika. Got it."

"Balalaika owns a company in Luxembourg, which in turn owns a company in Ireland, which in turn owns a place in Marbella."

"Tere's hairdressing salon."

"All these companies invoice one another, and make bank transfers for nonexistent services. The final link in the chain is Tere's salon, which declared earnings of two million three hundred and forty-seven thousand euros on its last corporate tax return."

Jon gives a high-pitched whistle.

"That's a hell of a lot of perms."

"Internal Revenue charges twenty-five percent, and no questions asked. Lola's mom probably goes to the bank every morning with her fictitious takings. In garbage bags."

"I bet the bags are mauve."

"Now do you understand?"

Jon nods.

"I understood the second time."

"Then why did you make me repeat it four times?" Antonia asks with a groan of frustration.

"You need to improve your communication skills."

Antonia slumps back in her chair the way small children do when they fold their arms and threaten to stop breathing. She can think of eleven reasons why Jon is wrong, but is unable to communicate any of them.

Jon polishes off the ratatouille and signals to the waiter, whom he took aside earlier and who is at the ready. The man brings over a chocolate brownie with a lit candle on it. The whole restaurant—two German pensioners, a woman with a little dog, the waiter, and Jon—wreck, drag through the mud, violate, and murder the first two verses of "Happy Birthday to You."

"Who told you?" Antonia demands to know, arms still folded.

"Aguado, a while ago. I had it marked on my calendar."

"I'm not eating that. I need to lose weight."

"Aren't very sweet flavors the only ones you can taste? Come on, just this once."

"I'm not touching it."

"At least blow out the candle and make a wish. Then I'll eat it."

Antonia rests her elbows on the table, arms still folded. She blows at the candle. It doesn't go out. Again. Nothing. Third time lucky.

Jon picks up a spoon. So does Antonia. Without making excuses.

"It doesn't taste of cardboard," she says, raising the spoon to her mouth. She can't believe it.

"The filling is Funduk, señora," the waiter tells her. "I'll bring your coffees."

Jon suddenly finds himself fighting for his life with a spoon on a battlefield eighteen centimeters in diameter. Antonia is quicker at eating desserts than at expressing her thoughts.

There's no problem a brownie can't solve.

"Can we charge her with money laundering?" asks Jon, surmising that she has finished sulking.

"No," replies Antonia, still disgruntled. "The mother is paid a wage. Four thousand euros a month."

"That's not bad for scratching your crotch six hours a week."

"Besides, there are a few details about the investigation the public prosecutor wouldn't appreciate."

"You mean the tiny detail that you got all the information illegally?" says Jon, pointing to her iPad.

"And it wasn't easy. The only link between the Irish company and the hair salon is her wage. If you hadn't noticed how empty the salon was, I wouldn't have known where to start."

"Is that a compliment?"

"You can be useful at times," says Antonia, scraping the plate with the spoon.

She gives, then snatches it away.

"How much does someone make from laundering money?"

"They don't have a pay structure."

"But from your experience, how much is it usually?"

"Not much. One percent."

"Well, honey, Yuri's commission on the salon isn't enough to support the lifestyle those two had. We still have nothing on them."

Antonia pauses for thought. She even stops defying physics by trying to extract brownie crumbs from the interior of the china plate.

"We have two possibilities. The first is to go and talk to Aslan Orlov."

Jon looks at her as if she has just suggested they organize Hitler's bachelor party.

"Going face-to-face with the prime suspect for the murder. Who is also a Mafia boss. With hit men guarding him twenty-four seven. And who won't tell us a thing. Oh, and flouting Captain Romero's orders when, for the moment at least, she's leaving us in peace."

"It's an option."

"Me winning Miss Universe is also an option."

Antonia analyzes this possibility and says solemnly:

"That's not going to happen."

"Neither is what you suggest. What's the other option?"

"We follow the money. See where it leads."

"I can hear a 'but' in your voice."

"We struck it lucky with the salon. There are regular bank transfers that are traceable to the Irish company. Normally, it isn't so easy. Why do you think the UDYCO, the Finance Intelligence Unit, and the Internal Revenue can't stop these people? They use the tiniest chink, subterfuge, or legal loophole they can find. They have all the money in the world to pay the best lawyers. It would take months to disentangle everything. We need a thread to pull on."

"You could start with Funduk," Jon says.

Antonia looks at him, blinking furiously.

You can be useful at times, thinks Jon, sipping his coffee.

RECORDING 01

ELEVEN MONTHS EARLIER

CAPTAIN ROMERO: Voronin, you and your whole gang are busted.

YURI VORONIN: Captain, I'm afraid my Spanish not so good. What you say?

DEPUTY INSPECTOR BELGRANO: Don't play dumb, Voronin. You speak it better than I do: I've heard you bragging in the Astral bar.

YURI VORONIN: It must be pressure.

CAPTAIN ROMERO: Listen, Voronin, there are two ways we can do this.

YURI VORONIN: I don't understand well your language.

DEPUTY INSPECTOR BELGRANO: I said, don't play dumb!

CAPTAIN ROMERO: Sit down, Belgrano. I admit you're very smart, Señor Voronin. Our experts are impressed. You've achieved something few others could manage. But you've seen the evidence. We can link you to last week's shipment.

YURI VORONIN: I am only honest entrepreneur. A businessman.

CAPTAIN ROMERO: Sure, that's what your kind always say. I'm a businessman; I work to earn a living.

YURI VORONIN: It is true.

CAPTAIN ROMERO: So how do you explain this?

(The rustle of paper on the table. A thirty-three-second pause.)

YURI VORONIN: I have nothing to explain. I have nothing to do with that company or that shipment.

DEPUTY INSPECTOR BELGRANO: So now it seems you do understand Spanish.

YURI VORONIN: I'm not going talk to you.

CAPTAIN ROMERO: We have evidence connecting your company to the one that shipped this container from Saint Petersburg.

YURI VORONIN: All proves is that I did business with a company you say made mistake.

CAPTAIN ROMERO: That is enough probable cause for the Revenue and the Finance Intelligence Unit to act.

DEPUTY INSPECTOR BELGRANO: They're going to shove a microscope so far up your ass, Voronin, they'll see your fillings.

YURI VORONIN: I said I'm not going talk to you. Tell him not speak to me.

CAPTAIN ROMERO: Then talk to me. What do you think will happen when they investigate your business, Voronin?

YURI VORONIN: Nothing. I know how Spanish justice works. Oligarch, they take six years. Red marble, eight.

CAPTAIN ROMERO: It's true the courts are very slow. But we have you in our sights now, Voronin. It may take us years, but this is bad news for you.

YURI VORONIN: Don't understand.

CAPTAIN ROMERO: We know what you do. We know you control the *obshchak*, the shared funds. You have the keys to the money. And you have little side deals of your own, right? What do posh people call that, Belgrano?

DEPUTY INSPECTOR BELGRANO: Er . . . I don't know what you're referring to, Captain.

CAPTAIN ROMERO: I'll tell you. "Outsourcing." You offer services to Colombians, Swedes. Financial assistance. Logistics. Consultancy. You're running a narco franchise.

DEPUTY INSPECTOR BELGRANO: A fucking McDonald's.

YURI VORONIN: You have no proof that.

CAPTAIN ROMERO: Belgrano?

DEPUTY INSPECTOR BELGRANO: Listen to what we recorded the other day. *(The sound of conversation in another language. Almost inaudible.)*

YURI VORONIN: That's just people talking. Everybody talking about everybody.

CAPTAIN ROMERO: It's true, everyone's talking. And what do you think your clients are going to say when we place them under constant surveillance? The procedure is very clear. Their accounts will be frozen, and their residency permits will be scrutinized.

DEPUTY INSPECTOR BELGRANO: Slash. Slash. A big *X*. A marked man.

CAPTAIN ROMERO: How many of your clients will want to work with a marked man?

YURI VORONIN: I—

CAPTAIN ROMERO: Your clients won't want to touch you. And your boss . . . you'll be a danger to Orlov. So he'll send you back to Russia. What time does the next flight to Moscow leave, Belgrano?

DEPUTY INSPECTOR BELGRANO: There's an Aeroflot flight at ten tomorrow morning. You'll be able to order a borscht for lunch in Red Square.

(A fifty-two-second pause.)

YURI VORONIN: I can't go back my country.

DEPUTY INSPECTOR BELGRANO: Then you're fucked.

YURI VORONIN: You don't understand. If I go back, they kill me.

CAPTAIN ROMERO: In that case, you're going to have to help us, Voronin. You need to give us something.

YURI VORONIN: What?

CAPTAIN ROMERO: Information.

YURI VORONIN: *(Inaudible, in Russian.)*

DEPUTY INSPECTOR BELGRANO: I don't understand well your language.

YURI VORONIN: I said, I'm no *shpik*. I'm not snitch. If I rat on them, they kill me here. I won't need Aeroflot.

(A twenty-seven-second pause.)

LOLA MORENO: Excuse me, Captain. I'd like to make a suggestion.

4

A WRAPPER

Two hundred thousand.

That's the number of shipping containers that pass through the port of Málaga every year.

Three million.

That's the amount of tonnage they contain.

Eleven.

That's how many customs officials there are in the port.

Jon shows his ID to the security guard at the port terminal, and the man opens the barrier.

"I'm looking for the person in charge," says Jon through the car window.

"Straight ahead, the office is right next to the hopper."

"The what?"

"A giant funnel for sifting," explains Antonia.

"The corrugated iron building next to the crane."

"Thanks," says Jon. "First left, then right."

It's sixty kilometers from Marbella to Málaga. Jon has covered the distance in forty minutes. It took Antonia twenty-three of those minutes to discover the name of Voronin's import company.

"It wasn't in his name," she explains. "It's a holding company based in Barbados. I tracked it down through a subsidiary in Macao, which owns Yuri's house."

Sooner or later, criminals have to come ashore. Someone has to own the houses they live in. The cars they drive. The credit cards they go on sprees with in jewelers and restaurants. But laws are made by people and people are fallible. It isn't illegal for Yuri to live in a house worth €5 million bought in the name of a foreign company registered in a tax haven. As long as society doesn't protest, everyone is happy.

The décor might be criminal. But the property isn't.

So all they can do is follow the trail of bread crumbs to find their way through the forest.

This forest is made of steel.

It's gigantic: twelve square kilometers of the best Basque concrete filled with enormous six-meter-long steel boxes, in some cases stacked five high. All painted in primary colors.

A few years before, a private company, Noatum Maritime, won the concession for the container terminal. Since then, the volume of traffic in Málaga has gone through the roof. A constant flow of goods, which have gradually won a greater share of the market from nearby ports.

The terminal manager is standing in front of his office. In one hand he has a cell phone, in the other, a walkie-talkie. He's wearing an orange vest and a white safety helmet. And with his ruddy cheeks, light skin, and blond hair, you expect him to speak to you in a foreign language. Until you hear him talking to an employee.

"*Aliquindoi* at Zone H4, okay? When the *Karaboudjan* arrives tomorrow, we're going to need space. Have them fill H5 first."

He turns toward them.

"You're from the police, right? How can I help you? Customs is already closed for the day. In fact, I was just leaving."

"We'll only take a few minutes of your time," says Jon. "You see, we're investigating the activities of an import company called Lemondrop Málaga Limited. If you could possibly help us—"

"I'm afraid I can't," the blond guy interrupts. "You need a customs official to check the import dockets, so you'll have to come back tomorrow."

With that, he turns on his heel and walks briskly over to the office door.

"Does your wife know you have a thing going with one of your employees?" says Antonia.

The man stops, one foot on the threshold. He stiffens.

He comes back to them.

"That's a filthy lie, señora," he says, lowering his voice and glancing about him.

"Pupils dilated. Pulse racing. I don't think so," Antonia comments to Jon.

"Me neither," says Jon, thrusting his hands in his pockets and shrugging his shoulders.

The man moves closer.

"Listen, you shouldn't say anything about this to anyone. I don't want to lose my girls."

"We don't care about that. We're only interested in the activities of Lemondrop Málaga Limited," says Antonia.

"Where you put your dick is all the same to us. You help us, we keep quiet," says Jon.

The man draws his hand across his face, which is even redder than usual. He has the pitiful look of a little lapdog going around and around a table. All that's missing is the wagging tail.

It's an easy decision.

"All right, dammit, all right," he capitulates, opening his laptop. "What did you say the company was called?"

Jon repeats the name.

"Yes, they're clients here," the manager says. "In fact, they have a TEU in the hot zone right now."

"A TEU?"

"Twenty-foot equivalent unit. The standard size. If all the containers measure the same, they can be easily transferred from ship to truck or train. Actually, this should have been loaded a couple of days ago. That's strange."

Antonia and Jon exchange glances.

"We're nearly there," says the manager, illuminating the letters painted on the ground that mark the different zones. "This way."

The dull afternoon has turned into early nightfall. Jon and Antonia are lagging behind the manager of the terminal enough for Jon to satisfy his curiosity.

"How did you do it?" he asks.

"Do what?" replies Antonia, innocent as pie.

"You know what."

She shrugs.

"You make me feel like a trained monkey when you ask me that kind of question."

"Come on. You know you want to."

Antonia sighs and begins to recite wearily.

"He isn't wearing his wedding ring, the mark on that finger is very visible and recent. He's buttoned up the second button of his shirt in the third hole. You heard his conversation with his employee. This is a man who pays attention to detail, which means he must have undone his shirt a short while ago, otherwise he would have noticed it during the day when he went to the restroom. And when he turned his back on us, I saw the soles of his shoes."

"And?"

"He's got a used condom wrapper stuck to his left sole. It might fall off before he gets home. Or not."

Jon suppresses a guffaw. He has no intention of warning the guy, and neither does Antonia. At moments like these, Inspector Gutiérrez is happy. He wouldn't change places with anyone else. Too bad these moments are so rare.

"Here it is!" says the adulterer, indicating with his flashlight.

The container is at ground level, and has two others on top of it. When Jon and Antonia catch up with the manager, he reads from the manifest on his laptop.

"GD772569. Arrived from Saint Petersburg three days ago. It was meant to be picked up the day of its arrival. That's why it's here in the hot zone, but no one has come for it. The company will have to pay a fine."

"Hasn't it been inspected by customs?"

"Not every container is inspected. There are too many of them, and not enough officials. But it's even worse in Algeciras. Here we deal with two hundred thousand TEUs a year: they have five million. They lack the staff."

Jon slaps the dark blue metal.

"Well, your reinforcements have arrived. Open it."

The manager shakes his head.

"I can't do that without a customs off—"

"Kiss my ass," says Jon, and grabs hold of the bolts, pushing and pulling. "Let's see how on earth this thing opens."

"You don't understand. Even if you find something, the law is very clear—"

The screech of the steel rod turning on itself drowns out the man's protest. Frustrated, he turns away, raising his arms to the sky.

"I'm washing my hands of it," he says. "Washing my hands of it."

Jon slides the bolt free of its catches. Then yanks hard: there's another loud screeching sound. Salt crystals fall from the container door as it swings open.

The stench hits them in the face.

Intense. Poisonous.

It's not something Jon has ever encountered before. Feces. Urine. The sweet smell of rotting flesh. All of that mingled together, and a thousand times worse.

The manager raises his hands to his face to try to hold back the nausea, but can't prevent the vomit splashing through his fingers and landing on his shoes.

Jon is luckier. He manages to turn and lean on the side of the container before bringing up all the contents of his stomach. The spasms are so violent he can barely control his body.

"Don't go in there," he warns Antonia. "Let Forensics deal with it."

She pushes past him, heading for the dark rectangle.

5

A CONTAINER

Antonia watches impassively as the two men struggle with the stench.

She can't detect much. Her anosmia isn't a complete lack of the sense of smell. Nearly all her olfactory receptors are dead, but a few are still more or less functioning. They faintly register the foul odor pouring out of the container's open door. It's like the distant memory of cheap, sickly sweet perfume.

"Don't go in there," Jon repeats, trying to restrain her.

Antonia ignores him. She bends down to pick up the flashlight the manager of the terminal has dropped, and steps inside the container.

Her feet stick to the floor. It's wooden, but is damp and sticky. The interior walls are made of steel, but they're not painted with anti-rust paint like the exterior. So Antonia sees the bloodstains. Hands that have clawed the sides and slid down, leaving five jagged lines in the corrugated metal.

On one side is an exhaust fan.

That can't have failed, otherwise they wouldn't have lasted so long, she thinks.

The monkeys begin to screech, picking up things from what she can see and telling their stories.

The overflowing bucket.

The smashed water barrel thrown into a corner, covered in blood.

The knife on the floor.

Enough.

Antonia mustn't give in to it. She has to choke back her disgust—

which is rational, not instinctive—and feel inside her pocket. Open her mouth in this atmosphere contaminated with decomposing particles, many of them infectious.

Have you forgotten? Forgotten the river?

Mentor's voice echoes inside her head.

You cannot hold back a river. You have to give in.

No, Antonia protests.

I'm not going to lose control.

I can do this. This time she puts three red capsules in her mouth. She has to crunch them to release their precious, bitter contents. She has been trained to count down, to take a breath between each number, descending a step at a time until she is where she needs to be. But the amount of drugs she has taken alters everything.

She doesn't count down from ten.

She doesn't descend the steps.

She plummets down them, into the darkness.

Where silence awaits her.

Antonia feels her body shaken as if by a gust of wind. Then everything becomes clear, in a way she has never experienced before.

It's wonderful.

Terrifying.

It's *Chādanāca*.

In Bengali, the frightening pleasure of dancing at the edge of a roof.

She feels the same calm as when the blue pill reduces her faculties, but keeps them intact. For the first time since she began her training to become a Red Queen, Antonia *sees* what has happened at a crime scene, she doesn't simply deduce it.

She sees it.

And what she sees is a nightmare.

She sees the eight dead women on the floor leaving Saint Petersburg. Young. Possibly beautiful—it's impossible to tell now. Manacled—the dead bodies still have the marks on their wrists. The ninth girl isn't tied up, but lies apart from the others. They have food and water, but during the journey something goes wrong. They argue, fight over the food and other resources. One of them ends up wounded in a corner of the container. The others ignore her: she's the first to die.

Then a second one, whom the rest place alongside the first.

Seven survive the journey. But no one comes to fetch the container. The fan runs out of power and stops. The women bang on the walls, desperate to escape.

When they realize they're going to suffocate, some of them fling themselves on the others. As the flashlight beam bounces from one side to the other, Antonia doesn't see blood traces under fingernails, torn out hair, ripped clothes. What she sees are women fighting, she sees the hurt they inflict, how one woman smashes another against the wall before she in turn is strangled by a third. As they fight, they use up the remaining oxygen more quickly. Until they kill one another.

Except for one.

Antonia sees her climb up to the exhaust fan, tearing at the tube with her nails.

Perhaps.

Perhaps.

Antonia rushes over to the woman, who has fallen onto her back on the toppled device. She is covered in blood and has a nasty gash on her face that has disfigured her forehead and probably damaged one eye. Her dress, which might once have been green, is now a torn rag held up by a single shoulder strap. Her left leg is bent at an impossible angle. Broken by her fall from the fan when there was no more oxygen.

None of that really matters.

The only thing that matters is the faint pulse in her neck Antonia can feel beneath her fingers.

Alive. Only just.

She takes the woman by the shoulders, trying to pull her out. Slips on the blood.

She shouts for Jon in a strange metallic voice she doesn't recognize. A voice she didn't know she had.

Then she passes out.

6

TWO FIXES

"When your colleague fell to the floor, did she hit her head?" the paramedic asks, pointing over his shoulder.

Antonia is sitting huddled in the ambulance parked outside the docks. Her clothes, face, and hands soiled. A blanket over her slumped shoulders. Her unfocused eyes puzzled and lifeless. Miles away.

"I don't know. I think not," says Jon. "She was trying to pull out the woman your colleagues have taken away. I think the lack of oxygen made her collapse."

The paramedic shakes his head and wrinkles his nose. He's not convinced.

"We can rule out concussion. Did she see an ophthalmologist today?"

"No, I'm sure she didn't."

"Well, I've never seen pupils as dilated as that. So if it isn't eye drops or concussion . . . I'm going to have to report it."

Jon was afraid of this. The last thing they need now is for the paramedic to go to the police with tales about the drugs Antonia takes.

He places his hand on the man's forearm.

"Please don't."

The ambulance's revolving yellow lights seem to slow while the paramedic looks Jon up and down. Jon returns the once-over. Good-looking. Shaven head. Carefully groomed goatee. A rainbow-colored pendant leaves no doubt. As does what the man says next:

"I'm married, Inspector."

Jon gently removes his hand. He wasn't coming on to the guy.

Although he wouldn't have minded. He has kindly eyes, which is usually what Inspector Gutiérrez falls for. But it invariably turns out that the old sayings are a lie. The eyes aren't the mirror of the soul. Actions speak louder than words and all that kind of crap. Jon's heart clangs shut. Until the next pair of smiling eyes.

"Forget about the report," he says. "She's having a hard time, with the custody of her son and everything."

The paramedic studies the toes of his shoes closely, then looks at Antonia, and finally at Jon once more.

"Tell your colleague to be careful at the next drug test," he says, donning his jacket as he walks away toward the police gathered at the terminal entrance. The TV cameras focus on him, journalists on the other side of the police tape thrust their microphones at him. The paramedic wags a finger at them. Yet another who refuses to make a statement.

So he is *one of the good guys,* thinks Jon, his eyes trained on the man. *And of course, all the good ones are taken.*

He turns to the ambulance, readying himself for a talk with Antonia. But someone has gotten there before him.

"Hello, señora," says Belgrano. He taps his knuckles on the floor of the vehicle. "Hello."

Antonia doesn't react.

"Deputy Inspector—" says Jon.

Belgrano wheels round. He seems less friendly than a couple of days earlier.

"Ah, Gutiérrez. What's this disaster?"

"As you can see, it seems Señor Voronin included white slave trafficking among his hobbies."

Belgrano puffs out his cheeks, unzips his jacket, runs his hand through his hair.

"How many?"

"Eight dead. One alive. Just. They've taken her to the hospital in critical condition."

"Shit, this is bad timing," says Belgrano. "And what are you two doing here?"

"Following a lead."

"Which led you to a container. Tell me you had a customs official present with a probable cause."

Inspector Gutiérrez scratches his throat, waits, letting his silence speak for him.

"*Pfff*. The captain isn't going to like this one bit, Inspector. We won't be able to use it against Orlov. And it would have been great to pin eight deaths on him."

"What can I say?"

"At least you saved that girl. We could fix the report, say you heard cries and had to step in."

Jon stares at him in astonishment.

"No way the public prosecutor will swallow it," says Belgrano, "but at least you won't be sanctioned."

"Thank you for that," says Jon, extending his hand.

For once it's good we're all on the same team.

Belgrano gives it a firm shake. And warns him.

"But you won't escape the captain's wrath."

No, I don't suppose we will, thinks Jon, looking at Antonia. She has a veil black as pitch in front of her eyes.

"Is your colleague okay?"

"She's fine," Jon lies breezily. "She's just affected by what we saw."

"I can call a colleague in our psychological support unit if you like."

Inspector Gutiérrez shakes his head. At any other time, he would have given good money to witness that interview. But today he's feeling generous.

Poor psychologist. Let's spare her the trauma.

7

ANOTHER PROMISE

In the end, it all comes down to how to manage expectations.

For example, if you intend to have a very serious talk with your colleague, but your colleague isn't there, you have to manage your frustration.

And Antonia isn't there.

There are people who go on a journey and leave behind the dog. Or their grandpa at a gas station. Or the small kid, who has to confront burglars alone using clever tricks.

Antonia has left her body behind.

So Jon helps her out of the ambulance, puts her in the car, and drives her to their hotel. He accompanies her to her room, but still she doesn't respond. He halts just inside the doorway, in that place where every hotel room on the planet hides in plain sight the slot for activating the lights. The spot where you grope in the darkness holding your suitcase in your free hand, your ass pressed against the door.

Antonia is standing there, completely lost.

"Oh, for fuck's sake," says Jon.

He follows her into the room, guides her to the bathroom. Her clothes are a disaster, and her skin has more dirty patches than clean ones.

I can't leave her like this, she'll catch Ebola, thinks Jon, turning on the hot water.

Once, many years before, he went with his catechism class to hunt for mushrooms. It must have been back in 1990, or '91. He was fifteen, half a head taller and much broader than any of the others. Not that he was fat.

They were in the hills, fooling around more than looking for white-caps. Then one of the kids, Gorka, a real joker, pointed to a low oak tree branch. A hornets' nest. I bet you can't touch it, Jon, he says. I bet you I can. Jon goes closer and pokes it with the tip of the stick he uses to find mushrooms. With your hand, Gorka says, and Jon says: You've gotta be kidding. Then Gorka says what's the matter, are you a homo or something?

For Jon, this was the worst possible accusation. He was buried so deep in the closet he couldn't see the doors for the coat hangers. So he threw down the stick with a *fuck you!* and took three steps forward, his arm held aloft. Very slowly.

The worst part wasn't the dozen stings he got—one of them under his left eyebrow kept his eye closed for a week—or the other boys' laughter, it was the fear he felt as he took those three steps. The weight in the pit of your stomach as you cover the distance between what drives you on and what makes you afraid.

The fear he felt before he touched the hornets' nest is nothing compared to what he feels as he stretches out to take off Antonia Scott's T-shirt. He grasps the hem and raises it. First one arm, then the other. Up over her head.

No response.

As delicately as possible, Jon removes her pants, socks, bra, and panties. Stripped of her clothes, Antonia looks much younger, with her pubic hair removed with a laser and breasts the size of lemons. And yes, she does have cellulite on her buttocks. But not enough to warrant giving up brownies.

He's afraid she might slip and fall in the bath, so he lifts her by her back and thighs. She's a featherweight in his arms, as light as if her bones were filled with air. He lowers her carefully into the hot water. As he does so, it soaks his shirtsleeves up to the elbows, turning the blood-stains pink.

The water is scalding hot.

Better that way.

While the tub is filling, Jon stuffs Antonia's clothes into the laundry bag. He'll throw them away in the morning, along with what he's wearing himself. His favorite tailored dark gray wool suit. Three thousand and something euros. There's no point washing it. Dry cleaning might remove the dirt, but as Jon knows, there's no way of getting rid of the smell of death. A house can take years to be free of it; a car never is. If someone dies inside a vehicle and is left there for more than eleven hours, insurance companies don't even bother to send a loss adjuster. They send it straight to a broker's yard, no matter how expensive or new it is.

Jon fastens the bag with a triple knot, stuffs it inside the bathroom garbage bag. Then he turns his attention back to Antonia.

He starts with her body. He covers the sponge with green citric soap. He rubs her gently with it, concentrating on her fingernails and neck. Leaving the faucet on, he raises the plug a little until the water around Antonia is no longer so murky. As he rubs, the sponge reveals a mark on her shoulder the size of a dime. This was where the first bullet White fired entered. The other one lodged in her husband's head.

Jon resists the impulse to run his fingers over the scar.

It isn't easy.

Eight grams might seem a paltry weight.

The eight grams of lead fired from a 9 mm gun, capable of traveling across four soccer fields in a second, are a different matter.

If you're a cop, you often think of those eight grams. The same ones you carry in your shoulder holster, nearly always with anguish. But sometimes, if you've really screwed up, that anguish becomes longing.

Jon wonders if Antonia ever considers suicide.

There is another, more substantial scar on his partner's left shoulder. A jagged five-branched star, nestling where the skin chose to heal itself.

A doctor would call that the exit hole. But not Inspector Gutiérrez. The eight grams of lead might have gone through her body, but the bullet is still in there.

Traveling toward Antonia's heart.

He washes her hair several times, lifts her out of the tub, combs the wet strands. Dresses her in the bathrobe and slippers. The floor is cold, so he carries her to the bed and sits her on the edge.

As he bends down to take off the slippers, a drop of water falls on his forehead. Jon looks up, and sees that Antonia is crying. Jon straightens up, sitting back on his haunches so their heads are level. Antonia fixes her almond eyes on him. Her pupils have returned to normal. The tears continue to fall.

"Where did you go?"

"Far away."

"Far away where?"

"I don't know," she says. "I've never been there before."

Jon thinks of everything that's wrong, of everything he ought to say, of all the silences he finds himself forced to live with. He decides that tonight none of it matters.

"What about the girl?" asks Antonia.

"Critical."

Antonia sniffs, nods, and falls back on the bed without removing the bathrobe. They know the rules. The universe makes them pay a huge price, but doesn't always deliver the goods. No point in protesting or drowning in a pool of bitterness. You just accept it.

"Try to get some rest," says Jon.

He stands up and heads for the door.

"Please, don't go," she begs without turning around.

Jon stops halfway. His skin is tacky, his clothes are ruined. He stinks of the same foul smell he's been trying so hard to clean off his partner's skin. The smell of death she doesn't notice but that he can't ignore. He is tired, sad, confused, and frustrated. All he wants is to wash himself, first outside, then inside.

But he won't leave her on her own. Because he feels that in some way, he is the electromagnet preventing the bullet lodged in Antonia's body from making its way to her heart.

So he switches off the light and lies next to her on the bed. He wraps his huge arms around her. It's like enfolding a small doll.

"Those women," says Antonia.

These two words are enough to invoke the horror of everything they have seen that night. The smell of death may have been replaced by that of citric essences (FRESHNESS, SUN, AND FRAGRANCES OF THE MEDITERRANEAN!) advertised on the soap label. But nothing is going to erase the dark stain of the world. Nothing is going to be able to rid their minds and hearts of that atrocity.

"Whoever did that is going to pay," she promises.

A low whisper from a tiny, almost broken woman. A tiny particle in an indifferent universe.

It barely disturbs the darkness.

But the darkness knows nothing. Jon does, and a bucketful of ice travels down his spine. He wouldn't want to be the person that promise is aimed at for anything in the world.

God preserve whoever's guilty from the wrath of Antonia Scott.

RECORDING 04

ELEVEN MONTHS EARLIER

DEPUTY INSPECTOR BELGRANO: This is a load of crap, Voronin. There's nothing in these documents.

YURI VORONIN: I can't give you anything more concrete about Orlov. I told you. They'd kill me.

CAPTAIN ROMERO: They won't touch you if we don't want them to.

YURI VORONIN: You can't protect me from Orlov.

DEPUTY INSPECTOR BELGRANO: We're the police, Voronin.

CAPTAIN ROMERO: How many soldiers does Orlov have?

YURI VORONIN: Eight *bojevík*, two *brigadir*.

CAPTAIN ROMERO: Eight soldiers, two commanders. That's not a lot.

YURI VORONIN: You not understand.

DEPUTY INSPECTOR BELGRANO: It's easy. There are fifty of us, and ten of him.

YURI VORONIN: It's not about numbers. This not Russia. In Russia, he will have hundred, two hundred. As many as he need. Because that's the Wild West, understand? Police won't enter Tambov. They stay outside, on guard. Smoking, leaning on their cars, looking the other way. Never inside the town, because if you do that, you might see things you shouldn't. But here he doesn't need a *bojevík* army. What for? Here there's peace. And he has other methods.

CAPTAIN ROMERO: So you're not afraid of his men?

YURI VORONIN: Of course not. What I fear is a woman.

The roadside bar on the highway is the only possibility. *So she takes exit 244 from the Madrid–Cadiz freeway, in the middle of Despeñaperros, and parks as far from the café door as possible. A viewing platform that must only be used in summer protrudes over the ravine. The wind whipping around can't drown out the noise of the river, which roars southward fifty meters below.*

She twists her wrist, and the bike engine stutters off. She slaps the fuel tank by way of thanking her mount. She doesn't like Japanese bikes: she has always preferred the snarling Italian temperament of a Ducati or an Aprilia. But the dealer didn't have any available, so she had to make do with a Kawasaki Ninja H2R. Painted black, apart from its logo. It has overcome her prejudices.

"Sixty thousand euros."

"Give me paint as well," she says, pointing to a spray can.

The manager passes it to her, and she throws her credit card down on the counter. Titanium, with unlimited funds. Money isn't an issue.

The manager can't contain an envious smile when he sees the famous face of the Roman centurion. Even so, he feels he ought to warn her:

"This model is unlicensed, it's strictly for competition. If the Civil Guard catch you, they'll stop you and impound the bike."

It takes her some time to decode what the man is trying to tell her. Her Spanish is rudimentary, although she understands almost everything she hears. When she has assimilated and processed his words, she decides:

"Not important."

Having carried out his civic duty, the manager turns to insert the card in his machine. She, meanwhile, stuffs the license plate between her bomber jacket and T-shirt.

Several hours and *250 kilometers later, she takes advantage of the stop in the deserted parking lot to attach the plate. It's 0000ABC. Not very believable for anyone looking closely, but it will have to do until one of her contacts can supply her with a permanent one. Besides, if the Civil Guard try to make her pull over on the highway, it'll be fun to see if they can catch her: their Renault Kadjar against this 310-horsepower beast.*

The finishing touch is to spray over the bike's logo. It requires several coats to cover it completely, with a tedious wait of a couple of minutes in between, and the result doesn't match the color of the rest of the chassis.

But it's worth it. Only a professional witness can identify a motorcycle. Any idiot can read and remember eight letters.

She throws the spray can into the bushes, drops her pistol into her helmet and covers it with her gloves, then heads for the door to the bar. Her only luggage is the clothes she's wearing. Tight leather pants and black bomber jacket. Discreetly padded forearms, which can pass as ordinary clothing without attracting attention. Steel-capped Doc Martens boots. Everything as black as the bike, the only concession to color being the boots' red laces. She couldn't resist.

She walks slightly hunched over.

Not because of the cold, although the temperature high up on Despeñaperros is below zero. No, she has experienced Russian summers that would give Spanish winters pneumonia. Her back is protesting at all the hours bent over on the bike. Or so she wants to believe. She wants to believe the cortisone injection will last longer than a few days this time, before the vertebrae leave her paralyzed once more, contorted with pain.

The inside of the bar is unremarkable. She's been in places like this before. They survive in the middle of nowhere by dint of being a supermarket, a souvenir store, and a latrine. The bare brick walls are covered in hunting trophies, old photographs, red-and-yellow flags. The biggest of these has an eagle with folded wings in the center. It reminds her of the Russian coat of arms, but this bird has only one head.

There are a handful of men seated at the bar, watching TV and drinking beer. They turn around when she comes in, but say nothing.

She sits at a table near the entrance, her back to the wall. The waiter brings a menu. It is in two languages: Spanish and what purports to be English. She doesn't dare order octopus or grilled razor clams and merely points to photos on the menu. The waiter shrugs and brings her a steak sandwich.

She removes the bread and calmly devours the protein in small bites, at the same time following a course of Teach Yourself Spanish on her cell phone. The app shows photos of different objects. Choose the chair. *She taps on the correct picture, and the phone rewards her with a cheerful chime.*

On the TV, she sees an image that captures her attention. She can hardly understand a word, but can follow the titles: WHITE SLAVE TRAFFIC. *She knows those words in many languages.*

She soaks up the images intently. The police refuse access beyond the tape, but the camera is able to capture jerky fragments of what's going on. Camera flashes illuminate paramedics carrying away blue body bags. Zooming in, an unsteady shot of a small woman wrapped in a blanket waiting on the steps of an ambulance.

She looks for the news item on her cell phone, with the help of an automatic translator as bad as the one they used for the restaurant menu. But she gets the gist.

She curses under her breath.

This isn't good news. She'll have to modify her plans. This was meant to be a twenty-four-hour operation. Arrive, do the job, drive to Lisbon, then take the plane back to Moscow via Rabat and Ankara. Get out of the city in three minutes, the country in four hours, and the European Union in nine. A plan guaranteeing she wouldn't be caught.

Now she's going to have to change things as she goes along. To run risks. Improvise.

And there's nothing she hates more than improvising.

Feeling frustrated, she gets up to go to the restroom. She can't help but notice the way the drunks at the bar nudge each other and stare at her. Going there and coming back.

She judges the threat.

Five of them. In their thirties, with beer guts. High levels of alcohol intake. One of them is big. The one on the right knows how to fight; he may be a security guard or ex-army.

Threat level: minimal.

She hands the waiter a twenty-euro note. He takes it and whispers something she doesn't understand. But his glance toward the drunken group at the end of the bar is enough.

She nods, picks up her helmet, and saunters out of the bar. She hasn't made any gesture toward the five men, but she knows they'll follow her. Packs of vermin are the same the world over. Dogs. On their own, they're nothing. When they get together, they think they can do anything. Have a right to anything.

The gravel crunches beneath her boots as she strides back to her bike. She doesn't have time for games, nor is she willing to give them the satisfaction of seeing how they've made her speed up.

The bar door opens with a creak and the tinkle of a bell. Voices call to her. At first, they're just obscene, and then directly threatening. One of the men takes the lead; another follows, and soon all five of them are hurrying to catch up with her.

She leaves the helmet on the seat of the Kawasaki. She doesn't bother taking out the pistol; there's no need. All she has to do is get onto the bike, start the ignition, and set off. That would be the most practical choice.

As she is slowly and methodically pulling on her gloves, the five drunks surround her, yapping at her. She doesn't understand the words, but the tone is unmistakable. In a moment, the first of them will stretch out a hand to touch her.

She avoids looking at them, not unaware that ignoring them is making them even more aggressive. Instead of climbing on her bike, she takes a couple of steps toward the edge of the viewing balcony. Only a flimsy rail eighty centimeters high guards against a fifty-meter drop. The pack closes in on her, thinking she is surrounded, drooling in anticipation.

While she was eating, she looked up the name of the ravine: Despeñaperros, or Dead Dogs' Drop.

Such a strange name.

She glances at her watch. She still has another couple of hours' journey. But the bike is powerful, so she can easily make up time.

She smiles.

She can amuse herself for a while.

8

A DAWN

Jon Gutiérrez doesn't like getting up.

It's not a question of when, because his profession has forced him to work the oddest hours, sometimes going hungry and others gorging himself, fifty-hour stakeouts and eleven-hour naps.

Jon can tolerate getting up as long as he's allowed to go through his favorite hibernation routine. To program his cell phone alarm for an hour earlier, tap snooze when it goes off, stagger to the bathroom, pee for what seems like a century—look, Mom, with my eyes closed!— stagger back to bed, collapse, press snooze four more times while snoring loudly, and finally surrender to the demands of becoming vertical.

What Jon hates about getting up is having to do it all at once. A sudden electric buzz between the ears. Sunlight hurting your eyes. Pathological fatigue. The threat of a hard day ahead. The absolute certainty it's humanly impossible to go back to sleep, however much you bury your head under the pillow.

Antonia is up and dressed, seated at the desk, iPad in hand. The muted TV is tuned to the news channel. Images of the port of Málaga.

Too many bodies to put it down to a heist.

"What time is it?" asks Jon, his throat bone dry.

"Almost eight. Go take a shower. You stink."

"How would you know, with your handicap?"

"I *know* you stink. And worse still, I know what particles are stuck to your clothes and hair. Go take a shower."

Touched by Antonia's gratitude for all he did for her the previous night, Jon sits up. At his own speed, that of tectonic plates, of dinosaurs, or tax refunds. When, after a succession of creaks and clicks, he finally manages to straighten his back, he turns his attention to his colleague.

She looks normal. At least, as normal as the most intelligent person on the planet can seem, someone who is also an agent for a secret European organization that operates on the margins of illegality.

"I want doughnuts," says Antonia. "Go take a shower."

Jon has no intention of leaving the room without discussing what happened last night.

"Antonia . . ."

"What?"

"I have no intention of leaving the room without discussing what happened last night."

"When last night?"

"In the container."

"I fainted. Go take a shower."

"I already know that. I pulled you out of there. But why the dizzy spell?"

"Due to reduced blood flow to the brain, caused by emotional shock, a lack of oxygen inside the container, and the sudden effort of bending down to try to drag that woman out. Go take a shower."

"Is that all?"

"Isn't it enough?"

Her explanation is exhaustive, but, no, it isn't enough. Because she still hasn't explained why her pupils were so dilated if she hadn't taken any of the red pills. But Jon has run out of energy, and so for a second time he makes the mistake of leaving the matter until later.

The sun will come out tomorrow.

"What are you doing?"

"The company that imported the container is a dead end. It's just an intermediary. But a different company was supposed to pick it up. It's in the name of a front man: an Armenian by the name of Ruben Ustyan. His office is here in Marbella. Go take a shower."

"I bet he's just another link in the chain."

"Which will lead us to the next one. Go take a shower."

They don't have much. But after what she saw last night, Antonia is determined to stop Orlov any way she can.

Jon ties his necktie. His ruined clothes may have only one last journey to make—along the corridor to his room—but Jon is determined they'll do it in style.

LOLA

There was once a little girl who wanted a cloak of invisibility. Or a magic potion to change her face for someone else's. Or a map that would show her where her enemies were.

Lola Moreno doesn't have the luxury of any such magical devices, so she pulls the hood over her face and walks with a stoop as if she were cold. She is. The storm has lowered the temperature still more, leaving an unhealthy, sticky dampness in the air. Fall has made winter sick.

As of today, Lola no longer has anywhere to sleep.

The deadline Yaiza gave her has run out. She left the apartment a few minutes ago. She was tempted to knock on her friend's door to beg her forgiveness and let her to go with her to Estepona. She had raised her hand to knock, but withdrew her knuckles at the last moment. There was no future in taking the easy path. Not for her or the boy. Of course, it had to be a boy, a little Yuri, a handsome little bastard like his father, a good-for-nothing. *Or nearly nothing*, thinks Lola with a stab of longing in her southerly parts.

The energy and determination she felt on leaving Yaiza's apartment ebbs away as she walks toward Lomas Blancas. She's scared. All of a sudden, starting over doesn't seem such a bad idea. Even if it's off the books: cleaning stairs from nine to eight. Serving drinks from ten to six. It brings back memories of her days as a waitress at Dreamers and at Mirage. The rolling drunks pissing against the bar in the early hours so they wouldn't have to go as far as the toilet. Or the woman who took a dump between two loudspeakers at the far end of the dance floor.

Or all the foreign girls she had to fish out of the bathroom, drunk as skunks, half undressed, soaked in their own vomit.

We have to start a new life, but not that one, Lola promises little Yuri, stroking her belly through the hoodie's pockets. Not knowing if she can keep her word. But then again, who makes promises that can't be unmade?

On the way to Lomas Blancas, as she is passing Parque de los Enamorados, her heart gives a leap, and her mouth goes dry.

She sees her face, magnified six times, staring back at her.

The police's information truck was a recurring joke among Yuri's buddies. A six-wheeler carrying a 150-inch screen, displaying the faces of the most wanted criminals. Three of them belonging to the Orlov clan. Underneath, a telephone number and a website to contact if you bump into any of them.

"The photos are terrible, so bad I could take a selfie in front of the truck and they wouldn't recognize me," bragged one of the men who used to hang out at Yuri's place. Some guy called Fomin, Kolia, or Vania.

Lola stares at the two-meter-high image of herself, with her name and date of birth, and she doesn't feel like laughing. It's a very poor photo, but it's her. She's recognizable, and she even looks good, even though nobody ever does in their ID photo. And the cop standing beside the truck has a machine gun, or whatever they're called. Black, with a long barrel. Very threatening.

As if all firearms weren't, unless you happen to be the one holding them.

The truck is parked on the opposite side of the street, and the cop is looking in her direction. And even if he isn't, she has no way of telling—that's why they wear those caps pulled down over their eyes. Lola can't turn around or change direction. So she waits with a knot in her stomach for the traffic lights to change. If she had her cell phone, she could pretend to be checking Instagram, but after what happened at the funeral home, she threw it away. She's sure they are intercepting not only her and Yuri's numbers but also her mother's, not to mention her own favorite numbers. It's so easy to do that nowadays.

The last car speeds past her—an Audi A8 with tinted windows—the next one pulls up as the lights change. Lola has no choice but to cross toward the cop guarding the truck.

Don't stop. Don't change direction. Act normal.

Her heart is racing and she takes shallow breaths. Lola doesn't feel at all "normal."

By now she is almost level with the cop. She has to summon half her willpower not to look him in the face. The other half she uses to restrain the impulse to take her hands out of her pockets and lower the hood still farther.

"Freezing, isn't it?" says the cop as she passes by him.

It takes Lola a few seconds to realize the voice talking to her is only trying to be friendly. Maybe because her pulse thundering in her ears is as loud as a Mayumana concert.

"Sure is," she says without stopping.

She has passed him, and is trying as hard as she can to control her feet, which want her to break into a run to get away as fast as possible. *Slowly. Slowly.*

Half an hour later, she reaches her destination. Lomas Blancas is a middle-class development where detached houses alternate with semidetached ones. Lola is exhausted, dizzy, and thirsty. She's paying a high price for not having insulin. Her mouth is so dry her tongue clicks when it touches the roof of her mouth.

She can't take much more.

To make matters worse, she doesn't recognize the house. She took Zenya there once when her car was in the garage, but that was two years ago, and Lola is at her wits' end. *It's semidetached*, she remembers. *Near the end of the street.* But when she reaches the place she had in mind, beyond the second sleeping policeman, everything looks alien to her.

Her legs won't sustain her any longer.

She flops onto the sidewalk, between a garbage container and a Peugeot, and bursts into tears.

Fuck it, Yuri. How could you be so dumb?

"Señorita Lola?"

Still sobbing, Lola looks up, and there is Zenya. A stocky middle-aged woman with dark hair and a mournful smile. She is wearing jeans and a bomber jacket and carrying a couple of shopping bags.

Lola tries to stand up, but her head starts whirling again. She has to lean on the Peugeot's muddy fender.

"Come inside."

* * *

Zenya is a good woman. She has been with them for four years. She has always worked hard, cleaning the house, ironing, and doing other chores. They didn't give her a contract, of course, because that's how Yuri was. But they paid her well. The house she and Lola are in now is the only other one she used to clean. On Fridays, like today.

"Would you like some more coffee?" Zenya asks, bringing the coffeepot to her cup.

Lola lets her refill it, although it makes her uneasy. She feels humiliated having to ask her cleaner for help, sneaking into a house that isn't hers, accepting the involuntary hospitality of strangers. The house belongs to a chef and his wife in their fifties, both of whom are at work. Lola notices a photograph of them on a fridge magnet. A vacation in Rome. They are beaming at the camera. Wearing identical bracelets.

I could have had that with Yuri. That's all I wanted.

She and Zenya are sitting at the island in the kitchen, which is adjacent to the living room. Everything as it should be—modest but homey. Lola smiles when she sees they have one of those minuscule thirty-two-inch screens. She doesn't like big ones: she hates seeing the presenters' nose hairs, their false, fluorescent teeth. Yuri bought her one of those gigantic ones, which give Lola the impression of a bathroom mirror in someone else's home. One of the magnifying variety. Such mirrors rarely bring any pleasure.

Lola had been annoyed he spent more than €10,000 on that TV. She would have preferred him to surprise her with a watch or an eye-catching jewel. But Yuri wasn't the most romantic or subtle guy. Whenever her birthday was approaching, she would hint at how much she liked something. Even before she finished speaking, Yuri would smile broadly and offer her a bundle of €200 notes.

That's all over now.

This poisonous, liquid certainty courses through her veins. It's all the more lethal where she is now, sitting in the midst of somebody else's perfect life, a life she'll never have.

"Why didn't you call me, señorita?"

Lola hesitates to tell her the truth. It could scare her. But no, Zenya is a tough woman. She escaped government repression in Ukraine. There's no sense in trying to deceive her.

"I couldn't take the risk, Zenya," she says. "The police are bound to have your phone tapped."

Zenya explains that they asked her a lot of questions, which she couldn't answer, because she wasn't in the house when the murder occurred. It was she who discovered the body and called them.

"Where is Kot?"

"They took him to the municipal dog pound. There was no way I could keep him," Zenya says ruefully.

Lola understands. Kot weighs ninety kilos and consumes €5,000 of food a year. No matter how well he gets on with Zenya—which is strange because he doesn't like anyone—the poor woman couldn't keep him at home.

"I have a proposition to make," says Lola.

She explains her plan to Zenya, or at least the part she needs to know. And that wouldn't work without her.

Zenya listens in silence. That's always her way, head tilted to one side, chin pointing slightly to the right of the person talking to her. As if it wasn't really anything to do with her. It made no difference if you were asking her to load the dishwasher or to give up her house, her life, her job.

A rented apartment where she lives alone, and only one client who doesn't pay enough for her to keep it on. An easy decision, Lola thinks. And she's right.

Zenya accepts. But on one condition.

"I need five thousand euros to send to my country."

"I'll give you ten times that next week."

"No, I need it now."

"I don't have that much."

"I need it. My sister has to have a prosthesis so she can walk, and it's very expensive. If something happens to me, I won't be able to help her. You give me the money to send to her just in case, so I help her."

Lola grows desperate. She tries to reason with Zenya, to explain she has to be patient. She won't listen.

"All right," says Lola finally. "I'll get you the money. Meet me tomorrow night at the dog pound."

"Señorita Lola, that place is guarded. It's not a good idea."

"It's a terrible idea, but I'm not leaving without my dog."

9

A FRONT MAN

Nobody would mistake Ruben Ustyan for a visionary.

Not even Ruben himself.

In 2001, Ruben (with the accent on the *u*, as he always tells anyone he meets) had just emigrated to Italy. There was no future and no work for him in Armenia, even though Ruben was open to any offers. On the cusp of forty, he had done a bit of everything. Pickpocketing, drugs, pimping. A cousin helped him get to Rome, but he stayed because of all the tourists whose pockets he could pick in Piazza Navona. Not exactly a friend of the forces of order, he was the first to be up in arms when on July 20, a carabinieri shot and killed Carlo Giuliani, an anti-globalization demonstrator.

"This globalization is terrible. Terrible. We have to put a stop to it as soon as possible."

Ignoring the fact he himself was carrying on a business on foreign soil with multinational clients—indiscriminately robbing Spaniards, Japanese, Americans, or whoever was ripe for it—Ruben Ustyan's aversion to globalization was another in a long line of historic predictions.

Like Alex Lewyt, the inventor of vacuum cleaners, who in 1955 said that in ten years' time, they would all run on nuclear power.

Like Thomas Watson, the IBM chairman, who in 1943 said that there would be room on the earth for five computers at most.

No, nobody would mistake Ruben Ustyan for a visionary. And yet his zero capacity for prediction ended up being an evolutionary advantage. During a trip to Spain on vacation some years later, he met Aslan

Orlov. How? It's a long story involving a punctured tire, a goat, and a bottle of vodka. Let's just say, by chance.

The Beast studied Ruben Ustyan intently. Small, sallow-skinned. Rat-faced, all elbows and knees. His protruding teeth meant he wore a perpetual smile. Orlov recognized him as a man without imagination, and put him in charge of a brothel in Puerto Banús.

"We can trust the Armenian," he told Yuri. "He's too dense to cause trouble."

Orlov said literally, "as dense as bear shit," but some Russian expressions translate badly.

So Ruben's life bobbed along. Keeping the accounts. Maintaining a rotation of girls, selling them to other places when they began to wear out. Ordering pallet loads of soft drinks. A successful manager in the years of Spain's property bubble.

Ruben was the last to hear when the bubble burst. Gambling and prostitution are the two remaining vices people heading for ruin give up. In fact, by the time he was told the bubble had burst, the next one was already beginning to swell.

"Thank heavens we're out of the crisis," Yuri told him.

"What crisis?"

"Never mind, give me another beer."

Yuri used to go to the brothel a lot, running errands, delivering bags of coke for clients, among other things. As one of Orlov's thugs, he could enjoy the girls free of charge. He had to pay for the beer. Even with a staff discount, Ruben calculated that 80 percent of Yuri's earnings ended up in his cash register.

All of a sudden, Yuri stopped coming.

Seeing his bottom line affected, Ruben took Yuri to task when he met him one day in the perfumery section of El Corte Inglés. The Russian had a bag in each hand.

"Yuri, what's going on? I haven't seen you in months. Are you pissed at me?"

"I don't do that kind of stuff anymore. I'm in love," Yuri said with a stupid grin on his face.

Ruben laughed. Yuri was his number one client. If he'd paid for sex as well as beer, Ruben would have owned a yacht. Who was capable of making him give that up? He continued to laugh until his eyes followed the direction Yuri was pointing. He saw a tall, slim woman standing by the Louis Vuitton display. The photo on the illuminated panel showed the actress Léa Seydoux holding a flower. The woman rummaging among the perfumes, tapping the gold tops with pink-lacquered nails, looked just like her, only more beautiful and less French.

Ruben managed to pick up his dropped jaw as she came over.

"This is Lola, my wife."

Then came the proposition.

That was years ago. Six? Maybe seven? Ruben can't remember. It might as well have been a hundred. Every day since then has been just like any other to him. More peaceful, yes, but deadly dull.

That day Yuri had told him about a new line of business he wanted to start. Ruben laughed at the thought of that bloody-knuckled bully opening a beach kiosk with Orlov's permission.

Two weeks later, he stopped laughing when the Beast informed him he was to leave the brothel and do whatever Yuri told him.

What Yuri tells him is to rent an office in San Pedro Norte. In the Edificio Palomas. An interior space, without windows, and only a couple of rooms. A desk, chair, telephone, bare walls.

Yuri sits Ruben down in the chair and puts him in front of a laptop computer, where he can keep himself amused.

"What do I do?"

"I don't know. Nothing."

"What if someone calls?" asks Ruben, pointing to the telephone.

"Pick it up."

"What do I say?"

"That they got the wrong number."

Ruben scratches his neck, lights a cigar.

"And how much are you going to pay me for this?"

Yuri tells him.

It's five times more than he was earning at the brothel.

So now Ruben works for Yuri.

He spends most of his working day sitting in his chair at the office. He plays *Tetris*, watches YouTube videos on interesting topics. There's a Korean contortionist who does tricks naked—like pulling the cloth from a table with his bare buttocks—who fascinates him.

"I could do this at home."

"You have to be here, in case I need you," says Yuri.

It's true that Yuri appears almost every day, dragging along a briefcase full of documents, or sometimes a notary public. He asks him to sign here, here, and here. Ruben signs. He spends the whole week signing. Documents with blue stamps in blue folders. Checks, loans, applications. Credentials, record books, transfers. Contracts. Summonses. Powers. Declarations.

And deeds. Lots and lots of deeds. Up to thirty of them some days.

Ruben has mastered the art of signing without looking, continuing to play *Tetris* with his left hand while his right hand scribbles his signature. Yuri plonks the relevant piece of paper in front of him, says, "Here," and Ruben signs. The notary certifies it, Ruben raises his hand and repeats the operation. Without ever taking his eyes from the screen.

Yellow paper, deed; blue paper, check.

Ruben dreams of breaking the world record of 4,988 lines on *Tetris*. So far, he's reached around half that.

"It would be easier if you didn't make me sign so many," he protests.

"Don't complain. You must be the person who manages the most companies in the world. Or in Europe at least."

"How many?" asks Ruben, vaguely interested.

Yuri does a rapid calculation.

"Just over seven thousand."

"I'm a magnate," says Ruben, preening. "Like Ramón Ortiz or Donald Trump."

"Sure, Ruben."

Yuri pats him on the back and goes to file away the documents. At the far end of Ruben's office is a glassed-in cubicle with big filing cabinets and a computer. Only Yuri goes in there; only Yuri has the key.

Now Yuri is dead.

Like everybody else, Ruben was at the funeral. He received Aslan Orlov's message loud and clear. He's heard strange rumors about Yuri's death and the female assassin who has been brought in to deal with his wife. But none of that concerns him. He is loyal to the Bratvá, so nobody can touch him.

That's why he keeps coming to the office every day.

Because this is his job.

He doesn't know exactly what it entails, now that no one comes with documents for him to sign, but force of habit is a wonderful thing. He'd be bored at home, with nobody to talk to.

Besides, there's *Tetris*.

So he turns up, jiggles the mouse to exit the screen saver, and resumes the game he paused the day before. He has twelve hundred lines and he's made only a slight mistake in one corner—those damned red pieces, he can never get them to fit—so he's confident he can recover.

The doorbell rings.

Ruben pays no attention. Nobody ever comes here.

The bell rings insistently.

10

A DIRECTORY

The Palomas building is a long way from the center of the city. It's one of those relics from the glorious nineties. A time when the Mafias came not from the steppes of Russia but from those of Soria. A time when they didn't stay hidden, but campaigned openly in the press to become local mayors. A time when they won and grew rich erecting buildings without any regulation. More than thirty thousand illegal constructions, dozens of office buildings built out of nothing more than greed. Almost all of them have survived, despite countless legal orders demanding they be demolished. Some of them, like the Palomas building, were abandoned to their fate by unscrupulous owners.

There is no doorman downstairs. Three-quarters of the offices are empty. At least according to the list of companies in fake bronze at the front entrance.

"This is Ustyan's company. Services to Entrepreneurs Limited. On the eighth floor, door B," says Antonia when she spots the plaque.

"They may be mafiosi, but they enjoy a joke," says Jon.

"They're creating companies out of nothing and helping them to operate. So technically the description is correct," says Antonia, pressing the elevator button.

Jon sighs theatrically.

"Do you think someday you might laugh without me having to explain why something is funny? Just once."

"It's in the realm of the possible. You first," she says, letting him into the elevator before her.

11

AN ANKLE

Ruben curses, gets up, and walks over to the office door. He opens it, grumbling.
"Look here, you've—"

A white wall, a blinding flash, dizziness. Ruben has no words to describe it. Except now he finds himself on the floor, clutching his nose.

The punch has broken it, and sent a gush of blood cascading through his fingers and onto the floor. Sticky, thick blood. Ruben looks down incredulously at the red on his hands.

He's a small, fearful man. Characteristics useful for a pickpocket. And which didn't get in the way of him running a brothel, provided he had some tough guys on hand. But they make it hard for a front man who has spent six years sitting in a chair to defend himself when those same tough guys turn up at his door.

Ruben knows them. The Fomin brothers. Two big Georgian sons of bitches. Tree trunks wearing clothes. Shaven heads, tattooed arms. Souvenirs of their army days.

That's not all they have brought with them. They've also acquired valuable skills. Like how to apply pressure to a bone until it snaps. That's what they are doing now to the prostrate Ruben. One is frisking him, the other is pressing down hard on his ankle.

The front man is so confused it takes a while for him to remember to cry out.

His first scream coincides with the cracking of his fibula. A dry, unpleasant crack, like when you snap the stick of a Magnum in two before sliding it into its foil wrapper.

Ruben yells. It's a sharp, stabbing pain, yet he feels it outside his body, as if it were happening to somebody else. He is yelling because he can't believe it. There he was, only a few seconds ago, sitting quietly at his desk, playing *Tetris* on his screen and with more money in the bank than he could ever spend.

"What are you doing? What are you doing?" he sobs, as if it weren't obvious.

Then he adds, because he can't avoid it, because everyone who has ever been in his situation has felt it necessary to say it:

"Don't you know who I am?"

"Of course," says one of the Fomin brothers. The younger one. Ruben thinks his name is Vadim. Or Kolia.

"I have to speak to Orlov. I have to speak to Orlov," says Ruben, trying to get to his feet and return to his desk. He collapses on his broken ankle, decides to crawl the rest of the way.

One of his attackers pushes past him to the desk, picks up Ruben's cell phone, and stuffs it in his pocket. The front man doesn't see any of this, because he's still facedown on the floor.

"I have to speak to Orlov," insists Ruben to the feet inches from his face.

One of the feet takes aim at his right cheekbone and smashes into it. The crunching noise and the pain prevent Ruben from hearing how the other Fomin—Vadim, or whatever his name is—breaks down the door to Yuri's archive.

Ruben blacks out for a few seconds. The moment he comes to, he starts up with the same refrain. It's all he has to hang on to. As we have already mentioned, Ruben Ustyan is a man with no imagination.

"Please. Let me talk to Orlov."

Ruben's persistence is rewarded when one of the brothers pauses, dials a number, and puts the cell phone close to Ruben's mouth.

"Have you finished?" snaps Orlov.

"Aslan, Aslan, it's me."

When he hears who is on the line, the Beast's voice becomes calm, uninterested.

"Oh, it's you, Ruben."

Ruben gives a yelp of joy and relief when he hears the *vor* at the other end. At last he can clear up this misunderstanding.

"Aslan, the Fomins are here."

"Yes, I sent them."

The front man feels something wet on the back of his neck, arms, and back. Even with his broken nose, he can smell a penetrating odor. He manages to turn his head just enough to see that Kolia—he's almost sure it's him—is sprinkling the contents of a metal can over him.

"Tell them not to hurt me. I've done nothing wrong."

"I know. But you saw the news about the container last night."

"What news?" Ruben asks, dumbfounded.

Orlov cackles.

"It's true, Ruben, I'll be sorry to lose you. It's hard to find useful idiots like you. But I can't leave any loose ends," he says, then hangs up.

Kolia takes back his cell phone, sits on Ruben's back, grabs him by the scruff of his neck, and starts pounding his head against the floor. Slowly, but surely. It's an excellent method if you're in no hurry, like tapping an egg on the edge of a frying pan. Sooner or later, the shell breaks.

The front man loses consciousness between the third and fourth tap.

When he comes around, everything is dark. Ruben thinks he must have gone blind, but then the flames start to dance.

After that, the screams.

12

A WISP OF SMOKE

"I can prove what I'm saying. You didn't get the cat joke either," insists Jon, pressing the eighth-floor button.

"It climbed up the tree. It's a code he and his friend agreed on to soften a blow produced by bad news. Of course I got it."

Inspector Gutiérrez rolls his eyes. It's no use.

She's totally humor-proof.

He presses the button again, to see if he can speed up the elevator. The piped music is a version of "Despacito" that convinces Jon he'd be better off in hell.

"We should have a code too," says Antonia.

"What for?"

"To warn of danger, and suchlike. A key phrase. Like 'Vatican cameos,' for example. If one of us says—"

Jon raises a finger to his lips to silence her.

"Did you hear that?"

Antonia shakes her head, but Jon knows what he heard. A cry. Then a dull thud, like an eighty-five-kilo bag filled full of flesh and bones falling from more or less seventy centimeters. For example. And there's something else.

Even before the elevator doors open, Jon smelled burning. Paper, plastic, meat.

Ding.

The corridor outside the elevator is completely dark. It's only thanks to the faint light from inside that they can see the wisps of smoke curling toward them.

Jon takes the flashlight from his pocket.

To his right is the door to office A. It's closed. At the far end of the corridor, the door to office B is open.

Jon can guess which one the smoke is coming from.

"Tell the captain and Belgrano," Jon whispers, reaching for his gun.

There was no need—Antonia's fingers are already flying over the keyboard. The message is sent even before Jon has finished speaking.

"What do we do?"

Jon points to the ceiling. The light fitting has been torn out. The electric cable is dangling, and the bulb lies smashed on the floor.

Whoever wanted darkness got it.

"Vatican cameos," says Jon, walking toward the door to office B. In his left hand, he is clutching the flashlight, like a dagger. His right is resting on the other forearm, gun pointed in front of him.

"This isn't how it works," says Antonia.

"I know. Get behind me."

Inspector Gutiérrez has a clear recollection of what happened the last time he said this to Antonia Scott. A Porsche Cayenne appeared out of nowhere, almost plowed into them, and then there was a breakneck chase from which they escaped alive only by miracle.

Jon can feel a strange tingling sensation in his scalp. A hundred insects scurrying between the skull and his hair. Insects stirred up only when things are going to end badly.

He breathes slowly through his mouth. The smoke isn't dense, and is clearing. Whatever caused it is burning itself out.

Jon Gutiérrez doesn't believe in coincidences. He doesn't believe it's possible for an accidental fire to have started in the company they're going to visit moments before they arrive. Nor does he think entering a dark, potentially hostile space waving around the only light is the best way to creep up on an enemy. He's also aware that, unlike ordinary delinquents, the Russian Mafia has access to handguns and assault rifles.

So Jon bursts into Services to Entrepreneurs Ltd. feeling what in police slang is known by the technical term *scared shitless*.

"Stay out here," he orders Antonia.

He flicks the flashlight beam around the room exactly as he was taught at police academy. Left corner, right corner, the other corner, behind the door. No one.

An empty desk, a chair. On the far side of the office, what looks like another room. A door. In the doorway, a body. Blackened, smoking.

"Son of a bitch!"

His curse sounds like a magic password to be added to the list of words that makes things appear, like *Abracadabra, Dracarys . . . son of a bitch*. Antonia emerges from behind Jon's back, sees the body on the floor, and rushes over to it.

"Stay where you are, woman! Always the same story," Jon groans. He has yet to check the second room.

He steps over the body. He repeats the four-corners procedure, shoulder forward, pistol pointed at the ground.

Left corner, right corner, the other one, behind the door. No one.

All he can see are the smoldering remains of a fire in the middle of the room. Remains of melted tiles, the stench of kerosene and burned plastic that makes the air unbreathable.

Two more bodies on the ground. Jon checks the pulse of the first—or rather the lack of it. No need to bother with the second, the knife embedded in his eye makes that unnecessary.

"Is your one alive?" asks Jon, pointing the flashlight at Antonia.

13

TWO SECONDS

Kneeling next to the smoking body, Antonia realizes he *is* still alive. She turns toward Jon to tell him, but doesn't get the chance. She hears a metallic thud, a gentle *clunk* like when you close a metal drawer. A head looms out of the darkness, floating next to Jon's face. An arm is throttling him.

The flashlight falls to the floor, bounces, and goes out with a clatter.

Now the darkness is complete.

On all fours, Antonia gropes for the flashlight. The darkness in front of her seems to come alive, to fill with menacing presences.

A savage grunt.

Two bodies rubbing, fabric against flesh.

A metallic blow.

A crash.

A moment of uncertainty, a silence.

A displacement of the noxious air in the room as a body falls to the floor.

Panting.

Feet moving.

At last Antonia's fingers grasp the end of the flashlight.

So do somebody else's. The flashlight switches on, illuminating the inside of Antonia's hand in a reddish, phantasmal glow.

"Drop it," says a female voice.

Antonia opens her fingers, lets go of the flashlight.

For a moment, the beam is reflected on her white T-shirt and she sees the face of a young woman with hard almond eyes slicing the darkness in two.

The woman pulls back, pointing the flashlight at Antonia, who by now has risen to her knees.

A pistol appears in the glare, its barrel less than six centimeters from Antonia's forehead.

She half closes her eyes.

A 9 mm Makarov.

"Who?" asks the woman.

She says this in a way that leaves no room for doubt. Answer or I'll kill you. But this isn't the first time Antonia has faced the barrel of a gun. It isn't the first, or even the tenth. And she has no doubts either. Never show fear. Never give in.

"Who are you?" she retorts.

The gun barrel comes so close it grazes her forehead, but Antonia doesn't move, apart from a frantic blinking of her eyes as she decides what to do.

"Who?" the woman repeats.

The finger curls around the trigger, about to squeeze. Antonia has only a couple of seconds.

For other people, two seconds can be a negligible length of time.

Not for Antonia Scott.

In two seconds, Antonia evaluates three possible physical responses:

- Roll over.
- Drop to the floor.
- Try to get hold of the pistol.

She rejects all three. Any attempt to grapple with her attacker is bound to fail. She has just killed two big men and overpowered— Antonia can hear his breathing—an even bulkier one. Not that he's fat.

She tries to calculate how long it will take the police to reach this remote spot. Thanks to her photographic memory, she can visualize the page in the mission dossier Mentor prepared for them. It could be five minutes. How long has it been since she called them? Three and a half, with a margin of error of ten seconds.

Her only option is to play for time. To stay alive until they get there. What Mentor calls the CDP tactic. Confuse. Distract. Probe.

"I wouldn't shoot if I were you," says Antonia. "That would be a real mistake."

The woman switches off the flashlight. Darkness returns, heavy and dense.

She's smart. She doesn't want me to see her.

"I no speak good Spanish."

"My Russian isn't perfect either," Antonia replies in a perfect Muscovite accent.

As soon as they start speaking Russian, the other woman's voice becomes gentler, almost indulgent.

"Are you police?"

"Something like that. My colleagues are about to arrive."

As though the universe was awaiting her signal, at that precise moment the wail of police sirens is heard in the distance.

"I've never understood when that happens in the movies." The voice in the darkness now comes from farther to Antonia's right. "The bad guy has the protagonist at his mercy. Then the sirens start up, and he runs off. It takes just as long to pull the trigger as not to."

Antonia smiles at the impeccable logic.

"Is that what you're going to do? Kill us both?"

The sound of shoes moving across the floor, the air displaced again. Suddenly the woman's voice is just behind Antonia's left ear. The words she says in Russian are disconcertingly soft.

"You're lucky, cop. Today you two are not on the menu."

Antonia gives a start. By the time she has collected herself, behind her there is only darkness.

She's gone.

Antonia stands up, pulls the cell phone from her jacket, and switches on the light. Jon is on the far side of the room, flat on his back, out cold. Antonia kneels alongside him, pinches the skin between his thumb and first finger with one hand, and squeezes hard beneath his nose with the other.

Jon comes round with a howl of pain. His lower lip is split, with a trail of blood trickling onto his beard.

"What are you doing?"

"Recovery by sensory stimulation."

"It hurts like hell."

"That's the idea," says Antonia, rising to her feet and going back to the body on the floor. "Help me turn him over."

"Are you sure that's a good idea?"

Ruben Ustyan is at death's door. Antonia knows that. She also knows, because she has examined his wounds, that turning him onto his back will cause him excruciating pain.

And she is counting on that.

Jon doesn't know this, and there's no reason why he should. Antonia has to make some decisions on her own.

"Help me," she insists.

They turn Ruben over.

The Armenian gives a low moan. The kerosene sprinkled on him has burned more than 40 percent of his skin, destroying the epidermis and reaching the fat layer. The nerve ends across most of his back have been knocked out by the fire, except where his polyester clothes have fused with the skin: there the pain receptors are still functioning. It's the same principle Antonia used on Jon, only far more cruel. The nerves are activated at once, sending tens of millions of alarm signals to the brain, increasing Ruben's heart rate, dilating his damaged airways, and bypassing the cranial trauma. Unfortunately, though, also reducing his life expectancy from seven minutes to a few seconds.

He tries to sit up. Antonia seizes his hand, even though contact with his burned skin (crunchy, hot, and rough on the outside, cracked like a dried-up puddle and slippery to the touch on the inside) revolts her.

"Take it easy, Señor Ustyan," she says.

"I've done nothing. I've done nothing. Tell Orlov I've done nothing."

"The ambulance is on its way. Don't worry," says Jon.

They can hear policemen yelling outside. Inspector Gutiérrez stands up, raises his hands, and calls out his name and rank. He doesn't want to risk a bullet.

"Did he do this? Orlov? Did he send the woman? Do you know her name?"

Ruben coughs, gasping for breath. Fighting for each mouthful of air. His voice is rasping. He looks at Antonia, wide-eyed.

"*Chernaya Volchitsa.*"

14

A RETORT

Captain Romero is far from happy.

She's a stiff, reserved woman, little inclined to show her emotions. Jon, however, is able to sense her disapproval because she's shouting at him two centimeters from his face. With saliva droplets and everything.

"I asked you to be careful. Not to stir up the hornets' nest. And what do I find?"

Jon, who is sitting on Ustyan's desk to make it easier for the captain to shout at him, lets her get on with it. Partly because in his twenty-four years with the police, he has been bawled out countless times, and he knows the best thing is to let them spit out their poison as quickly as possible.

Literally, thinks Jon, unfolding his arms just in time to wipe a fleck of spit from his cheek.

And partly because he feels guilty.

In recent days, he's been looking up the captain's record. Top in her year at the academy, the first female to make captain in Andalusia, an impressive list of raids, arrests, and seizures. In the *Diario del Sur*, she is touted as the next provincial police chief. And then, inevitably, Madrid.

Like all women in this shitty profession, she's scrutinized two or three times as closely. So she has to try four times as hard. No children. No stable relationship. A hard-ass.

This must be her day off, because she's in civilian clothes: jeans and a white blouse. With her hair in the same tight bun, to the point where Jon wonders if it isn't a helmet. And in a fuming rage that even drowns out the smell of the fire.

"Two dead bodies in the shopping mall," she counts, rolling each number around on her tongue and flinging it in Jon's face. "Eight dead bodies and another woman in the hospital from the container last night. And two more corpses here this morning."

Belgrano whispers something in her ear.

"Make that three. Ustyan died on the way to hospital. That makes a total of thirteen."

"Fourteen. Let's not forget Yuri Voronin," Antonia reminds her.

Jon runs his hand over his neck. It's painful and swollen where the mysterious woman put him in a choke hold that knocked him unconscious. He doesn't know how to warn Antonia that now is the time to keep a low profile. Maybe it's not the best advice, because the last time she asked him to do the same, he ended up slapping a superior officer. The noise his open hand made when it hit Captain Parra's face still gives him hot flushes at night.

"I'm not forgetting him," says Romero, her eyes fixed on Jon.

"But you did forget to tell us he was your informer, Captain. And not only that. An informer who trafficked women," says Antonia.

Don't go there, thinks Jon.

"You must be the consultant," says Romero, turning to Antonia as though noticing her for the first time.

"Antonia Scott," says Antonia. She's also sitting on the desk, arms folded, only her feet don't touch the floor.

"Belgrano has told me about you. He says you're a genius at crime scenes. And we hear things. Was it you in Valencia?"

Antonia doesn't answer.

Jon glances down at her hands. They're shaking again.

"Would you mind giving us a demonstration?" Romero insists, pointing to the door of the office behind her, which is being lit up intermittently by flashes from the forensic team's cameras. "So we can find out what went on here."

"I'm not a trained monkey."

Romero's expression becomes even grimmer.

"Scott, allow me to remind you what's at stake here. We've been building the case against Orlov for four years. Four years, while we had to deal with a hundred and fifty kilometers of coast and thirteen organized Mafias. Every day that goes by without us arresting him, people die. So if you have something to offer, do it. Otherwise . . ."

Antonia remains entrenched in her stubborn silence, now fortified with machine guns and barbed wire.

I'm going to have to save her ass.

"If you'll allow me to explain, Captain," says Jon. "We came here following a lead that linked the container where the women were trapped to a company whose front man was Ustyan. We came to question him as to the whereabouts of Señora Moreno, but unfortunately someone decided to deep clean the place before we arrived. We know they kept some kind of documentation here, on computers. All of it has been burned."

"And these two men were dead. And a mysterious woman with a Russian accent attacked you in the dark. A young woman neither of you saw or are able to describe," Belgrano interrupts him. "We already know all that."

"What we don't know is how that woman managed to kill the Fomin brothers single-handed," says the captain, creasing her brow. "Those two have criminal records longer than my arm. Two thugs with army training. And without using a firearm."

"Very quickly," says Antonia.

"What's that?"

"She killed them very quickly."

Romero turns to Belgrano.

"Until Forensics says something different, we're working on the assumption the Fomin brothers killed each other."

"Evidently, Captain."

Jon tries not to react. To emulate the captain's formality, although he senses his face must betray that he doesn't care much for her disdain. That's how it is with people from Bilbao. Brachycephalic heads, Rhesus negative, daggers for eyes when their partner is insulted. But he says nothing. To keep the peace.

Not to mess things up any further.

Even though that's what will happen anyway.

"A housewife shouldn't be too hard to find, Inspector Gutiérrez," Romero says by way of a goodbye as she heads to the office to talk with Forensics. "Keep us informed if you or the *outsider* discover anything."

She spits the word *outsider* as a deliberate insult.

"If you mean to imply that I'm not part of law enforcement, you're mistaken, Captain," says Antonia.

Romero turns round. The air between them frosts over.

"Oh yes. And might I know in what capacity?"

"That information is above your pay grade."

The color drains from Captain Romero's cheeks. Her nostrils flare slightly, but that's her only reaction. She is a woman with almost supernatural self-control.

What is Jon doing, meanwhile?

He can scarcely believe what he's heard. Compared to what Antonia just did, the slap he gave Captain Parra was a kiss on the ass.

"Find Lola Moreno, which is what you're here for," the captain says icily. "And then get the hell out."

15

A PIECE OF ADVICE

Out in the car.

"Are you going to tell me what's wrong?" Jon asks as he checks his wounds in the rearview mirror. His lip is split and swollen, but nothing that can't be cured by applying an ice-cold piece of glass in the shape of a beer bottle. "You could have explained the crime scene to her."

Antonia's hands are shaking so much she finds it hard to buckle her seat belt. Again, Jon pretends not to notice.

Inspector Gutiérrez sets off toward nowhere in particular. To get there, he first has to drive past police cars and a useless ambulance. A uniformed officer lets them through the roadblock at the end of the street preventing pedestrians from coming any closer. Pedestrians, meaning journalists. There is only one camera from the local TV station, which is already packing up. The news today will feature a building collapse, a gas explosion, a fire that claimed three victims. Fortunately, there was no property damage.

"She didn't look as if she'd believe us," says Antonia.

"I think you're right," says Jon, caressing his still painful neck. "Although I've no idea where the hell that woman came from. I swept the room with the flashlight before checking the bodies."

"Left corner, right corner, the other one, behind the door?"

"The usual procedure."

"I know. And apparently, so did she. She was on top of the filing cabinet."

The filing cabinet. Five drawers, probably a meter and a half high. Jon thinks over what he did as he entered the office. He pointed at every corner, but at floor level, the way he was taught at the police academy. Because they don't expect you to be confronting Batman.

"Who the hell was she?"

"A professional. Extremely dangerous."

You don't say.

"Shouldn't we make sure Romero goes after her?"

"Forensics will explain to her that the woman killed the Fomin brothers. But that crime scene is irrelevant. We're not here to find your attacker. We have to find Lola Moreno. The captain made that very clear."

"You were pretty outspoken yourself."

Antonia leans her head against the car window. She's exhausted.

"I wasn't about to let her blame us for it. Especially when her informer is directly responsible for the death of those women."

"Look, angel. Let me give you a piece of advice. No matter how angry you are, you must never, I repeat, never, pull rank on a boss. Even if it's justified."

Her eyes closed, Antonia rubs the bridge of her nose.

"I was . . . I don't know how to express it."

"Express what?"

"That feeling. When someone goads you for the sake of it, but they do it slyly. Surreptitiously, waiting for you to respond negatively. There must be a word for it in some language or other."

They stop at a traffic light. Jon takes the opportunity to glance at her, intrigued.

"Try to explain yourself in our language, honey."

Antonia spends her usual thirty seconds weighing this. Then another thirty, and another. The lights turns green, but they don't drive on. Luckily, the street is empty in this out-of-the-way place. Jon resigns himself to switching off the engine and watching the light change.

Green.

Red.

Green again.

Life is what happens while this woman makes up her mind to say something, thinks Jon.

"Sometimes . . . sometimes I look for words in other languages. Words that are untranslatable. It's something I would do . . . I do with Marcos. We capture feelings. If we found a special one, we'd make a gift of it to the other. I would find more than he did, of course. His task was to write them down, he'd jot them down, I mean he jots them down on a bit of paper."

Jon waits patiently, without commenting on her flitting between tenses, which is highly unusual in a person as unhealthily precise as Antonia. He doesn't comment, and yet he notices how she increasingly uses the past imperfect when referring to her husband. He often wonders (secretly, with the lights out) when it will be the right time to talk to her about this.

It isn't easy.

In the list of conversational taboos with Antonia, Marcos's coma is deep inside a temple lost in the jungles of Peru, guarded by tarantulas, spears, and a giant rock.

"Give me an example," he says to spur her on when he realizes she has become mired in introspection, to the detriment of her story.

"Of special words? I don't know which one to choose."

"The first one that comes to mind."

She clearly ignores what he says and thinks it over. Perhaps rejecting some that are too personal. Perhaps searching for a perfect illustration.

"*Boketto*," she says at last.

Then she falls silent.

"Of course. *Boketto*. It happens to me all the time."

"No, it doesn't."

"How am I supposed to know that?"

Antonia seems suddenly to understand how conversations work. That they're based on using comprehensible terms.

"It's Japanese. It means 'that feeling you have when you're staring into the distance and you get lost inside yourself for no apparent reason.'"

"That happens to you, a lot," says Jon, trying not to smile.

Antonia also tries not to smile.

"Wait. Here's one I think you'll like. Let's see if you can guess who I'm thinking of. *Backpfeifengesicht*. It's German."

"Meaning?"

"A face that urgently needs a slap."

Jon pauses, lips slightly parted, before looking Antonia in the eye and announcing in unison with her:

"Mentor."

They both laugh.

"I think I understand why you like that game."

"No . . . it's not just a game . . . It's more than that. I can't explain."

And that's the problem, thinks Jon.

Someone like Antonia, who lives inside the prison of her brain, perceives much more clearly than other mortals an incontrovertible truth. That the limits of your language are the limits of your world. This is something every avid reader understands intuitively, even if they don't express it in those terms, and it's why they can never read enough.

Antonia has taken this to an extreme, learning ten languages and searching those she doesn't know for words she can't find in those she does.

Jon doesn't read books or learn languages.

He's into TV series and rock lifting. So he sums it all up with a Socratic:

This girl needs to get to know herself a bit.

"In this game of yours that's not just a game, does it count if it's more than one word?"

"An idiom."

"A what?"

"A phrase. It counts if it only exists in that language."

"In that case, I have one for what Romero was doing to you just now."

"What is it?" Antonia says, leaning slightly toward him in anticipation.

"Stop fucking with me."

Antonia freezes at the crudeness, like an assault.

"What's wrong, don't you like it?"

"I don't like cursing," she says, pursing her lips in distaste. "It impoverishes language."

Jon rolls his eyes. Pure prejudice. It would do her a world of good to spend some time in Bilbao. Go for a few drinks in Pozas and García Rivero. Salmon with piperade in El Mugi, *felipada* sandwiches in the Alameda bar. Three *txikitos* while listening to the local fauna, and she'd learn a thing or two.

"Honey, curses are culture. They can define emotions in a way lots of other words can't. Think of Captain Romero, for example."

He glares at Antonia until she finally realizes he is actually asking her to think of Captain Romero.

"Imagine she's in front of you. Now say it: 'Stop—'"

Antonia shakes her head. And turns bright pink.

"I'm not saying that. I'm too embarrassed."

Jon leans over her. Pulls on the door handle. Opens the door.

"Say it, or get out."

She glances at him, wondering if he's being serious. He is. She looks up at the sky, the color of depleted uranium. The clouds are threatening more rain. She decides to do as he says.

"All right, all right."

And then:

"Stop fucking with me," she whispers.

Not good enough, thinks Jon, shaking his head.

"Louder. You have to live it completely. You're not just saying what you feel. You're pissing to mark your territory, you're building the Berlin Wall. You're telling her: 'Keep off, bitch.' Do it again."

Antonia takes a breath as deep as if she were accepting an Oscar. And finally:

"Stop fucking with me!" she shouts out loud.

Jon applauds. Restrained, as always. But deep down inside, he's delighted. He feels he's achieved something, although he's not sure what.

"Now we're talking! How do you feel?"

"As if I've captured a feeling."

There's no need for her to say it. She's glowing like someone who's swallowed a neon light.

But actually, she does need to say it.

"Good for you," says Jon, driving off again. Suddenly he remembers he hasn't a clue where they're headed. "What are we going to do now?"

Antonia's face reverts to its normal gloomy aspect as the real world wins out over the *My Fair Lady* moment.

"Following the money was our only option. And that's gone up in flames."

"Everything centers on finding Lola Moreno. I'm beginning to think the earth has swallowed her up. Or somebody has made it swallow her up."

"I had the same thought. But no, the Russians wouldn't still be watching her mother's hair salon. Besides, I'm beginning to think they aren't just looking for her in order to avenge Yuri's betrayal. I think there's a lot more to all of this than meets the eye."

Jon rubs his neck furiously. He wonders whether there's an untranslatable word for when you massage yourself to stimulate the flow of ideas. He doesn't say anything to Antonia, just in case there is.

"I don't know. What meets the eye is sometimes all there is."

"Sometimes," says Antonia very slowly. "Yes."

Meaning in your world, that isn't true, angel. But since you're living in mine, we need to get you something to eat, thinks Jon, alerted by the rumbling in his stomach. Which isn't the kind that comes with a pause button.

"Lunch break. Afterward, you can turn it over in your mind all you want."

"I'm not hungry," says Antonia.

"Some things are inevitable."

"You're right. Some things *are* inevitable," Antonia says, a couple of seconds later.

Jon turns toward her. He heard the expression on her face before he saw it.

"Oh no, not that look."

"What look?"

"The look that says 'what you just said gave me an idea, although you haven't got a clue what it might be, and now my mental processes are running full speed ahead, and I'm not about to bother to explain it to you.'" She can't possibly be more annoying.

Antonia tacks a half smile onto the look, proving Jon wrong. She can indeed be more annoying.

She pulls out her cell phone, calls Dr. Aguado, and reels off a list of things she needs. Jon can't hear the pathologist's reply, but from her clipped tone, it appears the call didn't arrive at the best moment.

WHAT THEY DID TO HER NEXT

In the control room of the Red Queen project, Mentor is talking to a small, shaky eighty-year-old who is bald, half blind, and wearing a plaid jacket. He doesn't look in good shape; in fact, you might say he has one foot in the grave, and the other on a banana peel.

But age can be deceptive. He is possibly the greatest neurochemist of his generation. His name would figure among the candidates for a Nobel Prize if he weren't slightly deranged.

"She's not ready to start, Dr. Nuno."

On the other side of the glass, unaware that in the future she will lose a husband and have her son taken from her, a youthful Antonia Scott is making strenuous efforts to arrange sequences of numbers into logical patterns. She has electrodes attached to her head and is dressed in a plain hospital gown.

"How long has she been in training?"

"Longer than any other candidate. But I'm finding it hard to get her out of her comfort zone. It's extremely frustrating."

"How is she responding to the chemical compound?"

Dr. Nuno stretches out a hand streaked with protruding veins that resemble purple lightning. He takes the sheet of paper Mentor holds out to him.

"The data looks good. Better than good, in fact. No other candidate has such elevated markers."

"And yet I can't see any results. Her mind is still working either too fast or too slow. The red pill allows her to focus, but only for a short time."

Nuno clears his throat and takes a deep breath. Mentor senses a lecture coming. He has a strong urge to call security to restrain the man, lead him to a dark alley, and discreetly make him disappear. He could do it. And nobody would protest.

"Do you know what differentiates us from animals, Mentor?"

"The lottery?" he says, since any incorrect answer will do.

"The capacity for diagnostic reasoning. To see a broken jug on the floor and know it was previously a jug on the counter. And that the child's ball next to the fragments has something to do with it. Substitute a dead body for the jug, if you prefer."

"I'll stay with the jug. Please continue."

"Researchers have tried to detect signs of diagnostic reasoning in animals. We began with chimpanzees and bonobos, then went on to dolphins. Nothing. Finally, some bright spark thought of testing crows. We placed a piece of meat inside a horizontal glass tube, and watched. The crow was able to figure out that to reach the meat it had to use a tool. Also that it had to avoid a trap hole in the middle, so that the meat wouldn't fall out of reach."

"Isn't that what they do with octopuses?"

"No. Octopuses are capable of getting food out of a jar. This is far more complicated. It involves the tube, the trap hole, and the tool. And the researchers discovered that even when they moved the trap hole, the crow was able to get to the piece of meat."

End of preamble, Mentor thinks to himself.

"We humans aren't very good at diagnostic reasoning. As a species, I mean. Our brains have evolved a highly complex mechanism that looks for shortcuts. To simplify or avoid the need for diagnostic reasoning, we tell ourselves stories. The earth is flat, Paul McCartney has been swapped for his double . . ."

"The government is creating an organization of superintelligent secret agents . . . ," suggests Mentor.

"Even the clumsy parody you just provided is a valid example. What we do here goes beyond anything that's ever been attempted in the field of neuroscience."

"I don't need you to remind me of our true objective," says Mentor. "What I need is your help in finding a way to unblock Scott."

"If you'll hear me out—"

"I hope this is leading somewhere," Mentor says, leaning against the glass.

Nuno clears his throat again.

"To illustrate the importance of stories in diagnostic reasoning, I'm going to tell you a little tale."

"There was once a Jewish man who owned a store in Nazi Germany. One morning he arrived at his premises to discover swastikas and racist insults daubed on the window. He worked hard to clean off the graffiti before opening his store again. The next day, the same thing happened. And so, on the third day, the man stayed up all night, and when he saw the Brownshirts arrive with their pots of paint, he went up to them and said:

"I'll give you ten marks if you paint graffiti on this window."

The Brownshirts gladly accepted being paid for a job they were going to do for nothing.

Once they left, the store owner cleaned off the graffiti. The following night, he waited for them again, only this time he offered them nine marks to paint graffiti on his window.

This went on night after night, until finally he offered them only one mark to daub his window. The Brownshirts refused. They weren't going to work for such a pittance!

And that was the last he saw of them."

"What does this tale tell us about diagnostic reasoning?"

"That the store owner could have used his fifty-four marks to take a train and escape before the Nazis grew tired of painting graffiti and packed him off to a concentration camp."

Nuno blinks in surprise.

"That is certainly an interpretation of the store owner's flawed reasoning. But my intention is to show how easily humans are deflected from a correct diagnosis. The Brownshirts no longer remembered what the real reason for their acts was, because they had substituted it for a conscious analysis. For arithmetic."

"What does that have to do with Antonia Scott?"

"What does the soccer player Cristiano Ronaldo do when he's going to shoot? Does he think about swinging back his leg, raising his arm to steady himself, tensing his stomach muscles to keep his back straight?"

"No, he simply kicks the ball," says Mentor, finally understanding what Dr. Nuno is driving at.

"This woman is the most astonishing human being who has ever lived," says Nuno, tapping the piece of paper Mentor handed him with his horny yellow fingernail. "If you're failing to guide her toward her full potential, it's because you're teaching her to make diagnoses based on directed thought."

"Then tell me what I ought to be doing," says Mentor.

"You need to help her find her story," the doctor replies. "If she finds that, she'll stop thinking about shooting and simply kick the ball."

Nuno tears up the sheet of paper and tosses the fragments into the air.

"And when that happens, *boom*."

16
A LIST

Antonia Scott asks Dr. Aguado for the following:

- A list of the names and addresses of the people Lola Moreno follows on Facebook and Instagram.
- A file containing the private messages they have exchanged over the past two weeks, including any they may have deleted (but which the server stores permanently).
- Access to Lola's emails, especially the most recent ones.

There are only two possibilities. First, someone is helping Lola, in which case the information will be on her social networks.

Antonia will make every effort to find it, but it will be a thankless task. Except for the last item on her wish list.

Which brings us to the second possibility.

Either someone we've overlooked who is close to her is protecting her, or she's surviving on her wits, thinks Antonia. *In which case . . .*

"I need you to track all the 911 numbers made in the province of Málaga."

"Now they've been digitalized, I can send you the audio files as soon as the caller hangs up. But you'll be inundated."

Antonia doesn't reply. The tremor in her right hand is steadily worsening. She wedges it between her leg and the car seat, so that Jon won't notice.

"Scott?"

She needs a red pill again. It hits her in waves that intensify according to the stimuli she is confronting, especially if they're linked to her train-ing. When she arrives at a crime scene or has to consider fresh theories about the case, the monkeys in her head go crazier than ever.

Right now, the speed of Antonia's thoughts is putting her body under extreme stress. Her cheeks are hollow and she has dark circles under her eyes. When she looked in the mirror that morning, she barely recognized herself.

She needs a red pill. But she won't allow herself to take one.

"Is it possible to filter them using keywords?" says Antonia, drag-ging herself back to her conversation with Aguado.

"Yes. Which words do you want me to enter?"

"Send me any containing two or more of the following: *young woman, pregnant, theft, pharmacy, pawnbroker, supermarket, food.*

"One other thing," says Antonia before hanging up. "I need you to search the database for a code name: Chernaya Volchitsa. Black Wolf. Interpol, Europol. FSB."

Jon raises an eyebrow when he hears the last part. Russia's Federal Security Bureau doesn't readily share information with the European Union.

"This isn't a good time to be accessing Russian databases unautho-rized," says Aguado. "They'll find out it was us. And I'll be the one held responsible."

"I know that. Do what you have to do. We'll accept the conse-quences later."

LOLA

There was once a little girl who had everything.

She told Yuri so.

Not the morning he died. Such meaningful, transcendent moments before you lose a loved one never happen in real life. In fiction, a father can pass on an irrefutable truth to his son before dying of a heart attack a few seconds later. Or being carried off by a tornado.

In fact, Lola's last words to Yuri were:

"I'm going shopping!"

Yuri's muffled reply reached her through the door of the guest bathroom, where he did what Lola wouldn't let him do in their bathroom (Yuri ate a lot of spicy food).

And that was all. No perfunctory kiss, not even an *I love you.*

With hindsight, Yuri's murder was foreseeable, and could have been avoided. Predicting the past is easy, as all economists, columnists, and their ilk will tell you: they simply add *obviously* to the previous day's headline.

But then Lola had been warning Yuri for quite some time.

"We have everything. What more do you want?"

Yuri didn't answer.

What does somebody who has everything want?

They want more, like everyone else.

Lola's common sense was fickle, it came and went. Like the decision to learn a foreign language, go on a diet, or sign up with a gym. Ninety-five percent of good intentions happen "tomorrow." So Lola didn't press Yuri too hard.

Naïve Lola, who believed she was in love with Yuri. Or maybe truly was. When it comes to love, isn't believing you're in love the same thing as being in love?

Lola believed she was in love. She also believed she and Yuri needed to change their lives. Maybe that's why she threw away her contraceptive pills and used a very fine needle to prick all the condoms that found their way into the house. Because she wanted to get pregnant.

And she did.

Believing it would force Yuri to get his ass in gear.

And he did get his ass in gear, of course. Only the idiot, the numbskull, did so without consulting her. He thought for himself, as if that could possibly be a good idea. Ever.

And now here is Lola, up to her neck in it.

That greed, that wanting more and more, has resulted in Lola being hunted down, her life on the line. And yet it could also be the key to her salvation. This isn't a question of life's ironies. Ironically, that would be too simple.

Evening is drawing in, it's past seven o'clock, and the sun is snoring in the sea's cradle. Lola walks down Calle de Enrique del Castillo and comes out into Avenida de Ramón y Cajal. She takes a left. Edik Gusev's shop is three cell phone stores along.

There's a sign outside saying INSTANT CASH, although inside, anyone who is anyone knows the score.

Gusev is a fence, and an asshole. He excels at both professions.

He is also an acquaintance of Yuri's. "Friend" would be stretching it, although Yuri was always friendly toward Gusev, yet he kept him at arm's length. Yuri would pick up any lowlife who spoke the language of Tolstoy, so if even he could see Gusev was poison, the guy had to be bad news.

The door opens with an automatic *ding dong* that doesn't appear to alert anybody. Lola glances at the toasters NEARLY NEW! the coffee machines ON SALE! and even an optimistic BARGAIN! by a CD player.

Gusev appears.

He doesn't recognize her at once. Lola hasn't worn makeup for days, her hair is lank and greasy. She has purple rings under her eyes the size and shape of hammocks.

"How nice to see you, Señora Voronin," he says after a brief pause. "You look prettier than ever."

Gusev is a short, potbellied individual with a pockmarked face that looks like it was once used as a target in a shooting range.

"Hi, Gusev."

The two stare apprehensively at each other. Lola is aware she has put Gusev on the spot by turning up unannounced like this.

"We missed you at your husband's funeral."

"I was indisposed."

"It was well attended. Everyone was there."

Lola has heard enough. Gusev is obliged to tell Orlov he has seen her. Possibly even claim a reward, assuming the Beast has put a price on her foolish head. But Gusev isn't stupid, and he knows that Lola knows. And it follows that he also knows she wouldn't have taken this risk unless it was really important.

"What brings you here so . . . unexpectedly?"

Gustav's Spanish is better than that of many native speakers, although he makes occasional gaffes. He is speaking in a hushed voice that oozes nasty suggestions.

"I need to sell something, urgently."

She has no need to explain why.

"Let me see it."

"Not here," says Lola, glancing out into the street.

Gusev nods, goes over to the door, and locks it. He turns the OPEN sign around.

"Follow me."

The back room is crammed with boxes and security monitors. Without all the junk, the space would measure four square meters. There are bits of dolls, watch parts, ballpoint pen refills. Video games nobody wants anymore.

Lola isn't fooled. Gusev's warehouse is located somewhere else, far from prying eyes. His real business goes on at night, and consists of buying and selling everything. Absolutely everything.

He sold a child's kidney," Yuri told her once, when they were in a bar having a snack.

"You're lying."

Yuri shrugged and scarfed down another pork rind.

* * *

Lola hadn't believed him then. She does now. Being so close to Gusev in that cramped space, she believes very dark things.

"Let's see what you've got for me," Gusev says excitedly.

Lola bends down as if she were going to tie the lace on her trainer. What she does is undo her ankle bracelet, because it's all she has left.

The bracelet was a gift from Yuri, when she complained the one she had in rose gold didn't go with anything.

Yuri grinned smugly and bought her the bracelet. A bracelet she didn't need, a ridiculous extravagance, a pampered child's whim.

Now it's a lifesaver.

It's all she has left of Yuri.

There was no way she wanted to part with the bracelet. In the first place, nobody would buy it from her unless she showed some ID. And second, she is very attached to it. Going to Gusev's store is pure madness, but Zenya refused to take the bracelet as payment, and Lola needs the money. She has no choice.

She hands it to Gusev.

Holding it up to the light, the fence examines the bracelet with an expert eye. His other wandering eye squints at Lola, who lists the attributes of the merchandise.

"The bracelet is a De Beers. White gold, eighteen carats. It's studded with thirty diamonds, and must be worth—"

"Twenty-five thousand euros, Señora Voronin. A gift from your husband, I presume. People don't buy pretty things like this for themselves."

He turns it over in his fingers.

"Possibly more, it's in excellent condition. And the price of diamonds has skyrocketed this year."

Lola can't help heaving a sigh of relief when she sees Gusev isn't trying to undervalue the bracelet.

"I need five thousand euros. That's all. You can have it for that. You'll make a big profit."

Gusev grins, and runs his hand over the front of what was once a white shirt, now adorned with egg stains.

"I'm afraid I can't give you the money, Señora Voronin."

The smile vanishes from Lola's face.

"How . . . how much can you give me?"

"*Nichego*. Nothing," Gusev replies, waving his fingers in the air.

"All right, then," says Lola, holding out her hand for him to give it back. "I'll look somewhere else."

Gusev's grin broadens. He reveals a perfect set of gleaming white teeth—a startling contrast in this disheveled individual who revels in his own vileness.

"You haven't understood." Gusev turns round and rummages in a drawer. "I'm keeping the bracelet, and my money."

He has pulled a gun out of the drawer. He points it at Lola's head, making her shrink away in terror. She backs into a shelf piled with boxes.

"You can't do this to me. It's . . . disrespectful. We know each other. Yuri helped you when you were in need."

"Wrong again. I'm doing it because I can. And don't talk to me about your idiot husband. He's a traitor to the Bratvá. I can do whatever I like with you. In fact—"

Gusev's scrawny arms force Lola to turn round. He presses the gun to her neck with one hand, while with the other he feels for her pants zipper.

Lola suppresses a groan. She doesn't want to cry. She doesn't want to beg. But she can't help herself.

Gusev's fingers manage to unzip her pants and twist around her panty elastic. As he yanks them down, he scratches her with his nails. Lola feels an infectious prickle on her skin that makes her shudder.

Gusev is struggling with his own zipper. They are both upright, and Lola is a head taller than him, making penetration impossible. Even more so because Gusev's penis is soft and flaccid.

"If I'd known you were coming, I would have taken something so I could give you what you deserve," says Gusev, rubbing his limp member against her thigh. "You and your husband thought you were better than everyone else, didn't you? Well, you're nothing now."

Grabbing Lola by the hair, he drags her over to the door.

"Run, bitch. Run. Maybe I won't call Orlov after all. Like you say . . . that would be disrespectful."

RECORDING 06

TEN MONTHS EARLIER

DEPUTY INSPECTOR BELGRANO: We've been too soft on you. We've run out of patience.

YURI VORONIN: Wait a minute.

CAPTAIN ROMERO: It's too late, Voronin. We're here to inform you that tomorrow we'll be presenting our evidence to the public prosecutor. We have enough to make a case.

LOLA MORENO: I told you I could help.

DEPUTY INSPECTOR BELGRANO: Señora, you told us you'd bring us something substantial. So far, you've given us next to nothing.

CAPTAIN ROMERO: Let her speak, Belgrano.

LOLA MORENO: We can't get what you want. But we can give you something in the meantime.

(Papers rustling.)

(A forty-two-second pause.)

CAPTAIN ROMERO: This tells me everything except the date and name of the vessel.

LOLA MORENO: I'll give you that later. First you have to promise to leave us out of this.

DEPUTY INSPECTOR BELGRANO: If you think a lousy tip-off like this will save you, think again, señora.

YURI VORONIN: It's four hundred kilos.

DEPUTY INSPECTOR BELGRANO: Of hashish. No one gets a hard-on over hashish.

CAPTAIN ROMERO: Language, please, Belgrano.

LOLA MORENO: With all due respect, Captain, four hundred kilos is a large consignment. And the Moroccans who import it are evil.

CAPTAIN ROMERO: Señora Moreno. Very well, but this ship is just the beginning. I'll accept this as a gesture of goodwill on your part, and we'll carry out a raid. But it's small beer.

YURI VORONIN: It's four hundred kilos.

CAPTAIN ROMERO: So you keep saying, as if it was the quantity that matters. It isn't, what matters is the substance.

LOLA MORENO: Why does that matter?

CAPTAIN ROMERO: If tomorrow we seize six tons of Moroccan blond, at most we'll get a six-second slot on the national news.

DEPUTY INSPECTOR BELGRANO: And half the people watching will shrug and say, "Why don't they just legalize it?" As if that shit is good for people.

LOLA MORENO: So?

CAPTAIN ROMERO: Give me heroin. Give me cocaine.

DEPUTY INSPECTOR BELGRANO: As for Arabs, they're a joke.

YURI VORONIN: I assure you they're—

CAPTAIN ROMERO: We know all about the brutality of Moroccan criminal gangs, Voronin. But they don't buy us headlines.

DEPUTY INSPECTOR BELGRANO: Russians. Now, that's sexy.

CAPTAIN ROMERO: Either you give us Orlov all at once, or you feed him to us in little pieces.

LOLA MORENO: So you want us to work for you.

CAPTAIN ROMERO: What I want is to clear this coastline of trash. But this isn't about what I want, Señora Moreno. It's about what I can do to you and your husband if you don't give it to me.

LOLA

There was once a little girl who narrowly escaped the clutches of a dirty, foul-smelling ogre.

Lola runs out into the street. Her clothes are in disarray, the neck of her hoodie is wet from her tears. The light from the streetlamps seems dreamlike, the air fragile and precarious, as if the atmosphere were about to evaporate. She stumbles up the street, fastening her pants—unaware her panties are still halfway down her buttocks. Her feet barely touch the sidewalk, as if she's floating on air. A concerned passerby says something to her, but the sound is lost before it reaches Lola's ears.

None of this is real.

None of this is happening.

Lola feels attached to the ground by a fine, fragile thread, like cotton candy. One gust of wind and she would fly off. Be lifted up and away, like dandelion fluff.

None of this is real.

My one chance of escape can't have been snatched from me. It's not possible.

Lola, who always knows what to do. Lola, who always keeps her cool, as dry and hard as the earth in a graveyard. For the first time in her life, Lola, who ever since she was little has been making plans for when she runs out of plans, has drawn a blank.

Maybe that's why she doesn't recognize herself in what she does next. She feels as though she is outside her own body as it lurches toward the restaurant on the corner. The sole customers on that February evening are a couple of bemused pensioners. She approaches the first laid table and grabs a knife.

"Hey. Hey, señora!"

Lola doesn't hear the waiter any more than she did the woman who approached her in the street.

"Señora!"

The waiter doesn't follow her outside immediately, because he is carrying a plate of food (green salad, deep-fried frozen squid). By the time he sets off in pursuit of the intruder, Lola is already opening the door to the ATM. Seeing her go inside, the waiter slackens his pace, invents a quick syllogism—he's a philosophy graduate, of course—and decides he is better off calling the police.

Everything comes down to a simple choice: you either fight to live or die fighting, thinks Lola as she launches herself toward the back room of the store and at the unsuspecting Gusev.

She finds him busy rubbing his crotch while he watches something on-screen. Lola can't see what it is because she is busy stabbing him in the arm and back. The knife is the sort waiters give you so that you can wrestle with your steak before asking for one that's actually sharp. And so with the first thrust she only succeeds in scratching Gusev's skin and ripping his egg-stained shirt.

The second encounters his shoulder blade, which causes the tip to bend and the knife to veer off course. It penetrates six centimeters, slipping between bone and muscle, then tears through Gusev's flesh. As Lola yanks the knife out, he lets out a yelp of pain. The bent tip destroys a fair amount of muscle fibers on the way.

The third stab hits the chairback.

The fourth cuts her own arm when Gusev pounces on her. As they roll around on the floor, Lola realizes the fence has wet himself, and she is struck for the first time by the sheer crudeness, the brutality of what is going on.

She is still angry enough to make one last thrust, and buries the knife in Gusev's thick, hard belly, missing his navel by a few centimeters. It remains there, plunged to the hilt, while Gusev stares at it, bewildered. Lola recognizes this look of unreality: it's the same one that seeped from her eyes less than two minutes before.

Life is full of surprises.

"I called Orlov, *súka*. Bitch. You're dead, you're dead, you bitch."

Lola gets to her feet, clutching her wounded arm. She rolls up the sleeve of her hoodie and sees it's only a scratch and has barely broken the skin. It hurts, but not a lot. She can't worry about that now.

Gusev, on the other hand, can only worry about knife protruding from his round belly like Neil Armstrong's flag on the surface of the moon. Clasping it with both hands, he tries to ease it out. But the serrated wedge-shaped blade causes him unbearable pain. He lets out another howl as two streams of blood gush from either side of the wound and flow downward, staining Gusev's shirt even more as they do so.

"I wouldn't do that if I were you. Haven't you ever watched TV? You can bleed to death if you pull the knife out," says Lola.

Her bracelet is lying on the counter. Stepping over Gusev's sobbing figure, she rummages in the drawer until she finds the gun. Slipping the bracelet in her pocket, she points the gun at Gusev's face.

"The safe."

A fence must keep a lot of cash: it's what he works with. But at first, Gusev doesn't seem inclined to cooperate.

"The safety catch is still on, bitch."

Lola turns the gun over, studies it briefly, and finally decides what she is looking for must be the small catch above the grip. She moves it carefully, hears a satisfying *click,* and aims the gun once more at Gusev, who emits an even more satisfying *argh.*

"Thanks. Now the safe."

"I'm not giving you a thing."

Lola raises her right leg just enough to brush the handle of the knife with the inside edge of her sneaker. Gusev gives a fresh howl.

"I can do this all day long."

Actually, she can't, because she's feeling dizzy again, and her mouth is so dry she can barely move her tongue. She urgently needs insulin. This pig has called Orlov. Maybe the waiter has called the police. She has to get out of there.

But she has no insulin, and nothing to buy it with. Nor does she have the money for Zenya, and this son of a bitch rubbed his dick against her leg. So she isn't leaving there without stealing as much as she can from him. Even if she only makes it as far as the inside of a patrol car.

Or a hearse, Lola thinks, raising her leg again.

"Okay. Okay. Behind there," says Gusev, pointing to the end of a shelf.

Lola pushes aside a stack of old movies and discovers the safe. It has a numerical lock. It takes only three kicks to Gusev's ribs to obtain the combination. But it takes a lot longer in seconds, costing her another precious minute.

The safe creaks open. A bitter, earthy odor hits Lola in the face. The source is an open bag of cocaine the size of a tennis ball sitting on a pile of papers on the top shelf.

On the lower shelf are several bundles of fifty-euro banknotes bound with rubber bands. Tucked under them are scraps of paper with handwritten notes giving the amount in each bundle. Lola stuffs several of them into the pockets of her cargo pants, relishing Gusev's whimpers as she does so. The theft seems to hurt him even more than the wound in his belly.

"You're dead, you're dead, you bitch," he repeats, his voice fading. His eyelids are starting to droop, his fingers slacken around the knife.

He's bleeding to death.

A big loss, Lola thinks, heading for the exit.

She steps forward and gets as far as putting her right foot outside the back room.

That's when the police officer appears in the doorway. Tall, bearded, and tired looking. He reaches for the door handle. His expression instantly changes from world-weary to alarmed when he sees Lola brandishing a weapon through the glass.

This is also when Gusev, still sprawled on the floor, chooses to make a grab for Lola's left heel. His strength is waning and his grip is weak. His fingers slip on Lola's sneakers, leaving three red streaks on the white leather. But as her foot had already left the floor, she teeters slightly. Her stomach tenses with fear, and this causes the index finger of her right hand to contract.

Blam.

The bullet exits the barrel and speeds toward the police officer. It misses his head by a fraction, shattering the glass door. The police officer leaps to one side, with a squeal that's rather unmanly but understandable given the circumstances.

All of the above has happened in fewer than three seconds.

Lola steadies herself against the wall, points the gun at Gusev—who appears to have lost consciousness—and looks back at the gun, confused. The blue of the patrol car lights reflects in her staring eyes. Outside, she can hear yells.

FUUUUUUCK.

17

AN AVENUE

"Well, it looks as if she's finally turned up," says Jon, climbing out of their car.

"You said it yourself," Antonia replies, joining him at the police cordon. "Some things are inevitable."

Jon and Antonia appear thirty minutes late, in the midst of the commotion. Obviously, Captain Romero didn't call them to share her progress in locating Lola Moreno. Probably because she was busy surrounding the suspect with two patrol cars and a police van that have blocked off Avenida de Ramón y Cajal. Also positioning six armed officers, their weapons trained on a three-meter-wide storefront.

Antonia was immersed in the information Aguado sent to her iPad when the police emergency call arrived. Her intuition proved correct. Luckily. The same luck that spared the police officer's head from the bullet that smashed the glass in the door.

Nobody called them, which is why Jon is in such a foul mood. This is obvious from the way he is stomping across the asphalt, and from his red face. But a hostage situation isn't the best time to start mouthing off. Especially when a dozen pensioners on the neighboring balconies are filming the incident on their cell phones. Despite a megaphone on the police van ordering rubberneckers to keep away from their windows and return to the safety of their apartments: static crackle, *This is an urgent message from the National Police*, static crackle, *The suspect is armed and you could risk getting shot*, static crackle.

People are assholes, thinks Jon, rightly enough.

* * *

Belgrano's and the captain's faces when Antonia and Jon appear are as welcoming as a gulag.

"Who tipped you off?" asks the deputy inspector.

"We read it on Twitter," says Jon.

"Your participation is no longer required," says Captain Romero. "We've located the suspect."

"Lola Moreno, housewife. Has she joined Al-Qaeda?" asks Jon, pointing toward the police officers barricaded behind the patrol cars, weapons at the ready.

"She has a firearm and shot at an officer who responded to an emergency call. She has blockaded herself inside the store and is threatening to shoot the owner, a man named"—Belgrano checks his notes—"Edik Gusev, a Russian citizen with a residence permit in Spain."

"We appreciate your collaboration, but we'll take it from here," Captain Romero says frostily. She is putting a bulletproof vest on over her uniform.

"We'd like to remain as observers until the arrest—that is, if you don't mind, Captain," Antonia says meekly.

Romero looks at her, puzzled. She had expected a power struggle, not a humble request. She has too much to think about, and there are too many witnesses, for her to refuse.

"Try not to get in the way."

Jon leads Antonia a few paces off.

"I see you've made use of my etiquette lessons."

"This isn't the right time to be telling Romero to stop . . . stop effing with me. We need to stay here to help any way we can. There are lots of armed tough guys around," says Antonia, glancing about her with alarm.

The police officers are jumpy, they have loaded weapons and are ready to use them. It doesn't matter who fires the first shot, because the group takes equal responsibility. Besides, the woman in the store tried to kill their colleague, who has been taken to the hospital, suffering an anxiety attack. A common-enough occurrence in such situations, although they never show that in the movies. His anxiety doesn't leave with him in the ambulance: it stays behind and proliferates among his six colleagues. It coils itself around their spines, spreads its deadly tendrils around their lungs, accelerating their breathing. It brushes against their hearts, making them beat faster, and winds its way to their index fingers hooked around their triggers.

"We need to get her out of there as quickly as possible," says Jon.

"She already shot at a police officer," says Antonia. "If she doesn't surrender with her hands up, and soon, there's only one way she'll be coming out."

LOLA

There was once a little girl who found herself trapped due to the evil of others.

Lola is sitting propped against the shelves in the back room. Gusev is unconscious, his breathing labored. He smells of urine and blood. Of defeat.

"Come out with your hands up," a megaphone bellows.

"Leave me alone. Go away!"

The pain in her head is getting steadily worse. It has installed itself behind her left eye and is spreading to her temples. It's like having a pair of pliers twisting around inside her.

And she is so thirsty.

Her saliva is thick as glue. Her throat feels like tough leather, bleached in the sun. Her desire for water has become acute, distressing.

In Gusev's office, there's only a tiny bottle with a drop in the bottom. Disgusted at drinking his spittle, Lola gives in to her desperate need and tips the bottle upside down, allowing the precious liquid to drip onto her tongue. The relief is momentary and futile. As well as repugnant.

Lola lifts the bottle to her eye, and peers through the top, as if she could magically make it fill up. All she can see is a sixfold image of Gusev dying, or dead.

Lola tosses the bottle at him half-heartedly. It lands on his chest before rolling toward his double chin. It stays there for an instant before dropping out of view on the other side.

I'm going to die in here.

I'm going to die alone in here with this revolting pig.

As glucose builds up in her blood, the symptoms of hyperglycemia intensify. She feels faint and confused. Her vision is blurred. Her belly is swollen, not just from the pregnancy.

And she's so thirsty.

Her pockets are stuffed full of money, but she has no means of spending it. She imagines the nearby stores, with their stocks of water and other drinks. She imagines the unreachable water pipes running through the building.

I'm going to die in here.

Maybe it's better if I surrender, accept I'm done for.

She is still holding the gun—the cause of this whole mess. The thought occurs to her briefly to use it on herself, but then she laughs. A laugh as rough as an adulterer's mother-in-law, as a jailbird's file. Her laughter has a savage humor that echoes round the shelves filled with blenders, used boxer shorts, and broken dehumidifiers. The throw-away society's garbage that aspired and failed to be something, and yet refuses to die.

I'm not going to end up like a yogurt maker.

To stay alive. What she took for granted every day was never so hard. Staying alive.

I wish I knew how.

At that moment, the telephone rings.

The harsh metallic tinkle bursts in on the anguish piled up within these four walls smelling of dust, cocaine, blood, and urine.

Lola contemplates the device with a mixture of aversion and awe, like someone finding a scorpion inside a Kinder egg. She lets it ring until the call abruptly breaks off.

It starts to ring again.

She reaches out her hand. Picks up the receiver gingerly, raising it to her ear as if an armed cop, or one of Orlov's *bojevíks*, might spring out of it.

"Listen," a woman's voice says. "*Russki?* Russian?"

"*Nmenogo.* A little."

"Do I say. Take *pistolet. Ponimayesh.*"

Ponimayu. Lola knows the word, yet she understands nothing.

"Who are you?"

"No time. You live? You want live?"

Lola inhales deeply.

Oh yes. I want very much live, she thinks.

"Do I say."

18

AN ESCAPE

Romero gives instructions to her men. Their patrol cars are parked diagonally across the wide avenue. On the stretch outside Gusev's store are half a dozen trees—the sole occupants of an otherwise deserted sidewalk. The restaurant on the corner is empty and in darkness, and the phone stores shut their shutters a while ago. Only the window of the Instant Cash is still lit up.

"Where's the hostage negotiator?"

"They've located one in Cádiz. She was working on a domestic violence case," Belgrano tells her. "The local station house estimates she'll be here in three hours."

"Three hours," Romero repeats in disgust. "Three hours to get hold of a trained professional, who by the time she arrives will be dead on her feet. Same old story."

Jon has donned a bulletproof vest, and after much insistence has persuaded Antonia to do the same. Together with Belgrano and the captain, they are the only ones wearing them. Further disturbing evidence of police underfunding. Some months ago, Jon read a report about a raid on a warehouse used by Colombians to process drugs. A shoot-out followed in which, ironically, the narcos were kitted out with bulletproof vests and AR-15 assault rifles, while his colleagues had no body armor and only their regulation weapons.

Nobody died, because the narcos surrendered; in a country where prisons are three-star hotels, you think twice before shooting at a cop. The weapons were to deter rival gangs.

On that occasion, nobody died.

But the problem hasn't gone away.

"What should we do?" asks Belgrano.

"We're not waiting three hours. We'll force the suspect to come out."

"That won't be necessary," says Antonia. "She's on her way."

"There's movement, Captain," declares one of the officers barricaded behind a patrol car.

A shadow appears in the doorway.

"Hold your fire. I repeat. Hold your fire," says the captain. "I don't want any scandal, all right?"

"Come out with your hands up!" Belgrano shouts through the megaphone. The device distorts his Andalusian accent, somehow making it comically unthreatening. But there is nothing funny about the guns aimed at the lighted store window.

"I'm coming out!" replies a voice. Slightly hoarse, tinged with fear, but sweet nonetheless.

Lola Moreno is a complete wreck. Her hair is dirty and matted, she has dark circles under her eyes, and her lips are chapped. Her parched skin gleams in the high beams of the patrol cars, which cast her shadow onto the storefront.

Even so, she's gorgeous, thinks Jon.

He is the only officer present who hasn't drawn his weapon. Even the captain is wielding her gun. And Deputy Inspector Belgrano is holding the megaphone in his left hand while his right rests on his gun holster.

"She isn't dangerous," declares Antonia. "Nobody shoot."

Lola is holding the gun by its barrel, between forefinger and thumb. She has her arms raised and is hunched over. Very slowly, she moves away from the store entrance.

"Señora Moreno," bawls the megaphone. "You need to drop the gun."

"What happened just now was an accident!"

"You need to drop the gun right now, señora. This is your final warning."

Lola peers in their direction, eyes wide with fright. And yet they also express something else. They are scanning left and right. Expecting something.

"Something isn't right," says Antonia.

Until now, she has been standing erect. Now she crouches down very slowly. Not that she offers much of a target. A small hand clasps the edge of Jon's vest, pulling him down too.

"Señora, I won't say this again. Drop the gun!" shouts Belgrano, contradicting himself.

"It was an accident. I swear it was an accident. You have to let me go," Lola says, sobbing.

She takes another step to her right, moving farther away from the store entrance.

"Stay where you are, señora. Drop the gun!"

Captain Romero pulls out her walkie-talkie and presses the talk button.

"Bravo One, permission to shoot to incapacitate."

"No!" says Antonia, beginning to stand up. Jon catches her by the waist.

"Bravo One, are you receiving me?"

Static noise.

Silence.

"Soler! Where the hell are you?" Romero insists, pressing the button twice more.

"Your man out," a woman's voice rings through the earpieces of Romero, Belgrano, and the six other officers.

"This is a police radio," Romero sighs. "Get off the channel or—"

"Your man out. I use his radio."

The police officers stare perplexedly at one another. The glance Romero and Belgrano exchange is subtly different.

"Who is this? Where is Officer Soler?"

Romero nods at Belgrano. The deputy inspector places the megaphone on the ground and gestures toward one of the officers taking cover behind the patrol cars.

"Your man okay. You no move."

"Look here, I don't know who you are, but—"

"Right wheel," the voice declares in their earpieces.

Traveling at more than eight hundred meters per second, the bullet bursts the tire of the Citroën C4 before the sound of the shot reaches the men surrounding the Instant Cash. As it does so, the noise is dwarfed by the deafening blast from the exploding tire. The patrol car sinks to one side as the officers hurl themselves to the ground. They take cover as best they can, searching for the direction the shot came from.

Jon has also thrown himself down, but has done so to shield Antonia with his body. She wriggles and sticks her head out.

"Up there," she says, pointing to the roof terrace opposite.

Romero knows where the shooter is. Exactly where she stationed Officer Soler with a PSG1 sniper rifle. A precision model. Aged just twenty-four, Officer Soler can perform miracles with it. He can hit a watermelon at six hundred meters. Or rather, blow it to smithereens, because the PSG1 uses 7.62 mm ammo that can penetrate a cement block five centimeters thick.

Obtaining this precision weapon for the UYDCO Costa del Sol was a monumental achievement. Romero had her work cut out persuading Madrid to agree to send them one, because such rifles are usually destined only for special ops, or police departments in cities like Bilbao or Barcelona. *Handled by somebody who knows how to use it, this is an unstoppable weapon*, Romero said when the package arrived at the police station. They all celebrated.

They're less enthusiastic now.

"You have to get up to where Soler is. Right now," Romero insists, shoulder to shoulder with Belgrano.

The deputy inspector starts to crawl toward the police van. He hasn't gotten very far when the voice crackles in their walkie-talkies once more.

"Big car left wheel. Small car back wheel."

The blasts ring out in quick succession along Avenida de Ramón y Cajal, clearing the area round the cordon of rubberneckers and reporters. And the balconies of bothersome old folk. The tire on the car bursts cleanly, the one on the heavier van sends bits of black rubber flying in all directions.

"Captain, the suspect is escaping," warns one of the men, spotting Lola's feet from beneath his patrol car as she slips away from them.

"Stop her!" orders Romero.

The officer raises himself slightly and takes aim.

This time there is no warning.

The bullet enters his left thigh from behind. It snaps his femur in two places, sending out a spray of tiny bone fragments from the exit wound. They lie there, bright white on the blood and asphalt, like a roll of the dice in which the bank wins.

A moment of silence follows the report from the fourth shot. A frozen moment of stillness, but not one of peace. A delayed moment of twisted faces and wide-open eyes. Of bewildered horror and wounded pride, like the kind experienced by the hunter who has become the quarry.

We're fucked, concludes Jon.

Then the wounded officer's screams pierce the silence as he clutches his shattered limb with both hands. Another man approaches him, removes his belt, and makes a tourniquet around his colleague's leg.

"You not move," the voice repeats over the walkie-talkies.

Meanwhile, Lola Moreno reaches the street corner, where she comes upon a TV cameraman taking cover on Calle de Enrique del Castillo. He and the female reporter with him stare at her in disbelief. Lola raises her gun and fires two shots in the air. The cameraman and reporter flee.

So does Lola. She ducks into Parque de la Alameda and starts running without looking back.

Captain Romero's face, meanwhile, expresses pure rage. Cheek to the asphalt, fists and jaw clenched. Every ounce of self-control and restraint is devoted to keeping herself pinned to the ground. Instead of raising her weapon and returning fire.

"How many bullets?" whispers Antonia, or at least the bit of her she has managed to ease out from beneath 110 kilos of Bilbao body armor.

"What?!"

"How many bullets in the magazine?" repeats Antonia.

Romero thinks hard, but she can't remember. Her mind is taken up with the screams of her wounded officer. His name is Vázquez. He has a wife and two little girls. They visited the station house once. To see where their dad worked, arresting baddies.

"The model. What's the model?" Antonia insists.

"PSG1," says Romero without hesitation. Filling in thirteen request forms has imprinted it on her memory.

"They have five. And she's used four," says Antonia.

She kicks Jon's shin, making him release his grip just long enough for her to stand up and roll quickly to her left.

The shot speeds through the air she occupied until a second earlier, and lodges in the yellow stripe on the patrol car door, leaving a perfectly round hole.

"And that makes five," gasps Antonia.

Romero reacts at last.

"She has to reload! Get moving!"

She has to hurry.

Although she has never used a PSG1 before, she knows how they work. The rifle is a powerful weapon, designed by the Germans in the aftermath of the 1972 Munich massacre. To enable their police force to eliminate armed enemies at a distance.

Unfortunately, it takes several seconds to reload. That small woman caught her off guard. She wasn't expecting her to stand up, and her reactions and training took over. Her finger pulled the trigger automatically, emptying the magazine.

She doesn't waste time reloading. Crouching down, she moves away from the edge of the roof terrace and clambers over the unconscious officer.

She knows the rules. Never kill police officers. It was easy enough to creep up behind him, less so to put him out of action without causing him serious injury.

Escaping won't be easy at all.

Especially since she has wounded one of them.

She can hear them coordinating their movements over the radio. But there are lots of words she doesn't understand, so she pulls out the earpiece and throws it to the ground. She calculates she has roughly forty seconds before they reach the roof. It will take them at least that long to run up seven flights, as she has disabled the elevator. Another seven to break down the door, which she has secured with rope.

It will be touch and go.

She darts over to the west-facing side of the building. This was where she left the climbing gear, the rope and hooks she bought for less than forty euros at the sports store two blocks away. If they check the security cameras, they'll get a good idea of what she looks like. It wasn't the ideal solution, but she was forced to improvise. The text from Orlov's people contained only an address.

Six minutes away by bike.

She arrived in three.

Too late.

Under no circumstances must Lola Moreno fall into the hands of the police. Not before she has finished with her. After that, they can collect whatever is left.

She slips on *her helmet and gloves and tests the steel hook twice. She hasn't time for snap hooks, harnesses, or rope brakes. She pulls the rope between her legs, wraps it behind one thigh, brings it over her chest and shoulder. Then she starts her descent. The reason why the technique hasn't been used for decades is because of rope burn. Her leather pants and jacket protect her from that, but the pressure it puts on her back is a different matter. She uses her legs to push away from the wall, and her hands to slide down the rope. But each fresh jump causes a searing pain, and each time she bounces off the wall, she grits her teeth. Flexing her knees as the soles of her boots brush the surface isn't enough. The impact sends a whiplash up and down her spine, an electrical charge that makes her cry out. Three meters from the ground, she nearly vomits inside her helmet, and narrowly avoids letting go of the rope. She can hear the cops yelling above her head, and is vaguely aware of somebody taking her picture, or filming her from one of the windows.*

At the last bounce against the wall, the pain causes her arms to give way, and she loses her grip. She spins around and becomes snared in the rope, like a strange yo-yo in the hands of a clumsy child. At the last instant, she manages to cling on, so that she lands on her front, not on her back. But she plummets a meter and a half onto hard ground. The helmet takes the brunt of the fall. The tinted visor smashes, leaving a hole where her eye is. She peers up at the roof terrace. The police officers are leaning over the parapet wall, weapons cocked.

Fueled by adrenaline, she ignores the pain in her back and rolls over. She flattens herself against the wall, where she won't give the men on the roof much of a target. The motorbike is close by, parked behind a dumpster.

Just a bit farther. Just a few more meters.

Enveloped in a fog of pain, she reaches the Kawasaki. The 310-horsepower engine roars when she turns the key in the ignition.

Shots ring out, but miss their target.

Seconds later, she is gone.

ASLAN

Aslan is a worried man; that much is obvious.

You only need to look at him. Sitting at his usual terrace café on the seafront, his favorite breakfast in front of him. The eggs have gone rubbery and the toast is hard. The cold sausages show their true composition: 80 percent fat, 20 percent meat scraps.

Aslan hasn't even touched his knife and fork. He has been sitting there for over an hour, trying to work out what went wrong. Why Lola Moreno isn't dead, as he ordered. Why the Black Wolf allowed her to escape from the police, instead of simply putting a bullet in her head.

He has been told exactly what happened. And the Beast is aware this has caused concern among the criminal community. The message he delivered at Voronin's funeral was very clear. Nobody who betrays Aslan Orlov lives to tell the tale. Kiril Rebo, his right-hand man, spread word that the Black Wolf was there to exact vengeance.

Aslan has ended up looking like a fool.

He shifts in his seat. An hour sitting in even the most comfortable wicker chair is excruciating for his bony old ass. He has no choice but to call Saint Petersburg and explain what has happened. It's up to them to call the Wolf to account.

The telephone rings several times before a croaky, liquor-sodden voice replies.

"Aslan. What a joy to hear your voice."

"*Pakhan.*" Orlov greets him deferentially, with the title they use to address the head of their organization, "Godfather." He can imagine him at the far end, with his perennial silver-topped cane and his empty, unseeing eyes. A book in braille open on the table next to him.

"What can I do for you?"

Orlov explains about the previous night's fiasco. She even shot and wounded a police officer, which crosses every line. The *pakhan* listens politely, without interrupting.

"Everything is going according to plan," says the old man once Orlov has finished.

The bewildered mafioso leans forward, glancing warily from side to side. He does not understand. And many years in the Bratvá have taught him that not understanding is the harbinger of certain death.

"*Pakhan . . .*"

"Don't trouble yourself, Aslan. I understand why you are uneasy."

"What's going on? Why isn't the woman dead?"

"Why did I send you there, *vor*?"

"To set up a—"

"I sent you there to launder our money. A task you have carried out somewhat carelessly."

"I only do my job."

"Ah, but that's the problem. You didn't do your job. Voronin did it for you. A simple *bojevík*, who in a matter of years transformed into a financial wizard. He seemed too good to be true. And he was."

A shadow looms behind Orlov. The mafioso wheels around with a start, convinced they have come to kill him. It has always been this way when you feel *tenmote* in the dark. A figure comes up behind you and sticks a knife in your throat.

Only this time, the knife takes the form of a sheaf of papers.

"Look at the documents just delivered to you, *vor*. You'll see Voronin's betrayal is far more serious and damaging than simply talking to the police."

Orlov cringes as he leafs through the pages in Cyrillic that Kiril Rebo has just handed him. He cannot believe what he is reading.

"This means—"

"It means he was stealing from you. Emptying the *obschchak* under your very nose, Aslan. If this becomes known . . ."

Orlov feels a shiver go down his spine. To have a rat inside the organization is dangerous. A thief is an unimaginable disaster. If word were to spread among the Bratvá that the Tambóvskaya was letting itself be robbed, he might as well paint a target on his forehead. Among vermin, the least sign of weakness is a death sentence.

"I sent over the Black Wolf a week before you requested her, Aslan. She is following my instructions, not yours."

"If only I'd known—"

"Then maybe you wouldn't have sent your men to destroy Voronin's files. That was a mistake. Finding the money will be much harder now. But it's the only reason you're still alive."

"Voronin's wife knows where it is," says Orlov.

"The Wolf will find the money. And when she does, maybe you'll still be a *vor*. Or maybe not."

The call breaks off, although Orlov keeps the cell phone to his ear for a while, before laying it down on the table.

He hasn't escaped the death sentence for his mistakes. Merely postponed it.

Until the money turns up, assuming it does.

He examines the documents once more. The figures leave no room for doubt. Although Voronin had been smart, the trail he left behind finally surfaced, even if it leads to a dead end.

A hundred anonymous credit cards paying out vast sums of money, month after month.

Not for the last time, Orlov curses his stupidity in trusting Voronin. He did everything to help that asshole.

How did he manage to deceive me like that?

And what the hell has he spent €653 million on?

Part 3

LOLA

We have doomed the wolf not for what it is,
but for what we deliberately and mistakenly
perceive it to be.

FARLEY MOWAT

1
A RÉSUMÉ

Jon Gutiérrez is still smarting.

It's not his shin. Antonia Scott would need half an hour and a hammer to give him as much as a bruise. It's his soul, yes, his soul. Jon's soul is a delicate thing that's easily broken. And the fact Antonia was able to fool him so easily and break free still hurts. His mood is defiant. And today's agenda won't help improve things.

It contains only one item.

Call Mentor.

He has summoned them for a video conference at one o'clock sharp. He has also ordered them not to leave the hotel until then.

Jon has used the time to carry out two chores he had pending.

One.

Check if the guy on Grindr has shown signs of life. Curse despairingly.

Two.

Call Amatxo, who spends half an hour railing against her neighbor in 2-B. Jon, who is always happy to gossip about his mother's neighbor—*that two-faced bitch, she sure raised a stink over those geraniums*—listens with half an ear. Bad-mouthing the woman in question no longer brings him the same satisfaction as before. Time calms enthusiasms the way water douses a fire. He now sees this decades-long feud between neighbors as petty and nasty. But he regrets the thought immediately, because to turn a blind eye to people who offend you isn't right.

Not until Amatxo *says so. Unthinkable.*

When he hangs up, Jon feels worse than ever. Lately, calls to his mother have become a duty, a rusty, creaking routine. And it shouldn't be like that. Aged forty-something, Jon has finally become independent. But he doesn't like the feelings of guilt that go with it.

Jon is all she has.

But what about me? What do I have?

As with all unequal relationships—and not many aren't—one person always needs the other more. And the scale tends to tip more rice into the heavier bowl, until the chain breaks and the grains scatter everywhere.

Suddenly, Jon isn't so sure these reflections are only about his mother.

Antonia lets him into her room at 12:57. By 13:11, Mentor still hasn't called.

There they are, the two of them, each in an armchair, not speaking. He is watching the news on his cell phone. She is reading a book. At her own mystifying pace.

"What are you reading?"

This isn't the first time he sees her immersed in an actual book. Generally, they are thick criminology manuals. Scholarly articles about serology or psychopathology in foreign languages. With impossibly long, boring titles. Jon renames them in the best Spanish tradition. *My Neighbor Always Said Hello. How to Remove Blood Stains for Beginners. How I Became a Serial Killer.*

But the one she's holding now looks different.

"I'll tell you only if you promise not to laugh," says Antonia.

Jon swears on all that's sacred. His *amatxo*, T-bone steaks with french fries, and pin-striped suits.

Antonia shows him the cover. On it is the photograph of a sneaker lying on the floor. And a title that tests Inspector Gutiérrez's resolve and self-control.

Children: An Instruction Manual.

Keeping a straight face, Jon stands up and looks out the window. It offers a charming view of an interior patio, with damp stains running down the walls and patches of dark red on light red tiles.

"You'd better stop smirking before your face cracks," says Antonia.

"I have my back to you."

"And glass is a reflective surface."

Jon gives in and turns around, his expression a smoking gun.

"So . . . ? Any useful advice?"

"Not really. Variations on 'listen and do what you can.'"

"I could have told you that for a lot less than twenty euros."

"Yes, but you don't have baby photos on every tenth page."

"All the more reason."

When he appears on the iPad screen almost an hour late, Mentor looks dreadful. Even Antonia, who isn't much given to commenting on other people's appearance, can't help noticing.

"What's wrong?"

Mentor clears his throat and wrings his hands.

"Something very serious, Scott. We've lost two Queens."

Jon and Antonia exchange looks of alarm.

"Which ones?"

"England and Holland."

"Is that why you're in Belgium?"

"We're not in Belgium anymore. I can't tell you where we are."

Behind him is a plain white wall. The halogen lights emphasize the weariness etched on his face. He hasn't shaved for several days.

"But yes, that's why the heads of all the teams are meeting. It's an extremely complex situation."

"How did it happen?"

"I can't tell you anything more."

"Do you need us there?" asks Jon.

"No!" snaps Mentor. "I don't need you here. Until we've clarified the situation, I need you to stay exactly where you are, well away from Madrid."

"Was there foul play?" asks Antonia.

"I don't intend to tell you a thing, Scott. Don't try to manipulate me. Remember, I taught you all the tricks you know."

Antonia leans back in her chair, vexed.

"The situation here is no piece of cake either."

"I'm aware of that. I have the information you requested from Aguado," says Mentor, holding up some sheets of paper to the camera. "We'll discuss how you obtained it some other time, Scott. It was reckless of you. But I have bigger fish to fry right now. And so do you."

"Did you find out anything about the woman?"

"Oh yes. You're going to love this."

Mentor starts to read.

"Olena Jovonovich a.k.a. Chernaya Volchitsa. Daughter of a champion in the Russian martial art *sambo*, and a chess grand master. Born in 1990 in Kstovo, on the banks of the Volga. The authorities abducted her at birth, and told her parents their baby had died."

"How delightful."

"I don't see why you're surprised, it was also the custom in Spain until not long ago," says Antonia.

"The girl became part of a secret program run by the KGB, which by then was in decline. Those were paranoid times, before the Russians found out they could control the world with computers. Their aim was to create the ultimate human weapon. An experiment previously carried out by the Nazis and the Americans, although less successfully. The Russians learned from their rivals' mistakes. They were determined not to fail, which is why they snatched hundreds of babies. Some they disposed of. Others survived. Children like Olena Jovonovich, whose intellectual and physical qualities are exceptional."

Jon thinks he detects a hint of wistful envy in Mentor's voice.

Best to get them when they're young. That way you won't produce agents who think for themselves, he reflects, looking at Antonia.

"When the wall came down, the Osobyye Deti (Exceptional Children) program became the preserve of the SVR, the Foreign Intelligence Service. By the time the children grew up, the top brass at the SVR realized they needed to start selling off assets to pay for their dachas in the country, their Mercedes in the garage, and their *lyubovnitsa's* breast enhancement."

"That's why Asia and Africa became inundated with automatic weapons and surface-to-air missiles," says Antonia. "The arms traffickers feathered their nests with money from dictators and terrorists."

"And when they ran out of bombs, they sold the children," says Jon.

"I'm afraid so. Only they were no longer children. They were weapons. We don't know exactly how many Deti the SVR sold to the Bratvá. Accounts differ. Half a dozen, maybe a dozen. Nearly all are registered as deceased on the FSB database."

"Nearly all," says Antonia.

"Nearly all. Not this woman."

"Her activities?"

Mentor lights a cigarette and shuffles the papers.

"There's a lot of speculation, but little solid evidence. Two deaths in Amsterdam, four in Belgrade. One judge assassinated in Moscow, another in Dagestan. All enemies of the Tambóvskaya."

"Witnesses?"

"Very few. They all concurred that a mysterious woman appeared out of nowhere."

"That sounds familiar," says Jon.

"Of course, there's no photograph," says Antonia.

Mentor shakes his head.

"You have a second phantom to add to your collection, Scott."

"Anything else?"

"The other information I have is so muddled and impossible to verify it's not worth passing on. Implausible executions, enemies gunned down by the dozen. No doubt the majority of those stories are false. But they've helped the Tambóvskaya spread terror among their rivals."

"They have their very own bogeyman."

"The Black Wolf isn't a bogeyman. She's the person they send to kill the bogeyman."

Jon runs his hand over his face and folds his arms. He's just a boy from Santutxu.

"Fucking great. Just what we need, Keanu Reeves's baby sister. Was it you who said mafiosi are boring?"

2

A WARNING

"One other thing," Mentor says before hanging up. **"I've decided to terminate** your involvement in the Lola Moreno case."

At this, Antonia, who was lost somewhere inside her own head, raises it in astonishment. Jon does, too, but in disbelief. The three of them know what comes next. The only question is which words Antonia will use to tell Mentor where to go.

"That's not going to happen."

Mentor says nothing. It looks like the screen has frozen—it hasn't, he has simply gone silent. So has Jon. He hasn't forgotten the story Mentor told him a few months ago, about the dog he had to put down because he couldn't control it. And he therefore finds it odd that someone who knows Scott so well would choose such an inappropriate way to inform her of a stupid decision.

A few awkward seconds follow. The type that are labeled: *The first to speak is the loser.*

"Inspector Gutiérrez . . . ," says Mentor.

"Don't look at me. You know how things stand."

"How things stand is that we have a situation with too many dangerous variables. You're on your own, with no forensic backup. The Madrid team is busy trying to help us find out what went on in England and Holland. The only reason I'm not recalling you to Madrid is for fear something might happen to you."

"We need to stay here. I understand that. But since we're here, why not make the most of it?"

"Scott. You've come up against this woman twice now. It's a miracle you both escaped so lightly. You're not a SWAT team. Your abilities have a very specific use."

"Oh, come on. This is going to be another Valencia," says Antonia.

"You and I have very different memories of Valencia," Mentor sighs.

"Possibly. But Jon and I are going to find Lola Moreno and get to the bottom of what's been going on here."

"We can't afford to lose you, Scott, you're too valuable."

"How much?"

"What do you mean?"

"How valuable am I, give me a figure."

"I don't think—"

"I'd really like to know. How much am I worth? Two women? Three women? Eight women, like the ones in the container?"

Jon remembers the smell. The putrefaction. The blood he had to wash off Antonia's body, and his own. The promise she made. A soft whisper from a tiny half-broken woman. A speck of dust in an indifferent universe. It barely ruffled the darkness.

And yet . . .

"I don't get to choose where you send me. Or what I do with this," she says, gently tapping her brow with her forefinger.

"That's unfair."

"You decide when we go in. All right, I decide when we pull out. And if you don't like it . . ."

She pauses.

"If you don't like it, you can go take a hike."

The last image they see is Mentor's contorted face, his eyes protruding like golf balls. It freezes for an instant before Antonia ends the call.

"How did I do?" she says, turning to her partner.

The inspector scratches his beard, pretending to reflect.

"I'll give you a ten for execution, a five for choice of insult, and a four for timing."

"That's an average of six point three." Antonia says, pouting.

"Let's make it seven. You get extra for the expression on Mentor's face."

"Not bad. Better than my college grades."

Jon stands up. He moves back to the window, thrusts his hands in his pockets. His whole body is sending out a signal even Antonia's broken receptor can pick up. It says: *Ask me what's wrong.*

"What's wrong?"

"I enjoyed watching you put Mentor in his place. But I think he's right."

Jon doesn't need a reflective surface to see the dismay on Antonia's face. Or eyes in the back of his head, like Father Carlos in catechism class. That guy definitely had superpowers.

"Not you too."

"I'm not saying we should pull out," replies Jon, turning to face her, hands raised in a conciliatory gesture. "Lola Moreno is still the key to catching Orlov. But now Xena, warrior princess, has shown up. And it looks like she wants the same thing as us."

"We already came up against her once. We're not her target."

Jon rubs his neck, which still bears traces of the encounter.

"We're not her target as long as we don't get in her way. You saw what happened to the cop who stood up."

"We've confronted killers before. What about Sandra Fajardo?"

"A sly fox, who used deception. We can deal with people like her. But this one—"

"She's only human. She escaped by the skin of her teeth."

"Rappelling from a rooftop. That's not our area of expertise, sweetheart."

Antonia folds her arms.

"What do we do, then? Lock ourselves in our rooms and watch TV?"

"Not exactly. But the police are already working on the ground. And they won't solve anything. Lola Moreno has money now, which means she can hide. All I'm asking is that we stop running around like crazy for a couple of days. Look for her here," Jon says, tapping the iPad. "And in here," he adds, pointing at his forehead.

Antonia stares at the minibar. Her objections are lining up on her tongue, but in the end, she keeps her mouth firmly closed.

"Okay. Leave me alone. I need to think."

RECORDING 11

EIGHT MONTHS EARLIER

CAPTAIN ROMERO: This wasn't the deal.

YURI VORONIN: The deal was—

DEPUTY INSPECTOR BELGRANO: Shut up, Voronin. We know you're a big nobody.

CAPTAIN ROMERO: It's true, isn't it, Señora Moreno?

LOLA MORENO: I've no idea what you're talking about.

CAPTAIN ROMERO: Of course not.

DEPUTY INSPECTOR BELGRANO: You keep feeding us bullshit.

YURI VORONIN: It's good information.

CAPTAIN ROMERO: It's not the information we want.

DEPUTY INSPECTOR BELGRANO: We asked for information on Orlov. You're giving us tip-offs about his rivals.

YURI VORONIN: And you're arresting them.

DEPUTY INSPECTOR BELGRANO: You're eliminating the competition.

YURI VORONIN: You wanted cocaine, you wanted heroin. You've got them. Weapons too. The Belarusians will be shifting some stuff next month.

CAPTAIN ROMERO: We want Orlov.

LOLA MORENO: No, Captain. You want headlines. And that's what I'm giving you. What we're giving you.

DEPUTY INSPECTOR BELGRANO: Ah, the old Freudian slip.

CAPTAIN ROMERO: That's not what—

LOLA MORENO: *(Talking over her.)* You've been there before. With

Operation Oligarkh, and Operation Red Marble. Even if you catch Orlov, it'll be ten years before he goes on trial.

(A seven-second pause.)

DEPUTY INSPECTOR BELGRANO: By which time he'll be dead, or too old for prison.

(A three-second pause.)

CAPTAIN ROMERO: What are you proposing, Señora Moreno?

LOLA MORENO: I'm proposing you turn up the heat. Keep making raids, keep making headlines. Stop going after the big fish and gorge yourselves on small fry.

CAPTAIN ROMERO: Assuming your proposal interests me: Who is the first of these small fry?

YURI VORONIN: There's a consignment leaving in a few days. Serbs. Drugs and money. Destination: Barcelona. An escort and a mail van.

3

A CRAVING

The instant Jon leaves, Antonia raids the minibar and eats all the candy.

The chocolate bars have been calling to her all morning with their siren voices and tempting colorful wrappers. She gorges herself on them and washes them down with a Coke Light. She burps and feels better, but also like a pig. The paradox of ultra-processed foods. A subject on which Antonia could write a treatise.

As soon as she exchanges her sugar and fat cravings for a feeling of guilt, a different sense of urgency takes over.

For a long time, she has been putting off having this conversation with herself. It's a specialty she has never excelled at.

Antonia has always functioned like a skyrocket. Once her fuse is lit, she is able to travel in only one direction, burning gunpowder until she explodes in a cloud of magnesium, antimony, and strontium salts. This also means not asking herself during the ascent what is going to happen at the end.

But now, even she can see she has a problem.

The electric tingling in her hands, chest, and face is pretty much constant. She finds it harder to control her breathing, and yet it's not impossible. But the tremor in her hands is getting worse. She can no longer even hold the iPad in her right hand without the letters dancing about and becoming an illegible blur.

She finds it increasingly difficult to hide this from other people. She knows she can't fool Jon. She has seen him purposefully avoid looking at her trembling hands. Or looking askance at her when he thinks she won't notice.

Three capsules, thinks Antonia. *Just three little capsules. That's all I need.*

That doesn't seem like a lot compared to the four she took the day before, simply to stay on top of her thoughts. She split open the capsules and poured the powder into a glass of milk, hoping the fat content would help the drug enter her bloodstream more evenly.

It worked, partially.

The three she plans to take today may not seem like a lot, except that she is only supposed to take one, at those moments when her brain is unable to cope with external stimuli, or the high levels of histamines her hypothalamus produces.

Anu ọhịa-azụ.

In Igbo, the language spoken by eighteen million Nigerians, this is the beast on your back that gobbles up your food and leaves you the scraps.

She takes off her T-shirt and bra, kneels down by the bathtub, and turns on the shower. Ten minutes of ice-cold water on her scalp leave her shivering and stiff, but she has managed to combat her craving. At least until she dries her hair.

Anu ọhịa-azụ.

Antonia knows that beast's face only too well. Just as she does those of the hundreds of monkeys inside her head, leaping from liana to liana, baring their fangs.

In real life, she has seen that beast only once. One Sunday morning at the Barcelona Zoo, taken there by her mother. Coarse dark hair, black face. Long thin arms, prehensile tail. It moved ghostlike among the dangling ropes of its enclosure. She saw something eerie in its blue eyes. Not malevolent but definitely not friendly either. The creature seemed to know more than was good for it.

Antonia burst into tears when she saw it.

"It's a spider monkey," her mother said. "They're fruit eaters. It won't hurt you."

When she saw Antonia wouldn't stop crying, Paula tried to lead her away from the cage. But the girl stood stock-still, holding the gaze of that wise phantom as it pummeled the glass with its thumbless hands as though trying to warn her of something.

That was the last outing Paula Garrido took with her daughter. A week later, she was confined to the hospital. A month later, the cancer defeated her.

The monster knew, thought Antonia.

Anụ ohịa-azụ.

Antonia doesn't want to give in to her anxiety so rapidly, but she needs a clear head. She takes three capsules from her bag and places them in the little metal box. In case of emergency.

There are only six left.

After that she will have to ask Jon. Explain what has been happening.

He won't take it well.

She slips the metal box into her pants pocket, and the bag containing the remaining six under the bed. She would rather confront the beast than hurt Jon. It's bound to happen, sooner or later. *But, like the words of the song in that film, the sun will come out tomorrow.*

What baloney.

All at once, Jon's words ring out in her head. What he said about the Black Wolf.

We aren't her target.

So, what is?

There is only one way to find out.

Antonia gets dressed, goes out into the hotel corridor. She walks past the elevators and takes the stairs, where she is unlikely to bump into Inspector Gutiérrez. Outside, she hails a cab and gives an address on Calle de Salvador Rueda. The place with a lurid purple façade.

On the way, she programs her iPad to send Jon two messages. Two messages that will arrive two hours apart.

He's going to hate me for this. But it's the only way.

The cab stops outside Tere's hair salon. Antonia pays the fare, climbs out, and crosses the street.

"Hey there! Mafiosi!"

She waves her arms at the second-floor balcony. At a couple of Slav gentlemen seated on plastic chairs sporting their SOBAFRESH T-shirts and tattooed arms. When they hear a crazy woman yelling, they poke their heads out, puzzled.

"I want to see Señor Orlov. Tell him I know where Lola Moreno is."

4

A PROBLEM

Jon Gutiérrez doesn't like room service.

Not that it isn't convenient. They bring you a pile of food on a huge tray. Lukewarm, so you don't burn your tongue. You know it's going to taste exactly the same as the last meal you ordered at a hotel belonging to the same chain a thousand kilometers away. Because nobody likes surprises. You can eat it in the comfort of your room. More often than not contemplating yourself in boxer shorts and socks in one of the many mirrors.

The opportunity for human contact is also to be welcomed. You open the door to a stranger, who invades your space with a big smile. They pretend not to see the rumpled sheets, the underwear strewn around. You listen as they list the dishes you have ordered. You swear on your mother's life you don't need anything else: you studied the menu for a good ten minutes before ordering. You promise to call them to come and collect the tray. Knowing full well that you will peer outside the door, look up and down the corridor like Inspector Clouseau, and slide the tray out onto the carpet when the coast is clear.

None of the above is what bothers Jon Gutiérrez about room service. *Those are all positives.*

What pisses Jon Gutiérrez off about room service is that it makes him feel even lonelier. The loneliness of the castaway, the waterfront at dawn, the evening star. The loneliness of a Sunday afternoon when it's only Thursday. Which no amount of TV will alleviate, or scrolling to refresh his messages on Grindr, or the loud sex in room 604. The woman coming discreetly. As discreetly as a bronze bell rolling down-stairs. Twice.

It's four in the afternoon, señora.

Jon's loneliness turns into a nap, rudely interrupted by a call from Mentor.

"Let me guess, you want us to do battle with an evil albino from Opus Dei."

As expected, Mentor completely ignores Jon's opening remark. Jon has decided he will put his theory to the test: next time he'll recite Athletic Bilbao's entire lineup.

"Are you alone?"

"Yes, I'm alone," Jon says, rubbing salt into his own wound.

"I need to talk to you about Scott. Have you noticed anything unusual about her recently?"

Jon thinks back over the past week.

In no particular order. And without being exhaustive.

Running from the scene of a crime, tossing bottles into the river Manzanares, becoming catatonic after pulling a dying woman from a container full of corpses, confronting a hired assassin in the dark, swearing not once but twice, ordering the hacking of a foreign power's database, intentionally drawing a sniper's fire, and refusing a dessert.

"Look, you'll have to be more specific."

Mentor lets out an exasperated snort. Like a dog being denied his meat scraps.

"I'm referring to her behavior. And her physical state."

Jon visualizes Antonia's trembling hand. Attempting to conceal itself beneath her jacket.

"Possibly."

"I need to know for sure, Inspector. I need more information."

"That makes two of us."

Jon hears the click of a lighter, the slow exhalation of a first puff.

"How's the vaping going? Does it work?"

"Listen, Inspector. We have a serious situation here. I appreciate you wanting to protect her, but I need to know."

"And I need you to tell me why the hell you're asking. Then I can decide how best to protect my colleague."

Mentor pauses for three puffs and two taps into an ashtray.

"All right. We've detected a problem in the secure refrigerated cabinet at Madrid headquarters."

"What kind of problem?"

"Missing capsules. Fifty red and ten blue."

Aha.

"I assume you have a list of people with access?"

"Yes, and it's very short. Just me."

"Then you definitely have a problem."

"*Now* will you help me?"

First rule of interrogation. Formulate your questions as affirmations.

"You think it was Scott."

"Scott could easily figure out the ten-digit password if she wanted to. She could also obtain a copy of the key itself. She could even get around the biometric tests, including my fingerprints. But to do all of that without being caught on camera is difficult, Inspector."

Jon scratches his head vigorously. This makes no sense.

"What would happen if I swallowed one of those red capsules?"

"You'd mostly suffer from side effects. Upset stomach, reddened skin. Possibly dizziness. It depends what you had eaten."

"But it wouldn't make me any smarter."

"The chemical compound is specifically designed for Scott's brain. It regulates her dopamine levels and helps her control exterior stimuli. The capsules aren't the instrument, Inspector, she is. In fact, we don't believe she needs them. The problem is what *she* believes."

"What do you mean?"

"One ingredient of the compound is designed to stimulate the release of presynaptic gamma-aminobutyric acid. And sustained use creates an increased demand in the organism."

"Meaning?"

"It's damned addictive."

Aha.

"Which is why she can take only one capsule at the crime scene, when she's programmed to receive a maximum of stimuli. A bigger dose would be extremely dangerous."

Second rule of interrogation. Repeat your questions over and over until you get an answer.

"And you think she might be behind the theft," Jon insists.

"Believe me, I hope she is. That would be serious, but manageable.

I'm far more worried it might have something to do with this attack on the Red Queen project. So tell me, have you noticed anything different about Scott recently?"

Well, except that she hasn't asked me for a single capsule, has noticeable withdrawal symptoms, and is even moodier than usual . . .

"No, nothing at all."

"All right," replies Mentor, his voice dripping despair. "Don't mention a word of this to Scott, do you hear me?"

"Of course, I won't say anything to her. Who do you think I am?" replies Jon, who has already slipped on his pants and is heading toward Antonia's room.

5

AN EQUATION

It's been a short journey.

Fifteen minutes or less. They haven't blindfolded her, or put a bag over her head. They did press a gun to her ribs, but only briefly. Long enough to leave a mark on her skin, and to show they meant business.

Antonia isn't reassured in the slightest by their failure to employ the techniques you see in movies. That's where amateurs get their ideas. Professionals don't care if you see where they are taking you, especially if the trip is one-way only.

The house is rather ugly. Not a monument to bad taste, like Voronin's. This place is simply tasteless. A semidetached structure, with white walls and red floor tiles. Identical to the hundreds all around it. No photographs or paintings on the walls. Functional furniture.

They take her to the kitchen.

Only salt grains and a few traces of oil on the countertop. A half-eaten leg of cured ham on a stand. Fingerprints on the shiny coffeepot. A lost olive pit by a chair leg. Antonia can tell from this the house has been inhabited. A lone plate sits in the sink full of water.

A single person, who doesn't use all the cupboard space, she deduces, observing the dust on some knobs, but none on those lower down.

"Good afternoon, Señora . . . I'm afraid I haven't had the pleasure," says a voice behind her.

Antonia wheels around. Orlov. Dark, thickset, a shock of white hair. Deep circles under his eyes, which he didn't have at the funeral. Burdened with pressures, perhaps. Drowning in worries. He has exchanged his expensive suit for cheap sportswear. Recently purchased, with the mark of an anti-theft tag still on the collar.

"My name is Antonia Scott," she says.

She doesn't hold out her hand.

Nor does he.

Instead, he gestures to the two *bojeviks*. One hefty bodyguard would have been enough to lean Antonia over the kitchen table, frisk her, and take her backpack.

She doesn't protest.

They pull out her things one by one. That is, the things she has left for them to find. Her house keys, a couple of AirPods. A charger, some cables. A portable battery. The iPad, sunglasses. Her Europol ID. A packet of Smint. Her cell phone.

She doesn't protest. Not even when they extract the little metal pillbox from her pocket.

"What are these?" asks one of the bodyguards.

"For my migraines," says Antonia.

The bodyguard shrugs and empties the contents into the sink.

"You won't be needing these anymore."

Antonia represses a howl.

The iPad and cell phone are quickly smashed on the countertop, close enough to Antonia for a few glass splinters to graze her cheek. Afterward, they go to join the capsules and the plate left to soak.

The two bodyguards bind Antonia's wrists to the arms of one of the kitchen chairs with tape. Finally, they carry the chair over to the round table. Antonia presses her lips together, praying they will turn her to face the clock, but it's behind her.

Damn.

That complicates things a lot.

Orlov walks over to the table and sits down in a chair facing her. An arrangement designed for important negotiations, to enable two people to look into each other's eyes, to read each other's intentions. Or for an interrogation under torture.

"I remember you. You were at the funeral, *da*?"

"Might it be easier if we spoke in your language, Señor Orlov?" Antonia proposes in Russian.

"My, my. There's no truth in legs," Orlov says, pleasantly surprised. A common expression, urging your guests to have a seat and feel at home.

"I'm afraid your men have already invited me to sit down," says Antonia, motioning to her wrists.

"A necessary precaution. As you know, I have enemies."

"I suppose it comes with the job."

Orlov gestures with a bony hand.

"You told my men you wanted to see me."

"I need to talk to you."

"We are talking. Where is Lola Moreno?"

"We'll come to that later. First, I'd like us to make a deal."

The old man smiles. It's a smile with teeth.

"What makes you think your opinion matters?"

"Don't they all?"

"That's the West's greatest failing. One day they decided they could hoodwink people by endlessly repeating that lie. They've been doing it for nearly a century. Spreading the lie until it reaches even the most useless members of society. And look how well that has turned out."

"So you think it's better to use force?"

"Force is mathematics, señora," says Orlov with a shrug. "Now, for instance. Watch."

He makes a gesture, and one of his thugs moves next to Antonia and slaps her. Not too hard, but enough to stain her lower lip with blood.

"I'm sure you're able to solve the equation I just gave you."

"It's pretty easy," says Antonia, running her tongue over her lip.

"Then answer my question. Where is Lola Moreno?"

"I don't know."

Orlov tilts his head, puzzled. His eyes narrow and seem about to disappear into the hollow furrows of his face.

Like a moray eel, thinks Antonia. *Retreating under his rock.*

"So why did you come here?"

"Because I want to make a deal with you."

"So let's make a deal," says Orlov.

He gestures again.

A second slap on Antonia's face. The impact makes her teeth rattle. Her right ear buzzes unpleasantly.

"This is no way to negotiate," says Antonia.

"Once again, señora, you overestimate the value of your opinion. Where is Lola Moreno?"

"I don't know."

Orlov tugs at his ear, nodding gently.

"All right. Let's start with the simplest thing. Are you a police officer?"

"Something like that."

One of the bodyguards takes Antonia's ID over to Orlov. The old man lays it down on the table.

"Europol. I've never seen one of these before."

"There aren't many of us. But we do our job."

"And what is your job?"

"To find Lola Moreno."

"It seems we have . . . What's the expression? Competing interests."

"Not necessarily. We can help one another."

Orlov props his elbows on the table and leans forward slightly.

"Explain how, policewoman."

"Your problem isn't with Lola Moreno. It was with her husband."

"Ah, Yuri. When he arrived in this country, he was a nobody."

Then Orlov uses an expression straight from Antonia's compendium of impossible words.

Juyem grushi okloachivat.

In Russian, to knock pears from a tree by hitting it with your dick.

"Does that mean a lazy bum?" says Antonia.

"Yes, forgive me. You speak my language very well, but maybe I'm asking too much."

"Don't worry. What I don't understand, I can deduce from the context," Antonia says, turning away to spit out some blood. It dribbles from the corner of her mouth.

"Smart lady. Gosha, bring a napkin."

One of the bodyguards passes Orlov a roll of paper towels. He tears off a piece and gets up to wipe away the blood.

We've already established that Aslan Orlov is an affable man.

Antonia isn't sure what offends her more, the touch of his slender milk-white fingers or the fact that he didn't tear the roll along the perforated line.

"Yuri was a bum. Then suddenly, he got smart. Too smart for his own good."

"You don't need Lola Moreno."

"She has to die."

Antonia smiles. It's time for her to play her trump card. This is why she came.

"The Black Wolf could have shot her yesterday. She had her in her sights. And yet she didn't."

Orlov looks at her with interest. With intent. There are weights and measures in the scrutiny he gives her.

"So that's why you came."

"I think I've made it clear," says Antonia, who has no idea what she is talking about.

"Now I see your game. You want Lola Moreno in exchange for the money. How much is that woman worth to you?"

"A life. I don't suppose that means much to you. I saw the result of your *equation* at the port in Málaga."

"It was you," Orlov says, opening his eyes and mouth very slowly, as if something had suddenly clicked into place. "And you also paid Ustyan a visit?"

"Guilty."

The Beast throws back his head and lets out a harsh, obnoxious guffaw. Like an inflated bladder bursting in the heat of a fire.

"That's ironic. Do you know where we are?"

"No."

"In Ustyan's house. It was the perfect place to have a chat with you, seeing it's empty. He died because of your meddling, of course. And now you've told me everything I need to know."

He rises to his feet, goes over to his hostage, and leans down until their noses almost touch.

If Antonia could smell, she would detect a whiff of ointment, moisturizer. Arthritis cream.

"I don't think you know where the money is. But just to be sure, I'm leaving you in the hands of my men. They take a while, but they always make people talk," he says before heading toward the door. "You know. Mathematics."

Antonia swallows—saliva mingled with blood—and prays her own calculations are correct.

6

A WAIT

As Inspector Gutiérrez covers the distance to Antonia's room, he does his best not to let his simmering rage boil over. His footsteps seem to say: *I'll give her an earful!*

His knuckles rap impatiently at her door.

Nothing.

At the far end of the corridor, a room service waitress is pulling a trolley. Jon shows her his badge and asks her to open the door to room 512.

"I can't help you, you need to ask in reception," says the woman.

Jon sighs grumpily. People nowadays have lost all respect for the police.

He leans back, raises his leg, and gives the door lock an almighty kick.

"You can't do that!"

"So call the cops."

With the second kick, he smashes the lock, ripping out part of the doorframe. Jon bursts into the room and starts to rummage through Antonia's things. It takes him less than sixty seconds to find the bag containing her stash of pills. He might not be so good at other things, but this . . . he's been doing this for years.

Just then a message pings from Antonia.

> Jon, this is a programmed message. If you get it, it means I have a problem. Wait in the car for my second message. When you get that, I strongly urge you to drive as if you were me.

* * *

Beneath it is a sticker of a duck wearing sunglasses.

It's hard to describe with polite vocabulary the sensations running though Jon's head. He was already in a bad mood, pulse racing, prepared for a fight. Or an argument. Antonia's message has turned the pressure up to the boiling point.

The expletives he utters on the way to their car do not bear repeating.

He gets into the Audi—parked fifty meters from the hotel—pulls off his jacket, and slams the door. Then he fastens his seat belt and turns the key in the ignition to activate the electrical system, but not the engine. He curses some more.

Outside, it's already dark.

A casual observer passing the car, the inside of which is completely soundproofed, would turn their head in amazement. It isn't every day you see a man yelling in silence, like a TV with the volume turned down, while attempting to tear the steering wheel out with his bare hands. The casual observer would instantly quicken their step, because the man in question is very big. Not that he's fat.

Letting off steam doesn't calm Jon in the slightest.

And what comes next, still less.

Waiting for a call, a text, a WhatsApp, or a message on Grindr is one of the miseries of modern life. We are so accustomed to immediacy, to the double check mark, the instant reply, that we have become like spoiled children.

Take a look at Inspector Gutiérrez. Clutching his cell phone, checking every few seconds to make sure he has full coverage. Clenching his fists, glancing about in case Antonia decides to appear around the corner as if by magic. The passenger seat, painfully empty.

Waiting renders him helpless, imprisons him in a strange limbo between relaxation and action. And because what he is waiting for doesn't arrive, he starts talking to himself. An occasional useless *come on, come on, come on*. In between each exhortation, the threat intensifies. What's happening to Antonia right now, while he waits, becomes the worst kind of threat. The vague sort, where the monster of doubt keeps changing shape, making it impossible to decide how to combat it. Every child who has ever lived and been left on their own knows this monster well. It inhabits the time between our cry for our mother—because the shadows have revealed a claw, a bloodthirsty snout—and the moment she appears. While we wait, our mother has died a thousand horrible deaths, leaving us at the mercy of the darkness.

Each moment Jon waits, each passing second, causes him to recoil further and further, until his anguish and fear become a single incandescent point. A black hole of violence and despair consuming everything.

Then the message.

Come and find me. Please Click here.
P.S. I hope I'm not dead.

Below is a sticker of a vicious dog baring its teeth.

Jon turns on the engine and floors the accelerator.

I hope they haven't killed you yet. Because I plan to do it myself.

7

A KITCHEN

Antonia has lost count of the slaps.

They are being careful. They know they mustn't hit her too hard. Antonia is half their size. If they overdo it, they'll break her neck, crack her skull, or worse.

So far, they have split one of her eyebrows and both lips.

It isn't working for them.

Still less for her.

One blow causes Antonia to lose consciousness. Only for a few seconds. The unpleasant buzz of a bell ringing inside her head brings her around with a start. She realizes it's an incoming call. Although she can't hear the conversation, she sees the bodyguards' reflections in the shiny coffeepot as they talk between themselves.

Her left eye is beginning to close as blood accumulates in the broken blood vessels and the swelling increases. The area has gone numb. She can feel pain in her nose, but above all in her teeth. Every time they hit her, she clenches them tight to avoid biting her tongue or the inside of her cheeks. It hasn't always been successful, and she has cuts in her mouth. Her jaw muscles are starting to ache. As is her neck, which she tenses each time, trying to cushion the blow.

After the tenth, this no longer seems easy.

After the twentieth, she wishes they would finish her off.

All in all, it isn't working for them. Antonia hasn't told them where the money is: the main reason being that she doesn't know. And now the caller has transmitted something. Something *important*. Antonia is fairly sure what that is. One of her monkeys is clamoring for attention, it wants to show her something, but a fresh blow makes it vanish.

"Where's the money?" she hears from far away.

"I'd like to know what time it is," Antonia murmurs in Spanish.

"What? What did you say?"

Or just turn me around.

Or stop hitting me.

One of her three wishes is granted, as the bodyguard who spoke suddenly turns her chair around. After contemplating the same corner of the kitchen, convinced a tile would be the last thing she saw, to see a different part of the world seems like a blessing. That is, until she notices the taller of the two men open one of the kitchen drawers and proceed to extract objects that pierce, slice, and chop.

So they weren't being careful. Until now they were simply talking to me, thinks Antonia.

The other man, the one Orlov called Gosha, chooses a stainless steel utensil. Antonia can't see what it is, because her head is spinning and her vision is blurred.

She can barely see the kitchen clock, which is only three meters away.

"Now will you talk?" says Gosha.

He shows her the object he has just picked up. It's a seafood cracker. Designed to crack open the chitinous exoskeleton of crustacean decapods. In other words, a lobster. Or Antonia's left pinkie, whose distal phalange it is currently crushing.

"Where's the money? Do you know? Does the fat cop know? Talk."

The searing pain in her finger causes Antonia to open her eyes with a start. She manages to focus on the countertop. The place where the ham bone was until a moment ago.

"Okay, okay. I'm going to tell you something," whispers Antonia.

Gosha releases the cracker and bends over, moving closer to his prisoner's mouth. The other man leans in too.

"What?"

"Welcome to Hell."

The taller man must sense something. Which is bad news for him, because when he turns, his face makes a perfect target for the edge of the ham bone—also known as the mace—to slam into his forehead.

Antonia makes an involuntary calculation. An equation measuring the impact of a five-kilo object striking a skull.

- The object is moving at fifty kilometers per hour.
- The contact area is approximately four hundred square millimeters.
- The human skull is some six millimeters thick, and its average rupture point is 150 newtons per square millimeter.
  Total force of impact:
  Eight tons.

Antonia works out the equation in the interval between the sound of the mafioso's skull fracturing and the noise he makes when he falls to the floor. Most probably dead.

"I'm not fat," says Jon, dropping the ham bone. "I'm filled with hate."

The other *bojevík* pulls a switchblade from his pocket, flicks it open, and hurls himself at Jon. The inspector takes a step back, then another, doing his best to dodge the thrusts, which slice through the air with a shrill hiss.

Only when Jon has succeeded in drawing the man far enough from Antonia—which was his intention—does he pull out his gun and point it at the thug's face. The man halts mid-thrust and drops the knife, seething.

"I want lawyer," he says.

These guys sure know their lines, thinks Jon.

"Let me ask you something. If I told you I wanted a lawyer when you were about to stick a knife in me, what would you have done?"

The mafioso shrugs, his coarse features breaking into a half smile. Those aren't the rules.

"I get it," says Jon. He moves closer and presses the gun to the man's forehead. "You're only interested in the law when it's on your side. I should blow your head off."

The other man's smile broadens until it becomes a repulsive smirk.

"You not have balls."

"And you not have teeth," replies Jon, sinking his fist into the man's face.

The *bojevík's* body sways like a puppet on an invisible string, until finally he crumples unconscious to the floor.

Taking advantage of the situation, Jon kicks him in the mouth, adding another €3,000 to his dentist's bill.

Then he turns to Antonia.

He doesn't look pleased.

8

A SNORT

"It's good to see you," Antonia says, giving him a gory smile.

Jon snorts with a disdain worthy of the Queen of England.

He doesn't say a word.

He limits himself to walking over to the sink, where he runs his knuckles under the cold water for a while. Then he washes his hands with Fairy liquid, because they're still greasy with ham fat. He notices with disgust the black rim that has formed round the cuff of his Egyptian-cotton shirt. He tries to rinse it off with water, which, of course, only makes it worse.

"What's left of your iPad and cell phone are in here. How the hell did you send me the locator signal?"

"Look inside the box of Smints."

Jon sees the box on the countertop. He opens it. Hidden among the candy is a GPS device, like the ones elderly folks with Alzheimer's hang around their necks. Fifty euros at any MediaMarkt store.

"Are you mad at me?"

Jon laughs softly as he rummages in the freezer.

"Whatever gives you that idea?"

"In the first place, you haven't untied me."

Jon can't find any ice in the freezer, but there is a bag of frozen peas—the next best thing to deal with bruising or swelling. He takes the bag over to Antonia and tosses it on the table.

"There you are."

Antonia waggles her fingers to draw his attention to the tape still strapping her wrists to the chair.

"You're on your own," replies Jon, sitting down in the chair previously occupied by Orlov.

Antonia pushes herself forward with her feet. The metal chair legs scrape on the tiles, creating a most unpleasant sound. When she is opposite the frozen peas, she leans forward until her face is centimeters from the longed-for cold.

"Would you mind?"

Jon reaches forward and prods the bag with his finger until Antonia can lay her head on it.

"I'm sorry," she says.

"I need information—"

"Please untie me."

"First, let's have a little chat."

"I said I'm sorry."

"I realize you understand nothing about human behavior," Jon says, managing to sound reasonably patient. "But try at least to understand that 'sorry' isn't a magic word we use to make our mistakes disappear."

Antonia remains silent. Jon doesn't know whether she is thinking, has fallen asleep, or has expired from her injuries. After a while she changes position slightly.

"Marcos was always telling me that."

"And what did you say?"

"That in that case, I didn't see the point."

The point.

She doesn't see the point.

"You move forward. You try not to repeat the same mistakes. You tell the truth."

"I didn't lie to you about this."

"No. Not about this."

Jon pulls her stash from his pocket. He empties the contents of the plastic bag onto the table. Then he empties the box of pills.

Antonia sits up straight and stares at them.

Jon knows that look. He has seen it in people with brown teeth and very little personal hygiene. Defeat, submission. The void they once leaped into that now seems bottomless. They no longer scream, or try to grab at anything.

He manages to tear his eyes away from her.

"You've been taking capsules behind my back."

She makes no attempt to justify or deny. Just keeps gazing at him.

"Why?"

"You know why. Because we haven't found her."

Sandra. Everything always goes back to that crazy woman. Ever since we met, I feel as if she and I have been playing the same game. One for which neither of us made up the rules.

"You stole the capsules from the cabinet in Madrid."

"No," says Antonia.

One of her eyes is half closed, the other is still fixed on him. She won't let it stray to the tiny red and blue cylinders strewn over the table. But she can't fool Jon. He knows she has counted them, that she knows exactly how many there are. How much they weigh, the shoe size of the technician who filled each capsule with the powder.

Maybe not that last one. He doesn't think Antonia is lying. There's only one way to find out.

"But you know who did."

Antonia smiles. His mistrust offends her.

"Aren't you going to tell me who gave them to you?"

"No."

She is telling the truth.

Which makes everything even more complicated.

"Mentor is totally paranoid right now."

"Tell me you haven't said anything to him."

"What do you think?"

She shakes her head, tilts it back, and then slowly exhales before looking at him again.

"You're right. I'm sorry. You never let me down."

"That's more like it," says Jon. He rises to his feet and steps over the dead mafioso. He finds a pair of scissors in the drawer on the counter-top and stoops over Antonia's chair. That was a proper apology.

"Is this because I took a deep breath before I said sorry?"

Jon pretends he hasn't heard and begins to cut through the tape.

She gives, then snatches it away.

"You look like shit."

Her face is swollen in several places. Her eye is the worst. Her T-shirt is spattered with blood.

"Bruises and superficial cuts. All I need are some painkillers and an ice pack," she says, rubbing her wrists.

"Good," says Jon. "Because this is done with."

With his huge paw, he sweeps the pills on the tabletop into his free hand and tosses them into the sink.

"What are you doing?" yells Antonia, jumping up and running after them.

Jon blocks her path.

"I did what was necessary. You're losing it, girl."

"I'm doing my job!"

"The container, Ustyan's office. Last night. And now coming here."

"Orlov would have refused to talk if you'd come with me."

"So did you manage to get anything out of him? Was it worth the beating, the deceit? The heart attack you nearly caused me?"

She lowers her eyes.

"Let me past."

Antonia grapples with Jon briefly, desperate to reach the sink where the capsules are slowly dissolving in the dirty dishwater. Until she realizes she would have more luck reducing a wall to rubble by blowing on it.

"You don't need them," says Jon.

Antonia is sobbing.

"You don't understand. You have no idea where it is I have to go."

Jon contemplates this speck of dust in an indifferent universe, and he wraps his arms around her, stifling any protest.

"No, I don't. But I'll be here when you get back."

WHAT THEY DID TO HER NEXT

"This woman is the most astonishing human being who has ever lived," says Nuno, tapping the piece of paper Mentor handed him with his horny yellow fingernail. "If you're failing to guide her toward her full potential, it's because you're teaching her to make diagnoses based on directed thought."

"Then tell me what I ought to be doing," says Mentor.

"You need to help her find her story," the doctor replies. "If she does that, she'll stop thinking about shooting, and simply kick the ball."

The room is black and filled with light. The walls and ceiling are covered in thick padding so that no sound can escape. When he talks over the loudspeaker, Mentor's voice seems to come from everywhere at once.

He has been waiting for this moment for weeks. The story. The narrative that will stop her from thinking.

That's the problem with consciousness. You don't instruct your liver to secrete bile, you don't order your kidneys to produce urine.

But you can control your lungs. You can think about breathing. And once you've taken control of your breathing, sometimes it's impossible to relinquish it. You're forced to think about breathing.

Mentor has reflected about all the metaphors he could employ to stop Antonia from thinking.

He believes he has found the right one.

"You can't tame a river, Antonia. You have to give in to the current, make its power your own."

"To control by giving up control? That makes no sense."

"Not everything makes sense, and it doesn't have to. Give in to the current, Antonia," says Mentor.

Antonia tries.

Antonia fails.

9

AN INSTANT

Antonia tries again.

She closes her eyes.

She immerses herself in the past hour. In the time spent talking with Orlov. She recaptures the details she gleaned from their exchange. His clothes, his watch, his shoes. His pauses, the inflections in his voice. She finds nothing, except what she already intuited. That the hunt for Lola Moreno relates to something much more complex than a mere settling of scores to save the Bratvá's honor. Orlov is urgently looking for something.

Something Lola stole from him.

The money he assumed Antonia knew about, until she made a mistake that showed him she was lying. But which mistake?

She continues searching. Sifting through her memory, the long minutes tied to that chair with blows raining down on her.

Snippets of information, nearly all of them useless. Details about the clothes the thugs wore. The chain around one of their necks, the big gold ring—the imprint of which lingers in the painful wound on her eyebrow. The cell phone. The call.

The call she couldn't hear.

And yet she could see the men's reflections in the shiny coffeepot on the counter. Gesticulating.

You saw it. You did see it, you can remember.

The monkeys are back.

They appear in front of her again. Screeching, clamoring for her attention. They encircle her.

She is alone in the kitchen now. In the scene she has re-created inside her head. Jon is no longer there. But the monkeys are. On top of the cupboards, on the surfaces, leaping about the floor, clasping all the clues they have found, waving them in front of her eyes.

Each of them thinks it is important, that it possesses the solution: they wave their fragment of truth, claiming it's the key to everything.

Antonia spins around in a circle, attempting to separate each element, to understand it, see how it will combine with the final result.

You can't tame a river, Antonia. You have to give in to the current, make its power your own.

"No."

I can't give up control.

You can't or you won't?

She closes her eyes.

She opens them again.

She is no longer in the kitchen.

She is seven years old.

She is on her mother's arm at the zoo. She asks for an ice cream. Her mother agrees to buy her one. While they are waiting at the stand, Antonia stops to look for the first time.

The marks on the back of her mother's hand from the hospital drip. The glass of water into which she has just dissolved the sachet of antibiotics.

The extreme pallor of her skin. Her hair, no longer her own, but a wig. The yellowish whites of her eyes. The weak, dry cough from lungs that have lost the battle.

"Let's go and see the monkeys, darling," her mother says, defeat etched on the corners of her mouth.

The signs were there, right in front of her.

She knew. Back then she knew.

Now she understands why she burst into tears outside the monkey house. Because she was suddenly afraid of that animal that seemed to be keeping a secret. When she was the one who had been concealing it right from the start. The secret of what she was capable of.

I've always known how.

But I was too afraid of myself.

* * *

She closes her eyes.

She opens them again.

She is back in the kitchen.

The two thugs rise from the floor, guided by an invisible force making time travel backward.

It sits Antonia in the chair again, puts back the tape on her wrists, reduces the swelling on her wounds.

Once more she sees the men's reflections in the coffeepot.

She sees them exchange words.

She reads their lips. She doesn't catch everything; she is dizzy from the blows and her vision is blurred.

But she catches one sentence.

She opens her eyes.

Jon still has her in a bear hug.

"I think I know where Lola Moreno is," she says, wriggling free.

Jon frowns, scratches his head in frustration. Today has been a roller coaster of emotions. The sensible thing would be to give up while they are even.

"Let's go to the car. But first we'll stop at a pharmacy," he says, signaling the wreck that is her face.

Antonia nods gratefully and walks toward the kitchen door. To do this, she has to navigate the two *bojevíks*. As she steps over the first man Jon hit, a strange conviction strikes her, which she can only express as a question.

"Do you love me?"

Jon gives a weary smile.

"Ah, angel. I love you so much I haven't strangled you yet."

KOT

The runt of the litter.

His brothers and sisters are the first to feed, to find the warmest spot to sleep. The shepherd enters the hut, sees the little puppy, and walks past him. After many years and many litters, he understands the workings of nature. Some are bound to die. This time, the bitch has produced eight. With any luck, by spring, three will be left.

The winters are harsh in Goris, in the Armenian province of Syunik. The temperature drops to minus twelve degrees Celsius, and never rises above three. The village is beautiful, rugged, belonging to another century. Of course, the virus of civilization has infected even this remote area, so they have cars and cell phones. And yet a different race of people inhabits the houses clustered at the foot of the Zanzegur mountains, seeking shelter from the wind. People who possess an ancestral, atavistic fatalism. Born between an empty sky and an open tomb, they remain impassive when the one turns a deaf ear to them, and the other claims them.

This is why the shepherd regards the puppy with indifference. Somebody else in his situation would have brought a dish of milk to the hut, wrapped him in a blanket. The shepherd walks by and lets nature do its work.

He has enough worries of his own. It's hard work tending the sheep in winter. Crammed together in their pen, they need hay and water, and produce huge quantities of droppings that have to be cleaned out. With only his youngest son to help him—his eldest died in the war seventeen years earlier—the shepherd only manages to collapse, exhausted, onto his bed after he has carried out all his tasks.

When spring arrives and the snows melt, the world becomes a gentler place. The flock goes out to forage on the grass at the foot of the hills, and the shepherd only has to drive them from one place to another. Mounted on his Percheron, stick in hand, a full bag of food on his back, the shepherd feels he has regained his strength and dignity. The sun restores power to his weary limbs, and once again his life becomes bearable.

The dogs will help, when the time comes.

The Caucasian shepherd dog is an ancient breed. The Soviets claim to have created it after the Great War, crossing mastiffs from the mountains of North Ossetia with those from Armenia and Azerbaijan. The shepherd grimaces whenever he hears that lie, which is often. He is sixty-five, and grew up with the nagazi, which is their true name, as did his father and grandfather before him. How typical of the Russians to want to claim everything they see.

Land, women. Children.

Nagazi are powerful, and can grow as big as a man, sometimes bigger. Their thick brown coat has patches of black, and their legs are long and sturdy. Some weigh as much as ninety kilos. The shepherd recalls one huge male, the grandfather of this litter, who weighed a hundred. They are intelligent, fearless, and have a strong territorial instinct, all of which makes them ideal protectors of livestock as well as people. In that role, they excel at one thing in particular.

Killing wolves.

The puppy survived the winter.

One chilly dawn in early spring, the shepherd discovered him outside the shed with a dead pigeon between his front paws. A powdery coating of snow covered his snout. Mixed with the pigeon's blood, it sparkled in the morning sun like dusty rubies.

The shepherd gazed at the puppy in astonishment. By then, the runt must have been twelve weeks old. Yet five weeks earlier, the shepherd had assumed he was dead, killed and eaten by his mother, who knew that not all her pups would thrive, and simply hastened the process.

"Isn't he the runt?" asked the shepherd's son.

His father nodded.

"I don't know what to do with him. We already have too many."

Four of the pups had survived. Five including this one. A particularly hardy litter. And to feed four dogs weighing ninety kilos is difficult enough. They can eat thirty sheep a year between them, as well as chickens, vegetables, and fruit. You don't give dog food to nagazi when they can eat what grows and reproduces on water and grass. Not if you want your flock to survive. Seven years ago, a pack of wolves got into his neighbor's enclosure. In one night, they killed 120 sheep.

The memory of it still makes him shiver.

But they cannot afford to keep the pup.

"I'll take it down to the village. Nikol will buy it."

The shepherd frowns with displeasure. Such an animal should be free. Not bought and sold. It isn't stupid and servile the way sheep are.

He refrains from stroking the animal with his gnarled, weathered hand. He is not a sentimental man. And yet he knows that if he does, he won't let his son take the dog.

And God knows they need the money.

"Very well."

"What's his name?" asked Nikol, looking at the deceptively calm bundle of fur. Nikol owns a supermarket and an animal feed store, and is familiar with the temperament of the nagazi.

"I don't know. Kot."

"*Kot*. Puppy. Okay," he says, holding out a fistful of notes.

Nikol looked after the dog for six days, the length of time it took for the dog trainer from Volgograd to reply to his advertisement. On the seventh day, Kot was shipped out of Yerevan on a cargo plane bound for Russia. There he spent three weeks at the dog trainer's ranch. The man was in the business of finding and training pedigree mastiffs to sell to wealthy owners. The trainer knew his merchandise well. Proud, intelligent dogs. Not born simply to be pets, to obey commands. They were used to patrol the perimeters of Russian prisons, and if a convict tried to escape, the guards would release the dogs to do their job. Lurid photographs of the results were on permanent display along the prison corridors.

He had to tame them without breaking their spirit. An ovcharka— the trainer used the Soviet name with pride, believing they were a Russian breed—would rather be killed than give in.

When the dog was ready, the trainer put a photograph on his website, advertising a perfect example of an ovcharka, born among the snow-covered peaks. He would fetch €4,000, plus transport costs, a hundred times what Nikol gave the shepherd's son.

On the other side of the world, a drunken young Yuri Voronin beckoned to his wife. He sat her on his lap at the computer.

"Look, honey. I think I've found the perfect addition to our new home."

LOLA

There was once a little girl who went to rescue her dog. She managed to free him, and they escaped to a place where the evil men would never find her.

Lola knows her nightmare is almost at an end. Jack is about to escape from the ogre's lair by climbing down the beanstalk.

The past few hours have been awful. She was able to run away on foot. The police mounted a search operation, ran her picture on the news, but they mainly focused on what she was wearing. Lola was able to do a lot with the money she had. First, she went into a Chinese supermarket. She threw the hoodie in the trash. Now, dressed in a drab raincoat and baseball cap, a backpack slung over her shoulder, she looked nothing like the photo the police made public.

She took a cab to Estepona. She had no difficulty finding an apartment hotel that didn't insist on seeing her ID. *Which, of course, she had left at home, and she had an important job interview the next day in Estepona. If they agreed to let her stay, she would pay twice the going rate for a couple of days.* There was an all-night pharmacy nearby that stocked her precious insulin. Lola turned around and pulled a banknote out of her backpack. Her hand trembled as she deposited it in the metal security tray, fearing the pharmacist might recognize her at any moment. The pharmacist's eyes lingered on her slightly longer than necessary, but in the end, he placed the insulin along with her change into the tray and snapped it shut.

Less than two hours after she had fired into the air on the corner of

Avenida de Ramón y Cajal, Lola was sobbing in the tiny shower cubicle in her room, unable to stop quaking from fear and trepidation.

That night she barely slept, despite jamming the table against the door. The slightest noise made her jump. She imagined they had found her and were outside the room. Her exhaustion got the better of her finally, and she managed to drop off when the sun was already filtering through the shutters. She slept well into the morning.

She got up, injected her insulin, and had breakfast at a café. Then she went to a Mango store, where she bought some comfortable clothes, sunglasses, jeans, and sneakers. Despite turning her face to the wall as she walked down the street, despite every passerby seeming to eye her with suspicion, and keeping her eye trained on the entrance the entire time she was in the store, nobody approached her and nobody recognized her.

After all the events of the previous few days, life went on in a disconcertingly normal way. Laden with shopping bags, Lola stopped to have lunch at a restaurant on Avenida de España. She momentarily forgot about her situation as she rummaged in her new bag (containing only a few banknotes) for her cell phone to call and see how Yuri was getting on.

In a flash, life brought her back to reality with the subtlety of an avalanche.

She wept into her main course.

She was still on the run from the police. She had no ID, and no means of getting one. Nor did she have friends she could turn to, or relatives who weren't being watched.

I could run away, take a bus to Madrid or Valencia, lose myself in the city's streets, find a job, disappear.

No.

I'm not going anywhere without my dog.

Returning to Marbella was extremely risky, but Lola had regained her strength and self-belief. Besides, she would only be there for an hour.

One more hour, and this will be all over.

What a horrible place, thinks Lola as she walks around the perimeter fence.

The dog pound is on the outskirts of the city, at the end of a narrow, single-track road. Dog pounds have something in common with funeral homes, old people's homes, and cemeteries: we put them in places where we are least likely to have to see them. Because nobody wants to know what really goes on behind those tall fences, although we suspect they conceal a reality we have no wish to confront.

Time, measured in money, is the most efficient and dangerous drug in existence. We dispense it in a selfish, miserly fashion, renouncing any shred of sincerity. We use time to justify the selfishness that separates us from the truth, from the devastation we cause that eats away at people, and ultimately at ourselves. *We don't have time*, we tell ourselves. And so dogs continue to be crammed into cages and old people crane their scrawny necks toward the door each time it opens.

There is no time for the truth.

Time is also running out for Kot.

As a potentially dangerous dog—and few could be deadlier—the law says he must be put down unless he is adopted within ten days.

Before returning to Marbella, Lola bought wire cutters at a hardware store in Plaza de las Delicias, Estepona. Also some work gloves to be able to pull back the wire fence.

She selects an area at the back of the lot and goes to work.

It takes her less than six minutes to open a hole measuring approximately eighty centimeters in diameter—big enough for her and the dog to make a quick exit: she doesn't want to get snagged on the wire. She throws the section of fence aside and enters the pound.

There are no guards or other personnel in the dog pound at night. Along the outside of a low dilapidated building are two rows of cages. It's a chamber of horrors. Lola averts her gaze when she sees all those dogs whose owners one day decided they no longer had room in their life for that Christmas present, their child's whim. The cages are filthy, and the dogs' spirits crushed. The pound is privately owned, with predictable consequences.

Many of the animals don't even stir when Lola approaches. A few growl apathetically. One lets out a hopeful bark that falters the moment Lola walks past.

Another captive struggles to its feet when it hears her footsteps on the concrete.

Lola reaches Kot's cage and opens it at once. There is no padlock, only a long steel bolt.

The dog doesn't move. Even amid the gloom—the only light in the pound comes from a line of streetlamps on one side and the highway farther off—the animal is impressive. He is as tall as a dining table, as wide as a coffee table. The fur on his neck is thick and dark, and he has a black mask round his eyes and muzzle. All Lola can make out in the semidarkness is the gleam of his coffee-colored eyes, and his soft pink tongue gently panting.

Lola calls his name.

"Kot."

It's like a kiss; the *o* brings your lips together, rolls the consonants, the tongue emerging with *k* and the *t*.

"*Ko mne*," she orders, crouching to greet him. "Come here."

She loves the way he only obeys commands in Russian.

The dog goes to her immediately and licks her face greedily. He may be a mass of muscle and bone capable of ripping a person's head off in a few seconds, but love is the only emotion he feels for his mistress.

"Look at you, silly dog," she says, caressing his head and neck. "You're filthy. They've taken your collar off. And you've lost weight."

Kot doesn't resent her having abandoned him. But now she is there, the other dogs are making him nervous. He smacks her with his paw, the size and weight of a frying pan. He only means to warn her, but even so, he manages to hurt her leg. Living with Kot was always like that. Legs covered in scratches and bruises.

"That's enough. *Molodets*. Good boy."

She heads toward the hole in the fence, the dog at her heel.

"*Gulyat*. Out."

Kot slips through and sniffs the air briefly. Lola follows behind him.

At the far end of the lot, she can see Zenya's Ford Fiesta parked under a streetlamp. Zenya is waiting for her at the wheel. She flashes her high beams.

Luckily, it's finally over, Lola thinks. She can't believe how easy it has all been.

And with reason. Something makes her turn around as she grasps the car door handle.

Kot's body is stiff, ready to pounce. He puffs out his chest. A low, menacing growl rises from his throat.

"Where you go, Lola?" says a voice in the darkness.

Lola feels a steel ball in the pit of her stomach. She knows that voice. That false amiability.

Kiril Rebo steps forward into the lamplight with his wispy blond hair, his wiry body, all muscle, covered in pale flesh.

Brandishing a smile, his empty sharklike eyes, and a gun.

Of those three things, the weapon isn't what terrifies Lola the most.

"Why?" Lola says, looking at Zenya.

"They threatened to kill my sister if I didn't give you up, señora. She's still alive, but no one cares if you suddenly disappear."

Lola understands. Zenya did what she had to do. Just like her. And everybody else.

"I'm very sorry."

Lola smiles at her ruefully. In the past, only days ago, she would no doubt have insulted, threatened, or cursed Zenya. Now Lola doesn't even know if she is that person, the woman she once was. Or if she will ever go back to being her. She feels so tired. Of everything. Of everyone.

"It's okay."

Kot growls more loudly when a second thug positions himself next to Rebo. He is also carrying a gun, and is aiming it straight at the dog. His hand is unsteady, his eyes glazed. He has snorted at least a gram.

"Better you control your dog," says Rebo, pointing at Kot.

"I only have to give the command," says Lola.

"We only have to shoot, *da?*"

Lola grits her teeth, suppressing the syllable that would launch Kot at those sons of bitches' throats. He would kill one of them, even if they put a few bullets in him. It would take a lot more than a gun to stop him once he was committed to defending his owner.

But even if he kills one of them, the other will still be standing.

And she isn't going to let them kill her dog for nothing.

"Let's do a deal. The dog goes with her, and I go with you. *Khorosho?*"

Rebo frowns, considering her proposal. Shooting the dog isn't a good idea. They have already drawn too much attention to the organization these past few days.

"Okay."

Lola opens the car door and orders Kot to get in. The dog looks at her warily, but eventually obeys.

Lola leans toward Zenya and discreetly pulls an envelope from her jacket.

"Take him to the place I told you about," she says, slipping her the envelope. You'll be safe there. I'll join you later."

Zenya surreptitiously looks inside the envelope. It contains more than €5,000. Enough to pay for her sister's operation, and for her to disappear for a few days.

"They won't let you go," she says, repressing a sob.

"I'll be fine."

Zenya starts the car and drives out of the lot. Taking Lola Moreno's hopes with her.

Lola turns slowly to face Kiril Rebo.

"So, you found me."

10

FRIENDS

"You surprise me," says Rebo. "You not just Voronin's crazy bitch. Not just decorative, *da*?"

Lola stays silent. Professional recognition isn't among her priorities right now. Besides, she has been hiding in plain sight for too long to let her guard down the moment a psychopath with a gun pays her a compliment.

"You say nothing. Okay. You talk soon."

Lola feels sick. Freedom was within her reach and she squandered it because of a stupid mistake. She is so angry with herself. Afraid as well, but she won't let that show.

"Why not save us all a lot of bother and kill me now?"

Rebo is smiling again.

It's the most repellent smile in the history of smiles.

A smile that freezes on his face when a car's headlights come into view on the far side of the lot.

"Who are they?" asks the other *bojevík*.

Rebo grabs Lola's arm and pulls her toward him.

"Friends of yours?" he says, thrusting the gun against her belly. "You call them?"

The pressure of the steel barrel makes Lola gasp, sending a wave of electricity and panic from belly to throat. Her instinct—a tingling sensation in her hands and fingertips—is to push the gun away from the life growing inside her.

Terrified, all she can do is shake her head.

Rebo considers making a dash for his car, but he parked far away so as to sneak up on Lola in the dark. The headlights are looming closer. Two more beams are following a few meters behind.

Behind them, a third set appear.

The first two are a police patrol car and a black Audi. Behind them, another patrol car. The three vehicles screech to a halt, tires skidding on the gravel as they surround them. Several armed officers pile out and take cover behind their open doors.

"Police! Drop your weapons!"

More cars approach, sirens wailing.

Furious, Rebo glances around him. He still has hold of Lola's arm, and the gun pressed into her side. The car beams have trapped them in a circle of light, their shadows lengthening gigantically across the ground.

The other *bojevík* is pure nerves. Perspiring freely, his breathing ragged, heart in his mouth. The cocaine has raised his aggressivity, paranoia, and fearlessness to dangerous levels. He points his gun at the shadowy figures he guesses at behind the wall of light the cars have created. Shouts and confusion follow. Half a dozen throats making a jumble of noises.

The wired *bojevík* waves his gun and steps toward one of the patrol cars.

Somebody fires a shot.

The bullet hits him in the back. As he wheels around, a second shot penetrates the side of his neck, ripping out the trachea. For a split second, a cloud of blood and cartilage drifts through the headlights, before it disperses and falls.

The *bojevík* is dead before he touches the ground. But his body is unaware of this. It continues to twitch convulsively, scraping his face on the gravel for a few grotesque seconds.

"I want lawyer," says Kiril Rebo, letting go of Lola and dropping his gun on the ground.

"Hey . . . Where do you guys learn this stuff? Do they send you on courses, or what?" Jon's voice echoes behind the headlights.

ASLAN

First and foremost, Aslan is a man who doesn't allow himself to be ruled by his emotions.

When he learned of Voronin's betrayal, he thought it over for several days before taking action.

When he had to stand before the Bratva and his associates at Voronin's funeral, he weighed every word he was going to say to them, contemplated every inflection of his voice, every pause, even his gestures. He rehearsed in front of the bathroom mirror, placing his hands on the edge of the basin as though they were resting on the Bible of the Orthodox Church itself.

And when he had to answer to the *pakhan*—with the secret hope of discovering what the Black Wolf was up to—he sat for a long while over the remains of his fried eggs on toast before deciding.

But now it's different. Not only has he lost all hope of recovering the money, as he was ordered, but Kiril Rebo has also been captured.

Aslan hasn't felt unconditional affection for anyone in years. He has heard himself say on occasion that a friend is someone you haven't yet killed. But that was just for show, he never quite believed it, although he realized he had to live by the principles to which he paid lip service. They preceded him like a shield, and yet they exacted a price. The secret of a contented old age is nothing more than an honorable pact with loneliness, especially for a mafioso.

But if there is anybody with whom Aslan does enjoy a degree of friendship, a healthy, genuine comradeship, that person is Kiril. He has forgiven him all his transgressions and excesses—he accepts them as quirks of his character. Orlov has always known he himself was amoral. And that Kiril was plain evil. As a younger man, Aslan used to laugh contemptuously at the out-and-out villains so beloved of Soviet cinema. The sort that cackle dementedly as they abduct virginal maidens, preparing the way for the entrance of the proletarian hero.

Then he met Kiril Rebo.

When, at a certain age, standing on the threshold with one foot already in the grave, you can't help but look back at the past. Orlov, who has always done what necessity dictated, and what his instinct permitted, has killed a dozen people with his own hands. He never derived any particular pleasure from it. For him, it was a means to an end. Which was to dance on his enemy's grave. To go on dancing.

"Are we cold-blooded?" he asked Kiril one day, in front of a bottle of vodka. Lying dead on the floor was the eleven-year-old son of one of his rivals.

"We have good taste," was Kiril's enigmatic reply.

Orlov understood this later on, when they arrived in Spain. Good taste isn't about what clothes you wear or what furniture you have in your house. The tsars' palaces were laden with jewels and possessions that interior design magazines today would regard with horror.

Good taste isn't fashion. It's harmony. And the best way to achieve harmony is by killing.

This is why Orlov feels affection for Kiril Rebo. Because he is a free artist in his own right, someone who has decided to love what he does, passionately.

Even to be a mafioso you need talent, thinks Aslan. *And there is no talent without passion.*

Orlov is debating with himself. He is restless, unable to get comfortable in his favorite armchair. The terrace at his villa in La Zagaleta juts out over the hill. On clear days, he can see Gibraltar and the coast of Africa. Half a kilometer above him is Putin's villa in Spain. Orlov has never met the man, nor would he know what to say to him. Perhaps he would whisper a timid thanks.

Night has fallen, and the view is limited to a line of trees that reveal a pale moon and the murmur of a breeze in their branches. Nothing to see, nowhere to go.

Only a decision to make.

There is calculation in it. Consequences and repercussions. A betrayal. And perhaps the only way for him to carry on. To go on dancing. At seventy, with a limp and feeling his age, yet reluctant to leave the party. Because beyond the threshold there is only cold, howls, and razor-sharp teeth in the darkness.

Aslan is a man who doesn't allow himself to be ruled by his emotions, and so he is able to pick up his cell phone and dial a number he never expected to use again.

The person at the other end picks up on the first ring.

They were expecting his call.

"We need to deal with the problem," says Orlov.

"No matter what?"

"No matter what."

He hangs up and makes another call. He needs to arrange things in case the first plan fails. And he can't turn to anyone else, because there is no one else.

This isn't how he envisioned old age. He thought that as he grew older, he would transcend the body's desires and sufferings. But instead, he has seen it drag him further down, into its inner workings. Its brutal, vengeful, harsh, and increasingly rusty inner workings.

He rises to his feet.

11

ANOTHER BAG OF ICE

In the end, everything happened very quickly.

Jon and Antonia are in the car on their way back to Madrid, the same way they came. At night, watching the lines on the highway chase one another beneath the hood of the Audi. With an odd feeling of unreality. Shoulders tense, legs too light. Like soldiers who turn from the mud and the bullets and run once more across dry ground.

As if things couldn't be this easy.

"Things can't be this easy," Jon says to Antonia.

"We've done our bit." Antonia is speaking through half her mouth. Which is only half a metaphor. She is clutching a bag of ice (a different one) to the other half.

They bought the first bag on the way to the dog pound. While Jon was paying at the gas station, Antonia called Captain Romero. Any tension between the two women evaporated when Antonia informed her, in a serious, professional way, with no trace of any sly vindictiveness, of where Lola Moreno was going to be within the next few minutes. Captain Romero thanked her politely for taking the trouble, asked her for a meeting point, and gave her specific instructions.

At any rate, this is how Antonia described their conversation to Inspector Gutiérrez.

"What was her parting shot? Word for word, please?" asked Jon, who is familiar with Antonia's habit of skimming.

"'Don't fuck this up.'"

"I see. And where is the meeting point?"

* * *

The meeting point was a service road close to the dog pound. A slope gave them a slight visual advantage, so that when Lola left the enclosure with the dog, it was easy for them to approach from both flanks. During the time they took to reach the parking lot, the operation nearly derailed when the suspect was about to climb into a Ford Fiesta. But it ended up driving off without her.

The surprise, as they converged on their target, was the appearance of the two Russian thugs. Arresting an armed suspect was difficult enough, but now they were facing a hostage situation. They had seven weapons trained on the Russians, who only had two. When things kicked off and everyone started yelling at the same time, Antonia knew there was no way of avoiding bloodshed.

"Sixteen dead," Captain Romero commented once Kiril Rebo and Lola Moreno were handcuffed and placed in the back of a patrol car.

"Yes. Well, now, about that . . . ," Jon began, rubbing his neck and staring at the tips of his shoes.

And so they explained to the captain how they had found out about Lola Moreno's whereabouts. And that the body count had already gone up to seventeen.

A very tense, drawn-out, and uncomfortable conversation followed.

"You'll have to testify before the examining magistrate. They'll be in touch. In the meantime, I'll be glad to see the back of you," Romero said, by way of thanks.

Jon went to the hotel to pick up their luggage. Antonia stayed at the scene until a van with two officers from the judicial police arrived. By then, Jon was back. The police had driven from Málaga and were to transport the prisoners to Madrid.

"They asked for the transfer. They don't consider this a safe enough environment in which to take their statements," Belgrano told Jon, who waylaid him as he walked past.

The two judicial police officers, both in civilian clothes, handcuffed the prisoners to the metal bars screwed to the sides of the blue-and-white Citroën. One on either side. The officers slid the door shut and climbed into the front.

Jon and Antonia also headed off. They overtook the van at the first traffic circle, and that was that.

* * *

Jon is in no hurry, he hasn't exceeded the speed limit once. He is playing Joaquín Sabina's *19 Days and 500 Nights* on Spotify. The speakers in the Audi blast out songs about icefish, bad company that is the best, and platinum blondes.

They barely say a word except to exchange candy and other junk food they bought at a gas station (their second stop, as they had lots of time). Neither feels satisfied. How could they? And yet this is the job they signed up for. To give assistance from the sidelines, knowing they would receive zero reward and zero satisfaction. And, of course, knowing that if they hadn't been there, things would have turned out very differently.

They call Mentor briefly to update him.

"Good work. I'd rather you didn't return to your respective homes quite yet," he says once they have finished. There's no joy in his voice. "Tomorrow morning we'll talk about what's going on. Find a hotel and get as much rest as you can."

He hangs up.

Exhausted, Antonia falls asleep in her seat.

Jon lowers the volume on the music.

LOLA

There was once a little girl who was captured by monsters that bundled her into *a black carriage and took her to a sinister castle.*

Lola tries to stretch, to find a comfortable position. But she can't, because there isn't one. Her right wrist is cuffed awkwardly to the metal bar attached to the bodywork. The four seats in the rear of the van are arranged two on each side, facing one another. Kiril Rebo is sitting opposite her, not in the seat across from her, but in the other one.

There are no windows, or any music. They can't sleep. Only look at each other.

That is what Kiril does. He stares straight at her.

There is something in those dead blue eyes of his that could steal your life from you. In tiny morsels.

They bite. Those eyes bite, thinks Lola.

She closes hers, and tries to think what to do.

She doesn't have many options. The police will interrogate her, demand she tell them everything she knows about Orlov's organization. About how Yuri managed all the Tambóvskaya's money-laundering operations in Spain.

I didn't know much, Officer. Only what I overheard from the kitchen.

Snippets of conversation she picked up in the living room at home, while she was serving smoked eel blini and bowls of kissel, or wiping down the kitchen surfaces.

They nearly always spoke in Russian. I only know a few words, like "hello," and "Can I have the bill, please."

The companies? All in Yuri's name, as far as I know.

Our house? Our cars?

Ruben Ustyan? Never heard of him.

Lola breaks off her rehearsal. There could be photos, from some party or another. What she wouldn't give to be able to wipe her Instagram account right now! Not that it makes any difference, as they probably already have all the photos.

Oh yeah, the little guy. Yeah, I think he came to our house once. No, we weren't introduced, or if we were, I don't recall.

She can wriggle out of anything using that combination: 412 "I don't know," 83 "I don't remember," 58 "I've never met him," and 7 "Is that a fact?"

Lola has the same color blood in her veins as everyone else, but she has an advantage. She remembers seeing that horrible black-and-white movie about Jews in a concentration camp. When the bad guy asks a group of prisoners standing in a line who stole the chicken, nobody replies. So the bad guy shoots one of them, who falls dead on the ground. Then a young boy steps forward. The bad guy asks him if he stole the chicken. No. Then you know who did? And the boy points at the dead man on the ground. Come on, you've gotta hand it to the kid.

Lola has her own dead body to finger.

There is no paper trail. Lola's name doesn't appear anywhere. Her father was a good teacher. He was a loser, but he knew more about accounting than anybody. And she misses him dreadfully. All those evenings they spent together in his last years, when he explained the tricks of the trade to her, the legal loopholes. How to disappear by creating one screen after another, until you became invisible.

Her situation isn't great. But it could be a lot worse.

She just needs to hold out. Or, if things go badly, to make a deal in exchange for the information she has. Even if that's a lousy solution.

Also she needs money to pay a good lawyer, because they could easily put the heat on her for what happened in the store. But where can she get the money from?

She can't ask her mother. That's another thing: What will become of her now? Of them both.

What will happen later? *Will I end up being like her?* she thinks, fondling her belly. An obedient parasite. Her life marked out by a deathly calm, the vague yet persistent stench of decay. Sticking to the same script every time they speak on the phone. When her mother runs out of gossip, Lola senses the Significant Pause that precedes the Inevitable Question. *Don't you think you should find something better?* Like two actresses destined to repeat the same tired scene each time they meet.

That didn't stop her taking the money, did it? Lola's thoughts become increasingly bitter and confused as tiredness overwhelms her.

She is falling asleep. Despite everything. Despite her thwarted plans, her mistakes, despite traveling toward an unknown future with a psychopath's eyes drilling into her, she falls asleep.

And then it happens.

12

A TAMIL WORD

At some point a few hours later, Antonia emerges from a deep slumber. And from her snoring—she snores like a dragon. The familiar glow of the uniquely designed streetlamps on Avenida del Manzanares slowly rouses her. She blinks and stirs, drifting in and out of sleep as they drive over Puente de Praga. A few hundred meters from where only a few days earlier, they discovered the unidentified corpse in the river.

When they reach Calle de Santa María de la Cabeza, she straightens the crick in her neck and frowns, shaking the bag of what was once ice but is now water, dripping onto her pants.

The effects of the painkiller are wearing off. Reaching for the water to swallow a couple more tablets, she glimpses her bruised face reflected in the glass.

"What a mess," she says in the croaky voice of someone who has just woken up.

"Voronin's was worse," says Jon.

Antonia grinds to a halt.

So does the universe.

Voronin's face.

Voronin's face was obliterated. With a shotgun fired point-blank, straight at his head.

Erupararkkiratu.

In Tamil, a Dravidic language spoken in India and northeast Sri Lanka: to lead the ox astray by looking at a fly.

Suddenly, all the pieces fall into place for her:

- Yuri Voronin, killed by a single shotgun blast, at home in his bathing trunks, with no sign of a forced entry.
- Shot at point-blank range. They were aiming at his head.
- The dog, a Caucasian shepherd extremely suspicious of strangers, was locked in the pool area.
- Lola Moreno receives a text from her husband warning her they are coming after her.
- Somebody tries to kill Lola Moreno, about the same time as her husband.
- The bleach at the crime scene.
- Yuri Voronin was a police informer.

It all points back to the same place. To Voronin's death. Antonia remembers how uneasy she felt at the crime scene. How the monkeys became agitated, trying to make her see something that was there all along. The position of the body. The angle of fire.

Erupararkkiratu.

Lead the ox astray because you're looking at a fly.

"The dog. The dog, Jon."

"What about the dog?"

"Stop the car."

Jon puts the blinkers on and pulls over to the right. They are in the middle of Gran Vía, on their way to the hotel, but at that hour, there's almost no traffic.

"Let me drive."

"But we're almost there."

"We have to go back. Now. And you're not in any fit state."

Even as Jon swaps seats with Antonia, he can't quite believe what he is doing. The cold air outside—it's -3°C—helps wake him up.

"Are you going to tell me what's got into you?"

Erupararkkiratu, thinks Antonia, pulling the seat forward to adjust it to her body size. Not that Jon is fat. She buckles her seat belt and starts the engine. After performing a somewhat illegal maneuver to return to Plaza de España, she crosses a solid white line and runs a red light, followed by two more.

Inspector Gutiérrez, who could already smell the hotel bed, adjusts his seat belt and curses the exhaustion that made him lower his guard and hand over the wheel to someone like Antonia, who drives like a complete lunatic. Again. Having sworn he would never repeat the experience.

"You're scaring me."

"Call Mentor."

"Why?"

"Just call him."

Jon dials. A sleepy voice answers.

"The van carrying Lola Moreno," says Antonia. "I need you to locate it. Two judicial police officers are traveling in the vehicle. They're heading for Madrid. According to my calculations, they should be somewhere between Villaverde and Usera. It's a matter of life and death. Do you understand?"

"Consider it done," Mentor says gravely. Recognizing her tone of voice, he doesn't ask for an explanation.

Jon hangs up. He does want one.

"Do you mind telling me why we're risking having a serious accident?"

Antonia doesn't reply. She's too busy driving at ninety kilometers an hour down Cuesta de San Vicente. She narrowly avoids a cab coming out of Calle de Arriaza, which screeches to a halt. The sound of the car horn barely reaches them.

"The dog, Jon, the dog," she says when they are on the M-30 beltway and the clear road allows her to double her speed.

"**Okay, okay. The** dog. The cleaning lady took it. Why the interest in the dog now?"

"Not now. The day they shot Voronin. Don't you see? Where was the dog?"

"Shut away in his swimming pool," says Jon, his fatigue quickly dissipating thanks to the adrenaline rush produced as they pass other cars—thankfully not many—at more than sixty kilometers an hour above the speed limit. And because he is holding on to the grab handle quite hard.

"Why did Voronin shut the dog away? Because he was expecting visitors."

"He knew his killers. We already know that."

"Yes. But the people who killed him didn't intend to do so. They wanted to frighten him into talking. Why kill him first and *then* search the house for whatever it was they were looking for?"

"You're right, it doesn't make sense. So why kill him?"

Erupararkkiratu.

"It was an accident, Jon. They threatened Voronin with a shotgun, the dog got nervous and started barking. The pool is right next to the barbecue."

"Whoever was holding the shotgun got frightened. And . . . ," they declare in unison:

"Boom."

"Okay, but that doesn't explain why we've turned round," says Jon, recoiling as they pass perilously close to a truck.

"Minutes later, they tried to kill Lola Moreno. Why?"

"Because they messed things up when they shot the husband," says Jon, who is beginning to understand.

"We've been looking at it the wrong way from the start. We always thought it was a settling of scores, and that they intended to kill them both."

"But Orlov made it clear at the funeral Voronin was a traitor. An informer."

Antonia bites her bottom lip, closes her eyes, and tries to think. She doesn't realize this isn't such a good idea at high speed. The steering wheel turns a fraction of an inch. They come so close to a red minivan that the Audi's left side-view mirror snaps off, leaving only a cable that waves about frantically.

"Goddamn it, Scott!"

"Sorry," Antonia says, straightening the wheel. "Orlov didn't know about the money then. Otherwise, he wouldn't have killed Ustyan and burned all Voronin's files. That was his big mistake, because it led to us finding the container."

"So?"

"Think about it, Jon. According to Orlov, Voronin was a bum. He knocked pears from trees with his dick."

"He did what?"

"I'll explain later. Yuri was a lazy bum, until he met Lola Moreno and became the da Vinci of money laundering and illegal imports."

Jon nods, slowly. It feels like one of those optical illusions: once you find the hidden image, you can't help seeing it all the time. Lola Moreno has been laughing at them all along. Hiding behind a bunch of social stereotypes. Even now, they are treating her like a helpless victim.

"Son of a bitch."

"Lola Moreno has been the brains behind the operation from the outset. Manipulating her husband, stealing from Orlov. And one day they made a mistake, and someone put the screws on them. What's the deal with informers, Jon?"

"You look the other way, and they give you information. Everyone's a winner."

"But sometimes you get dirty," says Antonia gently.

Jon doesn't reply. He knows what happens, even with the best will in the world. You can't wade through a river of shit in a bridal gown.

"Now tell me why Lola Moreno fled from the police instead of handing herself in?"

Jon is tying up loose ends too. With alarming clarity. Of course, it's only a tiny spark: Antonia has done most of the work, showing him who Lola Moreno really is. An incredibly smart, manipulative woman. It's only a tiny spark, and yet for a split second, Jon glimpses what it must be like to be inside Antonia Scott's head.

"She knew her attacker," he replies.

"Somebody who had gotten too involved with Voronin and Lola Moreno. Who then poured bleach all over the crime scene," says Antonia, talking faster and faster. "Who suffered a superficial injury. Somebody with broad shoulders who barely moved one arm when we first met."

Jon swallows slowly.

"Holy shit, sweetheart. Ho-ly shit. You better be sure."

Antonia grips the steering wheel resolutely. He is right, there are still things she doesn't understand. Unanswered questions. A lot of them. In particular, those relating to the Black Wolf. There are more forces at work here than she can discern from the information at her disposal. But she has eliminated the impossible. Now all she is left with is the improbable.

"I'm as sure it was Belgrano as I am that they won't let Lola Moreno reach UDYCO's headquarters alive."

RECORDING 16

TWO WEEKS EARLIER

YURI VORONIN: I want out, now.

CAPTAIN ROMERO: I think we've already made it clear that what you want doesn't come into it, Voronin.

YURI VORONIN: You don't understand. Lola has no idea I'm here. I didn't bring her on purpose.

DEPUTY INSPECTOR BELGRANO: That's strange. Seeing as how she leads you on a leash.

YURI VORONIN: She does the thinking. I'm the one who rummages through the garbage, talks to people, finds out things to tell you. In Bratvá and outside Bratvá.

DEPUTY INSPECTOR BELGRANO: And you're very good at it. We had an agreement. We scratch your back and you scratch ours.

YURI VORONIN: Well, now it's over.

DEPUTY INSPECTOR BELGRANO: And what brought about this sudden change of heart?

YURI VORONIN: Lola is pregnant. We want out.

CAPTAIN ROMERO: I'm afraid that won't be possible.

YURI VORONIN: I did everything you asked!

DEPUTY INSPECTOR BELGRANO: And you're going to keep on doing it.
    (*An eight-second pause.*)

YURI VORONIN: No.

DEPUTY INSPECTOR BELGRANO: What did you say?

YURI VORONIN: I said no.

(The sound of a chair falling on the floor.)

DEPUTY INSPECTOR BELGRANO: I'm going to kick the shit out of you, you runt.

YURI VORONIN: You aren't going to touch me. You aren't going to touch either of us.

DEPUTY INSPECTOR BELGRANO: I'll wipe that smile off your face.

CAPTAIN ROMERO: Deputy Inspector, I'm interested to know why the suspect is smiling, when he knows we've got him by the short hairs.

YURI VORONIN: I'm good at finding things out. You said so yourself. I know how much money was in the car you seized from the Serbs.

DEPUTY INSPECTOR BELGRANO: How are you going to know that?

YURI VORONIN: Six hundred thousand euros. You declared forty thousand.

CAPTAIN ROMERO: It's funny you should know that, Señor Voronin, considering the driver died resisting arrest.

YURI VORONIN: That's because I put it there myself.

DEPUTY INSPECTOR BELGRANO: You told us it was a Serbian consignment.

YURI VORONIN: I lied. It was from Orlov. To pay a debt. I set it up. I even helped poor Jovovic load the car. Before he left, I asked if he was armed.

DEPUTY INSPECTOR BELGRANO: He must have picked up a weapon later.

YURI VORONIN: We lost the consignment. We lost the driver. Life goes on, Orlov doesn't get angry.

DEPUTY INSPECTOR BELGRANO: You'll soon see how angry he gets when he finds out you're a rat.

YURI VORONIN: You won't tell him. Because if you do, I'll tell everything. I've recorded all our conversations.

DEPUTY INSPECTOR BELGRANO: You're fucking kidding.

YURI VORONIN: I also hid a camera in the car. *Streaming* 4K. Everything is recorded. Even when you dragged poor Jovovic out and shot him, Deputy Inspector.

(A scrape of metal, banging, yells. Indistinguishable noises lasting forty-two seconds.)

CAPTAIN ROMERO: Let's all calm down and discuss how we can fix this.

YURI VORONIN: There's nothing to discuss. You leave me and my family alone. If not, there will be consequences.

13

A SILENCE

It happens in just three seconds. But what a three seconds.

The van is on the last stretch of its journey on the A-4 near La China—the treatment plant that purifies water for one and a half million people in Madrid.

The driver, a woman named Noelia Pardeza, is forty-one years old, the mother of a six-year-old boy. Normally, she wouldn't be working today, but her partner, Officer Alonso, is off sick. And so here she is.

In the passenger seat is Mateo Carmona, aged thirty-six, single, no children. He owns three dogs and lives with his elderly father. Mateo is dozing and has unfastened his seat belt, because nobody can fall asleep with that thing on, and besides, who's going to fine us, we're the police. His foolish, irrational sense of impunity is what saves his life.

Shortly before reaching the water-treatment plant, the van crosses the river Manzanares. They pass the settling tanks on the left and continue on their way. They are now parallel with the high-speed train tracks running along to their right, about four meters above them. The highway crosses over the extension of Calle Embajadores, where it narrows into a dead end.

The road is deserted, it's a perfect night.

Officer Pardeza maintains the speedometer needle at a hundred kilometers per hour. On a four-lane highway, in the early hours of the morning, it's a very safe speed.

Unless someone intentionally rams your vehicle.

The off-roader (with no lights on) emerges from the area beneath the high-speed rail tracks and joins the highway at seventy kilometers an hour, the maximum speed the driver has been able to reach in such a short distance. The Citroën's passenger door and part of its front are hit diagonally.

At that speed, a one-and-a-half-ton vehicle receiving an impact for which it wasn't designed becomes a kind of lottery of physics. Anything can happen, taking into account the principle of energy conservation. The kinetic transfer energy is similar to that required to halt in its tracks an elephant falling from an eight-story building.

Where does all that energy go?

First, to the driver's cabin, which is a separate structure from the rear passenger compartment. The bodywork around the engine block buckles from the collision, absorbing some of the impact. But not all of it. The kinetic energy of Officers Pardeza and Carmona, who are still traveling at a hundred kilometers per hour when the vehicle is knocked sideways, sends them in different directions. Carmona is forced upward and forward. His chest hits the dashboard with a force equivalent to fifty times that of gravity. One and a half tons, absorbed partly by his ribs, partly by the airbag, which fails to open immediately due to the violence of the impact. Inside his thoracic cavity, Carmona's heart bangs against his sternum, causing a severe, if not fatal, myocardial contusion.

Unencumbered by the safety belt, his body continues to move. This is what saves his life when the passenger door is smashed in, and occupies the space where his head would have been. Two jagged teeth of aluminum and steel spit out broken glass but don't even scratch him.

Pardeza doesn't share Carmona's momentary good fortune. The seat belt keeps her trapped, giving her nothing more than two broken ribs, a pulmonary contusion, and a lacerated spleen. The airbag inflates to prevent her from hitting the steering wheel, which at that speed would have been fatal. Six months of painful rehabilitation, a pay increase as a result of injuries sustained in the line of duty, and a son who would still have a mother.

But no.

Carmona's good fortune has kept him out of the danger zone but has turned his eighty kilos into a projectile. The spin the kinetic-energy transfer has given his body has reached his arm, which collides at wrist level with Pardeza's temporal lobe, just above her ear.

It's like punching a brick wall. Carmona's wrist snaps, and his hand bends back on itself until the nails brush against his forearm. The fractured bone pokes through the torn skin.

It's like being punched by a brick wall. Pardeza's skull smashes into the window, which halts the movement. But in every car crash, there are three collisions. That of the vehicle until it comes to rest, that of the bodies inside the vehicle, and that of the organs inside the bodies. Propelled by her cerebrospinal fluid, the officer's brain is jolted within her skull. Normally, this fluid would act as a cushion, but in a high-speed collision, it has the peculiarity of moving at a different speed than the cerebral mass, due to its different density. And so it sends the officer's brain in the opposite direction from that of the impact, causing it to bounce about inside her skull. Rather like a toy inside a box in the hands of a curious child who isn't allowed to open his presents until he has blown out the birthday candles.

Pardeza is dead before the three seconds are over.

Meanwhile, the compartment holding the prisoners has fared much better. The unusual seating arrangement, which might have proved fatal had the angle of collision been different, has worked in the prisoners' favor. The centrifugal force of the initial impact caused the van to spin around, away from the direction of travel. This transferred a large quantity of energy to the van's two left tires, which burst as they scraped sideways along the asphalt.

Inside the compartment, Kiril and Lola scream in panic, pinned to the backs of their seats by the force of inertia. Their safety belts keep them in position.

The Citroën continues to spin, circling the off-roader, which hasn't moved much from when it rammed the police van. It is more than a ton heavier, and has a higher center of gravity. It has better fenders and a stronger structure, and has suffered relatively minor damage. One side is caved in, the hood is as crumpled as a schoolkid's picture card, the left headlight is smashed, and when the engine stops, it probably won't start again. Even so, fuel continues to pump through the engine at six megajoules per liter. That's a lot of energy.

When the spinning motion that has caused the Citroën to circle the off-roader stops, gravity comes into play. The disparity in height between the two tires that are intact and the two that have burst causes the van to roll over onto the driver's side. It collapses on top of the guardrail, crushing it. Bits of twisted blue metal plunge four meters onto the street below. Half the van is left hanging in midair, while the other half reveals its underbelly, like a wounded animal.

The three seconds are over. But the drama continues.

The off-roader goes into reverse and rams into the van a second time. As it has less distance to cover and isn't traveling as fast, the impact is less strong. It's more like a sustained shove, the off-roader's tires smoking as they try to grip the asphalt and propel the other vehicle forward. Gradually, they bulldoze the van off the highway, and once again, gravity takes over. The Citroën plunges off the overpass, landing on its side. The impact destroys the bodywork and shatters the few remaining windows. It also hurls Officer Carmona—badly injured but still alive—onto the twisted shards of metal on the door that he escaped earlier. One of them pierces his jaw, ripping through his neck and throat. Sliding off the jagged tip, Carmona—injured, and now dead—collapses on top of his colleague.

The driver and his companion climb out of the off-roader. They are both wearing motorcycle helmets. They contemplate the wreckage through the gap in the guardrail the van made when it plummeted. The air is impregnated with the smell of burning rubber and brake linings.

"It's done," says Belgrano, raising his visor. His breath forms clouds of vapor in the cold dry air.

"Close your helmet," orders Romero.

"There aren't any cameras here."

"Better safe than sorry."

Cars are arriving. One stops, the driver pulls out his cell phone. He is calling the police. His female companion points hers at them. She is filming.

They have no time.

So they run.

They have left the motorbike on Calle Embajadores, hidden beneath the overpass. They scramble down the embankment, climb on the bike, and speed off. Just as they did that morning at the shopping center.

Only this time, they have finished the job.

Or so they think.

LOLA

Lola is no longer in the mood for fairy tales.

The accident has been a horror movie lasting only a few seconds. First, the violent impact. Next, the spinning that pressed her back against the seat. The worst moment was when the van turned on its side. Lola felt the earth, the entire planet, tilt beneath her feet. A whole ninety degrees. She gave a brief thought to what must be happening to the buildings, the people, their homes. All destroyed.

She finished up suspended from her chest and waist, one arm dangling down, the other still clamped by the handcuffs, her hair spread out in front of her. Only the safety belt was holding her up.

Then, the blow from behind. Lola felt the shock in her backside, transmitted to her seat through the chassis. A jolt, followed by the vibration and strain of the one and a half tons of steel and aluminum as it resisted being pushed forward, centimeter by centimeter, by a greater force.

The van was moving toward the abyss. A moment of weightlessness, which Lola felt in the pit of her stomach. Like when her father used to accelerate up the hill at Arroyo de la Miel, when she was a kid and they were going on vacation to Torremolinos.

The van plunged over the edge, and Lola knew she was going to die. Her last conscious thought was of her father's face, stepping on the gas as they approached the crest of the hill, pushing up his glasses, which kept sliding down his nose. With a mischievous grin, knowing she and her mother would shriek with delight when the car reached the top, the force of gravity giving them butterflies in the stomach.

The van hit the ground. There was a crunch of metal as the chassis crumpled under the impact. The sound of breaking glass. And that was all.

Lola doesn't die.

She doesn't even lose consciousness.

She is simply left dangling.

She doesn't feel relief at not having died, only surprise. A puzzling anticlimax. The universe had lined up all the elements to produce a certain result, and then delivered quite another. Like a scam from which you've ended up profiting.

The fact is, the Citroën's passenger compartment withstood the impact well. Lola only has a few bruises. Blood is trickling down her fingers from the rim of the handcuffs, which lacerated her wrist. Her wounds are superficial.

So much for the good news.

The bad news: Kiril Rebo has survived as well.

One of the rear doors has been flung open, and in the dim light, she can see him opposite her. He is sitting with his back turned, legs raised as he yanks the bar attaching him to the side of the vehicle. The impact probably loosened the screws, although Lola can't see this from her position.

With a *snap* and a *clank*, Rebo frees himself. He unclips his seat belt.

Lola shudders with fear. Although she can't see Rebo's eyes in the semidarkness, she remembers his empty stare that hadn't varied since they climbed into the van. And so Lola waits for him to attack her. Belted in, hanging upside down, handcuffed.

Defenseless.

But Rebo doesn't move.

For several long seconds, Lola observes him, until she realizes what is happening. And she also sees her chance.

"They tried to kill you," she says in a gentle voice.

Kiril Rebo stirs, lets out a hoarse groan, but doesn't reply.

"Orlov didn't care that you were in the van. You thought Orlov was your friend, didn't you? Well, here's the proof of his friendship."

Dragging himself from his seat, Rebo crawls toward her. In the gloom, his empty eyes have lost their pale blue glint and look even more threatening.

"You not talk like that," he says, grabbing her by the throat.

Lola doesn't back down. She remembers hearing Yuri talk about Orlov and Rebo. About how they were the first to come here when the Russians moved in on the Costa del Sol. The two were inseparable. The velvet glove and the iron fist.

"How many years have you worked for him?" Lola says in a strangulated voice. "How many are enough for him to double-cross you?"

Rebo relaxes his grip on her throat.

"Set me free. Get me out of here and I swear I'll make it worth your while."

"Take me to money."

"Do it quick, before the cops arrive."

The thug gives her a disturbing look.

He drags himself out of the van. Thirty seconds later, he returns carrying a length of metal. He slides it between the bar and the side of the van. At the third attempt, he prizes the bar free of its fixings.

Lola extricates herself, unfastens the seat belt, and lets herself drop down.

Rebo is waiting for her outside the van. He is shivering, it's bitterly cold. For some reason Lola can't fathom, he has taken off his jacket and flung it on the ground. He has so many tattoos on his forearms they look carpeted.

"You cheat me, I kill you," says Rebo, showing her the piece of blue metal.

Lola nods. She doesn't doubt it.

"We need a car."

They hear voices approaching on the highway above them. She and Rebo start to run under the railway line, and keep going down the deserted street. On the right is a solitary warehouse surrounded by a high wall. On the left, a turnoff to Madrid. Yet another street without a car in sight. Beneath a yield sign, a hopeful entrepreneur has stuck an advert announcing in black print on a yellow background:

CASTLE ROCK REHEARSAL STUDIOS
300 M AHEAD

Lola follows Rebo in that direction. Four minutes later, they arrive at an industrial estate. There is a half-empty car lot by the entrance.

Rebo walks between the cars until he stops next to a Renault Clio.

"This very easy," he says. "French cars, *pff*."

He goes to the rear window and forces the end of the metal bar between the rubber and the bodywork. The rubber refuses to yield. After several attempts, Rebo opts for the Russian method of breaking and entering: he smashes the window and crawls through to the driver's seat. He presses the unlock button, opens the door, and rips off the plastic casing around the starter cables.

He examines them for a while, touching them with his small, bony fingers like drumsticks. He pulls one end, exposing three red wires.

He gets out and walks over to Lola, who is watching him, hugging herself to try to keep warm. Her thin black jacket is perfect for the mild weather in Málaga. A joke on a freezing February morning in Madrid.

Rebo raises his hands to Lola's head, causing her to step back in alarm.

"You no move," he says. "I need this."

He feels in her hair and pulls out two bobby pins that are keeping her hair off her face. She put the pins in back at that motel in Estepona, a million years or twenty-four hours ago.

Rebo bends them until they snap in half. After some tinkering, he manages to use one piece as a conductor between the twelve-volt source and the auxiliary source, another between the twelve-volt source and the dash panel, and finally a third to connect both to the starter motor. The engine turns over with a gentle purr.

"Where?" he asks Lola.

"I drive," she says.

"Tell me where."

"Not far."

"How long?"

"An hour. Maybe longer. It's a lousy car."

Rebo eyes her suspiciously.

"Okay," he says after a while.

He relinquishes the driver's seat and climbs in the back of the car.

Lola sits behind the wheel and adjusts the rearview mirror.

She sees Rebo's eyes, menacing as ever.

She puts the car into gear and drives out of the lot. She heads east via Puente de Vallecas and Avenida de la Paz toward the M-30 beltway.

Without the satnav, she finds it much harder to get her bearings. Yuri always drove whenever they visited this place.

Everything is so much harder without him. Why did he have to be so stupid?

Why did he go after Romero and Belgrano? And above all, what made him believe he could think for himself?

Lola reassesses her situation: Yes, she has a psychopathic killer in the back seat, one armed with a sharp metal object. But for the moment, she is in control, although she's under no illusion.

Men are easy to manipulate. Some more than others. For almost all of them, sex is incentive enough. That's something she has always been capable of insinuating with a wink, a lowering of the eyes, a strap that accidentally slips off her shoulder. From an early age, she has known she possesses a weapon of mass destruction. Purely because her features are arranged in a certain way, her fleshy protrusions in another. And she has used it, boy has she used it. Yuri was the perfect camouflage for her, and he became a more lucrative tool than she ever imagined. But not all men are that straightforward.

If they don't respond to sex or money but to an inner passion she is unable to kindle at will, they are far more dangerous. More than the possibility he might hurt her, what scares her about Kiril Rebo is that he is immune to her charms.

So she does not kid herself. Rebo is only pretending to let her manipulate him.

It'll have to do for now, she thinks, glancing in the rearview mirror. His cold eyes are still fixed on her. *There's a surprise waiting for you when we arrive. You're going to love it.*

14

A TRAIL

The powerful Audi arrives at the scene of the accident eight minutes late.

Antonia pulls up next to the off-roader, which is still blocking the middle section of the highway. A couple of drivers have stopped to find out what happened, and if they can help. Others simply slow down long enough to stick their head out and see whether there's any blood. One stops, takes a selfie, and jumps back in his car to look for a Wi-Fi signal.

Antonia and Jon descend the embankment, picking their way through discarded bottles and used syringes. The wreck of the Citroën is still warm, wispy plumes of smoke are rising from the mangled lump of metal that was once the hood. The flattened radiator continues to drip onto the white line on the road.

Through the gaping hole in the windshield, they can see the dead bodies of the two officers, joined in a gruesome embrace. There is no need to check whether they are still breathing. The report will state: *Injuries incompatible with life.*

"Nineteen," Jon says with a catch in his voice.

Antonia doesn't reply, but walks straight to the rear of the vehicle. One of the doors is smashed in. The other lies on the ground, attached only by a hinge.

Inside, nothing.

"Did they escape, or were they abducted?" asks Jon.

Antonia takes a while to reply, first walking around the van, studying it intently. She borrows Jon's flashlight, climbs inside, examines the bars they were cuffed to. One has been torn out. A pair of handcuffs hangs from the other.

"Rebo freed himself. Then he released Lola Moreno," says Antonia, still crouching in the van.

After emerging, she heads toward the foot of the overpass. Her hands have started shaking again, though not as badly as before. She has lost none of her fragility, that brittle air that tells him she will snap at any moment. And yet . . .

There's something different about her, thinks Jon. *Something dangerous.*

She spends some time kneeling down under the bridge.

"They left on a motorcycle," she says, showing Jon the rubber residue on her fingertips.

"How do you know it was them?"

"They drove off from here," says Antonia, pointing at the asphalt with the flashlight. "Not somewhere you'd choose to park unless you were using a getaway vehicle. And there's no dust on the off-roader."

"So, they brought the bike and the off-roader. They passed the Citroën, set up the ambush, and then took off," says Jon.

"Believing they had killed the prisoners."

On such a long journey, two powerful vehicles like that would have a clear advantage over the van. They only needed to step on the—

Suddenly it dawns on Jon.

"They didn't just overtake the Citroën."

Antonia looks at him and nods silently.

"We saw a motorcycle and an off-roader on the highway, Jon. You couldn't have known it was them."

Jon drops a hand on her shoulder.

"Neither could you."

At first Antonia shrinks from the contact, but then lets Jon's big paw remain there. It's bitterly cold, and the warmth Jon gives off is like a balm.

"Believe it or not," she says, "I'm beginning to believe I can't save everyone."

Jon withdraws his hand very slowly.

He's overwhelmed by a wave of sorrow. It isn't possible to know Antonia Scott, but it's possible to understand her. And Jon has always understood the source of the ferocious energy driving her on. Because he recognized in her the same purity he had when he started out; the same desire for justice, the same compassion for other people's suffering. Only now he can put a name to a feeling he has had for days. The center of Antonia Scott's energy has shifted slightly. Compassion has given way to a desire for revenge.

Maybe this makes her even more effective. More powerful. Compassion is a fog we can get lost in. Revenge comes from hatred, and hatred is tangible, something you can wield like a weapon.

When he sees his dead colleagues in the van and thinks back to the container in the port of Málaga, Jon cannot blame her.

They must do whatever it takes. Or at least whatever they can.

If you can't save them, at least you can avenge them.

This thought doesn't make Jon feel any less sorrowful.

They can see the Guardia Civil's headlights up above them. Some are peering down from the overpass, others have started to descend the embankment in their yellow jackets.

Inspector Gutiérrez explains the situation to them, which takes up precious time. Antonia waits in the passenger seat of their car, eyes closed.

Jon climbs in, rubbing his hands together and breathing on them to warm them. It's getting colder by the minute.

"Did you fall asleep?" asks Jon.

She shakes her head, lips pursed, without opening her eyes.

"What I wouldn't give for a red capsule," she says.

"Yeah, and I'd love a rich husband. You can *do* this. You've done it before."

Antonia's breathing is shallow.

"It's a lot harder. And more . . ."

She doesn't add another adjective. But Jon adds a noun. Fear. Antonia Scott is afraid. This woman who doesn't seem to fear anything, apart from herself.

"I'm going to need your cell phone," she says after a while.

Jon passes it to her and watches as she switches it off and then on again. Then she presses down the volume button. Instead of Jon's home screen, an app appears. Antonia taps in a long number, after which the app carries out a facial recognition check.

"How did you install that on my phone?"

"This isn't your phone. We swapped it months ago. This one's better. And Apple can't spy on you."

"But you can?"

"I'm sure Asier_29 will text you eventually. He seems like a nice guy," says Antonia as she continues to type into the app.

Jon knows exactly which web pages he has visited, which messages he has sent, and what he has photographed on that phone. And that he wouldn't want anyone else to know. A dry heat flushes his cheeks, and a torrent of protests threatens to burst from his lips. But then he remembers the saying about people who play with fire getting burned. So he simply hugs the steering wheel and looks the other way. Until he gets over it.

"This is interesting," says Antonia.

"What?"

"Lola Moreno went to collect her dog. She was about to climb into the car with the cleaning lady but she didn't, because Orlov's men showed up to abduct her."

"That guy gives me the creeps," says Jon, recalling Kiril Rebo.

"I suspect this woman tipped them off. Zenya Kuchma, a Ukrainian citizen resident in Spain. No doubt they threatened her."

"She left before we got there."

"Zenya lives on the outskirts of Marbella. Why, then, is her cell phone telling me she's on the move somewhere in the Sierra de Guadarrama, close to Madrid?"

Antonia shows Jon the screen with the location of Zenya Kuchma's cell phone. Ninety-nine kilometers away.

"This is Heimdal, right?" Jon says, starting the car.

Antonia nods.

"And it located her phone via satellite, right?"

Antonia nods again.

"So you see, it *does* have a magic fascist satellite function."

LOLA

There was once a little girl who bought a house in a forest, not far from a fairy-tale village.

Lola loves Rascafría.

It's an incredibly beautiful place. The monastery of El Paular is over six centuries old. Carthusian monks constructed it around a chimney and a paper mill. It took two hundred years to build, and a great deal of effort to preserve, in the wilderness at the foot of Peñalara mountain. In the midst of a landscape full of icy, rocky streams and woods of poplar, spruce, and birch.

Lola had known that she and Yuri would need a refuge one day. A place nobody knew about, far away from everything and everyone. She found the house on a real estate website. A seventeen-hundred-square-meter plot of land, next to a forest track in the middle of the Sierra de Guadarrama National Park. Built in 1975, the house would be completely illegal nowadays.

"Buy it," she told Yuri.

She made sure that nobody could connect them with the property. This meant not using Ustyan as a front man but paying extra for the services of a Maltese lawyer.

The house cost €300,000. The same again to purchase it anonymously. And it became their romantic hideaway. They had driven up there on several occasions in secret, with Kot snoring away happily on the back seat. How he loved their long hikes through the endless forest. Especially in winter, when the snow could reach half a meter deep.

Today looks like one of those days.

* * *

They first encountered snow at the Pinilla reservoir. The black road gradually turning dirty gray. And then white.

The tires on the Clio began to struggle as they came to Alameda del Valle. Lola turned off the road and drove into the village.

"Is this it?" Kiril asked, suddenly alert.

"No. We need chains or we can't continue."

They pulled up behind a Mercedes parked outside a restaurant. The tires had chains on them. "Impossible break-in," said Rebo. Since they couldn't take the car, they stole the tire chains. They toiled for the best part of thirty minutes to remove them and fit them to the Clio's back wheels.

"You're Russian. Aren't you supposed to have done this before?"

Kiril shrugged.

"Prejudice, *da*? Like Black people dance good, *da*?"

That's all I needed, thought Lola, *a politically correct mafioso*. They climbed back inside the car, which was still chilly even with the heating full on. The Russian method Rebo used to break into the Clio had turned it into an icebox.

And so they arrived, shivering, in Rascafría.

Yet again, Lola is overcome by the beauty of the little town. Even at night, with half a gale blowing through the Clio's rear window, it feels like a relic from another century. The people there are calm, relaxed. The town boasts no discotheques or brothels. Barely fifteen hundred souls, and one police car that leaves the town hall garage only on feast days.

Paradise.

Lola drives through the town and takes the turnoff toward Puerto de Cotos. They come to a police sign warning that the road is closed due to the snowstorm.

Lola gets out to push it aside, and drives on. A hundred meters farther up is the turning to Arroyo del Cuco.

It's another twelve kilometers along a beaten track through the middle of the forest. The snow is already several centimeters deep. Lola slows down, staying in third gear to avoid losing traction, and steers as little as possible. Even so, this last stretch is a nightmare, and the tires slide perilously every few minutes.

Suddenly, the Clio grinds to a halt in the middle of the road.

"We'll have to continue on foot," says Lola.

Rebo looks outside, where the snow is now falling thick and fast, and then at his flimsy clothes.

"If we stay here, we'll die," insists Lola.

"Far?" asks Rebo.

"Near," she replies, although she hasn't a clue where they are.

Only the road markers every few meters prevent them from losing their way. And the fact that they were less than a hundred meters from the house. Because they couldn't have lasted much longer, not with the wind gusting at eighty kilometers an hour.

Another half hour and we wouldn't have made it, thinks Lola as she sees how fast the layer of white is rising.

Even so, they are half frozen by the time they reach the gate to the property—their lips blue, their muscles exhausted. Lola presses hard on the intercom button. If Zenya ignored her instructions and didn't come there, they'll have to climb over the wall. This won't be easy, as the dense hedge surrounding the property is three meters high.

"*Please. Please,*" Lola says, her finger still on the button.

"Yes?" a voice comes through the intercom.

Lola utters the magic words that, since time immemorial, have granted access to any door in Spain, regardless of the hour.

"It's me!"

The gate opens with a shrill, petulant buzz.

A light goes on at the front of the house, barely visible beneath the white blanket. Lola makes her way toward it. She has to lift her feet to walk through the snow, now forty centimeters deep. Her jeans are soaked up to the knee, and her feet are going numb.

By the time they reach the front porch, Lola is close to collapse. Rebo isn't doing much better: his skin has turned bright pink and he is gasping for breath. They reach the entrance. Every step is an effort.

Zenya is standing by the door, carrying a blanket. Before Lola can take it, Kiril grabs her from behind. Zenya recoils in fright when she sees the Russian.

"The dog," he says, forcing Lola to turn and pressing the jagged tip of the metal bar to her neck.

Lola looks at him, infinitely weary. At some point in a distant past, part of her plan was to order Kot to attack Kiril the moment they entered the house. A plan she had already forgotten, but which Rebo appears to have taken into account from the start.

She raises her hand, from which the handcuffs are still hanging.

"Zenya, where's Kot?"

"In the kitchen," replies Zenya.

Claws scratch at the adjoining door.

"Go fetch him," Rebo orders Zenya in Russian. "And tie him up where I can see him."

Zenya disappears through the kitchen door and returns a few seconds later with Kot. The dog is wearing a harness with a leash attached. Kot is pulling so hard Zenya finds it difficult to restrain him.

"Give command," says Rebo, pressing the metal harder into Lola's throat.

"*Myeste.* Stay," orders Lola.

Kot instantly freezes. But his gaze is trained on Kiril Rebo. There's a hungry gleam behind those coffee-colored eyes.

"Tie him up over there," Rebo says, pointing to a wooden beam in the middle of the living room.

Zenya obeys. She wraps the leash around the beam and ties a tight knot.

Only then does Rebo release Lola. She lurches away from him and collapses in front of the fireplace. Zenya has switched on the central heating, but hasn't made a fire. A pile of logs is ready waiting.

There is no kindling, no fire starters. Only a mound of old newspapers (untouched) and a copy of *Fifty Shades of Gray* missing half its pages. Her fingers stiff with cold, Lola tears out a chapter to use to start the fire.

Once the flames have caught, Lola tears off her soaking clothes. Naked, she wraps herself in the blanket Zenya offers her.

Rebo hasn't moved from the doorway, waiting to see what Lola will do. He doesn't look away while she undresses, relishing the strange geometrical shapes the fire makes on Lola's breasts and belly. With no clothes on, it's impossible to hide her condition.

"Yuri, *da*?" he says, approaching the fireplace.

Lola doesn't respond. She is gazing into the fire, a million miles away. Or in that same place, but a million minutes ago. Sitting by the fire with her husband. Running her hand through his black hair, twisting the curls around her fingers when he wore it longer. God, he was handsome. With his fleshy lips and wide, manly nose. He wasn't very tall, but he knew how to make her happy.

We could have had it all. You idiot.

"I never kill pregnant woman," says Rebo.

"And you aren't going to now. We made a deal. We split the money."

Rebo goes over to Zenya and orders her to sit on the sofa beside the fire. He pulls a pair of handcuffs from his pocket and fastens her hands behind her back. Lola realizes that at some point during the journey, he must have managed to undo them.

No doubt using one of my hair clips.

"I prefer to speak in my language," Rebo says in Russian. "You answer me in Spanish. Okay?"

Lola nods. There's no point keeping up the pretense.

"Is the money in this house?"

"It's here, in this room."

"Good, so show me."

Not only is there no point in arguing, it's also pointless to resist. She isn't going to make any demands on Rebo, or fight him.

Wrapped in the blanket, she stands up and walks toward the beam where Kot is tethered.

"Where are you going?" says Rebo, stepping between her and the dog.

"I'm getting the money."

"You're going to untie him, bitch."

"If you want the money, you'll have to trust me."

Rebo, who has never trusted anyone in his life, isn't about to begin now. He tears Lola's blanket from her, pokes the metal bar into the small of her back, and makes her walk ahead of him.

Kot tenses as they approach, and rears up as far as the harness will allow. He gives a continuous threatening growl.

"*Myeste.* Stay," says Lola, her voice quaking.

It's been hours since her last insulin injection and her throat is dry again, and her vision is starting to blur. But she mustn't mess it up now.

She crouches, caresses the backs of Kot's ears.

"Careful," Rebo warns. The tip of the bar breaks her skin, and she can feel a trickle of blood run down her back.

Kot becomes agitated. The scent of *blood* makes him anxious.

"*Molodets.* Good boy," says Lola, fingering his neck until she finds what she is looking for under his thick mane. A slightly raised area, where the Russian trainer made a thumbnail incision with a scalpel, before inserting a plastic sleeve under the dog's skin.

Impermeable and invisible.

Like having a safe-deposit box with teeth.

Lola murmurs reassuring words to Kot as she digs with her nail until she manages to extract the microSD card. 512 GB. Shockproof, waterproof, magnetically undetectable. Able to withstand temperatures of 85°C.

Without turning around, Lola waves the card at Rebo. He snatches it from her, grabs her by the hair, and drags her away from the dog.

Lola retrieves the blanket from the floor without a word. She wraps it round herself and returns to the fireside.

"What is this?"

"It's what everyone is looking for. How the Tambóvskaya's shell companies are structured. Evidence against Captain Romero and Deputy Inspector Belgrano."

"What about the money? Is it here?"

Lola nods.

"There's a folder containing 74,568 bitcoins."

"Six hundred million euros," says Rebo, unable to believe all that money can fit on a piece of plastic the size of his pinkie nail.

"When we took it from Orlov, it was worth that much. The last time I checked the exchange rate, it had gone up to about eight hundred million," says Lola with astonishing calm. "And before you get any funny ideas, the folders are all protected by a different password. I'm the only person who knows them."

"I'm not worried about that. You'll give them to us in the end," Rebo says smugly.

His use of the plural causes Lola to turn around in alarm.

Rebo waves a cell phone at her.

"Our things were in a bag in the front of the van. I had to poke around for them under those cops. But I doubt they minded," he says. "And I took this from one of them as a bonus," he adds, dropping the metal bar on the floor and pulling a gun from the back of his pants.

Zenya, who hasn't stirred from the sofa or opened her mouth, starts to sob.

Lola looks at the heavy black metal object and realizes how foolish she has been. Rebo hadn't taken the gun out until now so that she would trust him. Believe she had a chance of defeating him somehow. But he has outwitted her.

"We had a deal," she says in desperation.

"WhatsApp has a very interesting function." The way Rebo pronounces the word in Russian sounds comical: *Guat-sa.* "Real-time location tracking. Even though there's no coverage here, I doubt they'll have much trouble finding us."

"You stupid son of a bitch!" shouts Lola, leaping to her feet, furious. "Orlov was ready to kill you without a second thought."

"But I'm alive," says Rebo with a shrug. "All's fair in love and war."

At that moment, the front door opens.

Tailing them was *easy, at least to begin with.*

The van was *traveling slowly, so she had to rein in the Kawasaki on the highway. She even permitted herself a stop at a gas station to rest for a few minutes. She had a bite to eat, used the restroom, and quickly caught up with them again. To avoid the risk of being seen, she kept around eight hundred meters between her and the Citroën.*

Her plan wasn't as easy. To carry it out, she needed them to stop the van, so she was biding her time. The best moment would be when they reached Madrid. She would take advantage of the officers' fatigue after the journey, at a traffic light or pedestrian crossing.

The opportunity never arose. Somebody got there before her.

When she saw the off-roader ram the van, she braked sharply and pulled over onto the hard shoulder. She turned off her headlight and continued to move forward slowly. And so she witnessed the entire scene.

By the time she reached the overpass, the two attackers were already fleeing on a motorcycle. Another car had stopped by the crashed off-roader, and somebody was calling the police.

She stifled a curse inside her helmet. All that effort for nothing. She was overcome by rage and frustration.

Then she saw Rebo climb out of the back of the van. She saw him rummage among the dead bodies, pick up a metal bar. And saw him emerge once more with Lola Moreno.

She smiled. Her plan had suddenly become much easier.

She weighed up the pros and cons of executing it straightaway, and decided it was better to wait and leave it to Rebo to act.

She switched off her engine, wheeled the Kawasaki down the embankment and along the road a short distance. Only when Rebo and Lola set off in the Clio did she climb back on the bike and start the engine again.

Without the headlight on, the black machine and her were simply a darker shadow in the night.

Thirty minutes later, she felt her cell phone vibrate. She stopped at the roadside to check her messages. Orlov had sent her Lola Moreno's exact coordinates. Apparently Rebo had managed to get in touch with him. Orlov told her a team was heading that way. He ordered her (ordered her!) to join up with them and capture Moreno once and for all.

She laughed aloud at the foolish old man's arrogance. No doubt he was in for a surprise. But not before she had accomplished her mission.

She set off again, quickly catching up with the Clio. But a little farther ahead, things got complicated. The weather worsened the higher they climbed. The snowstorm in the mountains had covered the road in slush; no more smooth, safe highway lanes, only a meandering two-way track.

She saw them stop to steal some chains, but she couldn't allow herself that luxury. And even if she could, she wouldn't find any chains to fit the Kawasaki's wheels.

And so pursuing *them suddenly turns into a dangerous game, even though they are traveling at a snail's pace. The Kawasaki wasn't designed for conditions like these. If only she had studded tires, or rubber spray to improve the grip. But she might as well wish for a helicopter.*

She keeps going as best she can, trying to steer the front wheel in the Clio's tracks. This helps, but she still comes off twice. When the car turns onto a dirt track, the situation becomes impossible.

They are advancing so slowly by now, she has to stop several times to prevent them from spotting her. And the rising wind makes it hard for her to stay upright on the bike. Her leathers and the thermal vest she has on underneath offer some protection from the cold, but with the wind chill, she can feel that she is losing body heat fast.

Even so, she doesn't give up.

She decides to leave the bike among the trees and continue on foot.

Before long, they do the same. She looks on, astonished, as they head off into the storm in their flimsy clothes. They won't last ten minutes, *she thinks.* Stupid asses.

Fortunately for them, the house is very close by.

She has no difficulty following them through the main gate. They didn't even bother to lock it behind them.

And so she overhears everything they say from the entrance, protected from the wind by the columns on the porch.

Once she has heard what she needs to know, she pushes open the door.

"All's fair in love and war," Kiril Rebo is saying.

Suddenly he hears the door open, and he wheels around, pointing his gun at her.

"Who the fuck are you?"

"Chernaya Volchitsa," she replies, removing her helmet and walking toward him.

Kiril Rebo laughs maliciously and turns to Lola Moreno.

"The Black Wolf is here," he says mockingly. "Now you'll discover the true meaning of fear."

She smiles in her turn, pulling a gun from inside her leather jacket. She carefully presses the muzzle against the laughing Rebo's temple and pulls the trigger. The bullet blows off the top of his head, slicing his laughter in half.

15

AN UPSET

"This snow is too fucking much," says Jon.

"I think you swear too much."

"I think we're going to have a fucking accident."

Jon is driving at walking pace through Rascafría. He hasn't stopped to put on the chains, because Antonia won't let him.

"We're in a hurry. Turn on the assisted steering," she says, pressing a button on the dashboard.

The car has an onboard computer—*at that price, it should drive itself*, thinks Jon—which corrects any sudden sharp turns of the wheel. It doesn't perform miracles, but has already prevented the car from sliding on two occasions.

Beyond the town, they lose the signal.

"There's no coverage," says Antonia. "Where we are now is the last place Zenya's cell phone was recorded as active."

Where they are now is the middle of nowhere. There are two tracks in front of them: one goes back to Rascafría, the other to the Coto Pass. Altitude 1,830 meters. A police sign warns the road ahead is closed.

Somebody has dragged it to one side.

Jon looks at Antonia, and she nods.

"These are fresh tire tracks," she says as they head for the pass.

The tracks are very faint, and Jon has difficulty following them. The snow is still falling heavily, and a little farther on, the tracks disappear completely.

"This can't be it," Antonia says, climbing out of the car. She crouches in the high beams, surveying the ground.

By the time she gets back in, her teeth are chattering. "Nobody has been along here," she says, her voice shaking.

"We must have missed the turnoff," says Jon, putting the car into reverse.

"Go as slowly as you possibly can," Antonia warns. She lowers her window, pokes her head out, and shines the flashlight among the trees. The forest is dense, the trunks rising around them like ghostly sentries.

A few yards back, Antonia glimpses a gap barely visible in the darkness. And a faint tire track.

"Down there," she says, pointing to their right.

Jon steers the car onto the forest road. The ground is blanketed with snow, making it much more difficult to follow the tracks. There is zero visibility up ahead.

As the road curves around sharply, a stationary car suddenly looms in front of them. Jon automatically swerves, triggering the Audi's steering assistance, which turns the wheels back toward the stationary vehicle. A Renault Clio, Antonia notices, as they sideswipe it before the Audi veers off, slides a few yards down through the forest, until a tree brings it to a halt.

"And another one bites the dust," says Jon, once his airbag has deflated enough for him to speak.

"Two to one," says Antonia, extricating her face from the nylon bag.

"This one doesn't count as dangerous driving. We were only doing thirty kilometers an hour."

"I guess you're right," Antonia admits, stepping out of the car to inspect the damage.

A birch is sprouting from the Audi's ballooned hood. The front fender is staved in where the car has wrapped itself around the trunk. Without a tow truck and thirty hours at the repair shop at €200 an hour, it won't be going anywhere.

Jon walks to the rear and opens the trunk. A summer jacket is all he has against the cold. Antonia isn't much better off: she only packed a corduroy coat.

"Let's walk back up to the road."

"Wait a minute," says Jon.

He takes out their luggage, sets it down in the snow, and removes the piece of matting at the bottom of the trunk, revealing the spare tire.

"I think we're going to need more than a new tire."

Jon lifts the tire out and tosses it to the ground. Beneath is a recess, in it a tray several feet long. Jon slides it toward him and pulls out what's inside.

"A Remington 870 Nighthawk shotgun with telescopic stock, neoprene strap, and a belt with five additional cartridges," says Antonia, impressed. "This is not regulation issue."

"The forest is a dangerous place at night," says Jon, hooking the strap over his shoulder, the barrel of the gun pointing at the ground. He grabs a couple of bulletproof vests from the trunk, slips his on, and forces Antonia to do the same. "Come on, do it up."

The climb back up to the abandoned Clio is arduous. By the time they reach the top, their legs are heavy and they are gasping for breath.

"Let's keep going."

A little farther on, the trees suddenly come to an end. It isn't snowing as hard, and the wind has dropped considerably. So they are more or less walking upright when they come to the wall surrounding the property.

The main gate is open.

They are halfway up to the house when they hear the shot.

"You stay here," Jon says, heading toward the porch.

Naturally, Antonia ignores him. The front door is open, and when they enter, what they see isn't what they were expecting.

The rustic-looking living room is spacious: exposed wood beams on the ceilings, with several more dotted about the room. A fire is burning in the grate. There is a sofa, two armchairs, a table. None of the vulgar eccentricities of the house in Marbella.

On the sofa sits a handcuffed Ukrainian woman. Lola Moreno is standing by the fireplace, a blanket wrapped around her. Tethered to a beam, a Caucasian shepherd dog growls menacingly. On the floor, stretched out like a rug, is Kiril Rebo's dead body, half its skull missing. Two steps from the corpse stands a red-haired woman in black bike leathers. Her skin is so pale it reflects every flicker from the fire. She is holding a helmet in one hand, a gun in the other.

Jon walks in, the Remington cocked in front of him.

"Put the gun down. Now."

The woman looks at him, and then at Antonia.

"I know you. Police."

Just then, Lola leaps forward and pushes the woman in the chest.

The attack takes her by surprise, and she trips over Rebo's body, falling backward.

"*Fas*," Lola says.

Kot snarls and launches himself at the supine woman. He can't reach her arm, so he buries his teeth in her left thigh. The woman lets out a stifled yell. She points her gun at the dog's face, but doesn't shoot.

"Order him off her," says Antonia.

"But she works for Orlov!"

"I won't say it again," snaps Antonia.

She is unarmed, and a head shorter than Lola, but something in Antonia's voice tells her she means business.

"*Myeste.*"

The dog instantly opens his jaw. When he withdraws his teeth, they are stained red.

"Your gun," Jon says, walking over, his Remington still pointing at her.

The woman is breathing heavily, trying not to cry out in pain. Teeth gritted, she resists handing her weapon to Inspector Gutiérrez.

Antonia crouches, and prizes it from her stiff fingers.

"Let me look at the wound," she says.

It's a deep one. The Caucasian shepherd's huge incisors have torn a hole in her thigh, which is bleeding profusely.

"Keep an eye on them," says Antonia, signaling toward Lola and Zenya.

"Don't worry."

Antonia returns shortly with scissors, fresh towels, a bottle of vodka, and some masking tape she found in a kitchen drawer. She cuts through the leather pants and does her best to patch up the mess.

"She needs antibiotics."

"And I need insulin," says Lola, who is crouched over Rebo's body.

"Step away," says Jon.

"You don't understand. This is what you're looking for," she says, waving the microSD card at him. "The money. The information on Orlov. The evidence against Romero."

"I'll take care of that," says Antonia, snatching the card from her.

"There's more money here than you two could earn in a hundred lifetimes. If you help me get away from them, I'll share it with you."

"How much?"

Lola repeats the figure.

Jon whistles.

"You say there's evidence here against Romero. What evidence?"

"My husband was a police informer. We had an agreement. He gave them names, they carried out the raids. Then things got complicated. Yuri laid a trap for them. A courier transporting money and drugs. They stole some of the money and killed the courier. It's all there. Video and audio recordings. Everything."

Antonia and Jon exchange glances.

"You were right," says Jon.

"Unfortunately. It was Belgrano who tried to kill you, wasn't it?" Antonia asks Lola.

"Yuri threatened them. He wanted to end the agreement."

"And it didn't go too well," says Jon.

"He was an idiot. There were better ways of handling it. If only he'd told me," says Lola, who has started to feel dizzy again. She sits down next to Zenya.

"Okay. But now it's all over. And we've even captured the Black Wolf," boasts Jon.

Antonia looks at the woman sprawled on the floor. Then at the gun she took off her. She looks at Kiril Rebo's dead body. At the dog, who keeps his eyes fixed on them, licking blood from his muzzle.

"Except she isn't the Black Wolf," she says.

Jon turns toward her, eyes popping.

"What are you talking about, sweetheart? Have you lost your mind?"

Antonia points at the dog and then at Rebo.

"Tell me why our professional killer shoots Kiril Rebo in cold blood, but doesn't shoot the dog in self-defense."

Jon definitely has no answer to that question.

"Are you the Black Wolf?" asks Antonia, leaning over the injured woman.

"No, I follow her, I kill her."

Inspector Gutiérrez laughs sardonically.

"*You* killed the Black Wolf. The assassin who has the Mafia quaking in their boots?"

"She good. I better," replies the woman with a shrug.

Jon scratches his head.

"Okay. You're not the Black Wolf. Then who are you?"

"Name not important. Important is, Orlov coming."

"Let us decide about that."

The woman stifles a grimace of pain and takes a deep breath. She hasn't spoken these words for many years. So many that she sometimes doubts who she really is.

"My name is Irina Badia."

Part 4

JON

The little girl felt no pain when the nail scratched her face below her left eye.

1

A STORY

This story should be told in a soft, leisurely, lilting voice, with all the time in the world.

> *There once was a little girl*

Soft vowels, hard consonants, sounds spoken with an accent from far-off lands.

> *who used to play at hanging*

Short sentences, a lot of silences, some of them lengthy.

> *from the branch of an old oak tree*

Until it describes the same story she recounts to herself endlessly.

> *until one day there arrived*

To soothe her pain, relieve her need, help her fall asleep.

> *some evil men.*

There once was a little girl who used to play at hanging from the branch of an old oak tree until one day there arrived some evil men.

The little girl's name was Irina Badia. Her sister's was Oksana. They lived on their parents' farm in Chkalova, Ukraine.

These are simply words.

How many does it take to tell a person's story? A thousand? A hundred thousand?

That isn't enough either.

To try to describe the little girl's terror when the men came looking for her would be pointless. Her family died, and she escaped, that's all. It wasn't easy, but she went on living. Until she had become strong enough to travel two thousand kilometers in search of somebody who made her even stronger. Who taught her to rise above herself.

"*How long should* a fight last?"

"*Five seconds.*"

"*You will never be the strongest. If your opponent resists your first attack, it will be hell. Go for his weak points, mercilessly, finish him off before he even realizes he's in a fight.*"

Years went by.

She traveled even farther, to the far side of the world, in search of those who had taken everything from her.

She found love, or something akin to love.

She left it behind, because she realized it wasn't enough. The only thing that could fill the immense void in the center of her heart was blood.

She came back. Alone.

The more alone a person is, the more solitary they become. Solitude grows around them like mold. A protection against the thing that could destroy them, but which they so fervently desire. Solitude grows, spreads, and proliferates of its own accord. Once the mold takes root, it takes a lifetime to get rid of it.

The girl moved on. She grew more violent, more effective. Her fights were over quickly, but each one took more of a toll on her. Her body was starting to feel the strain, her back was its own universe. Inhabited by an excruciating pain that took over everything.

She has fewer and fewer fights left in her. And her heart hasn't even begun to satisfy its hunger.

One day, in Saint Petersburg, she discovered the whereabouts of the last of the men who ordered the invasion of the Badias' farm. A pimp named Orlov. Since then, he had come up in the world, and now had his own clan. In Spain.

But the heads of the Tambóvskaya weren't happy with Aslan

Orlov. They had sent a female assassin to destroy him and correct his mistakes.

A dying man told Irina all of this after she had tortured him for hours. A *shestiorka* in the organization who wanted to stay alive. He didn't, although his death was not in vain. He put Irina on the trail of the Black Wolf.

She traveled to Madrid with her on the same plane.

They stayed in the same hotel.

That night, when the Black Wolf went for a stroll by the river, Irina followed her with a knife and a length of wire. She caught up with her on the bridge. The other woman was relaxed, off her guard, like all predators who believe the night belongs to them. At the last minute, when Irina was already upon her, the Wolf sensed danger. She managed to parry Irina's first blow.

The fight lasted three seconds.

Irina stripped her body and disposed of it, not before using her thumbprint to unlock her cell phone one last time.

From that moment on, she became the Wolf. She knew all she needed to about her target. But just as she was preparing to go in search of him, it seemed Orlov required her services too. The game became even more interesting.

This story begins just like the ever-changing fairy tale Lola tells herself. Is there any other way to begin a story? And yet there is a big difference from the self-indulgent lies with which Lola attempts to rewrite herself.

Irina Badia's story is real.

As real as any story can be, when it comes down to it.

This is the story Irina Badia should have told Antonia Scott. But we don't often get the opportunity to hear a person's whole life story before we judge them. Where they are from, their dreams and aspirations. The hidden desires deep in their hearts. The obstacles they have encountered, and why their path has crossed ours. What razor-sharp smiles keep them awake in bed at night. Who planted the thornbushes that torture their soul and obscure their judgment.

How they got that scar below their left eye.

In reality, we don't get many opportunities to hear a person's whole life story. And being holed up in a mountain chalet under imminent attack from a team of assassins armed to the teeth isn't one of them. Life doesn't resemble a movie or a novel, where just before a defining moment, the narrator indulges in a lengthy flashback in pastel shades.

So in fact, the conversation went rather like this:

2

A SUMMARY

"My name is Irina Badia."

"You're really good. Russian special forces? Spetsnaz? Alpha Group?"

Irina shakes her head.

"Friend teach me."

"Why are you here, Irina?"

"Orlov kill my family. I kill Orlov."

Antonia realizes they won't get far with Irina's rudimentary Spanish.

"How did they die?" she asks, switching into Russian.

Irina replies in her language. She speaks more slowly. Her voice softens.

"We had a farm. They wanted me and my sister. They killed our parents, abducted my sister for their human trafficking ring. I escaped."

Antonia contemplates the woman lying on the floor, defenseless. She shifts slightly, and Antonia notices one of her ears is missing. She assesses her in the light of this fresh information. Then she raises her hand to Irina's left cheek, almost touching her scar. A thin, pale line that runs down the middle of her cheek. And throbs in time with the scar hidden beneath her clothes.

"How old were you?"

"Eight."

Thus far, the preamble covering her motives.

"Then what?"

Thoughts dart behind her eyes, like fish under green ice: impossible to reach. Irina inhales and recounts twenty years of commitment, violence, and suffering, in as many words.

"Then I grew up and killed them all. The perpetrators and the people who gave the orders. One by one."

A thought strikes Antonia like lightning out of a clear blue sky. A sudden, humbling awareness that her abilities, however great they may be, will never be sufficient for her to understand everything.

And without understanding, how can I do what is right?

She turns to look at Jon, who is observing every detail of the exchange even though he can't understand a word.

"You must leave," Irina says, tugging at Antonia's sleeve to get her attention again. "Orlov is about to arrive."

Antonia gently removes her hand.

"How do you know?"

"I have the Black Wolf's cell phone. They were right behind me, following Rebo's signal."

This is not good news.

This is not good news at all.

Antonia has to decide what to do about Irina, but first she needs to understand her.

"You came here for this," says Antonia, showing her the microSD card. "Why?"

"Orlov is the last person on my list."

Antonia reflects about what is on the card. All the names, the networks, the bank accounts. Not only those of the Russian Mafia but their collaborators and associates in a dozen countries. People who are beyond the reach of justice.

"You've come to the end of your list. And you want to start another."

Irina presses down on her wound. It's obvious she's in pain.

"For all the little girls who haven't shared my good fortune."

She pronounces the word sweetly, with resignation.

Udachi.

It means "good fortune," in Russian.

Nothing more.

The word lashes Antonia. A whip braided with envy, contempt, and sorrow. They took everything from this woman when she was a little girl. How can she consider herself fortunate? Somebody invaded her life and destroyed it. Transforming her into a hate machine.

How can she think herself fortunate?

Why does that make me feel so guilty?

3

ANOTHER DAWN

After Antonia finishes talking to Irina, she has a brief conversation with Lola Moreno. Then she goes over to Jon. He is sitting at the dining table, where he can watch the three women.

"Well?"

"The situation is complicated," she says, lowering her voice.

And she explains.

"Shit. So we need to hurry up and get out of here."

"It's not that easy, Jon."

"We can take Zenya's car. The five of us climb in, and *adiós*."

"It's a Ford Fiesta, Jon. With no chains. And there's half a meter of snow outside. If the exhaust pipe doesn't choke, the wheels will spin. Or we'll run into Orlov out in the open."

"We could head in the opposite direction."

"Conditions will be worse farther up the mountain. And the road ends after three kilometers at a viewing platform. There's nowhere for us to go in that direction. We'd have to go back the way we came."

Jon rubs his face wearily. He's exhausted. His eyes are puffy, and he's ravenous.

"I'm asleep on my feet."

"Wait here," says Antonia.

She returns soon after, carrying two cups of instant coffee she has heated up in a microwave and a packet of stale crackers. The sort that exist in every larder, because nobody is ever hungry enough to risk eating them. Jon takes the cup his partner hands him. Then devours the crackers two at a time.

"It isn't far to the town. We could try to escape through the forest and make our way down there."

Antonia gestures toward their prisoners.

"One is wounded, I doubt she can walk. The other two aren't wearing proper clothing."

"Maybe there's some warm gear in the wardrobe."

"I already checked. There's nothing, except for a couple of designer T-shirts and a box of sex toys."

Jon drains his coffee, if you could call it that. He gazes out the window. A pale, dirty light heralds the dawn, illuminating the square garden covered in a thick blanket of snow. He glimpses the treetops, ghostlike against the sky as it changes from black to gray. In contrast to the powerful gusts earlier, the gentle breeze making the low branches sway is a soft murmur.

It has stopped snowing.

"That doesn't help," Jon says, pointing outside. "They'll find the house more easily."

Antonia eyes him solemnly.

"You and I might make it. We leave them here, take the card. Once we have coverage, we call the police. They might get here in time."

Inspector Gutiérrez brushes a crumb from his beard, and smiles.

"That's not going to happen."

"No," agrees Antonia. "But it was the last option I wanted you to rule out."

"So there's only one thing left to do."

Antonia nods slowly.

"Two against who knows how many," says Jon.

"Three," Antonia corrects him, motioning toward Irina.

"I'm not sure I follow you."

"She's on our side."

"That crazy woman?"

Antonia frowns.

"Not the term I would use."

"And what term would you use?"

"If I had to make a psychological profile? Post-traumatic stress, egomania, prolonged grief disorder, antisocial personality. Possible schizoid tendencies, though I'm not sure."

Some diagnosis, thinks Jon. *Enough to get her locked away.*

"What are you going to do with her?"

"I'm going to give her the gun back."

"You're kidding."

Antonia reaches for a cracker and munches it slowly, shaking her head.

"How can you trust a person like her?"

"How can you?"

Somebody presses the pause button on Jon's face, which freezes until he understands who Antonia is referring to.

"Ah. Really, all those things?"

Antonia shrugs. She isn't proud of it.

"But you haven't taken to killing people," says Jon.

"You know I've tried. But I'm not a very good shot."

Jon laughs out loud as he recalls the tunnel and Sandra Fajardo. It's the kind of nervous laugh you let out when the darkness is crawling with monsters.

"Well, this is your chance to practice. By the way, that coffee was great. Suddenly I don't feel tired anymore."

Antonia pulls a little bag of white tablets out of her pocket.

"Diphenylmethyl-sulfinylacetamide."

Jon recognizes the bag instantly. It's supposed to be in the glove compartment. He looks down at his cup, and then at Antonia, his eyes narrowing.

"That's a dirty trick, sweetheart. You spiked my drink."

"You'll thank me for it."

ROMERO

This is not why I joined the police, thinks the captain.

She looks at her watch. It's past eight o'clock, and will soon be light. It's been a long, depressing night.

Tiredness affects her mood, makes her melancholy. She has never been one to acknowledge her emotions. Still less to let them show. God knows they're the last thing a woman in her profession should reveal. Anything like that is taken as a sign of weakness. Having a cold, or your period, the least change in your mood. Complaining about a situation using negative language. Any character trait or quirk accepted in a man without so much as a second thought is considered a failing in a female police officer. Every day since she started this job, she has had to listen to words like *quota*, *gender parity*, *decorative*.

So she has eliminated any characteristic that might humanize her. Colorful clothes: certainly not. The same goes for makeup. She has even learned over the years to adapt her body language.

A formidable task that had begun to bear fruit.

Until one day she became obsessed with Orlov. And with Voronin as a way of getting to him. And that obsession, that commitment, has brought her here.

Here being a crossroads outside a remote town in the Sierra de Guadarrama. Where it's as cold as a witch's tit.

As good a place as any from which to look back.

It all started when they caught Voronin as a result of that business with the container. The evidence was flimsy at best. But Voronin took the bait. And so did his wife, that shameless tramp. Pretending to be all innocence, as if she wouldn't hurt a fly. But Lola Moreno didn't fool her for a minute. Voronin wouldn't so much as open his mouth without first looking at her. Even if you asked him the goddamn time.

Lola Moreno. What a repulsive bitch.

Romero lights a cigarette. She only smokes when alone. Another weakness she avoids revealing. But what does that matter now? Only Belgrano is with her at the crossroads. And he knows all there is to know about her.

Deputy Inspector Belgrano. Loyal to the end. With his hotheadedness and his foul temper. She wonders why she has never slept with him. They have shared everything else. All-nighters, bloodshed. Quarrels. Arrests that led nowhere, criminals who escaped justice. Others who ended up where they deserved to be. Frustrations, plenty. Triumphs, a few. But never bed.

Just as well, she thinks, glancing sideways at her deputy. He is propped against the motorbike, not saying a word. Tired, like her. But uncomplaining. They are like brother and sister. They share the same code, which unites them more than the other. They are family.

Family marks you. Life weighs you down.

She knew she was taking a risk using Voronin as an informer. That he would use them to eliminate the competition. Romero has been around long enough to know this is the first rule of the informer. But how could she have envisaged the trap he was laying for them, that bastard?

She hadn't been too greedy. No more than was usual, in any case. A few wads of bills always went missing when there was a big haul. Everybody knew that, and everybody turned a blind eye. What did they expect, on the miserable salary they were paid? Under €3,000 in her case, and Belgrano a third of that. What they earned in a month, a small-time drug dealer could make on a slow afternoon. A courier ten times that for one lousy trip. And yet every day she and Belgrano had to risk life and limb for peanuts. Wade through rivers of shit with a smile on their face, impeccably turned out. Of course.

She hadn't been too greedy. No more than was usual. The rules were clear. Don't get caught, be discreet. Don't do it too often. But everything apart from that was your problem. It's your choice and your conscience. No one will raise an eyebrow.

The detectives in Marbella who were caught eight years ago. Friends of hers. Colleagues at UDYCO. They made only one mistake. They got things the wrong way around. Instead of being cops and snatching up whatever scraps fell from the table, they set a place for themselves at the table.

She wasn't like that. She never had been.

All she wanted was to do her job well.

But that Serb courier. Six hundred thousand euros in used notes, and just the one driver. A slimeball with a history of violence. Murder, theft, abuse. The money went to Belgrano's head. And hers, too, no denying that. It would plug a lot of holes. They notched up the arrest, one more to add to Captain Romero's impeccable record. End of story.

When something seems too good to be true, guess what?

Fucking Voronin.

If she's honest, the guy had run out of road anyway. It was time for him to stop offering them small fries, instead of helping them hook the big fish. But he preempted them. Without telling his wife. She would never have let him do something so stupid. Threaten a police captain. You've gotta be . . .

He paid for it. Dearly. That hadn't been their intention. That goddamn dog spooked Belgrano, who's always been a bit jumpy. And things got out of hand. They had to go after her, quick. And they messed up.

A total disaster.

The incident attracted too much attention. Orlov called in person to demand an explanation. It was the first time she had spoken to him. And she offered him half-truths. Just enough for everyone to save face.

But somebody in Madrid got wind of it. And those two showed up to help search for Moreno.

When they arrested her, Orlov called again. She was supposed to die, whatever the cost. Orlov provided the off-roader. Another fuckup. And two officers dead. Two innocent people. Another red line crossed.

That Lola Moreno is like a fucking cockroach. Impossible to crush.

Orlov called a third time. To inform them Lola was still alive, and to issue them fresh orders. At that point, Romero understood the tables had turned. Now she was nothing more than a tool in his hands.

This isn't why I joined the police, the captain repeats to herself.

* * *

The two cars arrive at first light. The sun won't break through above the mountains today. The sky hangs low, bloated with gray clouds and ill omens. What they do today will be hidden from God's view.

Scant relief for a grim task.

The first off-roader pulls up at the crossroads. Romero glances inside. Only two men, who remain impassive when they see the two police officers.

"Is this the best Orlov has?"

"The best Orlov has is Orlov," a voice behind them says.

Romero turns around and sees the elderly mafioso climb out of the second off-roader, accompanied by two more bodyguards. The Beast. Pimp, rapist, drug trafficker. Murderer. She has to restrain herself from whipping out her gun and cuffing him right there on the hood of their car.

She feels a wave of revulsion. Toward him, toward herself.

"Is it just you?" says Orlov.

"Just us. Were you expecting someone else?"

The old man gazes into the distance. At the line where the forest starts to climb the side of the mountain before being swallowed by clouds.

"It doesn't matter. Did you locate the last position I sent you?"

"It's here," says Belgrano, showing a satellite map on his phone. "There's a house in the forest, twelve kilometers farther on. After that, nothing."

"Get in the car. Let's finish this once and for all."

4

AN INVENTORY

They lay everything on the table. Four pieces of metal and plastic on the wooden top.

It doesn't amount to much.

Jon's handgun has thirteen bullets in the magazine, another thirteen in the spare.

Irina's pistol has ten bullets. No spare magazine.

The pistol Rebo was carrying, twelve bullets. No spare magazine.

Jon's shotgun. Eight cartridges.

"It has a twenty-meter range. Beyond that, the shot dispersion reduces the likelihood of a fatal hit," says Antonia, resting her finger on the rifle butt.

Jon nods slowly.

"Roughly how far would you calculate twenty meters from here?" he asks, pointing out the window.

"Up to the birch."

"Sure. And just to clarify—"

"The tree to the right of the Ford Fiesta."

"You see how easy it is when you explain—"

Antonia gets to her feet and picks up Irina's gun, together with the one Rebo stole from the officers.

"In the end, we've managed to solve the Manzanares murder."

"You can't really claim that one. The case solved itself."

"Who caught the killer?"

"Technically? The dog," says Jon, rising and walking toward the prisoners.

He asks Zenya to stand up and picks the lock on her handcuffs.

"I need you to reverse your car as close as you can to the main gate. Leave the handbrake on, and come back to the house right away."

She obeys. Antonia goes to the front door and presses a button that locks the gate. In case Zenya gets any last-minute ideas.

Antonia returns and explains her plan.

"Orlov is about to arrive. We don't know how many men he has, or what weapons they're bringing. We'll just have to hold out as best we can. Two things are in our favor. The house is solid, and the windows all have bars on them. Which means the only entry point is the main door."

"What's the second?" asks Lola.

"They're not expecting any opposition," Antonia replies, picking up the gun by its muzzle and extending it to Irina.

An awkward silence follows. Even the dying embers of the fire cease crackling.

Irina makes no move to take the weapon. Her green eyes hold Antonia's gaze.

"Are you sure?"

"No. But I haven't much to lose either," replies Antonia.

Irina raises her arm. Her fingers close around the muzzle. For a split second, the energy transmitted by her hand communicates itself to Antonia through eight hundred grams of steel.

"What about me and Zenya?" asks Lola.

"You betrayed her," Antonia says to Zenya, pointing at Lola.

"And as for you . . ." Jon does the math, but it's simpler to generalize. "Well, you betrayed everyone. So go hide under the sofa and don't get in the way."

Irina stands up and goes with Jon over to the window. She has to lean on him at every step.

"Your plan . . . bad."

"Really? How many times have you been in a house that's under attack by the Russian Mafia?"

Irina tilts her head inquiringly. Then she holds up two fingers.

"And how did it go?"

"One bad. One good."

Antonia joins them at the window.

"Do you have a better plan?" she asks in Russian.

"We need a shooter on the roof," she replies in the same language. "To try to hold them off. If they reach the house, we'll all die, bars or no bars on the windows."

"I'll go," Jon offers when Antonia has translated into Spanish.

"You can cover a lot of ground from up there with the shotgun. They'll try to encircle you, so you need to watch your back."

"Okay," says Jon.

Irina takes Antonia by the elbow, draws her closer to the window, and continues talking to her in Russian.

"You stand here," she says, rapping the sill with her knuckles. "Break the glass, it doesn't help at all. Wait until you're sure of hitting your target."

"What about you?"

"I'll be outside, among the trees."

"With that leg of yours? No way."

"Do you know how to use this?" Irina says, pointing to Antonia's pistol.

"Not very well," she admits.

"Then don't argue. Hurry. They'll be arriving any second."

5

A ROOF, A GARDEN, AND A LIVING ROOM

Jon is the first to see them.

It had been hard work. The skylight in the main bedroom is the only one in the house without bars. First, he had to stand on a chair to be able to reach it. Then he had to force it open as far as it would go. Which turned out to be forty centimeters. The math told him he wouldn't get through. Not that he's fat. So he smashed the pivot hinges preventing him doing so with the butt of the Remington.

To judge from the sound of breaking glass down below, Antonia is doing something similar.

Inspector Gutiérrez hasn't been up on a roof in eleven years. And back then, it was to fix a satellite dish for friends. So his entire experience consists of remembering that they slope and are extremely slippery, especially when covered in snow. It's a pent roof with tapered mission tiles, and the chimneystack is to the left of the skylight; it's substantial enough for Jon to use as cover and is directly above the front door.

The bad news is that he offers an easy target for anyone sneaking around the back of the house.

Within a minute of Jon positioning himself behind the chimney, the off-roaders appear at the bend in the road. Close to where they crashed the Audi—which wasn't Jon's fault.

"They're here!" Jon yells down the chimney.

In the living room, Antonia uses the poker to smash the glass window panes, then drapes a blanket—stolen on an Iberia flight—over the frame to allow her to take aim without cutting herself. A blast of icy air hits her in the face.

Sixty seconds later, Jon's voice bellows down the chimney. To her right, she hears the living room door open. Irina is going out.

Antonia turns to Lola Moreno, who is getting dressed now that her clothes are dry.

"Watch the door, in case I need you to open it quickly. And you," she orders Zenya, "keep an eye on the kitchen window, in case someone tries to attack from there."

Irina descends the porch steps into the garden. The knee-deep snow hampers her movement. And yet, curious though it seems, being in contact again with this blanket of white energizes her in a way she didn't think possible anymore. It doesn't stop the pain, but it gives something back to her. From the time she spent in Magnitogorsk with the Afghan. The man who turned her into a weapon.

It's obvious discretion won't be on her side. She is leaving an unmistakable trail of footprints, drag marks, even tiny red bloodstains that turn pink as they dilute in the churned-up snow.

Use whatever you have at hand, the Afghan's voice echoes in her head.

Instead of heading straight toward the gate, Irina veers off along the wall, where she can see a hosepipe hanging. She opens the faucet all the way, and prays the water hasn't frozen inside the hose. After a few seconds, a powerful jet gushes out. Irina picks up the nozzle and drags it away from the hedge, letting the water flow toward the front door of the house. She may need to beat a hasty retreat, and the water will help clear a path for her.

Up on the roof, Jon sees them preparing to attack. They step out of their vehicles. Four from the first, three from the second. He recognizes Orlov, Romero, and Belgrano. To see them alongside that vermin—two colleagues, who swore the same oath he did—makes him sick to his stomach.

"There are seven of them, including Belgrano and Romero!" he yells toward the chimney, hoping Antonia will hear.

He sees Irina edging along the side of the property by the hedge. Limping noticeably on her injured leg, leaving a trail anybody could follow. Every so often, he loses sight of her, as the half dozen trees in the garden obscure his view. Suddenly, he realizes the trees could become a problem, if their assailants use them as cover to advance on the house.

Maybe it wasn't such a good idea to leave the Ford Fiesta in front of the gate. It'll make it harder for them to get in, but it means they'll know we're here, thinks Jon.

He can see they are organizing themselves. Somebody barks an order—Orlov, no doubt, although Jon can't see him. The first off-roader reverses on the road, drives up to the gate, and begins to push. There is a screech of metal as the off-roader accelerates.

And two people are going around the back of the house. Jon sees them turn the corner before they disappear behind the hedge.

Shit, shit, shit.

Outside, Irina has managed to reach the far end of the garden. A log pile juts out from the wall. She takes cover behind it, gun in hand, trying not to think about how hard it is to stay on her feet.

The off-roader, a black Range Rover, rams the gate with short, sharp thrusts. Reverse gear, foot flat on the gas pedal, first gear. The tires have made furrows at the entrance. The front fender already has a big dent in it, but the gate won't resist much longer. One more blow and it will come away from its frame. The air smells of gasoline, mud, and metal.

Clank.

The grating sound rings out above the revs of the Range Rover engine. This is something that has never ceased to surprise Irina. The way snow dampens some sounds and heightens others. Snow is capricious.

The off-roader reverses away from the gate to allow the men in. The first one squeezes through the gap between gate and wall. Irina sees a pair of blue sneakers, jeans, and finally a stocky figure, encased in a sheepskin jacket.

Irina lets him go past. She waits for him to walk onto the snow in the garden, and pull the gate back to help his companion through. When she sees the second man's legs, she takes a step forward, leaving the cover of the logs. She presses her gun to the first man's head and pulls the trigger. She doesn't stop to look at the second man's face, but simply turns, thrusts her gun into his stomach, and fires a second shot. The first man is still falling to his knees, head blown off, when the second thug begins to scream in agony. The bullet has gone straight through his guts, leaving an exit wound the size of a tennis ball.

Irina throws herself to the ground just in time. Shots fly through the space where she was standing. She rolls over, retreating to the log pile.

Now they'll try to shoot at me from above, she realizes, too late.

Up on the roof, Jon sees the two men whom Irina has shot fall into the snow. Then he sees her throw herself on the ground. Suddenly, a head pops up above the log pile.

They're trying to climb up that way. Jon lays the shotgun down, leans against the stone chimney, tenses his shoulders, and relaxes his hands. From this distance, he has no chance of hitting the head and hands poking out. But that isn't necessary. It's enough for him to do what he does: aim at the wall, ripping out a chunk of plaster, and causing the head and hands to vanish.

He has given Irina time to get up and retreat limping. Unfortunately for him, he has done something else.

Jon has given away his position.

The two who were circling the wall have discovered an angle of fire, and have spotted Jon.

Luckily, they can see only the top of his head and part of his shoulders. The thunderous noise splits Jon's eardrums as bullets strafe the roof ridge, shattering tiles and showering him in a cloud of clay and cement. He manages to flatten himself before a second volley rips one of the stones out of the chimney.

Bastards. It's an automatic.

"They have automatic weapons!" Jon's voice booms down the chimney.

By then, Antonia has already recognized the characteristic *rat-a-tat* of the AK-74. The modern version of its famous cousin, twenty-seven years older. Selective fire, thirty cartridges made of semitransparent polyamide, rotating bolt.

This is bad, thinks Antonia.

From the direction of fire, she deduces the position of Jon's attackers. At the rear of the property, the hedge is three meters high, and there is no way into the house. But if they can trap him on the roof so he can't shoot back, the defenders' options are severely limited. Irina is retreating around the edge of the garden. That leaves Antonia to face the attackers on her own.

The man Irina shot in the stomach is blocking the gate. His clothes must have snagged on the bars. He is still screaming in agony. *He's dead, he just doesn't know it yet*, Antonia concludes from a distance. A 9 mm bullet in the stomach at point-blank range requires urgent assistance within thirty-two minutes. After that, there's only morphine.

Orlov seems to have come to the same conclusion. The off-roader reverses, then rams the gate once more, twisting the metal bars against the wall and crushing the injured man. He emits a string of bloodcurdling screams. A single shot rings out. The screaming stops.

"He executes his own men. That's the kind of mercy we can expect," Lola says behind her.

She has gotten up and is peering out the window, eyes filled with fear.

"Go back to your position," Antonia orders. "And please stay out of my way."

In the garden, Irina has managed to reach the side of the property. She is limping badly. There is little or no strength left in her wounded leg. She takes cover behind one of the trees and tries to find a place she can shoot from. But no angle gives her a clear line of fire at the gate.

Shit, thinks Irina.

Up on the roof, Jon is still trapped. There's no way for him climb back inside without standing up and making himself an easy target. He raises a hand to check they are still there, and lowers it instantly. A fresh volley pins him down.

Shit, thinks Jon.

Inside, Antonia watches the off-roader ram the gate again, nudging forward the Ford Fiesta. The wheels spin in the snow, pushing the car back even though its handbrake is on.

With one last push, the Range Rover enters the property and starts to go around the Ford Fiesta, the last obstacle between it and the house. Behind the windshield, Orlov's face looms larger and larger.

Shit, thinks Antonia.

6

A NICE PEACEFUL MORNING

Antonia starts firing as the off-roader roars into the garden. One bullet skims the top of the vehicle, another hits the hood. A third goes straight through the windshield, snapping off the rearview mirror.

Weighing the results with some objectivity, Antonia concludes that for her it wasn't bad at all.

But it hasn't succeeded in stopping Orlov.

"If they get through, we're dead!" yells Antonia.

Someone starts to shoot through the lowered windows in the rear of the off-roader.

Jon hears, rather than sees, the Range Rover roar in. Hunkered down behind the chimney, he doesn't have the right angle to be able to aim with precision. But the advantage of the shotgun is that it doesn't need much.

He sticks out the barrel of the Remington one handed. The kickback from this beast would make anyone less strong buck like a rutting mountain goat. But Inspector Gutiérrez's right arm isn't any arm, and when he pulls the trigger, the shotgun remains steady, as if his five fingers were soldered on. Jon feels the punch reverberate through his forearm and elbow.

The first shot smashes one of the headlights and bursts a tire. Jon flexes his arm, reloads, and fires again. This time, the Range Rover's hood flies off. He reloads, *snap-crack*.

The off-roader has now driven round the Ford Fiesta. Any farther and it will have a free run up to the house. The attackers are protected by three tons of car, so Jon and the others won't stand a chance.

No.

He gets to his feet.

The third blast sends twenty-seven 6 mm slugs barreling through the radiator, the battery, and the auto mass airflow sensor. Only the last of these three wounds proves fatal. Deprived of the information essential to its functions, the Range Rover's engine decides to cease functioning.

Jon pays a high price.

By standing up, he has once again made himself a target.

A fresh volley rings out from below. Speeding upward, the bullets smash into the stone chimney, into Jon's back, and graze his right arm.

Jon cries out, collapses against the chimney, and loses his footing. This protects him from a second volley that sends fragments of stone in all directions.

He manages to grab on to the chimney just as he is about to fall off the edge of the roof. He jabs one foot on the gutter, which gives way beneath his weight.

Antonia sees Orlov and two of his *bojevíks* climb out of the Range Rover. Orlov darts behind the vehicle to the left, while the others run for cover among the trees to the right. They are closing in on Irina, who is still behind one of the birches, waiting for her chance.

Three in the front garden, two dead. Two more shooting at Jon, Antonia calculates.

Then an idea occurs to her.

"It's Belgrano and Romero!" Antonia yells at the fireplace. "Make them say something."

Jon is seeing stars before his eyes. His right arm is bleeding, although he is scarcely aware of the pain. The kick from the bullet in his back is what really hurts. Together, the ceramic plate and Kevlar armor have saved him from open heart surgery, but they have left him with a spreading bruise, a broken rib, and another coat to throw in the trash.

It has also cost him the Remington, which slipped off his arm and plummeted into the snow down below. Now he only has his handgun.

He hears Antonia as if she were speaking to him from inside a water tank.

Something about making Belgrano and Romero talk.

I can scarcely breathe, let alone talk, thinks Jon.

"Romero, can you hear me?" he yells at the top of his voice, which after the blow to his back projects about as far as his shirt collar.

Jon tries to roll over, move closer to the chimney and turn his head. His feet slip on the tiles. A few more come loose. Still, he manages to prop himself up on his elbows and raise his head slightly.

He calls to Romero again, this time more loudly.

"What do you want?" replies Belgrano.

"If you give yourselves up now, I promise we won't tell anyone you tried to kill us."

The deputy inspector laughs out loud.

"Are you an idiot, or what?"

Well, yes, probably, Jon thinks as he grips his pistol.

Then he hears five more words through the chimney.

In the living room, Antonia fires at one of the men behind the trees. Disappointingly, the bullet hits the trunk. The only effect this has is to make them take cover and to slow them down.

For a few seconds. The second *bojevík* steps out from behind the tree and fires. He, too, has an AK-74. And Antonia can't compete against that. She jerks away from the window just as the bullets ricochet off the sill and bars.

Then she hears Belgrano's voice.

"Irina," she calls in Russian. "The voice behind the hedge!"

She shouts five words at the fireplace.

Irina is trying not to cry out in pain. When she rolled on the ground by the log shelter to escape the bullets, her back clicked like dice rolling on a table. Her two friendly vertebrae, L4 and L5, desperate to fuse together. At least the excruciating pain in her back has made her momentarily forget the one in her leg.

Despite this, she has managed to cover fifteen meters. She has almost reached the house, near where the hose water has melted part of the snow. But her body refuses to go any farther, and she has had to crouch behind the last tree. She leans her face against the bark, feels its roughness on her cheek, allows herself to close her eyes for a second. Only a second.

Get up. Keep moving.

She looks up in time to see Jon cling on to stop himself sliding off the roof. A new stab of pain in her back makes her clench her teeth. She leans against the birch, gasping for air.

Her name. Somebody yells her name.

The voice behind the hedge.

Irina understands.

Tensing her calf muscles to stand up, she slides her back against tree and pulls the trigger in the direction of the voice.

One. Two. Three. With a fifteen-degree angle between each shot.

The bullets slice through the hedge. She hears a scream on the other side.

"When the Russian woman shoots," Jon hears through the chimney.

Three shots ring out. Followed by a scream.

Jon raises himself slightly. He sees Belgrano clutch his side and fall to the ground. The bullet has hit him just above the hip.

It won't kill you, thinks Jon. *But it sure will hurt like hell.*

Romero snatches Belgrano's rifle from him, levels it at the hedge, and opens fire. A spray of bullets makes jagged holes and sends sprigs of leylandii flying into the air, exposing the wall at the base of the hedge.

Click, click, click.

"No more bullets, Captain. Whereas I have plenty," says Jon.

Irina's biggest problem isn't the volley of bullets Romero fired back through the hedge. She slid down the tree in time, and the base of the wall the hedge is planted in protected her so that most of them flew over her head.

Irina's biggest problem is that the shots have given away her position as well.

The two *bojeviks* who took cover behind the trees have located her, and are encircling her. One keeps her pinned down with a burst of automatic fire while the other starts to move around behind her.

She is caught between them.

The stabbing pain in her back and wounded leg prevent Irina from escaping.

So she does something she has never done before. Something the

Afghan forbade her to do. Something she thought she would never need to do.

She calls for help.

Antonia has lost sight of Orlov, but she can see the two men in the garden. One is closing in on Irina, the other has stayed back, spraying the tree Irina is hiding behind with bullets.

Antonia clearly hears her cry for help.

She has been saving her remaining bullets for when one of them gets close to the house. To within two or three meters. To give her a minimal possibility of hitting her target.

The man with the AK-74 is twelve meters away, half concealed by a tree, one knee on the ground.

Antonia fires.

She misses.

She keeps firing, until she runs out of ammunition.

Irina hears Antonia's covering fire from the house. Now is her chance. She leans out to the left of the trunk, just as the *bojevík* on the move reaches the tree closest to her. She fires instinctively, hits him in the calf. The white fabric of his sweatpants—Real Madrid's official colors—is torn open in two separate places. They aren't white anymore.

The man falls on his face in the snow. He tries to return fire, but Irina is too quick for him. She puts a bullet in his throat, another in his jaw.

One more.

And one more bullet.

The *bojevík* with the assault rifle pauses to swap magazine. He raises his gun.

Irina drops onto her back in the snow.

Don't miss now.

The shot enters the mafioso's right eye and lodges in his brain.

Irina remains motionless on the ground.

The pain has completely overwhelmed her.

Up on the roof, Jon has Captain Romero in his sights.

"Drop the rifle and put your hands up," he orders her.

"Listen, Inspector. I'm sure we can find a way to resolve this."

"Sure. You and the judge together."

What gives Romero away is her lifelong attempt to eradicate the smallest trace of her humanity. Including her body language. The gesture she makes with her head would have passed unnoticed in anyone else. In her, it stands out like a neon billboard in the center of Madrid.

Jon moves the barrel of his pistol away from her and at Belgrano. The deputy inspector has raised himself on one elbow and pulled out his handgun, taking advantage of being screened by Romero.

He fires.

So does Jon.

Belgrano's bullet skims Jon's left ear. Maybe his unsteady aim has to do with his wound. Or maybe Jon shifted slightly at the last moment. The fact is, he doesn't die.

Belgrano does.

Jon's bullet hits him in the forehead.

Romero raises her hand to her holster and draws her pistol. She knows she doesn't have a chance against the inspector, who is already pointing his gun at her from an elevated position. But she has chosen her own path. Suicide at the hands of the police. A quicker path, less shameful, and infinitely less wearisome.

Jon isn't having any of it.

Instead of shooting, he jumps.

The likelihood of Jon being able to see Captain Romero's face clearly as he hurtled down toward her is negligible. The image that stays with him, and which he recalls vividly over the following days, is doubtless a product of his imagination. A face, eyes gaping, mouth twisted in a grimace of fear, a hand raised in self-defense. And a usually immaculate chignon slightly disheveled.

There's a sharp snapping sound, possibly two at the same time. An arm and a leg breaking, quite badly. Because 110 kilos of Basque falling on you from a height of five meters is a lot of kilos. No matter how much snow there is to cushion you.

7

A RESULT

Braced to return fire, Aslan Orlov steps onto the porch. There's a strange silence
all around him. The soft creak of boards beneath the soles of his sneakers
accentuates the tense calm.

There is no opposition.

Alert, careful of every move he makes—he is old, and in his profession, you don't get to be that without being cautious—he leans through
the window, gun pointing ahead of him.

He barely reacts to seeing Rebo's corpse. He'd already assumed he
was dead. He is only looking out for danger, but finds none.

He smiles when he sees what is awaiting him inside the house. A
dazzling smile, like a dental-implant ad.

Hands above her head, Antonia is shielding Lola and Zenya. Not
that she offers much cover, but her intention is clear.

They have left the front door open.

"Señor Orlov," Antonia greets the old man in Russian when he appears in the doorway.

"Forgive me if I don't remember your name. I recall we met under
different circumstances."

"They weren't much better," says Antonia.

"No, they weren't. I hope you remember our conversation."

Orlov steps inside. His gun covers the room from end to end,
searching for danger.

In front of him are only three women.

Easy work.

"I remember it very well," says Antonia, who wants to keep Orlov's attention fixed on her. "We discussed mathematics."

"The force equation," says the old gangster, leveling his gun at Antonia.

"How does two thousand kilos of pressure per square centimeter strike you?"

Orlov's eyes cloud over, uncomprehending.

Lola whispers one word.

Kot, who is lying on the sofa waiting for her command, snarls and launches himself across the room. He is only three bounds away from Orlov. The old man fires successive shots at the gigantic mastiff. Two hit their target. But that isn't enough. Kot is defending his mistress, and even bullets won't stop him. The animal's massive paws knock Orlov to the floor, and he sinks his teeth into Orlov's neck. He fires another two shots point-blank into the animal's side, into his stomach. Kot's body convulses, but he doesn't let up.

Even with his dying breath, the faithful dog's jaws remain locked around Orlov's throat. The last thing Orlov sees before his eyes cloud over with darkness is Antonia's face, making sure that the answer to her equation is correct.

8

A DECISION

When Antonia peers over the edge of the roof—getting up there was much more
of an effort for her than for Jon, because of the difference in height—
Inspector Gutiérrez is coming around down below. Captain Romero
has fared a lot worse. She has one leg bent unnaturally, a dislocated
shoulder, and to judge from her sobs, a pain that will take a while to
pass. But their heads banged together, and now Jon is rubbing his forehead as he struggles to remember his name.

"Your record says: 'lack of respect for his superiors,'" says Antonia.
"Underlined several times. I guess this is what they meant."

"You know me. I jump at the slightest provocation."

Even Antonia has to smile.

"Come into the house. I need you."

Antonia's words prove prophetic.

Returning to the living room, she finds Irina threatening Lola with
a gun. Lola is kneeling, the muzzle of Irina's pistol at her head, sobbing
and pleading for her life.

"What are you doing?" asks Antonia in Russian.

"She has to pay for what she's done," says Irina.

She is a total mess. Her clothes are dirty and sodden from the snow,
blood is dripping from her thigh. She can barely stand. But the force
equation needed to pull a trigger at point-blank range is minimal.

"This isn't the way to do it."

"I saw the images from the container. Nine women trapped inside,"
says Irina. "Like bits of meat waiting to be fed to animals, without a

conscience. How many more have they brought over here? How many more have died? How many more girls like my sister?"

"It was an accident!" protests Lola, sniffing loudly. Her face is flushed, tears roll down her pink cheeks.

Irina slaps her hard and presses the gun to her head again.

"Be quiet," Antonia orders Lola.

There is a noise at the door, and all four women—Zenya, flat against the wall, is watching the scene—turn as one.

"Would somebody please tell me what's going on here?" says Jon, who has entered the room, gun pointing straight at Irina.

Antonia gestures to him to lower his weapon. Jon looks askance at his colleague. Eventually, he obeys, very slowly.

"I understand what you've been through," Antonia continues to talk to Irina, in Russian. "I lost somebody too."

"You can't understand!" Irina cries. She is looking at Antonia, but still pressing the gun to Lola's forehead, forcing her neck backward.

"I understand what it is to feel despair. And guilt. To know the world is broken and there's no way of fixing it."

"Then you must know why I have to do this."

"She's pregnant."

"I don't care."

Antonia takes a deep breath and shakes her head.

"So you've lost any humanity you had left."

Irina jabs the gun even harder into Lola's forehead. She, too, seems on the verge of tears.

To Antonia she looks like a little girl.

"You don't sell drugs," Irina says softly. "You don't traffic women. You don't profit from other people's misery. The rules were established long ago. And they haven't changed."

Antonia slips her hand into her pocket and pulls out the microSD card. She shows it to Irina in the palm of her hand.

"This is what you came here for. I'm giving it to you. But in exchange, you have to let her go."

Jon puts his hand on Antonia's arm.

"You can't give her the money and the evidence," he says sternly.

She looks at him. He sees regret in her eyes, but also determination.

"I can't let her take this life."

Inspector Gutiérrez holds her gaze. A battle is raging behind his

brown eyes. A cruel battle that will claim victims. Jon's instinct as a police officer is fighting against his belief in Antonia. His desire for justice
against the need to protect Lola and her unborn child.

"There is no other way, Jon," says Antonia.

With a sigh, Jon releases her arm.

Antonia steps toward Irina and offers her the card.

"Take it," she says in Russian.

"How do I know he won't shoot me in the back as soon as I turn
around?" Irina asks, her eyes narrowing as she points toward Jon.

"You have my word. If I have yours."

Irina studies them both.

Jon's expression is stony, jaw clenched, arms by his sides. His gun
is lowered to the floor, but his crooked finger betrays what he would
really like to do.

Antonia is serene. Holding out the card between thumb and forefinger.

Irina makes her own calculations. Which take her long, nerve-racking
seconds.

Eventually, she withdraws the gun. Released from the pressure, Lola's
head jolts forward. The barrel has left a rectangle on her forehead, with
a circle at the top.

She takes a deep breath, relieved but also furious when she sees
Irina take the card from Antonia and limp toward the door.

"What about me and my son, what are we supposed to eat?" she
asks, clutching hold of Irina's boot to try to stop her. "Tell me, what are
we supposed to eat?"

It has taken thirty-two years—her entire life, minute by minute—for
Irina to arrive at this instant. She feels pure, unequivocal, invincible
when she replies:

"Shit."

9

A STRAIGHT LINE

Cleaning up after a party is never fun. Still less recounting it. A summary will do.

Antonia managed to walk to the crossroads, where she got a signal again. The snow was deep and thick, but she took advantage of some fresh tracks. The woman who left them was limping and bleeding. Antonia walked slowly so as not to catch up with her.

An hour later, this peaceful setting was swarming with police. Forensic teams circulated between dead bodies and bullet impacts, leaving triangles everywhere. There was a public prosecutor and an investigating magistrate. Plus some people from the police inspectorate. Even an official from the Interior Ministry. The involvement of two corrupt officers in the affair—a captain and her deputy inspector—meant it was a great big mess. Which, like all tricky scandals, ended up being brushed under the carpet.

As they are taking Lola Moreno away in an ambulance, huddled beneath a blanket, Jon eyes her with disgust.

"What really makes me mad is that she'll get off scot-free."

"For sure," says Antonia, who shares his frustration. "But we did what we had to."

It's cold. They also have blankets around them, but they offer little protection against the wind sweeping down off the mountains. It will probably start snowing again soon. Jon stamps his feet to try to warm up.

"I'm not sure if I agree with you, sweetheart. We took too many detours."

"Walking in a straight line never gets you very far," says Antonia.

It's so much easier to forgive people when they're wrong than when they're right, thinks Jon.

"Maybe. All I know is my journey ends here."

Under normal circumstances, Antonia might have taken a while to grasp what Jon is trying to tell her. Her partner. Her only friend. Her tenant three floors below. But she has been fearing this moment would arrive for several months now. The moment when he said *enough is enough*.

"So we're no longer a team," she says.

"I guess not."

The events of the past few weeks would have been too much for anyone to bear. She has tested his trust, lied to him, pushed him to his limits and beyond.

In reality, she can't blame him.

But she isn't going to make it too easy for him either.

"What will I do without you?"

Jon has no doubts about that.

"Over and above the lies, and the stupidity, you'll continue tirelessly to try to get to the bottom of things. Because that's who you are. You're a detective. Possibly the best there is."

"Possibly?" says Antonia.

"I can't claim to know them all, angel."

EPILOGUE

"How long is forever?" asked Alice.
"Sometimes, just one second," replied the White Rabbit.

A Goodbye

The room has changed a lot. All of Antonia's belongings have been collected up and packed into boxes.

Marcos hasn't changed.

He is still being kept alive by machines.

His body has deteriorated further these past few months. His limbs have shrunk, his skin is pale and hanging loose. Stark evidence of the diagnosis. The doctors wrote him off years ago. "Terminal," they said. But Antonia refused to believe them. She turned her back on reason, too proud to admit she had made a mistake that couldn't be fixed.

Then she met Jon. And he changed everything.

Somebody knocks at the door. She opens it, cautiously.

It's a tall, elegant man. The man she needs to be with her today.

"Hi, Dad."

Sir Peter Scott was surprised to receive his daughter's call. But he is there, even though they haven't seen each other for months.

He is there, and that's what counts.

"How is Jorge?" she asks.

"Growing. Eager to see you."

"Tomorrow," Antonia promises.

"I'll tell him to set up the chessboard."

"I miss him," she says. And she means it.

Antonia and Peter remain by the bedside for a while, contemplating Marcos's inert body. The empty shell that once contained an incredible love.

"Despite all the things I'm good at, all my skills, I couldn't save him."

Her father says nothing. He doesn't embrace her either. Year upon year of constant rejection has taught him not to get close to her. Even now, when Antonia needs it so desperately. When she would have wanted him to.

She receives no comfort, so she searches for it inside herself.

From the moment of our birth, we know our fate. The cradle rocks above the abyss that is ready to swallow it. Life is a flash of light between two infinite blacknesses. The end awaiting us appears more daunting than the preceding darkness, that instant when we didn't know our face before we were born. Perhaps we fear what comes next because deep down, a tiny part of our being recalls something terrible. Something we forget when we fill our lungs with air for the first time and cry.

And if nothing can protect us from death, then at least let love save us from life.

Antonia kisses Marcos's lips for the very last time. Then she gestures to the doctor, who is waiting patiently by the respirator.

When the machines are turned off, Antonia starts to cry. Grateful for so much love.

A Stroll

Antonia Scott allows herself to think of suicide for fifty-four long minutes.

She refused the offer to be taken home in her father's car. She prefers to walk, to have these moments to herself. To reclaim lost time.

Fifty-four minutes might seem a long time.

Not for Antonia Scott. Not when, truth be told, she is incapable of applying herself fully to the task.

When all she can think of is *now*.

Of how she can carry on without Jon.

In the forty-eighth minute, she decides she can't.

A Change

Meanwhile, at no. 7, Lonesome Street, Jon is packing up his things.

Truth be told, he isn't putting much effort into it either.

His rather expensive clothes require special packaging: suit bags, tissue paper, wardrobe boxes.

Since he hasn't purchased any of the above, the only thing he *has* done is toss his underwear into a suitcase, along with some of—though not all—his cuff links, a toiletry kit, and two towels. Also three jars of Antonia's store of homemade fig jam, which the other tenants pay her in lieu of rent, and which she refuses to eat with the flimsy excuse that she hates figs and jam is fattening.

He looks at his watch.

At this time of night, stores selling packaging materials are closed. But the Wok on Calle del Olivar is open. Ideal for a late supper. Then maybe catch up with the series he was halfway through when this whole mess started. Fall asleep in front of the TV.

And tomorrow, who knows. Maybe he'll think again about moving back to Bilbao.

Jon goes out into the street. He is about to turn the corner when he hears footsteps behind him. Light, female footsteps. He turns around, smiling. But it isn't Antonia. The woman is slim, well dressed, and cheerful looking. She has a friendly face.

"Excuse me. Could you tell me how to get to Calle de Atocha?"

"Keep walking straight, you can't miss it," says Jon, masking his disappointment.

The woman smiles back at him. Then pulls a syringe from her pocket and plunges it into Jon's neck.

"What the f—" says Jon, pushing her away.

Her friendly face is the last thing he sees before a pair of strong arms grab him from behind, before darkness descends on him.

Greeting

Antonia's phone rings as she is walking up Calle de Lavapiés, where it crosses Calle de la Cabeza.

"This isn't a good moment."

"Listen, Scott," says Mentor. "We have the evidence now. It turns out your phantom is very real."

"I don't understand."

"I can't tell you any more over the phone. But we've found out what happened in England and Holland."

Antonia finally understands what Mentor is talking about. And she enjoys the harsh reality. The only thing worse than being the lone voice of reason is when people admit you were right when it's too late.

"It was White."

"I'm in Madrid. Fetch the inspector as quick as you can and come here."

Antonia hangs up and quickens her pace.

Turning into Calle del Olivar, a stone's throw from her apartment, she sees it.

Two men struggling to bundle a third man into a van. He flails weakly. He has a black bag over his head, but Antonia doesn't need to see his face to know who he is.

An elegant woman wearing a raincoat and a friendly expression turns around and spots her. She is too far away for Antonia to see the surprise in her eyes, the small gift entailed in knowing Antonia is there to witness what is happening. But Antonia doesn't need to see it to know it's there.

Sandra Fajardo waves to her before climbing into the van.

Antonia runs toward them, knowing she is too far away. The van speeds off down the street, quickly leaving Antonia behind. Even then she doesn't give up. She keeps running until her lungs are burning, her heart pounding inside her chest like a jackhammer.

The moment she comes to a halt, hands resting on her knees, gasping for breath, is when she receives the message.

I hope you haven't forgotten me.
Do you want to play? W.

AUTHOR'S NOTE

Antonia Scott's story was ten years in the making. I promise that when the time comes, I'll tell you how it all began. Until then, please keep the secret of my novels.

Ah, and one more thing: Yes, Antonia and Jon will be back.

ABOUT THE AUTHOR

José Jeosm

JUAN GÓMEZ-JURADO is an international bestselling author of thrillers whose award-winning Antonia Scott trilogy (*Red Queen, Black Wolf,* and *White King*) has been published around the world, sold millions of copies, and is soon to be a Prime Video streaming series debuting worldwide in early 2024. He lives in Madrid, Spain.